Getting In The Game

By Phil Ferriell

PublishAmerica
Baltimore

© 2003 by Phil Ferriell.
All rights reserved. No part of this book may be reproduced, stored in a retrieval system, or transmitted in any form or by any means without the prior written permission of the publishers, except by a reviewer who may quote brief passages in a review to be printed in a newspaper, magazine, or journal.

First printing

ISBN: 1-59286-617-4
PUBLISHED BY PUBLISHAMERICA, LLLP
www.publishamerica.com
Baltimore

Printed in the United States of America

DEDICATIONS:

This book is for Carmen, and for all those who never got in the game.

ACKNOWLEDGMENTS:

After more than fifteen years in gestation, the book "Getting in the Game" was finally born in 2003. No one can be more surprised than I. The task of creating a palatable novel while working a full time job and playing sports is ludicrous at best. But, this wasn't done alone.

First, I need to thank Dan Diercks of Hagerstown High School and Dr. George Blakey of Indiana University East for encouraging me to continue to write.

Next, I'd like to thank my family for BEING a family. They molded me into the person I am today with all my attributes and idiosyncrasies. My sisters Jane and Rae Marie taught me sensitivity; the female power to keep an insane world together. My brother Mike made me tough. Without him I'd be arranging flowers in San Francisco. My dad, Ray, taught me willpower and determination. That man achieved anything he put his mind to. My mother, Jeannine, raised me to love, have compassion, and to care about other human beings. These five people are the pillars of my life.

My two daughters, Amanda and Rae Ann, deserve a thank you. They are my greatest creations, even above and beyond this book. I helped raise them from birth, and molded them much in the way I was earlier. I taught them to love and prayed they'd love me back. Today, they both teach in Indiana and will impact children's lives for years to come. They will make a difference in this world. I love and respect both of them.

And finally, I want to thank my wife, Karen. She gave me the encouragement to finish "Getting In The Game" and the confidence to present it to the public. Karen broke through a barrier I built up over the years and showed me how to truly be open, honest, and intimate with someone. Without the love and support of this best friend, you would not be reading me today.

PROLOGUE

Basketball is just a sport. It's a round orange sphere filled with air that's dribbled or passed up and down a wooden court, in an attempt to put it through a round, metal cylinder. It's that simple.

In Indiana, basketball is a religion. More people fill the stands on Saturday night than sit in a pew on Sunday morning: unless, of course, your team loses. Blame it on the cold winters, or the lack of entertainment in a mid-western farming community, or even the fact us Hoosiers are too stupid to learn to play chess. In any case, it's Indiana's game, and no one loves it more.

Each year, Indiana holds a State Tournament where every high school team participates. Prior to 1998, Indiana crowned only one state champion. The tournament was played in four rounds: the Sectional, the Regional, the Semi-state, and the State. Sectionals are played locally, and by the time they're finished, only 64 teams are still alive in the Tournament. Each following round reduces the number of teams by one fourth, until one winner remains at the State.

In 1944, 778 teams in Indiana participated in the State Tournament. In Richmond, Indiana, twelve teams from around the Wayne County area vied for the Sectional Championship. Since Richmond was the biggest school in the County, they usually won the Sectional and advanced to the Regional. In fact, Richmond had won 61 out of the 77 Sectional Tournaments prior to 1998.

Every year, the other eleven teams at the Richmond Sectional lived for one thing: Beat Richmond! Whatever happened after that was gravy. To beat Richmond in its own Sectional was indeed a State Championship for any of the eleven small schools in the County. In 1944, three teams had a chance to beat Richmond. Two of them failed.

"The Centerville Bulldogs are leading the Richmond Red Devils 26 to 24 with less than a minute to play in the game. Richmond's called a timeout to set up some kind of play to attempt to tie this game up. This is Richmond's third straight close game in Sectional action. If you remember, the Red Devils squeaked by Hagerstown 19 to 17, and then narrowly beat Fountain City by a score of 33 to 30.

"Centerville, on the other hand, had an easier route to this Semi-final game by destroying Cambridge City 52 to 13, and bouncing Greens Fork 42 to 30.

"Twice in this game, Richmond has held leads of seven points, only to have the Bulldogs charge back both times to tie it up, and right now take the lead.

"Both teams are back on the floor now, and we're ready for action. Richmond gets the ball in bounds and brings it down the court. The Centerville defense has fallen back and is going to protect the basket to prevent a final shot. Richmond is working the ball around the perimeter now, as we go under 10 seconds to play. Here's a pass to the top of the key, now it goes down to the right side of the lane. Deflected away by a Bulldog! There's a scramble for the ball! Richmond's Johnson picks it up and fires a 12-footer. It's good! Richmond ties the game! Three seconds left! Centerville tries to get the ball in bounds! They can't! There's the gun! That ends the quarter, and we'll play an overtime period!"

In the stands, three recent graduates of Centerville were watching the game together.

"Dad blame it!" George yelled to his friends, as he sat down in disgust. "I can't believe he hit that shot!"

"We're gonna lose for sure, now," lamented Milo, as he joined George on the bleacher. "The team that sends it into overtime always wins."

"We almost stole it, too." Kenneth agonized over what could've been. "That would've been the game if we just coulda stole the ball."

"Don't worry guys," George hoped, "I've got a good feeling about this one."

"Yeah, sure, George," Milo ridiculed. "You said that every year we were in high school, too."

"George is right, Milo," Kenneth corrected. "Have you ever heard of a thing called destiny?"

There were only two points scored in the overtime. Centerville's Bob Rosser hit a shot at the top of the key to put Centerville ahead.

"Time is running out! Centerville leads 28 to 26, and Bulldog Dick Null is just holding the ball at mid-court! The Red Devils are either too tired to go after him or they don't realize the game is slipping away! Null is just standing at mid-court with the ball under his arms! Four seconds, three! No one's going to touch him! There's the gun! Centerville has beaten Richmond by a score of 28 to 26!"

George, Milo, and Kenneth were ecstatic. They kept hitting each other with their hats until the bands popped clean off.

"I told you they were going to win!" Milo shouted.

"You told us nothing!" George corrected. "You're the sad sack who said they'd lose!"

"You've mistaken me for someone else!" Milo grinned.

"Oh, no you don't!" Kenneth threatened. "Centerville won and you lost! Now pay up on that bet! Drop those pants and run around the basketball court!"

Most of the Centerville fans poured onto the court at the sound of the gun. A mad jogger who wore nothing more than a broken brim hat and a snazzy new pair of boxers soon joined them.

Several fights broke out in the stands between the Bulldog fans and the Red Devils. A 17-year-old Centerville student named Aaron Belcher had one of his front teeth knocked out when he was blindsided by a wild punch.

"Are you all right, Aaron?" Betty shrieked, as the blood stained her cheerleader uniform.

"Leave me alone!" Aaron snarled, "I need to find the coward who did this!"

The police quickly dispelled the fights as the Centerville celebration continued.

Centerville still had one more game to play. They barely defeated Williamsburg 38-36, to win the 1944 Richmond Sectional. Dick Parker broke a 36-36 tie with a one-handed lay up with six seconds in the game. Centerville's starting five played the entire thirty-two minutes. None of the substitutes got in the game, but none of them cared. They had beaten Richmond and won a Sectional Championship. Centerville has never won a Richmond Sectional since.

SURVIVAL OF THE FITTEST

Are you ready to be bored? Not a very good opening line for a novel. It's the best I could do. Everyone's heard of the mid-life crisis. This is how I'm dealing with mine. As the Dragnet disclaimer states, "The story you are about to read is true. The names have been changed to persecute the guilty." (Is that right?) Of course, I reserve the right to exaggerate or stretch the truth whenever necessary.

There's nothing earth shattering contained in these pages. It's just a simple story. It's my story. Philip Aaron Belcher's my name. (No, I don't need any Tums, and my stomach acids are just fine, thank you.)

I was born a Hoosier farm boy. (Well, there go the East and West coast readers.) I was the fourth child in a family of two boys and two girls. My sister, June, was seven years old when I was born. My brother, Randy, was six and my other sister, April, was four. I was zero. To them, literally. (Actually, my brother and I were lucky we weren't named March and August. If my parents would've had ten more daughters, we could've enveloped the entire year.)

Now, it didn't take a math wizard to figure out the situation here, but the thought never crossed my mind until I started having kids of my own. *I was a mistake*! Birth control wasn't such a big thing back in '55, and that good 'ole Catholic rhythm method was no match for raging hormones. So, Aaron and Betty Belcher had a fourth child. I'm sure Aaron muttered something disparaging. Having another mouth to feed that he couldn't take to the Hog Market. "Fatten the little bastard up and we'll get top dollar for him."

Betty, on the other hand, was probably ecstatic. Maybe another child would bring her and Aaron closer together. Maybe they could raise their kids as a twosome and spend more time with each other. (Yeah, and Mickey Mouse prances around Disneyland naked!)

I was born the same day as my first cousin. She had an inney and I had an outey. Our mothers were at the same hospital together, so the radio and the newspapers interviewed them. The radio station gave our moms a 78-rpm album of the recorded interview. It never made the Top 40.

My fellow siblings anxiously awaited my arrival at the Belcher homestead. In fact, they already devised a farming accident for me to fall victim to.

"Drop him off the silo, why don't ya?"

"Yeah, we can hide the body in the hay baler."

"I'm tellin' Mom, you guys!"

Being the baby of the family was a tough job, but I was perfectly cast for the part. Apparently, I was a happy baby, or at least my mother prefers to remember it that way. Using a few coos and lots of giggles tends to put you in a prime maternal situation, and on the endangered species list of your siblings.

I only thank God I was too young to realize what those three probably did to me as a baby. I found out, later, my mom would make them take turns pulling me around the house in a little red wagon. Needless to say, they would make it halfway around the house and abandon the wagon and myself for more selfish pursuits. It wasn't my fault I had to cry to have them turned in to the authorities. I'm sure the more they suffered as a result of my ratting, came back two-fold in the form of one of those revengeful tricks I still don't want to know about.

Several years later, I heard about the pea-shooting contest. It was dinner time at the Belcher House, and as most dinners there went, it was a grand feast of fried chicken, mashed potatoes and gravy, and of course, *peas*. Aaron Belcher was late for dinner, which was usual during planting season, harvest season, or wild-oats-sowing season. Betty Belcher excused herself midway through the meal, to tend to some other household chores she wanted to complete before Aaron made it home.

Unfortunately, Betty left her three older children, June, Randy, and April totally in charge of their adorable little brother's well being. Mom! What in the world were you thinking?

"Wipe off Phil's mouth, will ya Randy," June bossed, since she was the oldest.

"You do it," Randy responded. "What do I look like, your slave?"

"He's grossing me out," June winced, "I'm losing my appetite."

"Have you looked in the mirror lately?" kidded Randy.

"Very funny, Frankenstein," June shot back. "You're not exactly Troy Donahue."

"Sticks and stones may break my bones, but I'm still not wiping the little baby's face off," riddled Randy.

"I'll do it," April sympathetically said, as she grabbed a napkin.

"Wait a minute," Randy ordered. "I think he looks neato like that."

"Wipe it off April," June overruled.

"Make up your minds, Heckle and Jeckle," April added.

"Just a minute," Randy said, "I've got an idea."

Randy grabbed a few peas off his plate and scooted over towards his baby brother. "Let's play ball," Randy said as he started tossing the peas at the mashed potatoes and gravy on the lower lip and chin of an oblivious little Philip. The first three peas bounced off my face and dropped to the tray of the high chair. Finally, on Randy's fourth try he got a pea to stick in the goop on my chin. "Bingo!"

"Let me try that," June said, grabbing some of the leftover peas off her own plate.

"Cut it out, you guys," April protested. "How'd you like someone to do that to you?"

"This is too hard," June complained, as she fired peas in rapid succession without having any luck.

"Take your time," Randy instructed. "You're not a tommy gun."

"I'm telling mom, you guys," April threatened.

"This isn't working," June said in disgust, "He doesn't have enough goop on his face."

"I can fix that," Randy boasted, as he scooped up some mashed potatoes. Randy proceeded to dab the squishy spuds on my forehead, cheeks, and nose, while I raised my arms up and down in the air and squealed in delight. Of course, no potato should exist without gravy, so Randy dabbed some of the brown liquid on each spot.

"I'm really telling mom now," April said, getting up out of her chair.

"Sit down, April," Randy glared.

"Sit," June added, "We're just having fun."

"Doesn't look like fun for Phil," lamented April.

"Look," June reasoned, "he's laughing about it."

"Okay," Randy said, wiping his hands after completing his artwork. "The forehead and cheeks are one point. The chin is two points, and the nose is three. I'll go first." Randy threw first and planted one on my cheek. "There's one. Your turn, June."

June bounced a pea off my forehead. "This isn't fair."

"You try it, April," Randy goaded.

"I'm not doing it," April said stubbornly, as she folded her arms. "I don't want to get in trouble."

"Okay, baby. My turn again," Randy said, as he drove a pea directly into my chin. "Bingo! Two points. Three to nothing."

"You're cheating," June protested. "You're too close."

"Well, get up there then," Randy insisted.

June closed in on her prey. She reared back like a relief pitcher trying to get the final out, and cut loose with a fast pea down the middle. Bam! It skidded onto the bridge of the nose. "That's three, that's three!" June cheered.

"Now, you're cheating," Randy complained about being tied.

"Let me try," April finally gave in, as she grabbed some peas.

"No. You said you didn't want to," June scolded.

Soon, all three siblings were flinging peas at their little brother's face as fast as they could reload. Their target became even more elusive, as little Phil bounced excitedly up and down in his highchair with all the attention. But, without warning, Betty Belcher came in from the back porch, causing the battle of the peas to end. Betty stopped in her tracks. Randy, June, and April froze in fear. Life became a snapshot for a good ten seconds.

"What on earth are you kids doing?" Betty tried to scold, as a smirk came over her face.

"Just playin' with Phil," Randy simply said.

"Yeah, look how messy he is," June added.

"I didn't want to do it," April confessed, "they made me."

"He may be a baby, but he's not that messy," Betty smiled. "How'd all that food get on his face?"

June and April instantly pointed at Randy.

"Rat finks," Randy whispered in disgust.

"I suggest you wipe him off right now," Betty strongly urged.

"But Mom," Randy protested, "He likes it. Watch!" Randy tossed a few peas at the messy faced baby as he bobbed up and down.

"Stop that," Betty laughed. "Philzy doesn't want to be a target."

About that time, one of Randy's missiles made a direct hit inside my mouth. I jumped and squealed at his accuracy.

"He loves it, mom," June squealed too as everyone broke down laughing.

When baby Phil chewed up the pea, though, he didn't like the taste and started spitting it back out.

"Look out!" yelled Randy. "He's firing back! Take cover!"

Everyone rolled with laughter. They laughed until the back door began to open. Then Randy, June and April dove back in their seats.

"Am I too late for dinner?" Aaron Belcher bellowed.

"No, you're just in time," Betty laughed out loud. "You can finish up what Phil's eating."

Aaron looked at his youngest son's potato and gravy face with an assorted pea topping.

"Cheeze, Betty," Aaron said seriously, "haven't you taught that kid to eat yet?"

At the same time, baby Phil spit a pea onto his highchair. Even Aaron had to laugh.

FIRST MEMORY

Some people say, they can remember things as a baby. Some even say, they can remember birth. Excuse me, but not only am I glad I can't recollect my head being in a vice grip in the birthing canal, but if I did I would have a hypnotist erase it from my memory.

Miraculously, my first memory was a pleasant one. I was somewhere between two and three. I was still sleeping in a crib, and it was Christmas Eve. While in a deep sleep I could hear voices talking to me. "Phil, get up. Get up, Phil. The presents are here. We can't open 'em without you."

I awoke to a dark room surrounded by my brother and sisters. They helped me out of my cage without taking the time to lower the side railing, and we proceeded to the living room where we opened our gifts. For one all-too-brief day, we were a family. All of us were together. All of us were happy. And all the gifts were the best they could be. Well, the Texas fruitcake still sucked.

Like most kids, Christmastime brought out some of my best memories. I'll never forget the two six shooters and toy rifle I got one Christmas. The ends of the bullets really shot out of the guns (this was back when it was ok for toys to hurt kids) and you put the greenie-stickum caps on the back to make the loud bang. I wiped out a good half dozen bulb ornaments off the Christmas tree before the sheriff and her posse lynched me in the bedroom.

For the first six years of my life I had it made. It was the Fifties. Eisenhower was President, and the United States was in a cosmic funk of peace and tranquility. Sure, there was a Cold War, but I was nice and warm. I never worried about any nuclear threat, but I did have one nervous habit to ease the tension. For some reason, I'd pick at the corner of pillowcases and the ends of my shirt collar. With my thumb and forefinger I could tarnish and disintegrate even the best made fabric. That habit drove my mom crazy, but it kept my nerves at ease.

There wasn't such a thing as a day care center. Mothers stayed home in the Fifties to raise the children they brought into this world. That does pose an interesting question, though. Are women joining the work force to get away from their demon offspring, or are their children demons because there's no one home to discipline them?

In any case, while my siblings were expanding the inner reaches of their minds, I was swiftly becoming a 'Momma's boy'. It was me and Mom, and Mom and me. It just doesn't get any better. (Those beer commercials lied). Who needs a Miller when you got Mommy?

I was probably as much an entertainment for my mom as she was for me. Being sheltered and naive has its humorous side when it comes in contact with the real world. One time, while looking at the pictures in a magazine, I learned a new word. Tampax. It was a neat word. It had a nice ring to it. And even though I had no idea what it meant, I proceeded to use it as much as I could. When my older sister, June, heard me say it for the first time, she cracked up. So, I said it again. She sent me to my younger sister, April.

"Tampax, tampax, tampax," I told her.

"What did you say?" April laughed.

"Tampax, tampax," I repeated.

"Can you believe it?" June asked in between giggles.

"Where'd he learn that?" April asked, not knowing herself.

"I have no idea," June nearly spit out.

"Go, tell Mom," April goaded.

So, I went to my mom. "Tampax!" My mom looked at me in shock. She looked at my sisters with surprise. Then, she doubled over in stitches.

"Tampax here, tampax there, tampax in your underwear," I chanted and marched, not realizing my accuracy, "with a nicknack paddy whack, give a dog a bone, this tampax came rolling home."

All three of them were on the floor in hysterics. My career as a comic had officially begun. Then Randy came in the room.

"What's going on?" he asked everyone. My mother and sisters could only point to me as they pulled themselves off the floor.

"What's up, stupid?" Randy asked.

I looked at him with my straightest face and shouted. "Tampax!"

The three women cackled again. Randy just looked at me with his flattop and mouth full of braces. "That's it?" he wondered. "Get outta here you little twerp."

Before Randy could slap me in the head, my dad walked in from work. Everyone suddenly got stone quiet.

"What's going on?" Dad asked looking around at all of us.

"Nothing dear," My Mom said nervously, with a faint snicker.

"Dinner ready?" Dad demanded.

"Almost," Mom answered. "Girls, set the table for me, will you?"

"Tampax," I calmly said, sending my sisters into another giggle fest.

"What'd he say?" Dad asked.

"Nothing," Mom said quickly. "Phil, go in and shut the TV off."

"Sure thing, tampax," I said on my way out, causing April to drop a plate.

"What's he talking about?" Dad demanded.

"Just, just kiddie talk," Mom said, while biting her lip.

"Well, he doesn't make sense." I guess Dad was more naive than me.

I was also an adventurer. When my siblings were off at school, I could excavate the privacy of their rooms. My sisters slept together upstairs. Next to their bedroom was a spare room where my parents stored things or collected trash until it came time to haul it away. One day, while on an archeological dig in that spare room, I came upon a curious discovery. The contents of a grocery bag were nothing more than a bunch of bloody bandages. Someone was injured. I looked in another bag and found more bloody bandages. Someone was seriously injured. I ran downstairs to get my mom.

"Mom! Mom!" I yelled. "Come quick!"

"What's wrong, Phil?" she asked.

"Someone's been hurt!" I shouted.

"Where?" she asked with concern.

"Upstairs!" I yelled. "Come quick!"

"How do you know someone's hurt?" she asked.

"There's blood all over the place!" I said, scaring her. "Hurry!"

Mom picked up a broom and followed me upstairs. When we got to the spare room I went straight for the bags of bloody bandages, and she looked around for a bloody intruder or an uninvited corpse.

"Here they are!" I bragged on my discovery. "There's blood all over the place! And the way they smell, there must be somebody dead."

Mom looked at the bags and sighed nervously with relief. "It's ok. Those belong to your sister."

"Has she been hurt?" I asked with concern.

"No," Mom laughed. "They're just feminine napkins."

Now I was really confused. I had no idea napkins had genders. And, if they did, what exactly were feminine napkins? Does that mean they make masculine napkins, too? I'd never used any napkins shaped like that. And surely, never to soak up blood.

"Don't worry about it," Mom assured, "It's nothing."

I didn't understand. Someone had surely bled to death in our house, and we were not to care. And, where the heckle was the body? Like a young kid, though, I had to trust my mom. Thus was the beginning and end of my education in feminine hygiene. Thank God they didn't make Summer's Eve back then. I would've used it for bubble bath.

LET IT ALL HANG OUT

My mom and I were inseparable. We were like a mother and her young baby, because . . .she was my mother and I was her young baby. Whether we were sunbathing in the nude in the backyard, or taking a bath together, it was an enjoyable time. My mom was a very attractive woman, and I always enjoyed looking at her body. She was barely five feet tall, but at my stage in life she seemed like a beautiful Amazon Queen. I was fascinated by her breasts, and took every opportunity to gawk at them. Maybe it was because I was bottle-fed and I felt deprived of getting a chance at those babies. It wasn't a sexual thing obviously, because I was way too young to have any type of sex drive. I think it's just a male thing to marvel at the beauty of a woman. And, when that first beautiful woman happens to be your mother, hey, who am I to argue? All the shrinks would have had a field day with the Oedipal Complex stuff and me. They'd be right too. I really did want to kill my father and marry my mother. As a matter of fact, I probably would've dusted off the two sisters and one brother while I was at it.

    My mom had a great singing voice. One of the earliest memories I have of naptime is Betty softly singing, "Don't Sit Under the Apple Tree" to me, so I would nod off. Next to getting a story, Mom's singing was the greatest. If you could bottle that contented feeling and sell it on special at Wal-Mart, the world would be a much better place.

    The nude sunbathing was the best. Actually, I never got totally naked. At least, not when I got older. I always wore a pair of shorts. But, Mom would drape a blanket over the cellar door, strip down to her birthday suit, and lay down to soak up the warming rays. We were out in the Country, and the house protected us from the occasional traveler along the gravel road. But, once in a while, a gasman or fertilizer man would stroll around the house looking for my dad. They seemed to get a bigger kick out of seeing my mom naked than I did. Sometimes, they'd stop in their tracks and just gaze at the vision before them for what seemed like hours. Eventually, Mom would figure out someone was there, give out a surprising "Ohh!" and cover herself up. Sometimes, I think, she would intentionally play possum just so she could put on a show. It was some show.

There was one time that really scared me, though. The guy who came to pick up dead farm animals tried to get a little too familiar with our surroundings. Mom was sunbathing, as usual, and I was halfway up a walnut tree not too far away. The dead-farm-animal guy came around the house and got a glimpse of the vision. For some reason, he felt it was an invitation, so he went over towards my mother and stood beside her. She sat up and grabbed her shirt to cover her breasts, but the dead-animal guy stuck his hand on her inner thigh and said, "Lemme show ya somethin', lady."

Instinctively, my mom jammed her right bare foot into the guy's crotch, and sent him rolling backwards. Then, she got up stark naked, grabbed a hoe which happened to be leaning against the house, and broke the handle over the side of the dead-farm-animal guy's face. He spun to the ground and started crawling away on all fours.

"That's enough! That's enough!" He yelled waving his arm, as my mom grabbed another garden implement. "I'm leavin', I'm leavin'!"

He crawled a few more feet, got up on his feet, and staggered around the house, as blood oozed from the top of his cheekbone. Mom stood there with a rake held high over her head, exposing every inch of her young womanhood. The dead-farm-animal guy didn't even bother to look back. Boy, did he miss a vision.

I was frozen in the tree with terror. Mom got dressed and went in the house to either find me, or make sure her assailant was leaving. She never called 9-1-1. (We didn't have it then.) And, she never called the police or told anybody about what happened that day. It was still the 50's. Stuff like that never happened. It was just a secret my mom and I always kept.

Not too long after that, we saw the dead-farm-animal guy drive his truck in the driveway to pick up one of his passengers. He had a bandage on his left cheekbone. He never even glanced at the house.

FIRST LOVE

When you're four years old, it's difficult courting a woman. Most are too old and can't hold a candle to your mother. Others are immature and talk in squeaky voices while wasting their time on dolls. That's why this broncobuster Belcher fell in love with his cowboy outfit.

There wasn't one piece you could single out as the best. The combination of accessories turned any mediocre child into the next Richard Boone. "Have Gun, Will Travel" was my motto; and the best part was … I Had Two!

I still get pistol-envy thinking back on those fine handguns. From their pearl handles to the ends of their barrels, they wreaked of the old West. The cylinder and casing were all metal, because cowboys never shot plastic. Even the shootin' shells were metal, and required hand loading. With the addition of greenie-stickum caps, they were awesome.

No ordinary holster could handle these gems. It had to be leather. When buckled to your waist and strapped to your legs, you knew you were a man.

Topping off the outfit was a red bandanna with white polka dots and the traditional cowboy hat. My hat was gray. That way, no one could tell if I was a good guy or a bad guy. It all depended on my mood. If my hat got crumpled with age, it never mattered. A tilt to one side of the head gave me that meaner-than-heckle appearance.

As with all first loves, mine didn't last. Whether my cowboy outfit was lost in a buffalo stampede or ripped off my rotting carcass by some scoundrel, I knew one thing for sure. You checked your guns at the parochial school saloon.

LIFE WITH PAROCHIAL IS LIFE WITHOUT PAROLE

The first six years of my life were probably the best I'll ever see. Just hang with Mom and do anything I wanted whenever I wanted to do it. I was pretty much the poster child for spoiled brats. I was the baby, so whatever I wanted, I got. My brother and sisters were just as much responsible for spoiling me as my parents were. Even though they were jealous of me, they always let me have my way. Maybe it's because I'd beg, plead and pester them until they did. My ultimate weapon was telling mom that one of them hit me. I was the baby. They were all older than me. They shouldn't be hitting me. Mom would go berserk if she found out they were abusing me, and they always had a hard time convincing her otherwise.

Yeah, I pretty much had it made. Heck, I didn't go to pre-school. Didn't even do kindergarten. It was the '50's. Boy, that was a good decade. Then, the '60's hit. Talk about your decade of civil unrest. It was time for me to enter first grade. First grade, heck! It was a freaking concentration camp.

It was bad enough I had to be ripped away from my mother at the tender age of six, but to top it off they had to send me to a parochial school, St. Andrew. The place was crawling with nuns. They were mean-looking and they were big. They weren't men. They weren't women. They were just 'Weebles' with ugly faces.

I tried my best to cooperate the first day. My Mom took me to the classroom, introduced me to the Commandant, and showed me to my seat. She left. No tears.

As I waited patiently for class to begin, I heard screaming in the distance. It gradually got louder and louder until I could tell it was right outside the classroom door. In came the most horrific sight I'd seen in all my six years of living. It was a mother, literally dragging her son into the room.

"Lemme go! Lemme go!" he cried, as he tried to throw himself on the floor. "I wanna go home!"

If the poor boy's mother sat him in his seat and walked away once, she must have done it at least fifteen times. After each reenactment, she would get a little closer to the door before her little boy would catch up to her and latch onto her leg. Finally, after a running start, she made the distance to the door before being caught. She wished the nun good luck and made a quick exit out the door.

The lady's screaming offspring was closing in on the door with a mad dash. Unfortunately, the nun positioned herself directly in the doorway and the only alternative the young lad had was to fly directly into her black robes. He could've pushed and squalled the rest of his life, but he was never going to move that black mountain. As he bounced and screamed off the nun's kneecaps, she reached behind her and slammed the door shut, made a quickened sign of the cross with her eyes closed, and, with a powerful right cross, slapped the snot off the screaming kid's face. Dead silence.

The poor kid never knew what hit him. He was so shocked by the blow and had expended so much tearful energy crying for his mom that he had nothing left to react to the slap. Without so much as a whimper, the Nun directed the boy to his seat and gave him an ultimatum.

"You stay in that seat until I tell you it's time to get up!"

For all I know, that kid is probably still sitting there today.

I never liked first grade much. Heck, I could say the same about second, third, fourth, or fifth grade. At St. Andrew, we were in the Army. We had to be quiet all the time. We had to stay in lines and march wherever we went. And, we were always separated into male and female groups. I lived in a house with six people and one bathroom, and I couldn't, for the life of me, figure out why we had to go to separate restrooms. Draining your bladder at my place was a public performance. It's no big deal.

It's my theory that families with one bathroom are closer. They have to be. When every morning you have members of the opposite sex all in one bathroom taking a bath with no curtains, brushing their teeth at the sink, and taking a dump on the toilet, we're talking about a tight-knit group. Either that or a bunch of perverts.

Look at most families that end up in divorce. They have nice houses with three or four bathrooms. Each member of the household has his own private room to do all his business, and he never even sees anyone else in the house naked. How do you bond to someone you haven't seen naked? How can you really know someone if you haven't seen him wipe his butt? It's impossible. Give me a family of ten using one bathroom, and I'll show you a group of people who know a whole lot about each other. It promotes better sexual health too. If sis sees big brother naked, she's not going to be wondering what that first boyfriend has in his pants. But, I digress.

As first graders, we marched to the bathroom about five times a day. It must've been a bladder control thing. The girls went one direction, and us guys went the other way. Seemed like a waste of time since my sisters and I always took group pisses. You'd have to stand over the person on the toilet, just to make sure you got your turn. Sometimes, since I was the one who could stand up, I'd threaten to pee on them if they didn't hurry. Well, after the first day I knew what the boys' restroom at St. Andrew looked like. So, I thought I'd check the other one out. I would've made it too if some of those girls weren't giggling so loud. Right as I got one step in the door, a hand grabbed me by the collar and pulled me off the ground. My feet never touched good ole' mother earth until good ole' Mother Superior whacked my asp. For the next eight years, I never got within a hundred yards of the girls restroom.

MAY I HAVE YOUR ATTENTION, PLEASE?

School and I didn't get along. (I picked on a lot of collars at St. Andrew.) Not only did my mind wander in every inappropriate direction, but I guess, you could say I was mildly hyperactive. Lucky for me, first graders didn't take prescriptions in the 60's. If there were something interesting happening outside, I'd walk over to the window to get a better look.

"Mr. Belcher, would you please take a seat," Sister Rose Marie would say.

I was busy. I couldn't hear a word she said.

"Philip Belcher! Sit down right this minute," she encouraged.

I guess I didn't know my name yet; cause I still didn't hear her. Maybe it would help if she got a little closer. She thought the same thing.

"Could you tell the entire class what's so interesting outside that you have to be over here by the window?" Sister Rose Marie nearly shouted in my ear.

Without skipping a beat, or even acknowledging she was so close, I answered, "That house across the street is on fire."

That was the cue for every student in the room to jump out of their seats and run over to the window. Sister Rose Marie was so amazed at the mass exodus to the windows that she couldn't speak. She stood there with her head vibrating on her shoulders getting redder and redder in the face. While all my classmates looked for the fire, I kept my eye on Rose Marie's eminent explosion. Every heated pot eventually boils.

"GET BACK IN YOUR . . . SEATS!" she bellowed at us. "NOW!"

I've never seen so many first graders scramble so wildly to get back in his or her seats so quickly, without someone being trampled. Me, I held my ground over by the window.

"You come with me, Mr. Belcher!" she shouted, as she latched onto my ear and pulled me toward the front of the room. "You can stand over here in the corner and watch the woodwork for a while."

And, as every adult does, she deflated the interest of the sight I had just seen.

"That house is NOT on fire, it's just the reflection of the sun bouncing off the picture window."

Five minutes later, as I faced my 90-degree prison, I felt somewhat vindicated when I heard the fire sirens heading in our direction. Sister Rose Marie slowed her reading considerably, when the sirens sounded, but she didn't dare go near the windows. Then, when the fire trucks stopped across the street, she knew she better think quick to keep control of the class.

"This classroom is 30 feet above the ground," she said calmly. "The next person to look out those windows will be thrown out head first."

We didn't lose anyone that day, but the battle of the nuns was far from over.

MY TWO JOHNS

I never needed any help to get in trouble, but I soon found the perfect accomplice.

John was tall. At least six and a half feet, if I recall right, as a first grader. He was lanky and had a head of hair like Phyllis Diller. He was your average rebellious Catholic School child, but what made him special was that this was his second year in first grade. He knew the ropes. Literally.

One time, in order to punish John, Sister Rose Marie made him stand next to her, as she sat at her desk. What a mistake! As she taught the rest of us, John took the cords that hung from her waist, and tied them to her chair. It made for an entertaining time when Sister Rose Marie jumped up to use the blackboard. It was the first and last time I ever saw a nun hit the deck. Even though we didn't see John for quite some time after that, (I thought for sure the nuns killed him in the basement), he became my first real life hero.

John and I kept in touch. He sat in the back of the room, for obvious reasons, and he would occasionally crawl up to my desk to see how I was doing. Usually, I was bored.

"Hey, Phil," John would whisper as he tugged on my shirt, "let's get out of here."

"I can't," I'd shoot back. "She'll see me."

"No, she won't." John said, as he pulled my shirt hard enough to tilt my desk. "She can't see you down here."

"Go back to your seat," I said, knocking his hand off my shirt.

"O.K., but you're gonna miss a lotta fun."

John shuffled on his hands and knees towards the back of the room, and he kept on going out the door. He jumped up and down in the hall making faces and waving his skinny arms and legs in every direction. He played at the water fountain briefly, and then he was gone. To top it off, I saw my brother Randy and several of his classmates out in the hall running around. Apparently, their nun was so old she nodded off occasionally during the day. Why was everyone having fun but me? Several minutes later, John arrived at my desk via the "slide and duck" highway, and pestered me anew.

"C'mon, let's go," John nearly shouted.

"No," was all I could answer.

"Do you have something to add, Philip?" Sister Rose Marie queried, suspecting foul play.

I just shook my head "No", and shrugged my shoulders. John gave a ferocious tug, pulling me out of my chair, directly on top of him. Sister Rose Marie found us two separate corners of the room to look at.

Did I mention John had some crazy looking hair? After Christmas, that first year of school, I had the perfect remedy for him. For some reason, as a man of six years old, I received as one of my Christmas presents, none other than a slew of Avon hair care and body products. Why? Don't ask me. I was totally perturbed like any six-year-old would be. But, being the quick thinking young Catholic I was, I just knew the Avon hair cream could straighten out John's follicles.

During a bathroom break on our first day back, I checked my pockets. I got the hair cream ready. We'll fix John's hair at recess. As I stood in front of the toilet, doing my business, a button popped off my pants and sank into the watery confines of the porcelain bowl. I had to have that button back. I knew I could get in trouble at home without that button. It happened before. *Big trouble*. So, I reached in the toilet bowl, beneath the depths of the tainted liquid, and retrieved my precious button.

I don't know if it was the chemicals they used to keep the toilet clean, or just the urine, but my hand seriously stunk. I washed up at the sink with the powdered soap they had. Now my hand stunk worse. Not only did it have a toiletry smell, but now it reeked of perfumed soap. Back in line to march to class, I nearly knocked out everyone who I let smell my hand. John smelled it. He liked it. He got an idea.

At recess, after plastering down John's hair with this rude smelling cream, we decided to offend everyone on the playground with an even ruder smelling concoction. We stuck our hands in the toilet, rubbed them down with hair cream, washed it all off with powdered soap, and then shoved our hands in the faces of every living, breathing human being whoever tried to enjoy recess. We stood in the hall for this one. But, not until we had our hands raked with a hard-bristled brush and some stinky soap. Did I mention that John's hair was very well groomed that day?

I barely made it through first grade. I was relieved at the time, but not half as much as Sister Rose Marie. When I made it to high school, I discovered it would've been better if I'd flunked. But, that's a later story.

CONSPIRACY THEORY

You've heard of bittersweet memories. That's what life at St. Andrew was like. At the time it seemed like the inquisition, but as I look back on it, now I realize it was part of the happiest times of my life. Without a doubt, John and I became best friends. We spent more times in the hall together, so we had no choice but to become best friends. About midway through first grade, John was the one to inform me of the big Catholic secret.

"They hate us you know," John said bluntly one day.

"Who hates us?" I asked.

"The nuns do," John replied. "They hate us more than anything."

"Why do they hate me and you?" I asked him half insulted.

"They don't just hate me and you," John laughed, "they hate all boys."

"Why?" I persisted.

"They're women, stupid," John said, half disgusted. "They're big, fat, ugly women. No man would ever marry them, so they become nuns. And, since they have to become nuns, they hate all boys."

"Do they have to be fat and ugly to become nuns?" I wondered.

"No, but it sure helps," John answered. "If they can't find men to marry them, then they go to the pope. He looks them over a while and then he says, 'yeah, your ugly so you're gonna hafta become a nun.' If they don't pass the ugly test, then he sends them off to become Lutheran."

"So, what do we do about them hating us?" I asked hoping for an easy solution.

"Just try to survive," John sighed. "Believe me, this is my second year in first grade, and I know. You just try to survive. We have seven more years of this, and I swear if I fail one more grade, I don't think I'll make it out of here alive."

Ever since that talk, I worked a little bit harder on keeping my grades up.

A KISS IS JUST A KISS

I kissed my first girl when I was in the third grade. Actually, she was my third cousin, but I really didn't know. Hey, it's legal! Third cousins are fair game. The fact was, she dared me to kiss her, so I did. I never liked to be challenged like that, and I never liked to be told that I couldn't do something. When she dared me to kiss her, all the people sitting around us heard her. They were laughing and goading me because they knew I'd never kiss anyone in the middle of a Catholic School class. I did it anyway.

It was just a quick peck on the cheek. Nothing more. Nothing less. But, the gasps I got from the interested crowd made it seem like a passionate, French-style extravaganza. It seemed like no big deal to me. It wasn't unpleasant. In fact, it felt kind of neat to do something to a girl my age that I'd only done to my mom and other older female relatives. And, in the same respect, I was only a third grader. It wasn't like I developed an immediate erection or anything. Kissing wasn't something I'd start giving up recess for. It was a peck on the cheek. I'd won the dare. It was over, so let's move on.

She told the Nun! I can't believe she told the nun on me! She dared me to do it, and now that I did it, she was telling the nun that I did it, just to get even with me, because I did it when she thought I wouldn't do it. No big deal, right? Yeah! While everyone else went to lunch, I was singled out and taken downstairs in the basement. They brought a priest in too . . . apparently, to exorcise the devil out of me, but what he really did, was confuse me even more. From what I could gather, my innocent peck on the cheek had instantly impregnated my third cousin with our child.

Do I know the difference between girls and boys? Yes, most girls have longer hair and wear dresses.

Do I know girls develop breasts? No. What are breasts, and can't they have them frozen off like warts?

Do I know how you have babies? Yes, apparently you kiss someone on the cheek.

Do I know what petting is? Yes, I do it all the time to my dog, Sneezer.

Will I ever kiss another girl again? No, father. As long as I live and breathe on this planet, I will never attempt to peck a girl on the cheek, so help me God.

I lied about that one.

After being forced to repeat my tale in the confessional, and ripping off five Hail Mary's as my penance, I was officially forgiven for my sin against womankind. Unfortunately, I ended up in a similar predicament when I began asking the girls if they had any breasts yet, and if so, could I see one. Boy, what a stupid kid I was. I should've asked to see both of them.

LOVE AT FIRST LAUGH

In the fourth grade, I found out that John had lied to me about one thing. Not all nuns were old, fat and ugly. Sister Bernadette, for the lack of a more creative term, was a vision of beauty. For three years we'd been subjected to the stereotype of old, fat and ugly, and I had resigned myself to hating nuns for the rest of my life. Then, Sister Bernadette appeared in the classroom and my entire philosophy on parochial schools changed.

In a matter of days, I was in love. Not only was she pleasant to look at, but the corners of her mouth actually curled up occasionally, forming what the Guinness Book of Records might call, the first semblance of a smile on a nun.

That smile plunged me into the depths of infatuation. And, it was those bright energetic eyes that led me deeper into a love I didn't even understand. When all you can see of a person are the hands and face, it's difficult to judge that person's total beauty. With Sister Bernadette, though, her face radiated from the pure love within her soul.

Not only was Sister Bernadette beautiful, she was young. The small areas of skin that were revealed to us had no traces of wrinkles. And, by no means was she fat. She didn't have to walk sideways down the aisles just to keep from knocking over the desks on both sides. Her habit and layers of robes and underclothing did nothing for her figure, but unlike any nun I'd ever seen before, she distinctly had a prominent set of discernable breasts. Not that I was looking, but for some reason they sure helped promote the feelings I had for her. Maybe it was because I was sure she'd look like my mom naked.

Sister Bernadette never yelled like the other nuns. She always seemed in a good mood, and got things done in a positive way. She had a sense of humor, and as God is my witness, (and at a Catholic School He usually was), she actually laughed when something funny was said. Once I found this out, I made my move to win her over. It became my daily duty to make Sister Bernadette laugh as many times as possible. If I couldn't say something funny, I did something funny. The best part was, instead of having to stand in the corner, I made the woman I loved laugh.

If another boy made Sister Bernadette laugh, I hated him. I was a jealous lover who had to work even harder to win her affections back. It was a full time job, but I enjoyed the challenge of the emotional roller coaster. For the first time, I was anxious to go to school. It was almost an inconvenience to go on Christmas break because I knew I wouldn't get to see Sister Bernadette. Who would make her laugh for those two weeks?

I was so anxious to get back to school in January, not only to wear my new Christmas clothes, but to see Sister Bernadette. But she never came back to school, and I never saw her again.

We were never given an explanation on what happened to her. She hadn't died, but none of the other nuns knew what was going on, or they weren't saying. I felt as if someone had surgically removed my heart to transplant it in some other body. For all intents and purposes, something died in me that year.

We were now the students of Sister Theresa Rose. She wasn't fat, but she was old and ugly, and she was meaner than heckle. She made all the other nuns look like Maria in the Sound of Music. Theresa Rose had a board with holes drilled in it called "Brown Betty". She used it several times. She used it many times. She used it on me. With Sister Bernadette gone, I could only hope that "Brown Betty" would put me out of my misery. It never did.

Sister Theresa Rose was nothing but a thorn. She beat and publicly humiliated so many students in her five months of terror that we came up with a nickname for her. "Attila the Nun." Attila came from the Order, "Nuns with bad habits". Instead of having knots on the cords that hung from her waist, Attila had little hangman nooses for each child she'd strung up in the cloakroom.

Most nuns had a paddle they'd use on bad kids. Attila had a two by four. If she wasn't whacking kids in the butt with "Brown Betty", she was making them slap themselves in the face. That's right. Slap your own face. And, you couldn't get by with doing it easy. If you tried that crapola, you did it again and again and again until you did it right. And, if you never did it right, "Attila" would do it for you, and then you could only wish you'd done it right yourself. It was the longest semester in school history. I know 30 kids who still have nightmares about "Attila".

I didn't realize it at the time, but I know what happened to Sister Bernadette. She left the Order and went back to being a normal person. She met a handsome man and fell in love, and had a slew of kids. Her new life made her happy, and her children made her laugh. She had one son who tried to make her laugh more than the others, and always felt a little jealous if another sibling intruded on his territory.

The smile I saw on Sister Bernadette's face in fourth grade was probably only a reasonable facsimile of the grand smile she carried into her new life. She wasn't made to be a miserable nun. She was made to spread joy and have fun. Sister Bernadette is probably a grandmother now, and her grandchildren continue to make her laugh. I only wish I could've seen Sister Bernadette one last time, so I could've thanked her for the joy she brought to my life. I want to tell her she was the first woman I ever loved. I just wanted to tell her goodbye.

FERAL CHILD

If St. Andrew was a showcase for my comic talents, then my home life was an isolation chamber. It wasn't all that bad. It's just that I was the youngest person in a household of six people. I was ignored, overlooked, misplaced, and shhhd so much, it was like I was nothing more than a haunting spirit that roamed the house in random disillusionment. Sure, they spoiled me, but that was just to shut me up.

Sometimes, I used to hide in various places around the house just to see if anyone would look for me. It seemed like hours rolled by before anyone missed me enough to go looking. Then, after a while, someone would say,

"Where's Phil?"

And, another voice would answer,

"Oh! he's probably just hiding again."

And, that would be the end of the conversation, and the end of their interest in me.

I didn't let them get away that easy, though. I began hiding in places where I knew positively they would eventually look. When it got close to dinnertime, I'd sneak in the pantry. At bath time, I'd stuff myself in the clothes hamper. In the mornings, I'd be in someone's closet. And, late at night, you could always find me underneath someone's bed. Each time, when discovered, I would jump out from my hiding place yelling "BOO", and just scare the pee-pee out of my victim of the moment. My siblings became paranoid. It got to the point before they'd open anything, they'd look around and say, "Where's Phil?" My mother swore she'd be the next heart patient at the hospital after each high-pitched scream, and one unfortunate time, after inadvertently scaring my father, I came the closest I ever was to actually being hit by him.

My scaring stunts gradually died out after taking a ride in the clothes drier, and being buried alive in the meat freezer. I always wondered if I'd suffocated or frozen to death first. I tried that experiment with a cat, but I got caught when mom went to defrost dinner.

If nothing else, I learned two things from my brother and sisters. Being the baby of the family was the best birth order you could hope for, and the other was how to pour a Coke. You didn't just throw ice in a glass and dump the Coke in. That was a cardinal sin around the Belcher household. Too much foam. You lose all the carbonation and most of the flavor. You pour a Coke poorly, and all you have is a Pepsi! First, you had to have a COLD Coke. A warm Coke over fresh ice is like creating a nuclear mushroom. After you put the ice in the glass, you fill it with cold water and pour it out. This washes the ice off and reduces its resistance to any liquid invasion. Then, you tilt the glass at a 45-degree angle and slowly begin to pour the Coke into the glass. As the Coke slowly finds its way to the bottom of the glass, you get a minimum amount of fizz, and a better tasting refreshment. It may sound stupid and trivial, but it's a commandment I've based my very existence on, since I was old enough to pour my own Coke. It was a Belcher code of Coca Cola ethics, and I've followed it religiously. Besides, consuming large quantities of carbonation made you a better 'belcher'.

JUNE BUG

My sister, June, was so much older than me. By the time I was starting school at St. Andrew, she was getting out. Boy, did I envy her? It seemed like we were a generation apart. While I was still playing with toys, she was experimenting with boys. I can't say we ever did much together, except maybe annoy each other.

Since June was the eldest, she took the brunt of parental abuse like all eldest children do. She was supposed to set the example for the rest of us, but she felt her life was not meant to parallel Mother Theresa.

"What time did you get in last night?"

"About eleven."

"It was more like eleven fifteen."

"If you knew, then why did you ask me?"

"Don't get smart with me young lady. The fact is your curfew is eleven o'clock, and not one minute after."

"I lost track of time, and I didn't want Rick to get a speeding ticket taking me home."

"Just don't let it happen again, or else I'll have to tell your father about this."

Those were all the words mom needed to say to get any of us to mind. "I'll tell your father." God forbid if father had to reprimand any of his children. I can't recall him ever spanking or hitting any of us, but if he ever yelled at you, it was as if he'd beaten you with a cat-o-nine tails. His words and tone of voice were so debilitating that it would take a code blue to resuscitate your pride.

One time, June was so mad at dad. I don't remember the reason, but since it happened once every week, it could've been for any reason. Anyway, she was in our parents' bedroom arguing with mom on why dad should be shipped to Siberia. June finished the conversation by yelling, "I hate him!" She stormed out and found dad sitting in a chair in the next room. She looked at him surprisingly. He looked at her with a stern expression. Neither one said a word; then June ran out of the room.

June and dad had a love-hate relationship. Rarely was there any middle ground. June was always in the process of vying for dad's approval, or trying to make him mad.

One classic instance was when she broke up with a boyfriend my parents loved, to date a boy they couldn't stand. He was a hood, but to me he was a nice guy with a Harley. I didn't understand why they hated him, but I guess most parents over-protect their daughters. If you date them, you better be pretty doggone good.

June left for college that Fall, and it was amazing how quiet the house became. No more arguments with mom and dad, and no more screaming at her little brother to leave her alone. Even though, I was only twelve years old and a big brat, I still missed her. One day I overheard my mom on the phone telling our grandmother that June had left college and entered a convent at Oldenburg. It seemed ludicrous to me because June wasn't old, ugly, or fat. But, she wasn't there to become a nun. June's hoodlum boyfriend had gotten her pregnant. That osmosis is a cruel jokester. Us kids couldn't see or talk to her for fear we might find something out. Stupid me; it was twenty-five years later before I ever got a clue. June's hoodlum boyfriend basically said, "So what?" And disappeared. Immediately after birth June gave her baby up for adoption. She was allowed to hold her daughter for a few minutes, and then . . . June never saw her again.

I don't know whose decision it was to give up the baby. I didn't want to pursue it. I only know that after it was all over, June and my parents didn't fight any more. There was no longer an angry father admonishing his rebellious daughter. The two of them talked like adults, with respect, civility, and . . . even love. The tragedy of the moment brought out the best in dad. His daughter was in trouble and now he had to get involved. My parents could've run June off for what she did, but instead, they rose to the occasion.

A positive result of the whole deal was the fact they let the baby live. Luckily, we were Catholic, and abortion wasn't popular in the Sixties. It was a positive choice, but June lives with the realization that somewhere she has a daughter she will never know. It can be a persistent memory, but would her guilt be any less if she'd mercilessly killed the invading fetus growing inside her? Somewhere, June has a daughter, and she might rob banks or find a cure for cancer, but at least she's gotten a chance to live. June's daughter can make her mark on earth, whatever it may be. Like June, I regretted the loss of a relative, and wished someday I could meet her.

Since then, June has become an advocate of pro-choice. I don't agree with her. I know I'm not a woman, and shouldn't try to tell others what to do with their bodies, but I just can't believe all those years ago June would've done anything to hurt her daughter.

APRIL HAD NO SHOWERS

My other sister, April, was closer in age to me. We could really relate to one another since we were a lot alike. Randy and June were similar in the fact they were more independent and rebellious. April and I were the more dependent-conformist type. We never liked to rock the boat because the other two were on the verge of tipping it over.

April taught me how to play with dolls without being ashamed. She loved movies, so we were always acting out a scene with her Barbies, or doing it ourselves on the back porch stage of our house. April dressed me in drag, and I played the most hyperactive, flat-chested woman you'd ever seen. I was performing in "La Cage Aux Faux" and I didn't even know it.

April and I laughed a lot. One of us would get the other in a corner and would poke and tickle until both of us would collapse laughing on the floor. Other times, one of us would sit on top of the other, pull up their shirt and pretend to play the piano on their stomach. It was a giggle fest worth remembering. It wasn't so much that everything was ticklish; it's just that we had so much fun together.

We really weren't brother and sister. It was more like we were friends. We kept secrets together, we sang, we danced, we even played doctor. I can't ever remember having an argument.

"Here, you take Ken and ask Barbie for a date," April ordered.

"Hey, Barb. Let's go find Tampax," I said.

"Oh, Ken. You're so cute."

One time, April and I laid a board across two fence posts, and we acted out scenes from a Fred Astaire and Ginger Rogers movie.

"You're easy to dance with," April sang, as we gyrated back and forth.

"Yes, I'm easy to dance with," I resounded.

"Except this board's a little bit shaky," April kept singing.

"And I'm a little bit shaky."

"Let's try this one," April thought. "Pump the oil, waltz with me. Pump the oil, waltz with me."

"Pump the oil, waltz with me," I toned in.

After a few too many pumps, I fell off. I thought it would be funny to slide the board off the fence post and make April fall. Bad idea. She fell off all right, but her leg caught on the barbed wire and ripped it open from her knee to her ankle. I was scared to death. As April lay crying in pain, I panicked. Not only had I killed my sister, but now I was in big trouble, too.

"Go get mom! Go get mom!" April finally yelled.

So I got Mom, and Mom took April to the doctor. I waited at home in lonely persecution, trying to decide whether to worry about my sister's life, or my own. When April got back, she had about three thousand stitches in her leg. She had trouble walking for a few weeks, too, but she never got mad at me for what I'd done, and she never told our parents it was my fault. No wonder I loved that girl so much.

"Watch it boys. Here comes Marshall Dan," a limping April would warn.

"Howdy Miss Kitty," I'd say as I came through the swinging doors. "I'm mighty thirsty."

"Drinks on the house for Dan!" April shouted.

"Thanks, Miss Kitty," I said, looking her over, "you sure look pretty."

"Cut it out Dan," April scolded, "you're drunk."

As time went by, I had to start sharing my time with April and her girlfriends. That wasn't so bad, but when the boys started coming along, I was left out in the cold. She wasn't as easy to tickle anymore, and she usually wasn't in the mood to sing and dance. One time, through my bedroom window, I saw a boy kiss April goodnight. He was so much taller than her that she had to stand on the front step just so she could reach his lips. I was so jealous that night, because I knew I could never compete with that.

I almost got even with them once. April and the tall guy took me with them to get some carryout pizza. Her boyfriend went in to get it, but a couple minutes later he came back empty handed.

"I'm a dollar fifty short," he lamented, as he got in the car.

"You're kidding!" April said in surprise. "I didn't bring my purse!"

I sat in the back seat quietly disappointed. How could such a tall guy be a dollar fifty short? Looked like bologna tonight.

"Look in the glove box," the tall guy said, "we've got to have some loose change in here somewhere."

As they frantically combed the car for cash, I realized what their last resort might be. ME!

April and her boyfriend stopped at the same time and looked at each other. They slowly turned around and stared me down.

"Phil. You have any money?" April said softly.

I played deaf.

"Phil!" April repeated, "We need some money to get the pizza."

"So?"

"So no one's eating tonight unless we get some money," April added.

I remained quiet.

"Do you have any money?" April said impatiently.

"I got a little," I shyly repeated.

"Then give us a buck fifty so I can go get the pizza," the tall guy demanded.

"Will I get it back?"

"Yes, you'll get it back!" April nearly laughed at the situation.

"How do I know?" I persisted.

"You'll get it back!" April's boyfriend shouted. "Now hand it over so we can eat!"

"With interest?"

"Don't make me come back there, little man!"

"Phil! Give us the money! We'll give you two dollars back!" April pleaded.

"Deal." I smiled, handing over the money.

"Whose idea was it to bring him along?" The boyfriend asked sarcastically.

"At least we're getting pizza," April defended.

A few years later she married that tall guy, just to make it legal. I'm still jealous! To top it off, he was a star basketball player for the Richmond Red Devils. I couldn't even make the team, and he was a star for the biggest school in the County. I hated him for that. Well, I didn't hate him, cause he seemed like a pretty nice guy, but he was taking my sister away. Pert near grounds for murder in Tennessee.

At April's wedding reception, I got plastered. I was losing a friend and I needed to drown my sorrow in a little booze. Champagne, beer, wine, I drank it all. Good thing I didn't have my drivers license yet, because I would've been a pathetic designated driver. Of course, back then, you didn't have designated drivers, it was just the first person sober enough to find the car keys. I'm sure I made a fool of myself there because I kept singing, "Though April showers may come your way..." Some people thought it was cute.

Eventually, my misery was complete when I threw up in the middle of the reception hall. My big brother got the pleasure of taking me home after that one. In the same trip, he took my three cousins and my grandfather home, since it was on the way. It was all I could do just to keep my head from bobbing back and forth. Finally, the ride got to me and I threw up again. This time, it was in the lap of my grandfather.

"Randy."

"Yeah, Pa," Randy answered.

"Phil's a puckin'!"

My grandfather had been holding some wedding cake that my mother gave him, so I graciously added some vomit icing to it. Fortunately, we pulled into my grandfather's driveway and everyone bailed out. My grandfather gave the cake to his German Shepherd, and my cousins said they'd just as soon walk the remaining half-mile home. Randy then ventured the five miles to our own house. On the way there, I belched a couple times, slowly erupting an alcoholic mixture down my chin.

"Stop it, Phil!" My brother ordered as if I had control over it. "Do that one more time and I'm throwing you out of this car."

When did I ever listen to my big brother? I did it one more time, so Randy slammed on the brakes, got out of the car, and threw up in the ditch. By the time we got home, Randy was mad, not to mention the fact he had a case of bad breath. He pulled off my clothes, rolled me in bed, and set a trashcan next to me.

"Now, if you get sick again, throw up in the can!" Randy ordered. I let out a short belch and smiled at him. "Sheesh!" was all he could say as he got the heck out of there.

BIG TIME RANDY

Randy was the second oldest, but since he was the first male-born child, he had the pleasure of following in our father's footsteps. Whether he liked it or not, he was going to be a farmer.

"Randy, it's time to get up," Dad would yell in our room at 4:30 in the morning. "Randy, get up."

Every morning I heard those phrases ten or fifteen times. Over and over again. Every three minutes. My brother was a heavy sleeper, and when he got his driver's license, he was a late-nighter. The combination made rising early to milk the cows a nearly impossible feat. As Dad's attempts to roust my brother increased, his voice got louder and angrier. My brother always knew at what decibel he finally had to give in and get out of bed. It was a ritual that was performed every morning, seven days a week.

One morning, though, something went wrong. Either my dad's tolerance level was greatly reduced, or Randy miscalculated the decibel meter. About the eighth, "Get up", my dad came in the room, grabbed my brother by the feet, and with one raging yank, he pulled my brother and all his blankets onto the floor. Randy hit his head on a chair on his way down.

"I warned you to get up, and I meant it!" Dad yelled with no sympathy for what he'd done. "Now, get ready for work!"

Dad left, and Randy slowly got up and tried to get his bearings. As he felt around for his clothes, I could hear Randy's occasional heavy breathing and see him rubbing his head. He was crying. I was helplessly scared. What could I do to stop the anger? What could I do to stop the hurt?

"You okay?" I finally whispered as I barely raised my head.

"Shut-up and go to sleep," Randy said in his proudest voice.

Soon, he was dressed. Then he reluctantly went off to follow in his father's footsteps.

Randy marched to the beat of a typical rural teenager. His interest included fast cars, pretty women, and John Deeres. And very much in that order. For his Sixteenth birthday, for all the work he'd done around the farm and probably because of a little guilt, our dad gave Randy a brand new, fire-engine-red

Camaro. No one ever caught him again. The odometer registered a quarter-mile at a time, and I can't count the times I shouted, "ready! set! go!" from the passenger seat just to embarrass another pretender in some has-been relic.

On a late "fire run" to get to school in time, Randy gassed the Camaro past the century mark. It was a fun ride and even got more exciting when the left front tire blew. Mario Andretti couldn't have handled that car any better as Randy swerved around three oncoming vehicles, coming to rest near a speed limit sign. June and April were in shock, and it must've really scared Randy, too. After changing the tire in two minutes flat, he only went 90 mph the rest of the way.

Randy and I were so different. He smoked like a chimney; I liked to play sports. He boozed on weekends; I drank Ovaltine. He could talk a girl out of her shirt; I'd just play shirts and skins. He was a cool dude, and no matter how bad I wanted to be like him, I couldn't come close. It wasn't just our age difference. We were just two separate personalities destined to follow our own paths.

Randy helped to make me tough. After years of being "Momma's boy", I needed a lot of that. "Big Time Wrestling" was our main attraction. He was Dick The Bruiser, and I was some no-name challenger sent in for the massacre. Randy could throw a fake punch better than Muhammad Ali. His favorite thing to do was pin my arms and legs to the floor, and slowly let the saliva dangle from his lips as I screamed and squirmed directly below him. It always amazed me how he could suck all the saliva back in just as it was ready to smack me in the face. But, of course, Randy wasn't always kind enough to suck it in. You just knew he had to let it plop sometimes, and he never failed to address that wet kiss somewhere in the vicinity of my flailing face. He'd laugh so hard I'd be able to free myself from his grip, wipe his spit off my nose or mouth, and go get him in trouble by telling mom. I despised him for that, but bullies at school never bothered me.

Randy had a real knack for making all of us sick at the dinner table. He could squeeze mashed potatoes through his teeth with ease; at least when dad was late. His braces made the event even more appealing, especially when he tried straining vegetables.

April and June really knew how to get Randy going. They used to tease and torment him until his temper reached a boiling point. On one occasion the two girls locked Randy out of the house because . . . well, just because. They stuck their tongues out at him, thumbed their noses, and danced around like fairies around a campfire. Randy steamed and screamed until he couldn't take it any longer. He rammed his fist through the plate glass window and abruptly put an end to all the festivities. All three of them looked at the glass in awe, then looked at each other.

"Dad's gonna kill you, Randy!" April finally said.

Randy puckered up for one of the few times he was brought to tears. "You guys made me do it!"

Sometimes Randy would do good things for me. Once he bought a harmonica off one of his friends and gave it to me. It came with a little case, and I learned to play all the songs that were in the instruction book. I used to take it with me everywhere.

Another time, my brother took me to see a Disney movie. I think he'd had a fight with his girlfriend, so I was more or less a substitute date. After the movie, we went for ice cream, and Randy filled me in on some of the great secrets of life.

Don't trust anyone you don't like.

Watch your butt around farm machinery.

Keep your tachometer out of the red.

And, never, ever, let a woman tell you what to do.

I didn't understand him at the time, but ever since then I've picked my friends carefully, I still have all my fingers and toes, I've never blown an engine, and . . . well, three out of four ain't bad.

It's surprising Randy let me live since I picked on him, too. Not only did I turn him in to mommy when I wanted revenge, but I set traps for him. I was ahead of my time in trying to convince Randy to quit smoking. Instead of badgering him with inane words of warning, I simply filled his cigarettes with match heads. Randy ignited one of my high-octane cancer sticks while driving his Camaro. He avoided a head-on collision, but he burned several nasty holes in his sweater. Not to mention a second-degree burn on his nose.

"I'm warning you, Phil." Randy would threaten. "If your raggedy ass touches my cigarettes one more time, I'm gonna beat you till you can't breathe."

I just laughed at him.

"I'm serious!" he added. "Mom'll hafta put what's left in a body bag!"

Another time, I took the hot-air register out of the floor and covered it with a bunch of Randy's clothes. When he went to see what smelled clean or dirty, he hit my trap and nearly broke his leg. Then there was the time I cut all the good stuff out of his Playboy. He said he only read the articles. The poor guy should've eliminated me just to save his own skin.

Randy's plans after high school were to be a farmer just like dad. He had no use for higher education. Heck, he had no use for lower education. So, two years after graduation, my brother was sent to Vietnam. I never saw him again.

I remember when they came to tell us. I ran upstairs and hid under April's bed. It didn't go away.

It nearly killed my parents. Mom cried and cried for what seemed like years. I never saw my dad cry, but he hid most of his emotions underneath alcohol. He'd always drunk a few beers before, but now he needed an entire blanket of suds to disguise the grief. My parents were two tortured human beings, but there was no way they could help each other. My dad would never allow it. He was too proud to admit he needed someone to lean on, and too stubborn to help console my mom. Both of them suffered alone.

I didn't cry as much as I should have. I felt bad about it. I don't know if I was in shock, or if I was just used to my brother being gone. I kept thinking that they'd made a mistake. Any minute a representative from the Army would show up and say my brother had been found in a Vietnamese Prison Camp. I felt the same way when Kennedy was shot. During the funeral I kept waiting for JFK to open the casket and say, "Hey, I'm OK. What's all the fuss?"

We buried Randy in December. Right before the calling, we had a brief family viewing. It was a closed casket with a lot of tears. After everyone left, I took out my harmonica and played Silent Night. It was appropriate, and it was my favorite song in the instruction booklet.

To this day, every time I see a soldier in uniform, I think of Randy. I'm proud of what he did even though Vietnam was a messy war. I'm proud of anyone who's put his or her life on the line for our country. I don't know if I could ever be that brave.

I still have my harmonica. I haven't played it since.

MAN ABOUT TOWN

Aaron Belcher was a stranger. He was my father, but he was just never around. He was either working his butt off on the farm or out on the town spending some of his hard earned money. The only time we saw him at home was to sleep and eat. When you get used to that routine, your father becomes more or less an occasional visitor, who isn't into the flow of the normal family existence. Needless to say, whenever dad came home, everyone was on his or her best behavior. It was like the warden visiting the cellblock. You didn't dare upset him for fear of getting a week in isolation.

My father started his farming career with nothing. He worked as a hired hand on my great grandfather's farm, right after he and my mom were married. He may have had nothing, but he was as proud as they come. When my great grandfather wouldn't fix the outdoor water pump handle at the house they rented off him, my dad told him what he could do with the job and moved out. Twenty-five years later, my dad bought that farm.

Dad worked hard and played hard. I got my hyperactivity from him, because he couldn't sit still long enough to carry on a decent conversation. Sometimes, I wondered if he even slept. He would come in late from a night of partying and would always be out at the barn before the first rays of sun would hit the earth. Most of the time, it seemed like he never even lived in the same house: Funny though, we all had food to eat, good clothes to wear, and a warm roof over our heads. He may have been absent, but he was the best provider there was.

My dad had two emotions: Extremely happy, and extremely unhappy. When he was happy, he'd sing "Rock of Ages" and call me Philly Bluebird. You could ask him for five pints of blood, and he'd slit open his wrist to give it to you. When he was unhappy, it was Beelzebub himself unleashing fury upon the house. All of us kids would scatter to our own hideaways to ride out the storm. That left my mom to deal with him alone.

"Is there anything in particular you'd like for dinner tonight, Aaron?" Mom would ask.

"Why are you asking me about dinner, Betty? I'm just now having lunch," dad sarcastically replied.

"I'm going to the store and just thought you might want something in particular," mom explained.

"You want me to start planning the meals around here too?" Dad ridiculed.

"No."

"Maybe I could make you out a schedule as soon as I milk the cows," he continued.

"No, I . . ."

"Better yet, I could just cook the meals too, and let you sit around the house longer."

"I just wanted to fix something you liked!" Mom shouted on the verge of tears as she got up from the table and went to the sink.

"You know I'll eat anything you fix, don't you?" Dad responded with as close as he would come to an apology.

"Yes."

"Well, then just fix what you want to and I'll be more than happy to eat it," he added. "Is that hunky dory with you?"

"Yes."

"I'll see you later then," Dad said, getting up from the table. He gently squeezed my mom's shoulder and walked out the door. Mom slammed some dishes in the sink and gave out a guttural groan. He had frustrated her again.

Mom never knew what to expect from dad. You could never read him. He was like Captain Quigg in the "Caine Mutiny". When Mom wrecked the car, all he said was, "Don't worry about it. You weren't hurt, and we've got insurance." But, if you lost that proverbial pint of strawberries, he could harp on it for hours until it just wore you down emotionally. Many times, mom would break down in tears and ask him, "Why do you do this to me?"

Being one of his children, you either loved my dad or hated him. Sometimes, both. There was never any indifference toward him. Even with his absence and even with his wild emotional swings, I knew dad loved us. My brother and older sister may have disagreed, but there was no doubt in my mind he really cared. Whenever one of us was hurt, he would never fuss over us and try to console. He would just get angry and uneasy. Dad would say, "Well, you shouldn't have been doing that". And we just felt worse. We all hated to feel worse. It wasn't until I had children of my own that I understood dad's reaction. Whenever my daughters would get hurt, I felt anxious and uneasy to the point of anger. I felt helpless not being able to stop their pain, so I would make up some stupid joke to take their minds off their problems, but it would only make them mad. I loved them so much that I wanted to make them better. That's when I realized my dad loved us. He had a peculiar way of showing it, but it was pure love just the same.

Dad always liked to be in control, too. If he was at a party, he was the guy buying drinks and keeping all the festivities going. If he was raising a family, he was the guy calling the shots and laying down the law. That's what made things so tough for him when all of us grew up. Yes, he could no longer control our lives, but more importantly he could no longer care or look after us. That's why he took our adulthood harder than my mom. He had missed out on all the school plays, the ball games and the swim meets, and he would never get a second chance. I knew he had some regrets, and that's why I knew he loved us.

Dad was also indestructible. He fell through the ice on a pond. He was a passenger in a car involved in a head-on collision without a seat belt. He was kicked in the head by a bull. Two angry sows attacked him. He flipped a tractor on top of himself. He was accidentally shot by a deer-hunter. And each time, he came out alive. The man was a literal God who could look the Grim Reaper in the eyes, and laugh. Dad also quit smoking cold turkey one day. He decided he didn't want to do it anymore, so he quit. No patches, no gum, no prescription drugs. Dad never needed help. He had the willpower of Zeus.

Sometimes, Dad's god-like power went to his head. You can never imagine your parents having sex. At least not without vomiting. It's even more difficult imagining them having sex with someone else. Dad was always the center of attention at parties, and many women kept their eyes on him, a lot of very attractive women, but none as pretty as mom.

As I look back now, I can forgive dad for any lustful habits. Since I've also experienced the abnormal affects the average male sex drive has on a person, it's difficult to condemn someone for giving into temptation.

Mom knew dad was popular and she loved the attention that went with it. But she never doubted him, and knew she had to be the faithful, trusting wife.

Late one evening, a man who had a problem keeping his wife faithful, came to our house. As I listened from the safety of my room, I could tell that Eric, our visitor, was as drunk as any man I've ever heard. Eric was also a big man. He was an angry, big man, and he knew his wife was having an affair. Fortunately, Eric had no idea who his wife was seeing. He just needed a shoulder to cry on, and his best friend was my dad.

"Open the goddam door, Belcher!" Eric shouted, as he pounded on the side of the house with a loaded pistol.

Dad took his shotgun to the door, and I'm positive he must've had the thought of putting Eric out of his misery right then and there. For all Dad knew, Eric could've been there to blow him away.

"What the hell's wrong with you, Eric?" Dad finally yelled through the door.

"Let me in dammit!" Eric continued. "Orrile kick yer ass!"

"Why you wanna kick MY ass?" Dad asked in fear.

"'Cause ya won't let me in!" Eric countered.

"If I let you in, will you behave?" Dad questioned.

"I am behavin', dammit!" Eric shouted. "Now, lemme in!"

"Take it easy." Dad pleaded as he opened the door. "Now, what the hell's wrong with you?"

"Shumbody's shackin' my wife! Dat's what's buggin' me buster!"

"Calm down," Dad said with a relieved sigh. "The kids are asleep."

"I don't give a shift!" Bill sputtered. "Less tells everybody. Shumbody's suckin' my wife!

"What d'ya mean, suckin' and shackin'?" Dad asked, trying to play stupid.

"Some ash ole's beddin' her down, for cryin' out loud!" Bill said, annoyed.

"What's going on out here?" My mother said in a loud whisper as she entered the kitchen.

"Make some coffee, Betty," Dad ordered.

"I don't nees no damned coffee!" Eric sputtered.

"What's going on?" Mom demanded.

"Just make some goddam coffee, will ya!" Dad said, in his politest voice.

"If I catchems, I'll kill the bustards!"

"You're not killing anyone tonight," Dad told Eric as he pried the 22-pistol out of his hand. "You're gonna sober up, and then you can sleep it off on the couch."

"No em notch!" Eric yelled as he lunged at dad's hand with the gun.

Dad threw his arm backwards, trying to keep the gun from him. When Eric hit dad's hand, the gun fired. Dad jerked to the left on the loud explosion as the shot deafened his right ear. Eric jumped back into his seat from fear, already regretting his stupidity. The revolver dropped to the floor and spun around three times.

After Dad shook his head for a few seconds to expunge the ringing, a sinking thought came to him. Betty had been behind him at the stove getting coffee. Getting coffee just like he ordered. He had cussed at her. Dad looked at Eric who was staring at a sight behind him in total amazement. Somehow the ringing in his ears didn't matter anymore.

"Betty!" Dad pathetically screamed, as he jumped from the chair and turned around.

Betty stood by the stove perfectly still. In her right hand, just a few inches from her torso, she held a saucer and a cup of coffee. The cup was split in two and the coffee dripped from the edge of the saucer.

"Are you alright, Betty?" Dad squeaked, as he grabbed her, knocking the cup and saucer to the floor.

"That was my mother's china," Betty muttered.

"Who cares!" Dad sighed as he bear-hugged her, "we can replace the china."

Eric looked around the room, not knowing what to say. He expended all his anger, and his antics had nearly caused a tragedy. Eric put his hands over his face and began to cry like a baby.

"I'm sorry, Awon. I jess went kazy. I ...I ...why'd she do 'is to me? What I do ta 'er?"

Dad walked over and put his hand on Eric's shoulder. He was too relieved to be mad. Mom put her hand on top of dad's hand and gently rubbed. He watched as she stroked back and forth, because he couldn't look her in the eye. Aaron Belcher realized he was a lucky man. He still had Betty. Before the year was out, Eric and his wife were divorced.

LIFE'S A GAME. CAN I PLAY?

I also had a mistress. She came to me in the fifth grade. Actually, she spurned me in the fifth grade, and that made me want her all the more. She was basketball. Like a true Hoosier, I fell in love with her from the beginning. She was just a game, but it was a game I wanted to last through the four quarters of my life. I only wish I'd been introduced to her sooner, but since my brother and father weren't interested in athletics, I got a late start.

I tried out for the fifth grade basketball team. A friend talked me into it, so I said, "Hey, why not." I got cut. I really wasn't that devastated, since it was only my first try. So I tried out for the sixth grade team the next year. I got cut again. And the next year, as a seventh grader, I tried a third time. And for the third time, I never made the coaches' top-ten list. At St. Andrew, the fifth and sixth grades made one team, and the seventh and eighth grades made a second team, so it was much harder to make the team with so many kids trying out. Everyone told me that so I wouldn't feel bad about being axed.

I was never one to give up. Especially, if it was something I wanted. I always felt if you were going to do something, then you should do it to the best of your ability. Never hold back. I used to wear out coaches and competitors alike because no matter how many times I got knocked down, I always came back for more. That philosophy served me well through the course of my life, as I usually achieved the goals I aimed for.

After my third failure, someone suggested I try practicing on my own, if I was so intent on making the basketball team. It seemed like a good idea to me. Unfortunately, like every other Hoosier homestead across the state, I didn't have a basketball goal. My dad and brother heated a metal rod, formed it into a circle, welded a bracket on the back, bolted it to a piece of plywood and hung it over the garage. I was in heaven. I had my own Market Square Arena.

Shortly after starting to practice on my new goal, I felt something was missing. It wasn't as much fun shooting at this rim. It wasn't like the one at St. Andrew. I needed a net. I gathered up all the loose baling twine I could find in the barn and began crocheting my own net. It took me about half a day, but I finally got enough knots tied, so the ball wouldn't slip through the twine. I attached my net to the rim with electrical tape, and I was ready to go.

Every night after school, I would do my homework first and then go out and shoot basketball until it was too dark to see. When it got cold, I dressed warmer.

When my fingertips bled from the gravel-stained ball slowly ripping the skin away, I put on band-aids and kept going.

Eventually, my snow-covered court would be impossible to play on, so I had to invent an indoor version of my game. I cut the bottom out of a shoebox, mounted it over a doorframe in the house, and began firing tennis balls at my new goal. I won hundreds of High School State Championships at that goal, and each time I won the Trester award for mental attitude. I was in love with the game, but I still had to convince her to love me.

FERAL CHILD II, THE SEQUEL

If I'd been better at basketball, it might have saved me from staring at so much wood trim in the corner of those classrooms. In fifth grade, after remaining anonymous in basketball tryouts, I turned to pyromania to entertain myself. For starters, I found out why you didn't leave altar candles burning in the cloakroom. Little Susie Bennett had to go home without her new winter coat, and the rest of the class smelled like they spent the night at a bingo parlor.

My second violation was a classic. One day, I took my great grandfather's magnifying glass (in its neat leather pouch) to school to show the other boys. The dirtiest girl in our class, Shelly Simmons, sat across the room from me with her long greasy hair bundled up on top of her head. And, the morning sun always shined directly into our classroom on the left side of my head. Are you getting the picture yet?

What can I say? It was a boring English lesson. Sister Elizabeth was reading an epic poem about the Lewis and Clark Expedition, and after I tired of cracking up the class with my pantomime of the poetry, I sought other adventures to pass the time. It really wasn't my fault. The magnifying glass was all I had to play with. Well, at least it was the only thing I could safely pull out of my pants. It seemed like an eternity, but it wasn't long before Shelly's hair ribbon burst into flames.

Luckily for me, and for Shelly too, we'd just had a firefighter talk to the class. When Shelly jumped up screaming with her pyrotechnics, the whole class screamed in unison.

"Stop! Drop! Roll!"

Shelly escaped with minor damage, and she actually smelled much better the rest of the day. As for me, I naturally got the blame. Sister Elizabeth wouldn't buy the concept of human spontaneous combustion. Actually, she should've been impressed I even knew the words "spontaneous combustion". She wasn't. I spent the next two weeks on trash duty, and writing "I will not set classmates on fire".

By now, most of you probably wonder how I stayed in school. But, you have to remember it was the '60's, and it was nearly impossible to get expelled. Most of the boys even carried pocketknives. In the '90's, all you had to do is pick your nose wrong to get in trouble.

In sixth grade, after joining the player relocation program in basketball tryouts, I tried other means of diverting my attention. The day after I was cut from the team, I planned to stay overnight with a friend in town, so I brought all my clothes to school. While waiting in line to go to lunch, I must've caused too much of a disturbance.

"Mr. Belcher! Is there a reason for you to be talking in line?" Sister Mary Catherine yelled.

"I don't know, Sister," I said, a little stunned.

"Well, if there is, why don't you share it with the rest of us?" Sister challenged.

She really shouldn't have said that. I thought for a 'brief' moment, dug in my bag of tricks, and pulled out my extra underwear.

"I'm not sure what to do with these," I hollered while twirling them around my finger.

The class broke out laughing, and Sister Mary Catherine stood there with her chin nearly touching the ground. I couldn't spin a basketball on my finger, and I wasn't the greatest with underwear either. They flew off my finger and landed on the head of one of the girls. Some of the boys were actually crying because they were laughing so hard. The underwear kept being flung from head to head, and the roar was deafening.

Sister Mary Catherine was still in shock. I'd never seen a nun move her mouth so fast without saying a word. Finally, she mustered some volume to override the mob.

"Stop it! Stop it! Stop it! Stop it!" she repeated. "Put those up! Put those up right now!"

Sister Mary Catherine might still be repeating herself if one of the goody-two-shoes girls hadn't grabbed my underwear and handed them to her.

"Don't hand those to me!" she shouted. "Give those to Mr. Belcher!"

I held them high one last time as all the boys cheered. At 50 years old, I'm still serving detention for that one.

BE FRUITFUL AND MULTIPLY

In seventh grade, I learned about sex. Yeah, I know. I lived a sheltered life. I was a farm boy remember. Even though I'd seen countless animals born: pigs, cows, dogs, cats, I was still pretty naive on how conception took place.

I'd heard my brother and older sister talk about girls in high school getting pregnant, and I'd seen dating couples drive down the road sitting on top of each other kissing, so I put two and two together and assumed girls got pregnant by osmosis. I really didn't know what osmosis was, but I figured if two people of the opposite sex indulged in too much physical contact, or exchanged saliva frequently, then the ultimate result was pregnancy.

Heck, one time at a Richmond High School game, my friends were talking about a cheerleader who got pregnant, and one of them jokingly remarked when she did the splits, something came up from the gym floor, poked her and got her pregnant.

"Really!" I said in amazement, believing the sons-a-buck.

"Yeah, really!" My friend said in mock sincerity.

Everyone got a good laugh out of that.

Not too long afterwards, when he was staying all night with me, my friend, John, decided to set me straight.

"You don't know much about sex do ya?" John bluntly asked, as we lay in bed.

"Well, I know a little bit," I responded, not wanting to seem a total idiot.

"Where do babies come from, then?" John challenged me.

I hesitantly told John about my osmosis theory.

"Holy scrotums, Batman!" he shouted. "You'll never have a family, Belcher!"

"Ok, ok, stop laughing and tell me how you have babies." I embarrassingly said.

John composed himself and began to explain the world of sex according to a 12-year-old. "Well, you know us guys got a penis, right?"

"A what?" I questioned, never hearing that term.

"A dick! You know your dick don't ya?" John prodded. "Or haven't you two been introduced?"

"Yeah, I know what a dick is," I said half-mad.

"Well, instead of a dick, women have a hole there," John articulately stated. Now I was really confused. "A hole?" I wondered. "You mean their butt?"

"No, not their butt! It's actually more of a slit, and it's on the other side. The GOOD side," John explained. "Most of us guys call it a pussy. Anyway, to get pregnant, when a man gets a hard on, he puts his dick in the woman's slit and they have sex. Then the man squirts this stuff in the woman and it swims to her eggs and gets her pregnant."

"He pees in her?" I said dumfounded.

"No. It's sperm," John said, slapping his forehead. "It shoots out after sex, and the woman gets pregnant and nine months later they have a baby."

I was totally shocked. For a few moments I didn't know what to say. I still had so many questions; I didn't know where to begin. Finally I asked, "How do you know all this?"

"My parents told me most of it," John said, "and, I picked up other stuff in Hustler. You can actually see a woman's pussy in the magazine."

I jumped up off my pillow like I just had a nightmare. "You've got to show me!"

"Sure," he said matter-of-factly. "Remind me when you take me home. I've got a Hustler under my mattress."

I could never thank John enough for telling me the facts of life. It would be so humiliating to be 50 years old and still trying to get my wife pregnant through osmosis.

"Well honey, maybe we need to sit closer at the dinner table or something?"

John could've lied to me about sex, too, and I would've spent the rest of my life doing it the wrong way. (If you asked my wife, she'd say I did it wrong anyway.) I'm also glad John was a straight guy. He could've told me how gay guys do it, and then taken advantage of me. Man, was I gullible? I hope to hell not THAT gullible.

I couldn't believe John's parents could tell him the disgusting tale of pregnancy. I began to doubt if my parents even knew about sex. Wait a minute; they've got four kids. They have to know how to make babies. Why didn't they tell me? I'm glad they didn't. I'd be too embarrassed in front of them. Hey, maybe they really didn't know about sex, but because they slept together it all happened by accident. Four times! I don't think so. They knew.

After all those baths as a youth with my mother, I couldn't remember what she had between her legs. I was too busy looking at her boobs. Did she have a penis? For the life of me, I couldn't remember. I knew dad had one. I'd seen him pee on the farm. He'd pee anywhere, anytime. The urge would hit him and he'd reel it out and let it go. That was a perk of living on a farm. You couldn't pull out your dick in town and let her rip. Town people are too paranoid. They have laws against that.

Anyway, when my mom took John home, I jumped out with him and ran in the house.

"Where are you going, Phil?" My mother screamed after me.

"John's gotta show me something!" I answered.

"Get back here! I've got to pick up your sister!"

I didn't look back. I couldn't go back. My naive male hormones needed an education. They were thirsting for knowledge. I was going to see my first slit. (If only I were that excited about Geography.)

John showed me the magazine. I was in awe. I stared, and stared, and stared. My body heated. My skin tingled. For the first time I was horny, and I had no idea what was going on, and there wasn't a woman in sight.

I still had a thousand things to ask John. "Does the slit ever heal up?"

"No, thank God," he prayed.

"Do women like doing it?"

"Oh, yeah!"

"Can you do it more than once?"

"Heck, yes!"

"Does everyone else in seventh grade know this but me?"

"You're the last to know, sweetie."

About that time, my mom came into the room looking for me. I instinctively threw the magazine out John's window.

"Hey!" John yelled. "That's the only one I got!"

Later, in the car, my mom asked me what I'd thrown out.

"Oh, not much."

I think she saw the magazine. My mom witnessed her first slit.

THEY ALSO SERVE WHO ONLY SIT AND WAIT

My last year at St. Andrew brought a glorious event to my life. I made the basketball team for the first time. At least it seemed like a glorious event when I heard my name announced. I was the only one in the team who hadn't played organized basketball in his life, so, needless to say, my talents were very raw. In fact, if my talents had been a steak dinner, the coach would've sent me back to the kitchen.

It didn't matter to me. I had the time of my life in practice. I was with my friends and I was part of the team for a change and that's what I'd always hoped for. I don't know what the coaches' thought, but I felt I improved every practice. Even the simple drills I tried to master, and whenever we had to run, I always finished in the top three.

Apparently, my enthusiasm for the game escaped the notice of the coach, because when the games began, I found myself on the bench. When the games finished, I still found myself on the bench. I wasn't a starter, I wasn't a sub, heck! I was barely a member on the mop-up crew. The coach had about 15 players on the team (which is probably why I made it) so by the time he got to me; the opposing team had already boarded their bus. And, to add insult to injury, since the 7th and 8th grades made up one team, there were 7th graders getting more playing time than me.

I hadn't expected much, but I was getting nothing. Sorta like my first date with my wife. Not only did I not score, but I never got the chance to get in the game.

I did see some action on the court. Usually the outcome had been decided about a week before and I was sent in to make the coach look good. One game I was so excited about getting in that I reported the wrong number at the scorers bench, which resulted in a technical foul. Another game I went in and committed three fouls within a 20-second span. Fortunately, the coach took me back out, so I wouldn't foul out. I guess, he wanted to save me for the final two seconds.

Some players would've been upset or embarrassed about being taken out of the game so quick, but it didn't bother me in the least. I was so happy just to get in. The players on the bench were cheering and slapping my butt in congratulations for getting the three quick fouls. I felt like a hero. I felt like a part of the team.

My greatest accomplishment occurred about mid-season. We were annihilating a team from St. Marys, and I actually was put in the game just after the start of the fourth quarter. I felt like a starter. I didn't have to hurry and do something in less than a minute to get the coach to notice me. I had all freaking day! The best part of the game was that I even scored four points. Yeah, you read me right. I scored. I can't even begin to tell you how I felt. Even though I'd never had sex, I knew for sure that this was better than sex. You might score in sex, but not FOUR times, and surely not as a sub. That's right. I was a sub that game, not a stinking mop-up scrub. The coach even told me I played well.

It was the highlight of my life, up until my honeymoon. I played well, I didn't foul out, I scored, and the coach complimented me. I just knew the next game I was going to be a starter. We were playing a tough Rushville team, and all week I plotted out my strategy on how to beat them. Pick and roll. Give and go. Post up. Unfortunately, I didn't plan on using the "sit and spin". That's right, I didn't even play against Rushville. The coach didn't even look that far down the bench. We lost by three points, and I knew the coach blew it. With my four-point contribution we would've won.

So, I rode the basketball roller coaster to the bottom of the hill. My roller coaster seemed to have quite a few more valleys than most. It would never be a popular Disney-ride. In fact, the rest of the season my roller coaster pretty much derailed.

My post-game ritual was to pout quietly, get dressed, and get the heckle out of there. At least I knew what it was like to have leprosy. After the games, everyone who played would celebrate and relive their exploits on the court, and you could see them purposely avoid anyone who hadn't gotten into the game. It was one thing to gloat over outscoring a teammate, but to rub the nose of a scrub in your poop was strictly voodoo. If anyone did talk to you after the game, it was usually in funeral wake phrases.

"Tough luck, kid."

"Sorry about your luck."

"You have my condolences."

"He looks so natural." Well, maybe not this one.

When I look back on it now, I can see how those splinters made me appreciate the sport even more. I didn't want to be a spectator. I wanted to be in the game. It was painful at the time. I would go home to my bedroom and cry. I'd sit in a chair over the warm-air register and cry so hard that I swore I'd fill the ductwork with tears. I wanted to die; I was so upset. Here I was just barely a teenager and contemplating suicide over a stupid basketball game. God, I wanted to play!

One time my mother caught me crying and tried to console me.

"What's wrong, honey?" she said softly.

"Nothing." I said sharply. It was bad enough not getting in the game, but I was an eighth grader and I didn't want my mom calling me "honey", or seeing me cry. "Just leave me alone."

"If those games bother you that much, then you should just quit," she said, as she walked away.

There was no way I was going to quit. I'm going to show them I can play basketball, if it takes me the rest of my life. It was the first real challenge put before me, and I was going to beat it or die. Quit? Heck, no! A Belcher never quits. I pounded my fist on the wall in anger until I made a crease in the plaster. If I'm going to beat this basketball thing, I need to go out in the cold and practice on my redneck goal. But, first I need to find a picture to hang over the crease in this wall.

I practiced until it was too dark to see the goal, and unfortunately my eighth grade basketball career never saw the light. My highlight was scoring four points in one game. My claim to fame happened near the end of the season when we played a team from New Castle. As I was mopping up in the last thirty seconds of the game, Kent Benson fell on top of me and pulled my shorts down to my knees. It's the closest I ever came to basketball greatness in my life.

MY WAY OR THE HIGHWAY

My frustrations in basketball and the onset of puberty made for a volatile mixture. Somewhere in that year of hormones, I developed a temper. It wasn't like me, a happy-go-lucky guy, to go bonkers at the drop of my pants, but it was happening. I was the baby of the family and I should be getting my way. If I don't get my way, I throw a tantrum. I still do today.

    I became a perfectionist. If something went wrong, I went crazy. My failures at basketball made me determined I was somehow, someday, going to excel at it. That point of view pertained to every aspect of my life, too. If I wanted to achieve something, I was bound and determined to accomplish it, even if it cost me my life. I was never going to be a quitter, and I would never be satisfied with being a fan. I wanted to be the current that sparked the fan. I wanted in the game!

    The eighth-grade nun was the principal of St. Andrew, and even though she wasn't as wicked as Attila, she and I had a definite personality conflict. Her alias was Sister Paula! (I ruined more shirt collars in eighth grade than all the others combined.) For all I cared, she could've been Sister Paul. She was the poster child for nun recruitment. Big, ugly, and a man-hater.

    She could set me off just by calling on me.

"Could you answer that for me, Philip?"

"My name's Phil, Sister," I corrected.

"Funny, but when your mother signed you up she filled out your name as Philip," Paula intimidated. "Have you changed it since then?"

"Not yet, I guess," I said in defeat.

"Then maybe you can answer my question."

"Sure thing, PAUL," I challenged, "let me see . . ."

    I finished answering that question out in the hall. In fact, I became quite an expert on hallway etiquette and tile formations.

    It was Sister Paula's daily duty to make me mad. Or was it my daily objective to get under her skin? Either way, we both succeeded. One morning, during mass, I decided I wasn't in the mood to kneel down, so I sat on the pew. Now, we went to church every single day of school. I've got so many masses stored up that I could live to be 100, and I'd still average more than one mass per week. Anyway, I felt one slight discretion wouldn't hurt anything. Sister "P" didn't agree.

"Are you sick Mr. Belcher?" she said after walking up to my pew.

"Just sick of church," I erroneously said before thinking.

"Come back and sit with me and maybe I can make you appreciate the mass a little more."

Talk about a long mass. I felt like I was stranded on a floating body of ice with the largest Penguin at the South Pole.

One time, in the cafeteria, I nearly started a riot: A pretty good feat for a Catholic boy in a place where you weren't even allowed to talk. For almost eight years, I'd endured St. Andrew cooking. For eight years, I stuffed food in empty milk cartons or convenient coat pockets, just to get past the nuns posted at the tray return. On every Friday, for eight years, I endured fish sticks. Hard, crusty, smelly fish sticks. (They were called fish sticks, but they tasted like a dead skunk.) I felt we deserved better.

I finally decided to stage my own protest. It was 1968 and I'd seen it done on the nightly news. At first I chanted quietly to myself. Then, I gradually got louder and louder. "All we are saying, is give pizza a chance."

I repeated it over and over. Soon, the kids next to me slowly and quietly began to join in.

"All we are saying, is give pizza a chance."

Gradually, everyone in the cafeteria began to quiet down to hear the eerie chant.

"All we are saying, is give pizza a chance."

Once people heard it a couple times, they joined in.

"All we are saying, is give pizza a chance."

Within a few minutes, almost everyone in the cafeteria was chanting, except for the brown nosers and the idiots already on probation.

"All we are saying, . . . "

The student body got louder. "All we are saying, is give pizza a chance!"

Sister Paula was frantic, blowing her whistle and waving in the air. But, the chant was too catchy to quit.

"All we are saying, . . . "

Even after Sister Paula drug me out of the cafeteria, I could still hear them chanting, "All we are saying, is give pizza chance!"

I felt vindicated.

Once a week, we went to confession. There were two of those torture chambers. Each confessional had a curtained entrance on each side where the sinners went in and kneeled, and a door in the middle where the priest entered to sit down. From first grade on, all of us were petrified of going to confession. You knelt in the darkness, waiting for the priest to slide back a small partition that enabled him to hear but not see you. Then, to top it off, you had to tell the guy what you'd done wrong the past week. Now, tell me. How much trouble can a first grader get into in a week's time? I had to make up sins just to have some legitimacy for being there.

As an eighth grader, though, I had to keep a daily journal of my sins, just so I wouldn't forget. I guess I added another sin during one of my sessions.

"May the heavenly Father forgive you your sins confessed here today," the priest said after sliding back the partition.

Now, I was supposed to say, "Bless me father for I have sinned. It's been one week since my last confession." What came out was probably responsible for Vatican II. You remember Vatican II, the sequel. The Pope is back, and he's mad as Hell!

"Hello, darkness, my old friend. I've come to talk with you again." Quoting my favorite song. "Because in visions softly creeping, left its seed while I was sleep . . ."

"My son, do you have any sins to confess?" the priest interrupted.

"You bet your sweet bippy I do," quoting my favorite TV show.

"Then let me hear them, and don't make a mockery out of this sacrament," the priest lectured.

"You know why nuns can't get married?" I asked. "Cause it takes 'em too long to get undressed for the honeymoon."

On that note, I made a quick exit. Before I got back to the pew, the priest threw open the confessional door, banging it loudly in the quiet church. He was redder than a matador's cape. He hurried over to Sister Paula, and Sister Paula hurried over to me. All three of us agreed it was time to talk to my parents.

Mom was the designated parent. Dad was out plowing some field or sowing some wild oats or something. Sister Paula talked to my mom privately for a while, and then they brought me in.

"So, Philip, is there any reason for your inappropriate behavior lately?" Sister Paula politely asked me in front of my mother.

It was useless trying to tell two women that my stupid coach was sitting my stupid butt on the bench too much and honkin' me off. And I didn't have the nerve to tell them I'd learned about sex last year and my testosterone level was quadrupling as we spoke.

"No, not really," I whimpered, realizing if I pissed anybody off now, that my dad would be called in next. I wasn't in the mood to be verbally cut apart.

"So, we won't see anymore temper tantrums this year?" Sister Paula slyly smiled, knowing she had me in a compromising position.

I felt the frustration and anger rising in me as I thought about her words. It was if she was the one sitting me on the bench, and making fun of it to boot. I wanted to scream at her so bad, but I held it in and boiled. Besides, it was December 5, and all she requested was no tantrums for the rest of the year.

"No, you won't see anymore this year," I said with a smile of my own.

"I think things will start looking up from here," my mother added, always being the optimist. "Philip's father and I will see to that."

Ironically, my dad didn't say a word to me about Mom being called into school. It hadn't interrupted his schedule, so he wasn't pissed. Actually, he made a big joke out of it. He told all his friends that his youngest son had been cursing out the nuns at St. Andrew. Just when I thought I knew my dad, he always had a way of surprising me. This one I liked.

VAST WASTELAND

Since I wasn't in demand in the sporting arena, I spent a lot of time in the fantasy world of television. "Johnny Quest", "Time Tunnel", and "Lost in Space" took my mind off the real world. I could always count on Will and his robot to give my life adventure and assure me that any predicament had a solution.

My career of writing was also in its infancy and I dabbled in humorous rubbish to take my mind off sports. I got my start in sixth grade, when one of the nuns gave us the assignment to write a paragraph using our twenty spelling words. I discovered a new world of creative writing and found out this type of activity could be fun. As far as television was concerned, I knew I could compete with the inane commercials and ads.

THE FOLLOWING MESSAGE IS A PUBLIC SERVICE ANNOUNCEMENT!

My name is Dr. Manny Tutors, and I'm here to talk to you about your health. In today's world of modern medicine and scientific advancements, many people are still laid up in bed needlessly. Of course, there are those who are laid in bed for profit, but I'm speaking of the millions of Americans who are forced to miss work due to minor illnesses that could have been avoided. Nausea, indigestion, headaches, and even diarrhea can be easily eliminated by applying my cost free, one-step method. The solution to enjoying a healthier life is simply farting.

Yes, farting is the key to staying physically fit. It's a built-in safety valve that helps keep our bodies naturally balanced, yet there are many who say farting is crude and vulgar and has no place in society. Well, I think that stinks! People are more concerned with proper etiquette than they are with their own health. They're afraid to exercise their rights in public places, or even in their own homes with company present, just because of a little embarrassment. I say, stop torturing yourselves. You fart when you're alone, don't you? Well, c'mon then, let go with a whopper and get your problems out in the open where everyone can smell them. Let's shove aside our archaic fear of baked beans and broccoli, and show the world we have nothing to hide: Stop holding back just because someone might hear or smell you. All you're doing is hurting yourself, because the Surgeon General has confirmed that fighting off a fart can be hazardous to your health. Of course, cutting one can be hazardous to everyone else, but don't let that bother you. Once we all get in the habit of free farting, you won't know whom you're smelling. Remember, for every fart you hold back, you add two minutes to the time you'll spend on the toilet. Besides, have you ever seen a briar with stomach trouble? So stand up and grunt for you rights. Farting is a privilege granted us by the Constitution, so let's declare our odor independence. Give your friends the satisfaction of knowing you really care by telling them you don't mind if they fart. They'll feel relieved if you do.

If you'd like to learn more about farting, and how it can keep you healthy, then write me, and I'll send you a free copy of my booklet, "Farting Can Be A Gas". In it, I describe various types of farts, and when they should be perpetrated. There's a chapter on when not to fart, like in a crowded elevator stuck between floors, or during a moment of silence at a memorial service. There's even a section for those still too embarrassed to fart in public. It details how they can relieve themselves and blame it on someone else. So, don't delay. Send ten dollars to: "Farting Can Be A Gas", in care of me, Dr. Manny Tutors, Sewer City, Missouri.

Also, in December, I'm sponsoring a telethon for non-farters. Give us a call and pledge your fart over the phone, or better yet, come down to the studio and we'll put your fart on the air. One lucky person will win a years supply of air freshener for the biggest stinker. Don't forget, that's this December, a time for giving. We'll be expecting a toot from you.

The preceding message was paid for by Red Faced Natural Gas.

STEADY DATE OR SHAKEY PRUNE

Eighth grade was also my year of sexual frustration. I was barely a teenager, and I was struggling with puberty. Frankly, it was getting the better of the fight. I had a steady girl, Rebecca, but going steady in a Catholic School meant that she was the only girl I never talked to. Don't ask me why. That's just the way it was. You communicated your messages to your friends and your friends told the girls, and the girls told Rebecca. Not exactly your ideal method of communication, but it's all we had.

"Rebecca likes you. You gonna like her?"

"Sure. Why not?"

"I'll have Elaine tell her, ok."

"Sure. Why not?"

About this time in my life, the "Sound of Music" was a popular movie. Since it was a "G" movie and since we were all good Catholics, all of us kids got free passes to see it. What a perfect chance for me to have my first date. Go to the movie with Rebecca, sit next to her, maybe put my arm around her, and hope I didn't get her pregnant. (Oh, that's right. You can't get pregnant that way.) And, the best part about the date is that it would be free.

Even when I found out Rebecca had already used her free pass; it didn't deter me in my quest. I traded Duane a pack of firecrackers for his pass, and wrote a nice little note to Rebecca about my intentions.

Rebecca,

Would you like to see The Sound of Music

with me on Saturday? We could meet at

the Tivoli at one o'clock. Let me know after

school. Please say yes! Phil

Sure, it sounded desperate, but I was a horny eighth grader and I needed a woman. I'd be too petrified to try anything, but I needed a woman.

After school, I waited patiently and anxiously by the church steps. Since I was in the right place, I even said a quick prayer. Some of my friends waited with me, but as the time dwindled away, so did my entourage. Eventually, I was sitting on the church steps by myself. I was about ready to give up when

Rebecca came walking around the corner with Elaine. I jumped to my feet without using my hands, and tried to act nonchalant. As they got next to me, I decided to use my verbal charm.

"Hi."

That was it. It was the best I could squeak out. If that didn't swoon her, then nothing would. I eyed her vigorously, waiting for a response.

Without breaking stride, and without even looking in my direction, Rebecca gave me her reply.

"The answer's no, and you better shut up." They walked around the church and out of sight.

What! What the heckle was that! I wanted to yell those words but I couldn't speak. "You better shut up!" We'd been going together three months, I hadn't spoken three words to her, and she's telling me to shut up! Get your skinny flat-chested butt back here and explain this to me! I don't understand!

I was stunned. I was mortified. I was depressed. Needless to say, I found out the next day through the grapevine that Rebecca and I weren't a couple anymore. My sexual exploits would have to wait for another time, another place. I found out later, my note to Rebecca had been altered on its way to her eyes. I never got the exact deciphering of the new message, but there was a good indication that fornication played a large part in it. I just thank God she never showed that one to Sister Paula.

LIFE, LIBERTY, AND THE PURSUIT OF BASKETBALL

Since I couldn't woo the women, I went back to my first love. Basketball. I spent a lot of time in my redneck gym. I cursed the gravel when it stole the ball from me in mid-dribble. I dusted myself off and went to the free throw line when the barn door fouled me on a driving lay-up. I stood on the back of the pickup to re-tape the net after too many three-pointers. And, I kept the ball usable with the use of an old rusty foot pump and a bent needle.

I was going to be a freshman in high school and I needed to work on my game. Being five foot five inches tall didn't leave me the luxury of sloughing off. No coach was going to look at me at tryouts and say, "He's a keeper" without even touching the ball. I had to show them something special that all the other midgets couldn't do.

I felt like I was getting better. With me as the point guard, we breezed by Richmond in the Sectional by 20 points. We nipped New Castle in the Regional with my last second shot from the top of the key. We slid by Anderson by one point in the Semi-State when I sank two free throws with no time on the clock. Then we shocked Marion at the State with a 15-point win as I set a record with 45 points in the final game. If I could lead the "Barn lot Crew" at the redneck gym, then I was surely ready for Liberty.

Liberty was my first high school stop. My brother and sisters had gone to Richmond. Illegally. We lived in the Liberty district, and no one caught it until I was ready to go to high school. So, instead of paying tuition at Richmond, I went to Liberty. Actually, it was a blessing. Richmond was a big school. It resembled a college campus. They probably held tryouts for student managers for all I knew.

As much as I hated St. Andrew at the time, at least I knew everyone in my class. The first day at Liberty I boarded a bus of 60 staring kids for the long ride to the school. I sat with the fat kid in the front seat. Apparently, he was scared to death, too. Neither one of us said a word.

Walking down the halls that first day was like parading naked through Cell

Block "C". All the upper classmen were lined up on both sides of the hall, and they treated the girls and all the freshmen like they were pieces of meat. Some of the praises I heard as I walked by did little to soothe my nerves.

"Who the hell's that?"

"Looks like he should be in elementary."

"I'll kick his ass."

"Check and see if he's got a dick."

"Looks dickless to me."

"He's probably a homo."

If I could just run into Sister Paula now, I'd give her the biggest hug and kiss. Since the seniors weren't addressing me directly, it was easy to ignore them. But then one of them zeroed in on me.

"Hey, asshole!" One of them ridiculed.

I tried not to look, but my instincts turned my head. After making eye contact, I stopped walking. We stared each other down for a few seconds. He was fantasizing about beating the shit out of me, and I was trying not to piss down my leg. At first, my vocal chords were frozen, but then it hit me.

"How'd you know my name?" I asked, using reverse psychology.

The senior looked at me like I'd just asked him to explain Einstein's Theory of Relativity. Then he laughed, "Hey, ya hear that, Butch? This freshman fag's named Ass Hole!"

"No, shit!" Butch replied. "'Bout time they named 'em right."

"Yeah, if you're looking for asshole, I'm your man," I continued.

"We'll keep that in mind, asshole," the senior added, getting distracted. "Hey, look at this babe with the ham hocks…" I got the hell out of there. The seniors knew me as "asshole" for the first month, but I was alive, and the name eventually wore off.

When we had our first school convocation in the gym, most of the guys threw pennies at the principal when he walked out on the floor. I was in hell.

My high school basketball career could be summed up by an angry movie director:

"Cut! Cut! Cut! Cut!"

My freshman basketball experience was like "The Good, the Bad, and the Ugly." The bad: I got cut. The good: when a kid quit the team the first week, I was reinstated. The ugly: after scoring four points in a game, the next day I broke my wrist in gym class and was out for the season. I even had a scoring average at the time of my injury that wasn't a fraction. It seemed fate was destined to keep me from my true love.

Once again, my sophomore year, I was cut from the Team. Surprise! But, since I'd been the JV and varsity manager my freshman year, I did it again. Toward the end of the season, a couple players had quit the JV, so I was given a uniform and actually played in two games. I still hold the record for the best shooting percentage for a JV player at Liberty, Indiana. I was one for one.

The best part about Liberty is that I got to meet Coach Reiser. Reiser was the JV coach, but I felt he should've been varsity. He was young, smart, and energetic. And, even though he ran a tough team, most of the players liked him and wanted to excel.

Jim Reiser was the gym teacher, and since I had him in class, he took me under his wing. Since I was the new kid on the block, (no, not an off-key teenage heartthrob), I became more introverted and decided to feel these Liberty kids out before I cut loose. Jim knew I was lost at Liberty, and he got me involved in activities and introduced me to the right crowd. He talked me into being the JV and varsity manager as a freshman, and as a result, I got a letter for both.

"Phil. Come in my office for a minute." Jim said one day after gym class.

"Sure."

"We need a Manager-statistician for the varsity and JV, and I wondered if you'd be interested in the job?" Jim propositioned.

"Oh, I don't know," I stumbled.

"You get in all the games free, and you get to come to all the practices." Jim explained, trying to sell me on the idea. "You'll probably have a lot of free time to shoot around at the practices, too."

"Really," I said, trying not to sound too excited.

"More than likely."

"Sure, that sounds pretty good," I replied in acceptance.

"Great. Practice starts right after school, so I'll see you then."

Jim would usually take me home after practices. Sometimes, we'd stop and eat at the local drive-in and he'd treat. Other times, he'd take me to the gym on off days and we'd play basketball or wiffle ball. He never let me win, and it took me a year and a half before I beat him at basketball.

"That's twenty!" I shouted. "I beat you, I beat you. I finally beat you!"

"It took you long enough," Jim said sarcastically. "Let's see, it's only been about 18 months."

"I don't care!" I said elated. "This is the coolest win I've ever had!"

"Well, just enjoy it mister," Jim threatened. "It'll be the only one you get for a while."

"Does this mean I'll make the JV team next year?" I weaseled.

"I can't guarantee that," Jim emphasized.

"I just beat the JV coach in basketball, and you're telling me I still might not make the team," I said half-mad.

"Hey, the varsity coach has a say in it, too," Jim said. "It's not all my decision. If it were, I'd pick you on heart alone."

"What's it gonna take for me to make it?" I asked.

"Just keep practicing," Jim said obviously. "Why do you think I'm here with you? Sometimes, it takes a lot of work to get what you want."

"Those other guys on the team don't have to work," I said with envy. "All of them make the team by just showing up."

"Those other guys take it for granted, too," Jim added. "They'll never appreciate what they have. If you don't have to work for something than having it doesn't mean anything."

"Just to get out on that floor, and hear the cheers from the crowd, would mean the world to me," I dreamed.

"Keep working, Phil," encouraged Jim. "Even if you never get to the end, you'll be a better person for the journey."

I never appreciated a win more because it took so long to earn it. Jim was trying to make me a better player.

Unfortunately, my father bought a farm in Centerville, and at the end of my sophomore year, we were going to move. I just got to the point where I was making friends and having fun at Liberty, and now I'm forced to start a new high school. It just wasn't fair.

"Give me Liberty or give me death," I told my mom in a mock argument.

All she could say was, "Honey, I'm sorry but there's nothing I can do."

It wasn't mom's fault. And, I didn't really blame my dad either. He'd rented farmland for the past 22 years and he finally got an opportunity to buy his own. All that hard work was paying off.

I didn't tell many people I was leaving. I kept hoping if I denied it, then it wouldn't happen. Sort of like what I did with final exams. I've got two parting memories of Liberty. At the end of each school year, we had a big carnival to celebrate. I rode a tricycle in the road race and picked up first place. That's not one of my memories, though. Anyway, before I left the carnival I found myself on the steps of the school alone with Becky Turner. Becky and I had become good friends in Biology class. I guess, you could say we did a lot of cutting up together. Dissecting and all. Never mind.

I liked Becky well enough to ask her out, but I never did or never would. I didn't know if she liked me, and besides, I didn't have my driver's license yet. We talked for a while on the steps, and I finally told her I wouldn't be back next year. She seemed upset, but she didn't break out crying and screaming "No, no, no!" like I hoped she would. I told her I'd miss her, and she returned the compliment, and I wanted to kiss her so bad, but the bad experience at the church steps with another Rebecca made me a little gun shy. I just touched her hand lightly for a brief shake, and said goodbye.

I wanted to call Becky after that, but I never got the nerve. Isn't it funny how the weaker sex can leave us men so helpless? Life is funny that way, too. One phone call, one chance meeting can change your life in so many ways. If I would've been brave enough to give Becky just one phone call, I might have been married to her today. As it is, I never saw her again.

My other final memory of Liberty is taking driver's ed' during the summer after my sophomore year. Coach Reiser was the instructor, and I never had so much fun in a class in all my life. He had a great sense of humor.

"Hitting a pedestrian in this class will lower you one grade level," Jim would joke. "And if I'm hurt in any way, you automatically flunk."

On the first day we parallel-parked, Coach Reiser bet me a Coke I couldn't park the car on my first try. Being the competitor I was, I whipped the vehicle in the designated spot in no time. I savored that soft drink. Even after I left Liberty, I went back to visit Coach Reiser at least once a month. I always appreciated what he did for me.

RELATIVELY SPEAKING

And so I began my new life at Centerville High School. It was my third school in three years, and once again, I entered the strange environment with a silent caution. A lot of people thought I was rude or stuck up, but my self doubts were just making me shy.

At least I knew some people at Centerville. My three cousins went to school there. Jerry Jr. was in the same grade as I. He's the guy who helped me get the girls. Greg was a year younger, and he was my main competitor in athletics. Danny was actually in elementary school, and he was the one who took the brunt of abuse from Jerry, Greg and me. Especially, when we were younger.

We used to put Danny in a big cardboard box with a football helmet on his head, stuff the box with blankets and pillows, then push him down a staircase. Talk about your slapstick comedy. Danny was the original crash test dummy. On other occasions, we'd use Danny for target practice. The three of us would tie him to a farm gate and throw snowballs at him. Cruel? No doubt. But, Danny always got revenge.

We also had a peculiar slant on pillow fights. All of us big guys would try to beat the snot out of poor little Danny. Now, wait a minute. It wasn't all that one-sided. We gave Danny a long leather belt to defend himself with, and us three could only be dressed in our underwear. Does that make it even? Darn tootin'! Have you ever had a leather belt wrapped around your face and smack you in the eye? The little scamp put welts all over us before we were finished. Danny usually held his own until Jerry whacked him a good one with the heavy down pillow. That baby caused brain damage.

Since all four of us were good Catholics, we invented our own form of cussing. We couldn't use the real four-letter words, so we made up our own. "Go to Mell" was a favorite. Just change the first letter and you had a different word that had the same affect. Whatever insult we could think of, we had an alternative to keep us out of adult trouble.

My three cousins had a barn on their farm that was more exciting than a carnival fun house. It had second and third story beams to walk across; ropes to swing on; chutes you could slide down to the lower level; a silo to climb; and hay mows to jump from. We abused that poor barn to death. The only thing we didn't do was burn it down. But, Danny did try.

They also had an old log cabin where you could pull plaster off the walls. Yeah, you guessed it. We threw plaster balls at each other. It was neat, too. The plaster would explode when it hit something, so it looked like a bomb going off. Only thing, the plaster balls pretty much caused permanent damage, if they made contact with body parts.

One hot July day, my dad and brother needed help castrating hogs. Not a fun form of entertainment, but a slick way to make some money. To be an accomplished castrator, you had to grab the hogs by both hind legs and vice their heads between your legs to keep them still. If you didn't hold them still it was up in the air on who got castrated. Randy was a pro at it. He could almost hold two hogs at the same time. Dad wielded the scalpel of eminent sex change. When the scalpel was inserted, it wasn't uncommon for the curious hog holder to get sprayed in the face with bodily fluids. Other times, the hogs just pissed all over you.

Jerry, Greg and me were adequate hog holders, but Danny was a little weak. Once he grabbed a fifty- pound hog by the leg and got drug about twenty feet through the blood and shit. He loved it!

Dad always dropped the hog nuts in a bucket to save for one of his friends. Why? They were supposed to be a delicacy. Don't ask me! I've never had a hog nut near my mouth. Anyway, Greg got a little too intimate with a hog one time and knocked over a half full bucket of nuts. Dad and Randy laughed as the rest of us gagged in disgust.

"Well, pick 'em up boys," Dad said with a grin.

"Son of a bench!" Greg lamented.

"He knocked 'em over!" Jerry said, pointing to Greg.

"I'll get 'em." Randy laughed, as he picked up a couple of nuts and bounced them off Jerry's chest.

"What the heckle!" Jerry backed up and started heaving.

"See how many you can juggle," Randy quipped, as he pitched another one.

" Ahhhh!" Jerry slapped it away with his hand and upchucked on a hog.

"Now, that's disgusting," Dad said.

It was frustrating the way the hogs would fight you, but I can't blame them. If someone held me down and put a scalpel to my balls, I'd probably piss, puke, bite, squirm and kick like a son of a bench. Heck, I acted like that on my honeymoon.

After the castration party, Dad took us to the Liberty soda shop to get a drink. When the four of us cousins walked in with our filthy clothes on, everyone else walked out.

"If all the hog pens in Union County were turned over it wouldn't smell as bad as those boys," said one man as he held his nose at the exit.

Another job I hated on the farm was baling hay. Not only did I have hay fever, I had to drive the tractor, too. Now, you might think driving the tractor is a pretty cushy job for baling hay, but when you baled in a field that resembled a roller coaster, it wasn't a picnic. The baler would invariably choke and sputter when we were rolling downhill, so if I put in the clutch we started to roll faster. If I jammed on the brakes, I ejected bales and loaders alike off the wagon.

"Don't put the clutch in going downhill!" Dad would yell.

"Don't slam on the brake!" he'd say, after picking himself up on the next hill.

I was damned if I did and damned if I didn't. Lucky Greg got to stand on the wagon and flex his muscles as he heaved the bales in place. Course, one time I threw him off the wagon then ran over his leg when I took off. Scared the poop out of all of us, but Greg just got a sprained ankle.

When we weren't working on the farm, my cousins and I challenged each other in our own rodeo. We'd jump on sows and ride as long as we could. The sows usually turned in circles and tried to bite your legs, so each rider ended up dizzy. Danny's small size made him the best rider. The sows didn't mind him so much.

A real thrill was grabbing baby pigs from their mothers. The little piggys squealed all the way, and the angry sows chased us down until we dropped their offspring. I always beat them since I was the fastest, and the biggest idiot. Heaven knows what those sows could've done to us.

The four of us had some strange rituals, too. We'd play "one potato, two potato" upstairs at our grandparent's house, and the last one in had to drop their pants and run in place. Greg would take it one step farther. He'd drop his pants and chase the rest of us around the room, acting like a sex-craved lunatic. We'd laugh so hard and trash the bedroom so bad, our grandmother would come up to see what the heckle was going on. The "loser" would invariably have to dive behind a bed to protect his modesty.

Greg also had a potty fetish. One time, two of us were on a lawn tractor chasing Greg around the barn lot. He mysteriously had his back to us as we buzzed in for the kill. He didn't even try to move and we soon found out why. Right before we hit him, Greg suddenly turned with his penis in hand and proceeded to hose us down with urine. We crashed into the barn and quickly washed ourselves off. And, if you ever climbed anywhere, God forbid you follow Greg. If I was baptized once by the yellow waters, I was baptized a dozen times. Eventually, you'd think we'd learn.

All of us even found the time to play sports. Usually, it was an all out effort to kill one another, and it invariably ended up in an argument.

"You were off sides!" Greg would yell after our third and goal produced a score.

"What the mell you talking about?" I responded, as I celebrated.

"You were in the frick frackin' end zone before he hiked it!" Greg persisted.

"No way, botchelism!" I yelled back. "That's six points!"

"Do over!" Jerry broke in.

"You benches are just mad cause we're winning," Danny added.

"Do over!" Greg echoed.

"What the heckle and jeckle you talking about?"

"Do over or we quit," Jerry threatened.

"Yeah, do over or we're done and you forfeit," Greg added.

As Greg turned around, I took off my football helmet and threw it at him. It rocketed just past his head and landed twenty feet away.

"Nice try," Greg said more calmly than I expected. "Too bad you throw like a girl."

We ran the play over, and of course, they stopped us. We hit them with the only word we could.

"CHEATERS!"

Years later, as adults, I had to apologize to Greg for throwing the helmet at him. We were playing basketball, and the muscle bound player I was guarding didn't like the way I stuck to him on defense. When we checked the ball, he threw it at me a little harder than I thought he should. I rammed it back at him. He dropped the ball and lunged at me with a swinging right fist. Luckily, I ducked but he got me in a headlock. Greg jumped on the guys back, pulled him off me and took him to the ground. I cheered for Greg to kill the guy until it was broken up. After the fight was all over, someone told Greg and I that the guy we were fighting had just been cut by the Dallas Cowboys. I owed Greg my life.

Jerry was a lunatic. Once, we challenged him to hold an entire tin of Skoal smokeless tobacco in his mouth for two minutes without slobbering. I never laughed so hard in my life as we watched him prance around the room turning red, purple, and green. That was the best five bucks I ever spent. Jerry won the bet, but he lost that sub sandwich he'd just eaten.

Jerry was also a lover: a ladies' man. He could charm a girl out of her socks, and a few other articles of clothing on his best days. Greg and Danny called him the all meat wiener.

"Voulez vous couche avec moi?" Jerry would ask in his best French accent.

"Aren't you dating Lucy, Mr. Frenchy?"

"You don't see her here, do you?" Jerry would question.

"You are a nasty little sexist."

"Hey, I'm a gentleman and I live by a strict code of conduct."

"Yeah, right."

Jerry usually got the girl, in the backseat.

It's amazing how all four of us survived. One of us should've been the lead story on the six o'clock news. We threw fire crackers at each other, had dirt clod fights, rolled each other down a hill in barrels, tried to run each other over with lawn tractors and mini bikes, jumped off barn roofs with umbrellas, and concocted home-made bombs with match heads. We were walking fatalities just waiting to happen. Somehow, we beat the odds. And, with the help of those three, I made it through Centerville.

I made it through Centerville, but basketball at Centerville made it without me. I was young for my grade. I could've been held back a year with no problem.

Since I was a junior, the coach didn't want to keep me on the JV. So, I was cut while three other sophomores less talented than me were kept. If only I'd flunked first grade at St. Andrew, I'd made the basketball team at Centerville. All I needed was to get in trouble with John at St Andrew a couple more times and I would've been set.

My senior year, I guess, you could say I cut myself. After final cuts had been made, I was still on the team, but I was practicing with the JV, while my cousin Greg scrimmaged with the varsity. Seniors can't play on JV. So, after a week of humiliation, I confronted the coach.

"Hey, coach. I need to talk to you," I said, hesitantly.

"Yeah, what is it?" he said, half-paying attention.

"Am I on the team or not? I've been practicing with the JV for a week."

"What grade are you in?" the coach asked.

"I'm a senior," I said with regret.

"Then I guess not," he replied, not even looking at me.

"Thanks a lot," I said, disgusted, as I started to walk away.

"Can't keep seniors on JV. Too bad you're not a junior," Coach said, turning his knife in my guts.

"Yeah, right," I said with anger and disappointment. "Too bad you're not a coach."

"What'd you say?" he shouted, looking up for the first time.

I didn't even turn around to acknowledge he'd spoken.

"Yeah, you're cut Belcher!" he yelled. "You're off the team"

I walked upstairs in the gym and joined the wrestling team. The basketball coach had to deal with his players who'd been standing around listening to our exchange. Several of the players told me later it wasn't right what he did to me. That coach lost a lot of respect that day. And not only from me.

For the second year in a row, I was one grade too old to make the team. I did go to the Regional as a wrestler, but it just wasn't the same as basketball. I was still in love with her, but I couldn't convince her to fall in love with me. The sad part about the whole thing is that in my four years of high school, the varsity basketball teams won a whopping total of ten games. Ten games! I could've picked out four nerds from the library and registered more wins with me as point guard. Hell, I could've recruited four cheerleaders and had more success. Would've been more fun in the locker room, too.

So, my anemic high school basketball career ended. In fact, my entire high school experience was so anemic, since I split two years with two different schools. I was a man without an Alma Mater.

Being on a basketball team now seemed impossible. How the hell was I supposed to play in college? I doubt if Bob Knight was looking for a slow, white, 5' 8" guard with an erratic shot. Besides, if you didn't make it in high school basketball in Indiana, then nothing else mattered. I had to find something or someone else to fall in love with.

DATING GAME

My high school love life paralleled that of the main character in "Revenge of the Nerds". Between getting chewed out in third grade for kissing my cousin, and having Becky turn me down so vehemently in eighth grade, I was extremely gun shy. I felt for sure if I ever got to the point where I knew a girl well enough to kiss her, Attila the nun would pop out of the back seat of my '59 Edsel with her board in hand.

Sure, I dated a bit, but I was either too shy, too slow, or not on the basketball team.

I know of at least three girls I dated for a couple weeks, who turned up pregnant within a year of breaking up with me. Guess you could say, I had a lot of close calls. Either that or my dating ineptitude drove women to sexual frustration. Even so, I graduated 25th academically in my class, and number one on the virgin list.

I was headed for Purdue University in the Fall. For what reason, I had no idea. But, I still had a summer to get through, without a steady girl. Finally, I asked my cousin Jerry, if he and his girlfriend, who he'd been dating since the Ice Age, could find me someone to go out with. I wasn't picky. I did prefer a woman. Some semblance of breasts would be nice, but not mandatory. All I cared about was that I didn't have to pack a lunch to walk around her, strain my neck to look her in the face, or have her beat me at basketball.

To me, the dating game is one big pain in the ass. Granted, it's been over three decades since I was a contestant, but one never forgets the anguish of reading minds. "Does she like me?" "Does she want me?" "What is she really like?" And of course, "What the hell does she mean by that?"

Someday, they'll invent a machine you can point at a potential dating prospect, and it will tell you everything you want to know about them. More than likely, it will tell you things you DON'T want to know. This fantastic new machine could be called a "Diagnostic Interpretation Center for Knowledge". DICK, for short.

At first, the DICKS will be bulky; about the size of a VCR. When they're new, you'll be able to pull one over on your dates, but once everyone gets word on what you're using, it'll be hard to point your DICK at a woman without her knowing what's going on.

Gratefully, when the new models come out, they'll be the size of a ballpoint pen. These small DICKs will be fun to use. No one will know when they're being analyzed. Point it at your potential date and watch it do its thing.

@^*)(#: BEEP! Specimen- female: age-23: dimensions- 34-24-36: (Padded bra adds two inches to chest) hair-blonde: (brown roots, bad bleach job) face-Max Factor makeup, hides acne scars and sagging cheekbones. Stamina of a race horse, and is presently on the pill. Has no desire for marital commitments. Looking for a good time with no ties. Female is presently not ovulating, conception highly unlikely. She thinks you're an ass hole! BEEP! @^*)(#

Pretty scary stuff. Women would no longer be so mysterious to us men. But, in the same respect, men would no longer be able to hide all their faults from the women they lust after. When a woman uses her DICK on a man, it's sure to raise a few eyebrows.

@^*)(#: BEEP! Specimen-male: age-27: dimension-32" waist, but has gut sucked in. Hair-thinning on top, strategic comb job hides it. Lives with parents. Socks and underwear on their third day. Abdominal area contains high traces of gastronomic energy. Brain waves indicate obsession on getting member of opposite sex naked. Specimen thinks you're ugly, but have a killer body. Wants to go to your place so he can skip out when he's done. Carrying a year-old prophylactic in wallet, but it's dry-rotted. He's married! BEEP! @^*)(#

As these new "DICKS" become more complex, the language will deteriorate to accommodate the average man and woman. No beating around the bush. Just get right to the point.

@^*)(#: BEEP! WARNING! WARNING! Just started period. TOTAL BITCH! No desire to be with a man, unless it's to castrate him. Have had more sex partners than Wilt Chamberlain; and in half the time. Drove hard, put away wet. Breast implants, Liposuction, nose job, and facelift. Has ears like Dumbo. Wearing Depends and an IUD equipped with razor blades. If you have any dignity, RUN LIKE HELL! BEEP! @^*)(#

Ahhh! Yes. These new "DICKS" will make dating a lot simpler. Probably a lot shorter, too!

LOVE IS BLIND. USE BRAILLE

I never meant to fall in love. It was just a blind date arranged by a cousin. How good could it be? I went into the date with hope, but prepared myself for mediocrity. The fact my cousin Jerry said she had a great personality didn't encourage me as far as having any success.

Before the date ever began, before I even met her, I made a promise to myself. I vowed this date would not fail because of me. I vowed I would not be backward and shy, and create long pauses of tense silence.

Ironically, my cousin and his girlfriend had warned my date I might not talk much. Without knowing it, I set out to prove them wrong.

"You must be Diane," I smiled, as I met my blind date at the door, flashing my dimples and bright blue eyes.

"That's me," she smiled back. I didn't know it at the time, but Diane had already fallen in love.

I met her mother and brother (her father was at work, thank God) and we left for our double date with Jerry and Marla. On the way to the movie, I was talking faster than an auctioneer. I had a billion questions to ask Diane. When I ran out of questions, I had a comment or statement about anything imaginable. I was a chatterbox that wouldn't allow any prolonged silences.

"Did you know 'stop' signs are octagons? They call this road US 40 because it runs along the 40th Parallel. Did you know fruit flies only live three days? That's not much time to arrange a funeral."

When we got out of the car at the theatre, I actually looked at Diane for the first time. She was 16. Almost a junior in high school. She had long blonde hair that hung well below her shoulders. Her eyes were blue, and her cheeks were naturally flush with a red glow. She didn't wear any makeup. As we walked toward the theatre, I took her hand in mine. A bold step for a guy, who usually drove women to a nunnery.

We were late, and the theatre was crowded, so the four of us had to sit in the front row. We went to see "Bullit" and it made me a little melancholy. Steve McQueen reminded me of Randy; with his brash attitude and the way he drove the streets of San Francisco.

Sometime during the movie, I put my arm around Diane. Sure, it fell asleep. Yes, I was in pain, but I didn't dare take my arm back. I'd rather have them cut if off than be accused of being a lousy date.

After the movie, we had a late dinner. Once again I hosted my own talk show, with the three guests in the booth.

"So, you liked the movie, Diane?" I asked.

"Yeah, I thought it was good," she said diplomatically.

"Did you think it was great?" I pressured.

"Well, I wouldn't go that far," Diane stated.

"Why not?" I prodded, being glad she didn't just agree with me to make me happy.

"I've seen better movies, and I've seen worse," she explained, "I thought it fell somewhere in the middle."

"Hey, you know what I like?" my cousin Jerry interrupted. "When strippers twirl those tassels in opposite directions. Can you do that, Diane?"

"I hadn't planned on trying," Diane smiled, as a blush overcame her cheeks.

I felt myself suddenly aroused at the thought of Diane in that situation. Jerry was always good about breaking the ice that way. Or just breaking up the conversation with his inane sexual humor.

Later, we went to Jerry's house and watched some TV. Soon, I found myself alone in the living room with Diane. Panic and anxiety frolicked through my veins.

{You've got to make your move NOW, you dummas! You may never get another chance like this!}

{What if I try to kiss her and she turns away? I'll be humiliated. What if I have bad breathe? What did I eat for dinner? Where's my tic-tacs?}

{Tic-tac my ass! Kiss her now, or go, buy a subscription to Playgirl.}

{What if she doesn't like me?}

{Tuff shit! Get it while ya can!}

Without dwelling too long, I turned to Diane and put my lips on hers. Oh, my God! She opened her mouth, and soon our tongues were exchanging unfamiliar saliva. I didn't know about her, but I was in heaven. And, if Sister Paula could've seen me, she'd say I was going straight to Hell.

If Jerry and Marla hadn't walked back in the room, Diane and I could've quite possibly tongue-wrestled all night. We both tried to act cool, but we were both steaming from the heat of passion. When our date ended, I walked her to the door and gave her another kiss. This one was short and sweet, because Jerry and Marla were in the car, and I just knew her mom was looking out from behind the curtains.

I got back in the car with my peacock feathers in full plume. It was the best date I'd ever been on. It was the best time I'd ever had with another girl. And, it was a freakin' BLIND DATE! Whether she liked me or not, I knew I'd shocked her.

Something must have gone right on that date. I got a second one. This time we went out on our own. I can't even remember what movie we saw that night, but the evening went well. The only drawback was that the next morning Diane was leaving with her friend's family to go to San Francisco for two weeks. We were at the beginning of a relationship, and now it had to be interrupted and possibly squelched.

I looked for signs she didn't want to leave me all alone in Indiana. I didn't see any. I kissed her goodbye, and I knew any second she would grab me in tears and beg me to take her away from her evil friends, who were going to separate us. It never happened.

"Call me when you get back," I nearly begged her.

"Give me your number," she answered, "or, maybe I can get it off Marla."

"No. I'll give it to you."

I wrote those seven digits as slowly as possible. I kissed her one last time and left.

"Not again!" I kept thinking on the way home. I've blown another relationship with a good-looking girl. I was positive Diane would come home from San Francisco pregnant, and I wouldn't have a hand in it. Or, any other body-part for that matter.

Years later, I found out, after I left Diane's house that night, she called her friend and nearly cancelled her trip. Why can't women tell us how they really feel? I had no indication how she felt about me. It drives me crazy how women refuse to tell the men in their lives what their true feelings are. Then, after you leave, they call their best girlfriend and spill their guts. Crazy, I tell you. I need one of those DICK things.

Two weeks later, Diane called me. I was ecstatic, but I couldn't show it. My mom and dad were in the room when I got the call. We had no other phones in the house, and since the kitchen, dining room, and living room were all one big area, I couldn't ask them to leave.

{Mom, dad, go to your bedroom please so I can make love over the phone.}

Yeah, I could just see my dad falling for that one.

"Hello, is this Phil?" Diane said in her welcomed voice.

"Yeah," I replied, trying to hide my excitement.

"This is Diane."

"Who?" I asked like an idiot.

"Diane. Diane Atkins. We went out a couple weeks ago."

"Oh, yeah," I struggled with my choice of words.

"You asked me to call you when I got back from San Francisco," Diane said in a voice indicating she was getting doubtful.

"Did I?" I tripped, "I mean, I did."

"So, I'm back from San Francisco," Diane said searching for words.

"Good."

"Marla said you wanted me to call?" she almost asked.

"That's right."

"She mentioned something about seeing a movie?" Diane added on the verge of doubt.

"That sounds good," I said approvingly, until I remembered my parents were ten feet away. Great! Now they think the girl on the other end offered me a night of orgasmic lust.

"O.k., I'll talk to you later," she said, giving up.

"O.k." I echoed.

"Goodbye," Diane said in disappointment.

"Bye," I said quickly and hung up. Oh, great! What a pathetic conversation. Diane probably thinks she was talking to Marcel Marceau.

"Who was on the phone, Phil?" my mom pried.

"Oh, just a wrong number," I thought quickly. I don't think they bought it, though.

Needless to say, I got to Jerry's house as fast as I could and called Diane back.

"I can't believe how cold you were," Diane scolded me.

"Sorry. I was half asleep," I lied, not wanting to tell her I was afraid of my parents hearing our conversation.

I did get another date, thank God! And, by the time I left for college, we were a couple. We were so much a couple that we didn't want to separate. Fortunately, Purdue was only two hours away and I came home every weekend. Seeing Diane was the only thing that kept me going. I didn't know why I was going to college, and to enter another school where I didn't know a soul was just too much to take. I was 17 years old, didn't know what I wanted out of life, and was lost. If only I'd failed first grade.

It was fun having a steady date. Someone you could count on. Someone you could share your life with. Ironically, Diane and I were both virgins.

Imagine that! Two virgins from the same high school, actually meeting each other. We had a lot of experimenting to do.

One of my best memories was, guess what? You're right! The drive-in movie. We double-dated with Jerry and Marla. Diane and I sat in the front seat, and fortunately, it was a bench-seated LTD. I had my right arm around her shoulders, and held her hand with my left. I worked ultra slowly. I started rubbing her hand, progressed to her knee, and gradually made my way up her thighs. After nearly an hour of the movie, I finally got inside her underpants. Paydirt! Or should I say, BUSH! They always say a bush in the hand is worth two in the pants. After another 15 minutes of fondling, I finally discovered what John was talking about in his seventh grade sex talk. Oh, my God! "I could've danced all night", but soon it was intermission.

During the second feature, I worked on her upper torso. Same slow, methodic style. Same glorious success. I felt like a Casanova stud by the time the evening was over. That is, until I found out later that Jerry and Marla had actually had sex in the back seat. Guess I was watching the wrong show.

The next night, I almost lost Diane forever. We were supposed to have a date at 7 PM that evening. I'd worked hard baling straw that day, but I got off work in plenty of time to make the date. I was cleaned up and ready to go by 6:15, so I decided to lie on the bed and relax for the first time in a hectic day. Bad Idea. I woke up three hours later.

"SHIT!" I shouted as I sprang off the mattress. "Why didn't you wake me up?" I said threateningly to my parents without thinking, as I cruised through the living room.

"You looked tired," my mother quietly replied. "Where are you going?"

I didn't even answer, as I went out the door. When I arrived at Diane's house five minutes later, she was sitting on the porch steps. Her legs were crossed, and her foot was bouncing up and down so fast it blurred in the glow of the porch light. She was pissed.

"I'm sorry Diane," I whimpered before I even got to her. "I fell asleep and just woke up."

"You're two and a half hours late," she replied coldly.

"I know. I'm sorry." I apologized again. "I just laid down for a minute and fell asleep."

"You may as well go home, now," she said mercilessly, "it's too late."

I was caught off guard by her reaction. I'd made an honest mistake, and she was treating me like I did it on purpose. I was dead tired, still half asleep from my nap, frustrated that I'd ruined our evening, and now Diane was scaring me.

"Please don't make me go," I begged Diane as my eyes began to water.

"Why shouldn't I?" she asked, looking away. "You stood me up."

"No, I didn't," I responded, as my groggy brain tried to think of an out. "It's not like I consciously avoided coming here tonight, or went somewhere else instead. I just laid down and zonked out. You can call my mom and dad and ask them. They were home when I left."

"So, what happened?" Diane questioned as she looked back in my direction.

"I was ready to go and I just laid down for a minute, and the next thing I know it's after nine," I tried to explain. "I 'bout pooped my pants when I saw the time."

"Really," Diane said, trying to hide a smile. "I guess I'm not important enough to remember."

"That's not true," I said, bending on one knee and taking her hand. "You're the most important thing in the world to me right now, Diane. Don't let this ruin everything."

"I don't like to be stood up," she persisted, just trying to make me suffer.

"I know. I'll make it up to you," I said in my sexiest voice. "It'll never happen again."

"Are you sure?"

With those three words, and a small inkling of a smile creeping on her face, I knew I was saved. "I promise."

Diane and I waited two years before we had sex. She wanted to graduate first because it disgusted her how all the other girls at school bragged about how many times they'd done it or how many boys they'd done it with. I still think the oversleeping incident had a lot to do with it. Me? I was ready any second to lose my virginity. Hell, I was hoping it was already in the lost and found.

We found other ways to entertain ourselves. Heavy petting was a favorite. Actually, it was OBESE petting. I was a perfectionist. Most of the time, I'd get Diane totally naked in the back seat of my '59 Edsel, (I didn't do as much farm work as Randy) and I'd strip down to my underwear and we'd indulge in foreplay until I couldn't hold back. Not exactly the best climactic opportunity for a female, but at least we both were still virgins. Sometimes, Diane wouldn't be in the mood to do the naked mamba underneath my jockeyed body. That's when I'd get mad. I was used to getting my way. Whenever I didn't, I'd throw a tantrum. Diane was the older sister of her family, so she was used to her brother always getting whatever he wanted.

"Where are you going?" Diane would ask, knowing the answer.

"I thought we could go park," I tried saying in my most seductive voice.

"I really don't feel like doing that tonight," she said with a sigh.

"Why not?" I asked pathetically.

"Trust me," she answered, keeping something from me, "I just don't."

I hated it when she kept something from me. My siblings always kept stuff from me. They never told me any good stuff because I was always TOO YOUNG. "Why not?" I persisted. "It's fun."

Then Diane brought in the heavy artillery. "It may be for you," she unloaded.

Now she was challenging my masculinity. "You don't like it?" I squeaked.

"It's just that I'm not in the mood to have sex tonight," she restated, trying to change the subject.

"We're not having sex," I rationalized in my best Nixon voice. "You said you didn't want to have sex until after you graduated. We're just fooling around."

"O.k., then I don't want to fool around."

"Why not?" I whimpered like the baby I was.

"If you must know, I started my period last night," Diane said, hitting me below the belt this time.

It only took me a second to return the fire. "O.k., no problem. You can leave your underwear on."

"Ahhhhh! You are driving me crazy!" she said in frustration. "Can't you take no for an answer?"

"That depends on the question," I answered with a big smile and a wink of my baby blues. "If I asked, if you wanted to date another guy, I'd love it, if you said 'No.'"

"You are impossible," she said with a grin.

Needless to say, we parked that night. Sometimes, I'd use charm, sometimes, I'd use guilt, and still, other times, I'd use sympathy. The sympathy didn't always work. She said I could find sympathy between syphilis and shit in the dictionary. I didn't always get my way either. Luckily, those nights were few and far between.

One evening, I wasn't getting my way. We were alone at her house and she didn't want to fool around. We had three bedrooms and two couches available to us and she didn't want to fool around. I felt like a fat guy at a smorgasbord without a plate. Finally, after an hour of begging, she agreed to go park. I was out the door like Edwin Moses with keys in hand. She shut the door behind me and locked herself in the house. Reminiscent of Randy and my sisters years ago.

At first, I was amused. I laughed and said, "Very funny, now open up." All she did was giggle, wave, and say "No." Slowly, my blood began to boil. I was a horny guy, and now I was being humiliated. I pounded on the door for her to open up. She only giggled louder. Now, I was mad. I beat the door for all I was worth, and on the last stroke I put my fist through the cheap thing. Suddenly, getting my rocks off was the farthest thing from my mind. Is 84 Lumber open this late?

Diane and I drove around for a while, contemplating my dilemma. We could just go back and act surprised like we knew nothing. But, what if a neighbor saw me pounding on it? We could blame it on the paperboy! Yeah, but the screen door wasn't damaged. We could blame it on an overzealous Seventh Day Adventist. Great! Just what every guilty Catholic boy should do. Maybe, they wouldn't even notice it in the dark?

As soon as we got back to Diane's house, her mom met us at the door.

"Do either one of you know what happened to the door?" her mother asked, without even saying hello.

"I'll tell you later," was all Diane would say.

"We almost called the police!" her mother added angrily.

"I'll see you tomorrow," I said to Diane, as I made a quick exit, nearly running for the car.

All that night I couldn't sleep. When I did, I had a nightmare about Diane's dad stopping me on a country road and cussing me out. The next day, I went straight to Diane's, apologized to her parents for my actions, and gave them a blank check to buy another door. I would've rather spent a week in the confessional at St. Andrew instead of admitting my stupidity to Diane's parents; but it did take a burden off. Diane's dad patched the door, and hung my check on their bulletin board. Each time I went to Diane's after that, I'd look for the check to make sure they hadn't made a down payment on a new house. I just knew they were going to screw me over for this one.

I wasn't always a spoiled little brat when it came to making love. Sometimes, I could be a hopeless romantic.

It's too simple just to say I love you
Or tell you I'll never let you go,
Because my words expressing love are few
To equal how absence will make it grow.

The days when you aren't near me linger on

Till night arrives and leaves me all alone
To dream of holding you until the dawn
When beams of light extinguish your sweet moan.

I long to wade your flowing stream of hair
And to caress your softly burning cheeks
When you are by my side. But do I dare
To chance a kiss that makes my will so weak?

I will dare to kiss you, and beg the night
Remain, and never let us see the light.

    Even poetry. Man, I was in love. I wrote the poem in a Creative Writing class at Purdue. I was disappointed in the B+ I got out of it, and even more disappointed when Diane didn't go "gaga" over it. She liked it, and kept it, but I expected more. Something like immediate nudity and a sexual romp that I'd never forget. All I got was a kiss on the cheek. Whoopee!
    At Diane's graduation party, one thought kept bouncing through my brain. "Now we can get to the good stuff!" I endured a host of long lost relatives with pleasure, knowing that soon Diane would be totally mine. Like most virgins, our first attempt at sexual intercourse wasn't very memorable. We were beginners, we were nervous and unsure of ourselves, we had a rubber to worry about and it hurt. Me, that is. I kept missing the mark. I ended up climaxing between the seat cushions. Took half an hour to clean up that mess. Frankly, until we got it right, I was ready to go back to foreplay and forget the intercourse part. But, like every newcomer, I developed a taste for the finer things in life.

WITH THIS RING . . .

Midway through my freshman year at Purdue, I decided on a major. My future was with Diane, and I was ready to get my degree. She had strength and confidence within her that I'd lacked, since I started high school. I needed that now more than anything. I didn't think I could make it without her. I quit Purdue after one year and started farming with my dad. In retrospect, I guess I used Diane as an excuse to quit.

I exemplified the typical teenager without a purpose. I didn't know what I wanted to be when I grew up, and I was quickly running out of time. I should've went into journalism and become a sports writer. I loved sports and I loved writing, but I was too stupid or too in love to see my obvious path. Unlike my brother Randy, I just missed out on Vietnam. I registered for the draft like a good boy after my eighteenth birthday. My number in the draft lottery was NINETEEN, so I was a shoe-in to be called. I never was. The last draft lottery was never put into effect, since Nixon was calling it quits. I lucked out. As naïve as I was, a virgin farm boy from Indiana, I wouldn't have lasted five minutes in the Vietnamese jungle. God looks after children and idiots.

Farming with my dad was like being Pete Rose, Jr. I knew I would never be as good as my father, (I would've bet the farm on it) but I was willing to try because he wanted me to. It was difficult, since my brother should've been the natural one to take over the farm. I started out more or less as a hired hand. I didn't have the money to buy land or equipment. I couldn't even afford a pair of work boots when Diane and I decided to get married.

When a small house became vacant on my dad's farm, I asked him if he minded if my potential wife and me moved in after marriage. He didn't try to talk me out of it. He didn't tell me I was crazy. All he said was, "If you want it, it's yours." The stage was set for the rest of my life. Or, so I thought.

I was never the type of person to do things the way they'd always been done. I wanted to be original and creative. The same theory went for the way I asked Diane to marry me. We went to a fancy restaurant to eat. (We both ordered Big Macs.) Afterwards, we found one of our lonely country roads and decided to park.

"Why don't you take off your clothes?" I requested in a sexy voice.

"What for?" she asked with a sly smile spread across her face.

"I want to see how beautiful you are," I replied, hoping to get her naked.

"Flattery will get you everywhere, you know," she said, taking off her coat.

"I'll keep that in mind."

I watched in awe and with sexually heightened amazement as Diane slowly undressed. She took off her sweater, revealing the fact she wasn't wearing a shirt. Then, she kicked off her shoes and dropped her skirt to the floor.

"Aren't you going to take anything off?" she asked before continuing.

"The only thing I want to take off right now is your underwear," I said, nearly drooling all over myself.

"Oh, really," she seductively said, "that's the same thing I was thinking."

Diane quickly unhooked her bra, (I was always jealous how fast she could do that) and she slid her underpants down to her ankles. Still, with a little embarrassment in the moonlit night, she put her left hand between her legs and her right arm across her breast.

"Put your hands by your side," I begged her.

"What for?"

"I just want to look at you," I whispered.

Slowly, she pulled her hands away and put them at her sides. Even in the dim light I could see a blush come over her face. I looked at every inch of her naked body. It was quite possibly the first time I'd really looked at it that hard without ravishing it first. It was the most amazing sight I'd ever laid eyes on. Her 18-year-old flesh was molded perfectly into the body of a Goddess. I hadn't even touched her yet, but I swore I could have a climax.

"Well?" she said invitingly, "now what?"

"I think there's a rubber in the glove compartment," I stuttered, not wanting the moment to end.

"Let's see," Diane opened the glove box and found the box that held her diamond engagement ring. "What's this?"

"Just something I thought you should have."

"Oh, my God!" Diane exclaimed after opening the box. "Is this what I think it is?"

"I don't know," I bragged, "what do you think it is?"

"Oh, my God!" she repeated after holding it up to the light. "It's beautiful."

Her hands were shaking as she pulled it out. It was such an extraordinary sight to watch my totally naked fiancé fuss over a diamond ring in my '59

Edsel. It was the sexiest experience I'd ever had.

"It fits too!" Diane boasted.

"Will you marry me, Diane?" I asked, not really worried about her response.

"What do you think?" she kidded. "Of course I'll marry you! This is so unexpected! Whatever possessed you to buy this?"

"I just wanted to get married," I muttered.

"We've got to go by and show Marla," Diane insisted.

"Can't we fool around first before we go?" I whimpered, as Diane picked up her clothes.

"I'm too excited right now to do anything!" she shouted, putting on her underwear.

I couldn't believe my luck. I'd finally gotten a woman too excited to have sex. Man, I couldn't get a break. I didn't mind though. Actually, I was excited too and wanted to broadcast the good news.

Marla was shocked. My cousin Jerry was at her house too, and I think both of them were a little envious since they were the ones who'd introduced us. After about 20 minutes at Marla's, I got a chance to whisper in Diane's ear.

"Now, can we go fool around?"

"We've got to go tell my parents!" she shouted, "let's go!"

Her parents were mildly happy. I think they were more concerned about how we were going to make it financially. After the shock had worn off, I made a suggestion to Diane.

"Let's go fool around now."

"I've got to call aunt Etta," she muttered, "this is all like a dream to me."

Needless to say, we never did fool around that night. But, I really didn't care. The night was already special. It would be the only time I would get Diane naked and not make love to her. I had the rest of the nights of my life to fool around with the woman I loved.

DON'T GIMME NO LINE AND KEEP YOUR HANDS TO YOURSELF

Months before our wedding, we worked on our honeymoon cottage. It was nothing more than a tool shed converted into a house. The kitchen and bathroom were basically broom closets. The other three rooms were even smaller. With the hours we spent working on that house, you would've thought we were building a mansion. I kept trying to talk Diane into making love on the floor of our future home, but she wanted to wait until we were married. Some superstition or something. Diane was a believer in the term "absence makes the heart grow fonder." She felt if we waited to break in our new home sexually, it would make the first time that much more memorable. My saying for her theory was, "abstinence makes the dick grow harder." She didn't like that one.

The big scandal of our marriage was that we were married in the Lutheran Church. Since I was Catholic, I guess I'd let the Pope down or something. But, my parents hadn't been to church for five years, and I hadn't been for two, so I felt it really didn't matter. For all I cared, Freddy Krueger in an Elvis Chapel could've married us and I would've been satisfied.

Diane had another great idea I hated. She felt we should abstain from sex for at least three weeks before we got married. First, we couldn't do it in our house, now we couldn't do it at all! This engagement stuff was really getting on my nerves. I was more than willing to just start dating again.

I didn't know days could last so long. You've heard of blue balls? Mine were a bit chartreuse. I've got to hand it to Diane, though. That abstinence thing paid off. When we got to the hotel, we were both naked before the luggage hit the floor. We'd only been at it about 15 minutes when there was a knock on the door.

"Room service," shouted a bellboy.

"Did you order something?" I asked Diane as I kissed her face.

"Only you," she gasped out of breath.

"We didn't order room service!" I yelled, wanting to get back to work.

"It's a complimentary bottle of champagne, sir," came the answer.
"You want champagne?" I mumbled in between her breasts.
"You're intoxicating enough," she whispered erotically.
"Sir, it's free!" was the impatient response.
"I've got to get rid of this guy," I groaned as I got up.
"Then hurry, before I lose the mood."

With those words, I was in fast forward. I jumped into my jeans, both legs at the same time, but when I zipped up, I nearly performed the first Ramada Inn vasectomy in history. I let the bellboy in, and he took his sweet time setting the glasses on the table. Then, to my horror, he lethargically opened the bottle of champagne and dribbled the glasses full.

"There you are, sir," he finally said, sticking out his hand.

"Thanks a bunch, guy," I replied, shaking his hand and pushing him out the door.

"I think he wanted a tip," Diane giggled beneath the covers as I dropped my jeans.

"This is all I had in my jeans," I exclaimed, holding my arms out from my body, "and I don't think he'd really appreciate it."

"Why don't you let me try it out?" Diane coaxed.

"You can only have half of it now," I kidded, as I dove on the bed. "The other half's for later."

I needed more than half for later. We had sex five times that night. I'd just get to sleep and Diane would wake me up. God, I wish honeymoons could last forever. We spent the next day soaking in the pool.

FAMILY MATTERS

Before we'd gotten married, Diane felt that something was wrong with her. She couldn't pinpoint it, but she was certain something was going on that shouldn't be. After about a month of marriage we got the news. Diane was pregnant!

Diane and I were engaged in February, got pregnant in July, and married in August. Not exactly the order it's supposed to happen in. Our first daughter attended the wedding ceremony as a six-week-old flower girl. If I'd known that, I wouldn't have been so X-rated during the honeymoon.

I remember the exact date I got Diane pregnant. It was July 4. I got to her house late that evening after working on the farm, (this time she knew I was going to be late) so we had to create our own fireworks. Alana was conceived in the back of that '59 Edsel, after a good hour of passionate lovemaking. It was without doubt, one of the best sexual overtures Diane and I experienced together. We attempted every position in the manual, and a few they were embarrassed to include. We were so involved that Diane kicked a hole in the lining of the roof.

It seems funny now, when I think about it, but after we found out Diane was having a baby, the thought of abortion never entered our minds. It wasn't even an option. Here we were, two young impressionable kids fresh off the farms of Indiana, and we were taking a stand against one of the most volatile issues of our time. Heck, we never even considered getting pregnant a mistake. It was just something inevitable that happened between two people who loved each other. You know. Osmosis.

The only hard part was telling our parents. I picked a lot of pillowcases and shirt-collar corners over that dilemma. Actually, my mom took it well. We told her when she was alone because we knew she'd relay the message to my dad, and if he had any complaints he could air them out with her. Sure, I was a chicken. It wasn't till after we left my mom, and she started doing the math that she figured out we'd had premarital sex. I assume, she nearly passed out. It shouldn't have been a surprise, but the fact her innocent baby had been seduced by a vixen might've made her weary.

I'm going against my religious upbringing here, but I think, every couple should have premarital sex. I couldn't think of a more horrendous fate than to discover on your wedding night that you and your mate have nothing sexual in common. Picture if you will, a journalistic effort of trying to combine Highlights for Children with Hustler Magazine. Absolutely none of the articles in either could be crossed referenced without dynamic repercussions. Have a Puritan spend the rest of their life with an S & M master? Talk about your living hells. Marriage is difficult enough without having to reach some unattainable happy sexual medium.

Diane's mom didn't take the news well at all. She did math a lot faster. She was pissed. Diane's dad came in a bit later, so we told the news to him. He took it a lot better.

"So, now I can call you grandma," Diane's dad joked with his wife.

She didn't think it was funny. She didn't say a word. She was pissed. We left about five minutes later. We didn't go back for about a week so her parents could get used to the idea. The next time we saw Diane's mother, she was excited about the pregnancy and wanted to do all she could to help. We asked her to take over the morning sicknesses, but she declined. Diane's dad gave us our first baby shower gift.

"I meant to give you this after you got married, but I'm sure it'll be of more use now," he said handing me my blank check off the bulletin board.

I was speechless. Diane cried.

WHO'S MINDING THE BABY?

Sometime, in the prenatal stages, I made a subconscious promise. I wanted to be a good father. I wanted to be there to guide them through the hardships of life. I wanted to be there to change the diapers and take part in the two o'clock feedings. To relish the highs and level out the lows. To make a difference in the entire life of my future child. I didn't want to be a standoffish figurehead who was always too busy to take part in their lives. I wanted to be a real parent.

Like every man, I wanted a son. I'd be a liar if I didn't say a male child was my first priority. Someone to follow in my footsteps. Someone I could work with and encourage. Someone I could instill with basketball knowledge and talent. Someone I could help make the team.

In the delivery room, I didn't feel as out of place as I thought I would. It was difficult watching the woman you loved in pain, but the birthing classes prepared us for what was to come. I even had a few chores I did to help make the delivery a little easier. After eight hours of labor, our child was prepared for its grand entrance. The actual event was easier to stomach than the movies we'd seen in the birthing class. Maybe, it was because it was our child erupting from the womb.

By the time our daughter was pronounced a little girl, I was numb. I didn't know how to feel. There were so many emotions striving to exit my body I didn't know which one to let out first. The only emotion that didn't exist was disappointment. I didn't care about what sex my child was. Alana was our daughter, she was healthy, and she belonged to us. That's all that mattered.

Sixteen months later, my second daughter, Renee, was born. She was the result of a blown out prophylactic. Diane and I were Planned Parenthood's nightmare. All the doctors and nurses had told us this child was definitely a boy. The way she carried it, the weight she'd gained, the hyperactivity of the fetus. There was no doubt it was a boy.

For the second time, there was no disappointment. Diane and I had thought it great we'd have a boy and a girl and we could call it quits. We had two daughters instead, and we were just as happy.

Not too long after Renee was born, I got a vasectomy. I could've had five more children and would've enjoyed it, but I wasn't the one having the babies burst out of me. Besides, with just two children we were able to give more of our attention and time to both of them. Years later, after the girls left for college, I regretted having a vasectomy so young. I longed for the toddler years when your child's world consists entirely of their parents. I longed to be so important, and to be loved so thoroughly. Actually, it wasn't the vasectomy I regretted. It was just that damn father time.

If I could freeze our lives at the time when my daughters were three and four years old, I'd be the happiest man alive. At that age, I was a hero to my daughters. I cooked for them, cleaned them up, played games with them, read them stories, and tucked them in. To my daughters, I was the world. It wasn't until they entered school that they discovered there were a lot more exciting things out there than dear old dad. It broke my heart.

Since I farmed and worked part-time in the early mornings at Speed of Light Delivery Service, I had a lot of free time during the winters and whenever farming was slow. Basically, I had two part-time jobs, and it wasn't until both of my girls were in school that I finally took a full-time job with SOL. (The topic of my next book, "Delivery", due out in the Fall). With the freedom of my jobs, I was able to spend lots of time with my family. I wasn't making much money, but we were close and we were happy. We only had one bathroom, too.

Ironically, since we lived rent-free in one of my dad's farmhouses, we were able to survive. The man who was constantly busy when I was little, now allowed me to spend countless hours with my two daughters. Diane could also stay home with the girls instead of having to reenter the work force. That's one thing we decided the moment we discovered we were pregnant. One of us had to stay home with the children.

Most parents today, for one reason or another, have children and then pay total strangers to raise them. Think about it. If your children spend eight or nine hours in day-care, then who's having the most influence? You see your children an hour in the morning when you're irritable and in a hurry, and a couple hours at night when you're tired and grumpy. And, in between, a nice lady in day-care with a great personality is taking over your child's life.

Money has a lot to do with it. Shift-work is also to blame, but I've seen parents who don't attend their children's school function even when they have the opportunity. Coaches and teachers are more or less baby-sitters that take over after day-care. Financially, I had a good opportunity to raise my children, but even without my dad's help, I would've found a way for one of us to stay home with our girls. If my wife could've worked and supported us, I would've gladly stayed at home. They were our children, we had the sex to bring them into the world, they were our responsibility, and by God, we were going to raise them.

So, I changed a lot of diapers. I mixed a lot of formula and sterilized a boatload of bottles. It wasn't always a barrel of laughs, but it had to be done. It was fun to watch Alana eat as a baby. We had a syringe-type feeding tube that held a cereal mixture that the girls sucked on to get their nourishment. Alana could empty that thing in 10 seconds flat. The poor kid acted like she never had a full meal in her life. And, if you tried to take it out of her mouth, it was like trying to pull a tree stump out of the ground. My favorite thing was teasing her with the nipple right before letting her eat. If I touched the nipple to her lips, she'd jerk her head around like Stevie Wonder in mid song trying to latch on to that nipple. Then, if I teased too long, Alana would let out a scream, which I'm sure included some baby cuss words. She was always the hungry child. One time, as a three-year-old, we were taking Alana and Renee out to eat. From the backseat, and out of the clear blue sky, Alana shouted, "I'm so hungry I could chew a horse!" I nearly ran off the road laughing.

Renee was a different eater. She ended up wearing so much of her food, you wondered if any of it had entered her mouth. Then, if you ever succeeded in keeping most of the food inside her, she'd invariably spit it back up on a belch. Letting Renee eat by herself was risky. We had to lay a tarp under her high chair, put a bib around her neck the size of a mattress pad, and have the garden hose ready to clean up. Twenty years later, Diane and I found Spaghetti-O's in the damnedest places.

The most important part of my child rearing was the fact I played with my children. I played with them because I was a child myself. I didn't want to grow up then, and I still haven't today. I don't like adults. People who are strictly adults have lost an integral part of their lives. They've lost the ability to have fun. Adults are ass holes.

The best games I played with my daughters were the ones I simply made up. First, there was the game, "Glue". Very simple premise. We had a crocheted afghan that usually was draped over our couch. I'd take the afghan, open it up, and cover one or both of the girls with it and tickle them ruthlessly. I'd warn them by yelling, "Look out for the glue monster!" Then I'd just repeat, "Glue, glue, glue, glue, glue!" They were scared to death of the Glue monster, but invariably one of them would drag the afghan up to me in a quiet moment and say, "Daddy, glue me."

The other game was "Pterodactyl." Now, I'm sure you're wondering how you can have a game named after an extinct prehistoric bird. It's easy. I'd be the terrible pterodactyl, flapping my wings through the air, and screeching, "Brrroooooocckkk, brrrrrooockk!" Naturally, I'd be chasing my two preys through the brush in hopes of feasting upon their carcasses. When I'd catch them, I'd give them tummy blows with my mouth to imitate the act of munching away. Then, I'd carry them off to my cavern nest, which usually resembled a closet. As I chased after my next victim, the first one would invariably get away. So, the hunt was pretty much continuous. Pterodactyl was a popular game. I was even commissioned for performances at family gatherings when all twelve of the nieces and nephews were present. It was an exhausting hunt, and I made them stay in the nest until someone else rescued them. Needless to say, I never devoured all of them. Gradually, the cousins got older, and the pterodactyl once again slithered into extinction. I'd give anything to play pterodactyl again.

I always enjoyed tickling my daughter's feet. When they were babies, it was fun to see their innate reaction to having their soles rubbed. I'd do it sometimes when they were asleep, and sure enough, they'd jerk their leg out of the way of the stimulus. As toddlers, I'd wake Alana and Renee up by tickling their toes. It was much better than screaming "GET UP!" all the time. They'd giggle and try to hide their feet under the covers to avoid the tickler. At least they woke up happy. As teenagers, though, neither one of them seemed to be too fond of my wake up call. I'd only hear something like, "Stop it! Give me ten more minutes!" I still got a kick out of tickling them anyway.

Diane and I always considered ourselves good parents, or at least we tried to be. We believed in spanking and making our girls behave, especially in public places. There's nothing more annoying than eating at a restaurant where parents have no control, no idea, or no care of what havoc their kids are creating. One time, I finally poured a half glass of milk on one kid's head when his parents weren't looking. Needless to say, he stayed in his seat after that.

A lot of parents don't believe in physically disciplining their children. They believe in taking "timeouts." I just think they're inadequate parents who don't have the balls to let their kids know who's boss. A "timeout" is something you use in a sporting event to change the course of the game. Give a child a "timeout", and they'll just find more ways to screw you. The "reward-punishment" system is the only way to train animals. Reward good behavior; punish bad behavior. Children are animals, and a "timeout" neither rewards nor punishes. If you want to stop inappropriate behavior, beat 'em on the ass.

There is a fine line between spanking and abuse. Parents have to be extremely careful not to cross it. I'll admit, I've straddled that line a few times, but I've never fallen into the pit of abuse. Parents who use "timeouts" never even get close to the line. In fact, they're so far to the left they can't see the line. Children should know what makes their parents angry, and what they should do to avoid it. If a child is never corrected, they'll trudge into the realm of kiddy promiscuity.

When they were babies, my girls became airplanes or bouncy toys that flew around the living room. When they got older, we played board games and outdoor sports. They learned from me, and amazingly, I learned from them. One time, while teaching them to play wiffle ball, I placed Renee on the left side of the plate where all right-handers hit. I tossed her several balls and she missed them all with her oversize bat. She kept trying to stand on the opposite side of the plate saying, "I can't hit that way, daddy", but I knew she threw right-handed so she had to stand on the right-handers side of the plate. After several more misses and a few more verbal complaints, I decided to let Renee stand on the opposite side of the plate. She nailed the first pitch for a ton, zipping it past my ear and sending me sprawling toward the dirt. Renee had officially become a left-handed batter.

GETTING IN THE GAME

With my new life as a husband and father, I seemed to recoup the confidence I'd lost in high school. Diane exuded confidence. She was intelligent, pretty, a great sex partner, and a wonderful mother. I couldn't help but gain confidence and self-respect by just being around her. I was a much better person with Diane.

This newfound confidence helped me realize my dream. I finally became a member of a basketball team, and I finally got in the game. I played in recreational leagues around the County with different teams. We played against ballplayers who'd graduated from the hated Richmond High School Team. They were tall, quick, and cocky, but I always felt I held my own against them. I didn't back down either.

I loved the game and never wanted to come out. I was nicknamed the "Energizer Bunny" because I ran around the court like a mad man to make up for my short size and lack of ability. I may have been short, but I had a bigger heart than anyone on the court. Most of the time, I scored around ten to fifteen points a game. A feat I considered good, considering I played against people who started on their high school teams. Several times, I scored in the twenties, and twice I chalked up 36 points in a single game. This was a shrimp that was cut from seven school teams. It was a dream come true for me. It never made up for not making the high school basketball team, but it was as close as I'd ever get. In Indiana, high school players are like Gods. Unfortunately, it was too late for me to be one.

I still play in 3-on-3 tournaments as a fifty-year-old, and Diane just groans when I bring another dust-collecting trophy home. The most fun I have now, though, is watching my grandson, Skyler, play ball. But, before I get too far ahead of myself, I need to tell you about the achievements of his mother and aunt. I coached those two girls in softball for 12 years, and we created some of the best memories a man and his daughters could ever have.

They both started playing softball the same year, and I volunteered to coach the team. Being the new coach on the diamond, I was the one who got the shaft. Out of the thirteen girls on my team, only three had played softball before. They didn't know which direction first base was and when I sent them up to bat they stood ON home plate. Instead of whining, I set out to make the best team I possibly could. We didn't win a lot of games that first year, but we showed some teams we could play ball. Late in the season, we played the only undefeated team in the league. They beat us by over twenty runs the first time we played them. We'd improved since then. This time we went into the last inning down by only two runs. It was hilarious watching the coaches on the other team sweat and scramble around trying to figure out what was going on. They finally beat us 5 to 2, but my team of inexperienced girls had proven a point. Don't take us lightly anymore. I was proud.

Three years later, we won the league championship. We won it again the next year, too, but unfortunately, Alana missed out on both of those because she'd moved up to an older league. Her team was only 3-12. She was not having fun. The next season Renee moved up on Alana's team, and fortunately, I was able to take over as coach. I had my work cut out for me.

The first thing I did was get two assistants, who I knew had the same dedication and determination to create a winner. Even so, we started off slowly. Actually, we weren't even moving. After the first four games of the year, we were averaging 17 errors. It might've been acceptable for basketball, but it was atrocious for softball. Finally, after the tenth error in our fifth game, I couldn't take it anymore. Our bats were lined up neatly along the inside of the dugout, that is until I sent them bouncing off the walls with one swift kick. It sounded like the bells of St. Marys in a hurricane.

"Coach, I'm gonna hafta throw you out of the game for that," the umpire said shyly, after walking to the dugout.

"Thank you!" I shouted back. "I'm sick of watching this team anyway!"

"Sorry, guy," the umpire returned.

I walked around the back of the dugout and straight to Diane. "Give me the car keys!" I demanded.

"Don't yell at me!" she responded, "I'm not playing."

"Give me the damn keys!" I yelled impatiently.

Diane threw the keys at me and I left the ballpark. I went home and ran two miles to blow off steam. My daughters finished the game in tears, and Alana told the other girls on the team, "You have no idea what we've done to my dad!"

Diane, Alana, and Renee had to find a ride home after the game. When they got there, I didn't say a word to the kids about softball. They were scared and quiet, but I kept my temper. At our next practice, I was civil to all the players and even laughed about my antics. BUT, and it's a pretty big but, all of my softball players finally realized I wouldn't tolerate a losing attitude. We finished the season by winning half our games and ending up 7-12. We even surprised the first place team by beating them.

The next year, we finished with a 13-8 record and got third place in the post-season tourney. We were on our way. The next season, we hit it big by winning the pre-season tourney and surprising everyone. It was a special moment, because it was the first time Alana and Renee had won a championship together. We then captured first place in the league, but only finished fifth in the post-season tourney. Our record was a respectable 19-5.

The next season was one I'll never forget. Alana was 18 and it was her last year in the league. I knew she wanted to make it her best. Like any coach, I was hardest on my daughters. I pushed them to excel in practice and in games to set an example for the rest of the team. Most of the time, Renee didn't need a push, but several times early on, Alana tried my patience. She would loaf in practice and I'd wear her out. She'd make a silly error in a game and I'd threaten to take her out until one of my assistants calmed me down. But, by the time Alana reached her last year, she realized what we'd accomplished. I needed a leader on our team. A leader that was a player and not a coach, and for the past few years I'd been grooming Alana to be that leader. That final year, I didn't have to yell at Alana once. She was a girl on a mission. She was determined to make her last year the best in softball history.

"C'mon you guys!" Alana would scream several times a game. "Let's get something going this inning!"

We won the pre-season tourney easily. We went undefeated in the league at 15-0. We were blowing people away. In the post-season tourney, we lost a 13-inning game 4-3, came back to beat that team once, but lost to them in the championship game. We finished the season at 29-2, with a second place in the post-season tourney. Now, you might think it was a disappointing way to end a great season. It wasn't. My girls had played six games in one day just to get back to the championship game. I was more proud of those girls for that second place finish than I would've been if they'd swept through undefeated. Not every winner ends up with the highest score.

That night, I saw just how bad my girls had wanted to win. When Alana took off her uniform, her knees were bruised and swollen and her feet were totally blistered. There was no way she could walk, let alone play softball. Renee didn't look much better either. They both had left it all on the softball diamond. I hugged them both and told them I was proud. As far as I was concerned, they had finished their softball years together on top. The combination of the two of them had forced the rest of my players into being winners.

The next year, without Alana, we finished second in the league and second in the tourney. Very respectable, but not as good as I would've liked. Alana and Renee were the heart and soul of my teams. Renee was the heart with her determination. Alana was the soul, and without her guidance we just weren't the same team.

Both girls only played basketball for a couple years in fifth and sixth grades. Alana never really had the coordination for the game and didn't try out. Renee was small, but she was a hustler. She went out for cheerleading in seventh grade instead of basketball. She made it. For the next six years she was on the sidelines at all the basketball games. Another case, where my heart was broken.

DEATH OF A DREAM

We were never the perfect family. We had our problems like everyone else, but most of them were small and easily handled. Little did I know that our happy foursome was about to embark on a dark journey into Hell. The bad part about it was that it always got worse before it got better.

As I said before, my family gave me confidence. Diane had always been my strength, but it got to where I could count on her less and less. She became a pessimist and tried to talk me out of doing anything special.

I succeeded in many ventures over the years. First, I went to night school at a local college and earned my two-year degree after 20 years. (Diane said it wasn't worth the time). Then, I always wanted to be a journalist and had regretted quitting college for that reason. So, one day I made an appointment to talk to a newspaper Editor. (Diane said I didn't have a journalism degree and they wouldn't want me.) After about fifteen minutes, he told me to submit a story and if they liked it, they'd print it. The next two years, I was a correspondent for the newspaper and earned a little extra cash.

I also had wanted to be a comedian. So, I started telling jokes at family birthday parties, and roasting the guest of honor. The more I did it, the more the word got around about my humor, and eventually, people were paying me to entertain at company parties, church gatherings, and for holidays. I was never good enough to make it on Johnny Carson, but at least I made a little extra cash.

Another profession I tried was Coaching. I coached my girls in softball and basketball. I coached Church and Youth League Basketball, and finally I was hired by the Centerville Schools to coach an 8th grade girl's basketball team. I'm not saying I was the greatest coach, but I worked on fundamentals and demanded that my teams improve.

All these professions took a lot of my time, but for the most part I never let them detract from my family. My kids always came first, and I planned my schedule around theirs. Unfortunately, I may have left Diane too much out in the cold. She was a homemaker, and frankly, the best damn homemaker I knew next to my mother. But, my other glories took me away from her quite a bit, and she was left in the shadows all alone.

The strength and self-assurance I acquired from Diane must have come at a price. She began to lose her confidence, and slowly fell into a depression. She ate to make herself feel better, but the food only made her gain weight. The excess weight depressed her, so she ate more to feel good again. It was one of those vicious circles where people have a hard time escaping.

Her depression came on so slowly it was hard to detect. But, I was so busy having fun, I probably wouldn't have noticed anyway. By the time Diane decided to go for help, she was clinically depressed. I felt as if I'd caused it myself. By using her to bolster my self-esteem, I'd drained all her resources to have pride in herself.

Fortunately, the doctors declared that Diane was depressed because of a chemical imbalance, so they put her on medication. It was a minor vindication for me and knowing the cause was little consolation. Living with Diane became a misery. She was always sad or mad or crying or upset, and she never had a reason why. There wasn't a quick remedy to simply make it go away. It was like she was bleeding to death, but I couldn't find the open wound.

Diane's depression had caused her to put our finances in a mess. Shopping gave her temporary relief from her sorrows, so she did it over and over again. Before I found out, she'd maxed out three credit cards. The incident caused yet another fight, torn up credit cards and a lot more depression. It seemed like we were spiraling down.

The real killer for me was when she found out I was writing a book. All she could say was, "Why waste your time. No one will read it."

Diane's medication was a bust. In fact, it made the depression worse. Three times I had to take her to the hospital when she overmedicated herself. Not exactly suicide attempts, but they weren't far from it. The last time, I had the brief thought of just letting her die. I still feel like a cad for that one. But eventually, she got the right medicine and improved slightly. Very slightly. We had a long road to travel.

"Are you all right, Diane?" I asked her, as I entered the bedroom.

"No," she replied from under the covers.

"What's wrong?" I said, trying to help.

"I don't know," was all she could say.

"There must be something bothering you," I persisted.

"I don't know what it is," Diane sobbed.

"How can I help you?" I begged her.

"Just leave me alone," she whined.

"I want to help you," I said again.

"Leave me alone!" she sobbed again.

"I love you, Diane."

She didn't answer me. All I could hear was her sniffles under the covers. I went downstairs into the bathroom and closed the door. I was shaking from frustration. I quickly took off my clothes and jumped into the shower. She didn't even answer me. I let the water hit me in the face, so my daughters couldn't hear me cry. Since she didn't answer me, then she doesn't love me. I was losing my wife.

FAMILY FEUD

To make matters worse, to make Diane's depression even deeper, our daughter Alana started dating a boy that Diane and I didn't approve of. (Does any child ever date a person that their parents really love?) His name was Joshua King and he was a year older than Alana. Joshua wasn't a juvenile delinquent, but he wasn't exactly the most pleasant kid in high school. He always seemed very emotionless. Never had any highs, and never had a low. At least that's the persona he displayed around Diane and me.

"How you doing, Joshua?" I said one day, when Alana brought him home.

"Not bad," he replied.

"You guys going out tonight?" I asked.

"Don't know yet," Joshua abruptly said.

"How's basketball going?" I asked, trying to get a longer response.

"It's ok," he said.

"Are you having fun?" I asked louder.

"Not really," he mumbled, "I don't much care for the sport."

Now, I really hated him. "Why don't you quit?" I persisted.

"I thought about it," Joshua bragged.

So, he was a quitter too. "Are you getting much playing time?" I went on.

"I don't care about that," he insulted, "I just need the letter for a jacket."

The kid should rot in Hell for a statement like that.

Joshua also seemed lazy. He had no motivation or purpose in his life. He played JV basketball, but whenever he got in a game, it was always half speed. Joshua had some talent for the game, but he didn't love it. He toyed with basketball like a kid at the Zoo would tease a chimpanzee. I hated that about him. Here was a kid who'd made the team, but was making a mockery of the game by walking out on the court.

Diane saw his laziness and she loathed it. Joshua would come to our house, sprawl out on the couch, eat our food and watch television for hours like he'd paid for everything. Diane talked to other parents who didn't like Joshua either. He hadn't treated their daughter right, or he was rude to their son, so very few people had much good to say about him. Joshua was a "B" student, he'd never been thrown out of school, and no one knew of any murders he'd committed, but you waited for him to do something terribly wrong just so you could run him off.

Joshua was also black. Actually, he was from a mixed marriage. His mother was black and his father was white. Joshua was fair-skinned, about six foot two inches, and quite frankly, he was a rather handsome kid. His personality made him seem unappealing.

Diane didn't like Alana and Joshua's relationship from the start. Diane didn't set out to break them up, but she never encouraged it either. Plus, she went out of her way to point out the benefits of being single. Sometimes, I couldn't tell if she was knocking Joshua or me.

I tried to stay on the sidelines and observe. I was a firm believer in the theory that the more you tried to pry two people apart, the harder they stuck together. I stayed out of their relationship, but secretly hoped for them to break it off.

Was racism an ingredient in why Diane and I didn't approve of Joshua? I felt not. I prayed it wasn't. But, you sometimes have self-doubts about your motivations. We lived in little Centerville, Indiana, and an interracial couple was a rare sight. Hell, Afro-Americans were a rare sight. People talk. People laugh. People accuse and degrade anything they don't understand. That's what we feared about their relationship. The problem with racism is not necessarily the blatant displays of it you catch on the six o'clock news. The real threat is the underlying current of racism that runs through mainstream America. What you don't see can kill you faster than what you can see.

As I look back on it now, I realize that the reason we didn't like Joshua King was not because he was half-black. It was because Joshua King was not a nice person.

And so, the Belcher Hell deepened and expanded into realms unmatched by human suffering. The cavern between Diane and Alana widened, leaving Renee and myself to bridge the gap. It took a toll on our family. Renee and I found more and more excuses to be away from home. Alana spent more time with Joshua. And, Diane found more reasons to be depressed. Searching for a better aid to her malady, she tried alcohol. It took two more visits to the emergency room and a near coma before she realized she had the wrong answer. We trudged on.

"You have got to stop letting this bother you so much," I scolded Diane.

"I can't help it," she answered, "as long as Alana's dating that Dickhead, I'm gonna be depressed."

"Why?" I wondered. "There's nothing we can do about them dating."

"We can force her to break up with him," she demanded.

"And, what good would that do?" I reasoned. "Then they'd just want each other more. They'd sneak behind our backs and we wouldn't have any idea what's going on."

"At least then I wouldn't know about it," Diane concluded.

"That's stupid," I added. "Besides, what has he done to make you hate him?"

"I just don't like him, ok."

"Is it because he's black?" I asked, fearing the answer.

"That doesn't help a whole lot," she muttered.

"So you're a racist, then," I accused her. "I'm living with the Klu Klux Klan?"

"I guess so," Diane scornfully added.

"Damn it, Diane! That's not the girl I married!" I screamed. "I know damn well you're not a racist or else I never would've married you!"

"There's a lot of things you don't know about me," she stabbed.

"Like what?" I asked once again, not wanting to hear an answer.

"Just tell Alana her and Dickhead are through and I'll be fine."

"I can't do that," I said doubtfully. "Until he does something that threatens Alana, then I have no basis for them to break up."

"Then leave me alone," Diane said, getting up and walking away. "I need a drink."

I wanted to run away so badly. I could've gotten into my car and driven anywhere and been happier. I was lonely and depressed. I felt like I'd completely lost my wife, and I wanted to have an affair. What kept me faithful and at home was the fact I wasn't a quitter. (No one wanted to have an affair with me anyway.) I was determined to battle for as long as I could to save my family. And, then there was Renee. I couldn't leave her alone to be the only sane person in the Belcher House. I fought for Diane and Alana, but I stayed for Renee.

"How's school going, Renee?" I asked my quiet daughter.

"Not bad," she responded in her shy two-worded answer.

"If you ever need to talk . . ."

"I know," Renee cut me short. "I can count on you."

"Totally," I assured. "What d'ya say to letting me pitch you a few softballs?"

Renee looked up from her homework and smiled. "Sure." Renee and I could always bury our sorrows in sports.

While in the middle of all this controversy, things continued to get worse. My grandmother died. It was my mother's mother. It was the lady my dad bought the farm from. She was my last living grandparent.

At the funeral service, a strange thing happened. As I went up for the final viewing, I looked over in the first row and saw my dad. He was crying! I'd never seen my dad cry in 38 years of life. I didn't see him cry at his own mother or father's funeral. He never lost it when my brother died. Apparently, the tears were catching up with him.

Anyway, my dad, Mr. In Control of His Emotions, had broken down in tears. I was shocked. I was empathetic. I was elated. Elated because I finally realized my father cared about something. I went over to him and grabbed him around the waist.

"I love you," I said in tears.

"I love you, Phil," he sobbed back at me.

I'd never hugged my father in 38 years. I'd never told him I loved him in 38 years. And, I'd never heard my father say, I love you. It was a metamorphosis I'd wanted 38 years ago, but gladly take now. I'd always known my father loved me in his own aloof manner, but now, I had proof. He actually said it. And, Dad never said anything he didn't mean. Ever since then, I've viewed my father in a different light. Now, I even make an extra effort to see him and my mom. In some strange way, I think my grandmother had something to do with it.

It had been a while since we'd seen Joshua (a.k.a. "Dickbert") and both of us prayed they'd broken up. When we finally got the nerve to ask her, Alana confirmed our hopes. Diane was elated. I warned her not to be too happy around Alana, who was definitely in her own depression. I prepared Diane for them to start dating again.

Two weeks later, we were called to the school to meet in the guidance counselor's office with Alana. She admitted to all of us that Joshua had choked and hit her. If you've ever seen the movie "Scanners" then you realize the affect my anger had on me that day. My head was ready to explode with rage. It was all I could do to keep from kicking down the door and running after the little bastard.

Even with the horrible news, we did have another ray of hope. Alana may never have anything to do with Joshua again. Unfortunately, by the next day, Alana recanted her story.

"What do you mean it's not true!" I screamed at Alana.

"I was mad at him and I made it up," she snapped back.

"You made this up!" I screamed again. "I don't believe it!"

"It's true," Alana responded, "I just wanted to get back at him for breaking up with me."

"I don't believe her, Phil," Diane interjected. "She's not that good an actress to make us believe a lie like that."

"You don't know that," Alana shot back. "I could convince you of anything I want."

"Well, let me convince you of something right now!" I said angrily. "You two are finished. No matter which time you were lying, it tells me something's terribly wrong with this relationship. Either he's bad for you, or you're bad for him. I don't know which, but I'm not going to let it go on. You are not to see him again! Do you understand me?"

"You can't keep me from him," Alana said, starting to cry.

"Don't you believe that, young lady!" Diane jumped in. "If I have to go to school and walk you to all your classes, just so you won't come in contact with that Dickhead, then I'll do it."

"If you did lie about him choking you, then you've set all of us up," I added. "We could be sued for liable! You're grounded, and you're going to stay grounded until I'm sure I can trust you again! You can drive to school and you can drive home, and that's it!"

I flung one of the swinging doors to her room so hard, it flew off the hinges and hit the floor. "And you can pay for that too!" I screamed, as I walked away. I fixed it later myself.

A couple days later, Joshua's parents wanted to meet with us to try and talk us into letting them date again. We met with them, but we held our ground. Joshua's father tried to convince us that it was just a minor teenage love spat. I told him that an accusation of assault was not a love spat, and to protect his son I felt it necessary to separate him from my daughter. Mrs. King didn't defend her son very much. Not as much as I thought a mother would. They left unhappy about our decision, but on good terms. Alana was still ours.

Our next step was family counseling. Boy, did that make me feel proud. Here I was the head of the house, the only male of the house, and I couldn't solve any of our problems. In one session, I told Alana she didn't realize how lucky she had it with parents that were still married, and a mother who stayed home. I told her she had the best damn mother in Indiana, and she just didn't appreciate it.

Needless to say, Diane and Alana couldn't even stand to look at each other by now. They were constantly arguing and threatening to hit each other, and Renee and I would do our best to break it up. One time, Diane started packing Alana's suitcase to take her to Joshua's house just to get her the hell out. I had to physically stop Diane and shake some sense into her before she'd quit. Luckily, Alana was not yet 18 years old. If she had been, I might've let Diane keep packing. But, I told Diane as long as Alana was a minor we had the responsibility for whatever she did. I also told Alana that if she still wanted Joshua on her eighteenth birthday, I'd personally help her pack.

One day, Renee came home from school upset. She told us Joshua had said something to her in the halls, but she refused to tell us what it was.

"Either tell us what it was, or else you can spend your spare time with your sister at home!" I finally demanded.

"Well, . . he said . . 'nice ass Renee, sure'd like to . . blank it," Renee stuttered.

"Blanket?" I questioned, not wanting to believe the worse.

"Blank . . as in a dirty word," Renee explained. "The blank was the "F" word."

"Jesus Christ!" I shouted, wanting to hit something so bad. If Joshua had been there, I'd killed him on the spot. There was nothing I could hit without breaking my hand, so I tried to think of something else. Why did I say the name of Jesus Christ when I was so mad? Was I blaming Him? Was I asking for help? When atheists get mad, do they scream "Jesus Christ"? Makes you wonder. For the moment, I cooled myself off.

The next morning, I went to the school parking lot to confront Joshua. As Joshua pulled into the lot in his shiny new IROC, I climbed out of my dingy, gray, 15-year-old Toyota and met him as he opened his car door.

"What did you say to Renee, yesterday?" I demanded.

"What are you talking about?" Joshua played stupid, as he got out of his car.

"What did you say to Renee?" I repeated.

"I never said anything to her," Joshua said sarcastically, as he grabbed his books and shut the door.

"That's not what I heard," I said, clinching my fist.

"Then you heard wrong," he shot back, as he started to walk away.

"I don't think so, ass hole," I returned. "You're the one who's wrong!"

"Why don't you get out of here?" Joshua said in a worried voice.

"You might have Alana fooled, but you're not going to mess with Renee!" I threatened. "If you so much as whisper to her again, you're going to regret it for a long time! Do you hear me?"

"Yeah, yeah, I hear ya," Joshua goaded with his back to me, as he walked even faster toward the doors where other kids were watching our confrontation.

"You don't want to mess with me," I warned him, "because I'll win!"

"Just get out of here," he said in a scared voice.

"You're nothing but a coward," I stopped and shouted after him. "You pick on people who won't defend themselves, but this time you're picking on the wrong person. So, just run away like a coward and hide in the school."

Without even looking back, Joshua entered the school and disappeared down the hall. I looked at the students who were standing outside watching us.

"He's a real brave little shit, isn't he?" I ridiculed. Then I turned and stormed away. Needless to say, he never spoke to Renee again. From then on, I don't think he even looked in her direction.

IT'S ALWAYS DARKEST BEFORE THE LIGHT

The turmoil went on for four months. We fought, we cried, we made up, and then we'd start the process all over again. Then, Alana turned eighteen. We told her she was on her own now, and that she would have to make her own decisions. If she wanted Joshua, she could have him, but she was never to bring him into our home.

Suddenly, it all came to an end. I never saw the magic wand at the time, but that's what seemed to happen. Alana didn't run to Joshua. She wasn't dating him. She wasn't even seeing him. And, the best part, Joshua had another girlfriend.

All was right with the world. We went into spring and summer and Alana had that great softball season I bragged about. It was like the sun broke free and we were all a family again. Little did I know we were only in the eye of the hurricane.

Alana attended classes at Ball State University for only a month when she came home and told us the news.

"I think I'm pregnant," she said matter-of-factly.

Diane and I didn't say anything for a moment. We kept waiting for a laugh and a "just kidding".

"You're kidding, aren't you?" I asked sheepishly.

"I wish I was," Alana said, as she put her forehead into her left hand.

"Oh, my God, no!" Diane gasped, as she clutched her heart.

"How do you know?" I questioned stupidly.

"I took a test," Alana sighed.

"Was it one of those home tests?" Diane pried, trying to find some hope.

"I went to the clinic at Ball State," Alana responded.

"Oh, shit," I whispered.

"Whose baby is it?" Diane demanded.

Alana looked up from her hand. Tears were running down her cheek, and she wouldn't answer.

"Whose baby is it?" repeated Diane.

"Calm down, Diane," I consoled, as I put my hand on her shoulder. "Can't you see . . . ."

"Tell me whose baby it is!" Diane cried. "I have to know who the father is!"

"It's . . . it's Joshua's!" Alana sobbed.

"No! No, no, no!" Diane screamed, as she leaned back against the kitchen counter and slumped down to a sitting position. "Oh, God, no! Please, God, no!"

"Take it easy, Diane!" I yelled at her, wanting to throw up myself.

"Ahhhhhhhhhhh!" Diane hollered.

"Stop it, right now!" I yelled out of anger for being scared.

"How could you do this to me?" Diane blamed, as she pulled herself up off the floor. "How could you do this now? Everything was going great. How could you ruin everything?"

"I was only with him once!" Alana sobbed between tears. "He came to see me in July and we went out. One time. I didn't think anything would happen!"

"Oh, shit." I mumbled, with the thought of Diane's and mine Fourth of July fireworks, some nineteen years ago.

"You didn't use any protection?" Diane scolded.

"I didn't expect anything to happen!" Alana continued crying. "He just wanted to talk!"

"And, he talked you out of your pants, didn't he!" threatened Diane. "Well, you're not having that baby. You can have an abortion and we'll be rid of both of the bastards!"

"Stop this right . . . ."

"I'm not getting an abortion!" Alana screamed.

"Yes, you will, or I'll do it myself!" Diane threatened again.

"Stop it! Stop it! Stop it!" I bellowed furiously, as I threw a cookie jar across the room, smashing it against the wall. My words were not so much for shutting Diane up, but to squelch the thought running through my mind of how easy a solution abortion would be. I felt ashamed. Alana was sitting in front of us now, because the thought of abortion never entered a young married couples mind, even though they couldn't afford the expense of another mouth to feed. Now, we were ready to kill a potential grandchild, just because we didn't like its father.

"Just what the hell do you propose we do then?" Diane interjected after a long silence.

"I don't know?" I said, trying to calm down. "I do know what we're not going to do, and we're not getting an abortion! There's all kinds of shit we've got to figure out, and we won't get it done by killing each other or an unborn baby."

"Have you told the Dickhead?" persecuted Diane.

"Stop talking like that!" I demanded.

"Have you told him yet?" Diane repeated.

"Yes, he knows," Alana said, regaining her composure. "He said he would marry me."

"That's great!" Diane lamented. "That's all we need. Bring the Dickhead into the family! That'll solve everything!"

"Will you shut the hell up?" I yelled. "You do realize Alana is eighteen and she can do whatever she wants?"

"You do realize that Alana is in college and we're still supporting her, and there's no way the two of them can afford to get married and have a baby, don't you?" Diane reasoned.

"Oh, shit!" I lamented. "We've got a lot of shit to sort out."

I picked the hell out of my pillowcase that night. I don't like problems. I don't deal well in stressful situations. I have a tendency to get mad and get nothing resolved.

After hours of arguing with Diane, I finally convinced her we needed to meet with the Kings. Before that, I wanted to talk with Alana alone.

"Your mother's not very happy," I understated to Alana.

"I know," she answered. "She hates me."

"She doesn't hate you, damn it!" I said half-mad. "In fact, it's just the opposite. She's always loved you so much, and she's always wanted the best for you and Renee, and when it doesn't happen, she goes bonkers."

"In that case, she loves me too much," Alana added.

"I'm the same way," I told her. "If you want me to feel sorry for you because you had good parents, then I'm afraid I can't oblige."

"I know."

"Look. There's no use messing with the how or why's of this pregnancy because it's all irrelevant now," I reasoned. "What we need to worry about is where we go from here."

"Where WE go?" Alana asked.

"Yeah, we're all in this still," I said. "I know you're old enough to make your own decisions, and that's what I intend for you to do, but your mother and I can't just turn you out on your own. We have to make sure we get you through this no matter what you decide."

"Thank you," Alana whispered with her head down.

"You said you intended to keep the baby?" I almost questioned.

"Absolutely," Alana said without hesitation.

"Thank God," I sighed, "I was so afraid I'd never see my grandchild."

"I couldn't do that, dad," Alana said proudly. "I've got to take responsibility for this, even though mom has a different idea."

"Your mother agrees with us," I reasoned, "she just doesn't realize it yet."

"Well, I hope she reaches total enlightenment soon," Alana joked.

"If she doesn't, I've got a sledgehammer in the garage that might help," I added.

"You do know, though, we want you to stay in college."

"Can we afford both?" she asked.

"We can't afford not to afford both," I jumbled. "You know what I mean. If we let you quit college now, you'll never go back. I quit college after one year, and it took me twenty years to get a two-year degree. Besides, I don't want you barefoot and pregnant the rest of your life."

"Don't worry," Alana said, "I don't plan on making this a habit."

"So, what's the deal with you and Joshua getting married?" I nervously asked.

"He said he wanted to marry me," Alana said sheepishly.

"Well, that's nice, but I don't have to tell you I really don't like the guy, and your mother hates his guts," I lectured. "I mean, we've been over this issue before and I don't think you're going to change our minds during this millennium."

"I can't do this alone, dad," Alana said with tears in her eyes.

"You won't be alone," I reassured, "you'll always have us."

"I know."

"All I ask is that you think about this," I said. "You don't marry someone just because you're pregnant. It might seem like a logical answer, but it's not the basis for a happy marriage. You marry someone because you love him. You marry someone because you can't live without him. You marry someone because you want to spend the rest of your life with him, not because it's a quick fix to a problem. If I thought it would do any good, I'd play your mother's side and tell you I forbid you to marry that creep. But, I know it's not that easy. You're going to do what you want to do. You should be able to do what you want, but on a decision like this, you better make damn sure it's the one that'll last a lifetime. And, if Joshua so much as raises his voice to you, I swear I'll kill the son-of-a-bitch."

"You won't have to," Alana cried.

"Just make up your mind, and I'll try and support you whichever way you go," I said.

"I think I want to marry him," Alana said, looking up.

"You think?" I asked sarcastically.

"I want to marry him," she confirmed.

"You don't have to decide this minute," I begged for a reversal.

"We've already decided," Alana said, "It's the best way."

I felt the rage rush toward my face. I wanted to rant and rave of the evils of marrying a Dickbert, but I kept my biases to myself. I wasn't in a position to forbid it, because if it worked out, then I'd end up losing Alana and any grandchildren. Sometimes, when you take a stand, you have to be prepared to deal with the consequences. Custer found that out.

I grabbed Alana by both sides of the head and planted a kiss on her forehead. Then, I got the hell out before I could explode. I never liked growing up, and this business of being an adult was getting on my nerves. I felt like I'd just pulled my daughter out of a burning building, only to lose my grip and drop her from the fifth floor. It remained to be seen if Joshua would catch her before she hit.

FIT FOR A KING

We had another meeting with the Kings. I hoped this one would be on friendlier terms. At least we were able to use their first names this time. Carla and Ed.

"Well, I guess we have a bit of a problem," I ventured to break the ice, after we all sat down.

"Our children have a problem," Carla corrected surprisingly. During the first meeting she hadn't said much. Now, with these words, I was afraid the women might end up in a fistfight.

"Well, Carla, we feel since Alana's still in school, we have a responsibility to help her," I said gently. "I'm not going to throw her out with a baby and no education."

"We feel the same," Ed added. "Some of us are having a hard time dealing with it."

"I just don't see where keeping the baby and getting married should be written in stone," Diane interjected. "We're talking about two young kids who are changing their lives forever."

"I agree," Carla added. "Most marriages like this end up in divorce anyway. Why should we sit back and let both of them make a mistake they're going to regret?"

"Who says they're going to regret it?" Ed chimed in. "If we make this decision for them now, then they might end up hating us for the rest of their lives."

"Joshua only has a part time job right now, Ed," Carla corrected. "You expect him to support a family on that? You heard Phil, they want Alana to stay in school, so how is she supposed to care for the baby and help support the family?"

"There's plenty of . . ."

"That's the same way I feel," Diane sided with Carla. "What they want just can't possibly be done."

I couldn't believe it. I was relieved that the two women agreed, but disappointed that their views balanced the opposite end of the spectrum as Ed and I. It seemed the Kings had as much domestic unrest as we had.

"It's been done before." Ed said.

"Where are they going to live?" Diane questioned. "I don't want them living here."

"They won't be staying at our house either," Carla added. "We have enough troubles of our own."

"Alana will be going to school, so they can get an apartment in Muncie," I reasoned.

"I have an aunt in Muncie," Ed revealed, "maybe they can stay with her until they get settled."

"So, Ed, do you actually think your son is going to straighten up and start taking responsibility?" Carla challenged.

"Now that he's forced to, I think he will," defended Ed. "He just turned twenty for heaven's sake, give the boy a chance."

"Phil, what do you think of our son?" Carla asked, putting me on the spot. I was not a good liar, and the question hit me like a fly ball falling out of the sun.

"Well, . . I never really thought of it that much," I stumbled.

"Oh, come now. You surely have an opinion of him, don't you?" Carla pressured.

"He's not very talkative or emotional," I strained.

"I'll tell you what I think," Diane jumped in, making me cringe at the thought of what she would say. "I don't like your son at all, to tell you the truth. I think he's rude and inconsiderate and he has very little respect for anyone; especially women."

"Now, wait just a minute!" Ed objected.

"Shut up, Ed!" Carla interrupted. "All she needs to add is the word lazy, and you know damn well that fits Joshua."

"He's not that bad, Carla," Ed said, trying to save Joshua's face.

"We've both had our battles with him, and you know neither one of us have won," Carla elaborated. "He's a spoiled little shit who hasn't amounted to anything."

There was a brief silence. No one had an argument for what Carla had said. In fact, it was the first time I'd seen Diane with a grin on her face.

"You scare me, Carla," I finally said. "We have a grandchild coming into the world and this is the best you can offer."

"We should all be scared, because this marriage is not going to work," Carla said bluntly. "I think the baby should be given up for adoption and let Alana and Joshua go their own ways."

"I'd have to second that," added Diane.

Ed and I looked at each other, not believing our ears. Here were two potential grandmothers on the verge of banning their only grandchild to obscurity.

"What we fail to realize here is that the two kids we're talking about are adults, and they can pretty much do whatever they damn well please without even considering what our opinions are," I stated in one breath. "We can condemn and suggest all we want, but the bottom line is they're going to do what THEY want. Our only choices consist of whether we want to try and help them succeed, or sit back and do nothing and watch our predictions of failure come true."

No one could argue with me. As much as we hated it, we no longer controlled our children. We were on the verge of teaching them to fly over the Grand Canyon. We agreed to help the new couple in whatever ways we could. Now, we could only pray the two of them could help each other.

TYING THE KNOT

Alana and Joshua were married in a small civil ceremony with only a few relatives present. A far cry from the Catholic extravaganza I'd foreseen. My sister June cried quite a bit at the wedding. I'm sure seeing the pregnant Alana getting married with plans to keep her baby brought up memories of her own ordeal.

"You did the right thing," June told me later.

"I don't know if it's the right thing or not," I responded. "It's just what they wanted and I had to go with it. Whether it's right or not we'll find out down the road."

"That's what I mean," June said. "You let them make the decision and didn't interfere."

"Well, they're past eighteen and they can make their own decisions," I added, trying to avoid talk of June giving up her baby.

"Yeah, you'd think we all would be grown up by that age," June said in self-pity.

"June, if I could've come up with another answer I thought was best for my daughter, I would've forced her to do it too," I consoled. "It's just that sometimes, too much help ends up hurting the person you're trying to rescue."

"Yeah, that's right," June smiled. "Sometimes, I just wish I had another chance."

"Sometimes, you get a second chance," I reasoned. "You just have to look for it."

June smiled again, as tears rolled down her cheeks.

"Thanks for being here," I told June, as we hugged each other. "It's nice to have your family."

Alana's wedding had enabled June to come to grips with her unwanted pregnancy. I didn't know it at the time, but it was at that moment June decided to find her lost child. She just wanted to explain herself. She wanted to say she was sorry.

LABOR PAINS AND OTHER FUN

Things gradually returned to normal around the Belcher place. Whatever normal is? Renee was having a great senior year, not having to worry about her sister anymore. Alana and Joshua were in Muncie starting their own lives. We worried about Alana a lot and called her often, but now she had to bear all the problems of her relationship alone. With the pressure off of us, Diane and I began to get along better. She was still in her depression, but we actually had sex once. I only lasted 37 seconds.

When Alana went into labor, we were the first ones she called. They paged me at work and I went home immediately, so we could make the forty-five minute trip to be with her. Before we left, we called Alana back.

"So, how are you doing?" I asked excitedly.

"Oh, .. not .. too bad," she said in distress.

"Are you in pain?" I asked worried.

"No, . . just . . scared," she sobbed.

"Well, we're on our way," I assured her. "If the pains get too close, just have Joshua take you to the hospital and we'll meet you there."

"He's . . he's not here . . right now," Alana stuttered.

"Where is he?"

"I don't know?" she responded. "He . . he just went out."

"If there's any problem, call a cab immediately," I said in a panic. "We'll pay for it so don't worry. You hear me?"

"Yes."

"We're on our way," I said in a hurry. "I love you."

"I .. love you, too."

Thirty minutes later, we were in Muncie. Alana was still at her apartment. I've never seen a person so glad to see someone in my life. When we walked in the door, it was like Alana had received a stay of execution.

We left the absent Joshua a note and we headed for the hospital. Three and a half hours later, they were ready to wheel Alana into the delivery room. Joshua had attended about half of their birthing classes and was supposed to go in with her, but he still was a no-show. As they wheeled her away, I kissed her hand and let her go. She was shaking.

Alana disappeared through the doors, and I stood there staring like a damn deer on an interstate looking into the lights of an eighteen-wheeler. Finally, I decided to act.

"I'm going in there," I said, heading for the nurses station.

"You can't go in there, Phil," Diane corrected me.

"Watch me," I responded, as I hit the desk. "Where do I change to go in for a delivery?"

"Right over here, sir."

I made a quick change that would've made Superman blush, and I crashed through the delivery room doors.

"This must be the father," one of the nurses shouted.

"That's MY father!" Alana shouted in shock.

"I'm just pinch-hitting for the slumping father," I joked.

"I don't want you in here, dad," Alana insulted.

"That's too bad, baby," I said, "Tom Cruise was busy."

"You can't see me like this!"

"Listen, I changed your poopy diapers for two years," I reasoned. "This will be a breeze. Besides, it's payback time for your mom. Now, you can see what you put her through."

As everyone in the room was cracking up, I grabbed Alana's hand with both of mine.

"Mission control, we have a go," I kidded, "baby launch in T minus ten seconds."

Whenever Alana hit a bad labor pain, I reminded her of the time she played six softball games in one day.

"You don't even have to chase fly balls now," I encouraged, "You're flat on your back and you call this difficult!"

"Shut up!"

After what seemed like a short sweet moment, I saw my grandson for the first time. I guess, I'd often wondered what color he would be, but when he came out I didn't even notice. I was the first one to hold him after the nurses cut the cord and checked him out. He was beautiful. What did you expect me to say? Actually, I think all newborn babies are ugly as hell, but when they're yours, that rule doesn't apply.

After I laid him on Alana's breast, I grasped the enormity of the moment. I cried. I cried like a freaking baby.

"Are you all right, Dad?" Alana worried.

I composed myself and brought my tears to a shaken laughter, "I've never been better."

When I left the delivery room, Diane was pacing back and forth in front of the nurses station. As I got up to her, I started crying again.

"What's wrong?" Diane asked in a panic. "What happened?"

I waved my hand in front of her face and tried to compose both of us. "We ... we have a son," I finally said, seeming more prophetic than I'd ever thought.

As we hugged and cried, the nurses behind us broke into applause.

THE SKY'S THE LIMIT

Alana went to recovery, and Diane and I waited in the maternity ward to see the new edition. When we got back to the hospital room, all of us got to hold the baby.

"What did you name him?" Diane finally happened to think. "I don't know what to call him."

"We named him Skyler," Alana replied. "Joshua picked it out."

"Skyler?" Diane asked.

"Skyler?" I seconded.

"Don't you like it?" Alana worried.

"Whatever you want," I said.

"It's an unusual name, I must say," Diane added.

"You don't like it, do you?" Alana asked.

"Hey, it's a special name for a special kid," I reasoned. "Skyler King. The kids will call him Sky probably."

"Sky King?" Diane wondered.

"That's a 60's TV show!" I said with surprise.

"You're kidding!" Alana said shocked.

"Yeah, I used to watch it," I told her.

"Now, I know you don't like it," Alana muttered.

"Hey, I think it's great," I reassured, "he'll never run into a kid with the same name. Will he, Diane?"

"I hope not," Diane said, as she rolled her eyes at me.

Just then, to spoil the moment, Joshua walked in. Alana didn't even break a smile at the sight of him.

"What's going on?" he asked innocently.

"Well, some of us are having a baby," I answered. "I don't know what the hell you're doing."

"Hey, give me a break," he chided, "I didn't know what was going on."

"Where you been?" Diane pried.

"Just out. Running around with some friends," Joshua answered.

"It would've been nice to tell your nine-month pregnant wife where you'd be," Diane scolded.

"Hey, shoot me," he said matter-of-factly.

"Don't tempt me," I whispered.

"Let's see the kid."

"We've got a son," Alana beamed.

"I told you that's what I wanted," Joshua said.

Diane and I got up to leave, but when I smelled the alcohol on Joshua's breath, I had to go after him one more time.

"I hope you're planning on taking some responsibility around here," I stated.

"Hey, I'm here, aren't I?" Joshua tried to brush it off.

"Just barely," Diane added.

"Hey, don't worry about it, old woman," he insulted, "this is out of your hands."

"She may be older than you, but I suggest you avoid any confrontations with her if you value your life," I threatened. "And, this is far from out of our hands. Until we see you can straighten yourself up, then you're going to feel a lot of our hands."

"We'll come back later, Alana," Diane said, kissing her.

"Bye baby." I added. "And, bye baby Sky."

At least Alana hadn't defended her AWOL husband. I began to regret letting them ever get married.

Two months later, we made a trip to Muncie to see Skyler and Alana. As we drove down her street, we saw Joshua and Alana getting out of their car. Alana was holding Skyler in one hand and Joshua's beer in the other. As Joshua got something out of the backseat, Alana set the beer on the car to tend to a fussy Skyler. The beer can slid off the car, rolled down Joshua's back and onto the ground. It was a funny sight until Joshua looked up, saw the beer on the ground, and slapped Alana across the face. He slapped Alana while she was holding a baby! She spun around, barely holding onto Skyler. I sped up, slammed on the brakes, and jumped out of my car, which I left in the middle of the street. When Joshua saw me, he ran.

"You son-of-a bitch!" I screamed, as I ran after him.

"Help!" he yelled.

He didn't make it fifty feet before I grabbed him by the collar and threw him on the sidewalk.

"Leave me alone!" Joshua pleaded. "I didn't mean it!"

"Get up, you bastard!" I kicked at him. "Get up and slap me!"

He laid there like the coward I knew he was, and tried to curl up in the fetal position. I grabbed his hair and started pulling him down the sidewalk.

"Goddamit!" he finally yelled, getting up and charging toward me.

I hit him in the nose before he got to me. I hit him with a left and a right, then grabbed his neck and shoved him against a tree. I popped him in the nose three more times before someone grabbed my arm.

"Don't kill him now!" Diane reasoned, "there's too many witnesses here."

The look of fear on Joshua's face was priceless.

"You're right," I said, calming down. "I'll finish him later. But, you're done you son-of-a-bitch! You're to get the hell out of here and never come back! Do you understand me?"

Joshua shook his bloody head.

"The marriage is over!" I threatened. "I don't give a shit what Alana wants! You're done! If I see you anywhere in the state of Indiana I'll finish this little job! Do you understand that?"

Joshua shook his head again. I kneed him in the groin and threw him on the sidewalk. By the time we got inside the apartment and looked out the window, he was gone. For the next two hours, we consoled Alana and waited for the police. I was sure he'd go to the police and charge me with assault. The police never came.

After hearing Alana, we knew why. She had suspicion Joshua was dealing drugs, but she couldn't prove it. Also, it wasn't the first time he'd hit her. The more we talked, the more I felt justified for my angry rage. It didn't take much coaxing to convince Alana the marriage was over.

For the next two weeks, Diane stayed with Alana in case Joshua came back to get his things. He never did. After the second week, I called the Kings.

"Is this Carla?" I asked, when a woman answered.

"Yes, it is," she replied.

"This is Phil Belcher," I said nervously. "I was wondering if you've seen Joshua at all?"

"It's been a while now," she said bluntly. "Are you the one who rearranged his face?"

"That's debatable," I dodged, not wanting to incriminate myself. "I just wondered if he was still around?"

"I don't think you'll have to worry about him, anymore," Carla assured me. "He came and got some money off us and said he was leaving for good. That's the only reason I agreed to give it to him; if he left for good."

"I guess you know the marriage is over," I said. "We're in the process of annulment."

"I took that for granted," she replied. "I tried to warn you about him in the first place, but you didn't seem to want to hear it."

"I'm not the one we had to convince, Carla," I shot back. "Alana was the one who wanted to marry him. Sometimes, you have to let your kids make mistakes before they learn anything."

"Good point," she agreed, "I hope things go well for her now."

"If you'd like to see the baby anytime, we'd be more . . ."

"I don't think that'll be necessary, Phil," she interrupted me. "We'd be happy to forget Joshua ever existed."

"I'm sorry you feel that way," I said.

"I am too," Carla added. "But, sometimes we have no choice."

I felt so sorry for the Kings. We had gotten our daughter back for the second time, and they had lost their only son. We had a new addition to the family to help raise, and all they had was an empty nest. I actually prayed for them to find some happiness. I also prayed that we could keep ours.

For a couple years, I'd been kidding Diane about having another baby. She'd always abruptly end the conversation by saying, "With all the trouble we've had with Alana, there's no way I'm having anymore kids." Now we had a chance to be parents again. We decided to keep Skyler with us. Alana could go to school full-time, work part-time, and come home on the weekends. Instead of relegating our new grandson to child-care, we'd help Alana by starting him on the right track. By taking summer school, we figured Alana could get her teaching degree in two or two and a half years, and she'd be set for life.

It was so much fun having a baby in the house again. I never realized how much I missed it. At first, Diane wasn't too crazy about the idea, but she did it to help Alana get through college. Diane had always said she looked forward to when her child rearing days were over, and now, they seemed to be starting again. The first time I saw Diane sitting in her rocker feeding Skyler, the memories of my teenage bride and her babies began to fill my head. Diane came across sometimes as a little callous, but she was a dedicated parent in the true sense of the word. I remembered why I had loved her.

Diane got a lot of help with Skyler. In the evenings, I took over the child rearing duties with a pleasure I'd overlooked the first time. Renee also loved children and she constantly wanted to play with Skyler. The poor kid very rarely got any privacy, because one of us was always grabbing him out of his crib.

Finally, our home was peaceful again. Sure, we had a new mouth to feed, and a new cry to attend to, but it was little inconvenience compared to a teenage tragedy. We missed Alana terribly during the week, and the following Fall we'd be missing Renee, as she planned to join Alana at Ball State. If either one of them made it as big as David Letterman, a Ball State alumnus, then I'd have no complaints.

The addition of Skyler helped relieve the absence of both our daughters. That helpless baby-boy may have needed us, but we needed him more. Skyler seemed to be the only thing holding Diane and me together.

DELIVERY, SEDUCTIONS, AND TEASES

I never meant to fall in love. I had no reason to. I wasn't looking for anyone. Diane might've still been depressed, but with Skyler, life was tolerable. Alana was on the verge of graduation. Renee was in her second year at Ball State. I didn't need any more controversy in my life, but I suppose my long neglected male hormones had another idea.

Some people believe in love at first sight, but I've always been skeptical. To me it's more like "lust at first sight". You can't love someone you don't know. I've met some of the most beautiful girls on the route, but as soon as they opened their mouths, it's like "get outta here."

This wasn't love at first sight. And, it wasn't love at second or third sight either. I'd known this lady for five years. She worked at an insurance agency on my route, and she was someone I had fun talking with. Most of the time her boss was out of the office, so when I delivered, we were the only two people in the building.

Now, I don't usually stereotype people, or make fun of them, but the first time I met Carmen Dellinger I couldn't believe how homely she looked. She had nice hair, but there were freckles all over her and she had no breasts. She wore clothes that looked like they came from the Salvation Army, and it was hard to tell if she even had a figure. I was not impressed.

The first time I delivered to Carmen, I didn't even really want to talk to her. She was about the fifth secretary I'd seen that month, so I figured why even get to know her because by tomorrow, she'd be gone. I was in a hurry anyway, and then there was that homely issue.

"Hello," I said to Carmen, when I went in to deliver. "I've got a couple packages for you, and I need you to sign your first initial and last name right here."

"I can do that," she said in a cheery voice. "They told me learning to write would come in handy some day."

"Thank you," I said, when she'd finished. "Do you have any packages for me to pick up, or did they even tell you about the pickup account?"

"No and yes." Carmen answered.

"What?" I asked puzzled.

"No, we don't have any packages, and yes, they did tell me about the account," she explained.

"O.k. Thanks a lot," I said abruptly, as I turned and headed for the door. I thought I heard Carmen say something else, but I was already around the corner and out of sight and so close to the door and in a hurry that I didn't even bother to respond. And, there was that homely issue.

The next couple of days, when I went in to Carmen's office I didn't have any packages to deliver. So, instead of going around the corner to see her, I just yelled *hello* and went down the steps by the entrance to see if she had a pickup. I'd sign for the packages, go back up the steps and yell *goodbye*. I thought, I heard her say something like goodbye, but I wasn't sure and didn't care, so I left. Actually, I wasn't even sure if it was her.

By the end of the week, I had more packages for Carmen. I was pissed. Now I had to go see her again, be friendly again, and waste more time in a dingy office with a homely secretary.

"Good morning," I said trying to be nice, "Looks like I've got something for you today."

"I sure hope so," Carmen said in a sexy voice. "It's lonely in here."

"Just need you to sign here," I muttered, since she'd thrown me off guard.

"I think I remember this," she said. "But, I do suffer from amnesia, occasionally."

"What?" I mumbled off guard again.

"Just kidding," she laughed.

"O.k. thanks," I said, as I grabbed for my board. She wouldn't let me have it. "Oh, aren't you done yet?"

"Yeah, I'm done signing, but I'm not going to give you this back until you tell me something," Carmen teased.

It was winter outside, I was layered in clothes, and this homely secretary was making me uncomfortable with her games. I was beginning to sweat. "Tell you what?" I asked.

"What's your name?" Carmen almost shouted. "You come in an out of here so fast I don't even know who you are."

"Oh, I'm Phil," I said with a laugh. "Phil Belcher, but I don't have gas at the moment."

"I would hope not, Phil," she said in that sexy voice again. "My name's Carmen Dellinger."

"Hi, Carmen Dellinger," I greeted her, as I extended my hand.

"Hello, Phil Belch a lot," Carmen replied, as she took my hand and shook it firmly. "Nice to finally meet you. Are you the regular driver on this route?"

"Yeah, you're stuck with me," I said in mock disappointment.

"Well, that can't be all bad, can it?"

"I hope not," I responded. "Are you going to be the regular secretary? There's been about fifteen here, the last two weeks."

"Yeah, I'm afraid you're stuck with me, too," Carmen said, mocking me.

"How disappointing," I said as a joke, but almost meaning it.

"Hey, you'll make me feel bad," she pouted, as she handed me my board.

"Just kidding," I apologized. "I better get going. If there's anything you need, just let me know."

"Oh, I will!" Carmen said in that sexy voice again, as I walked away. "Bye Philzy."

"Bye, Carmen." When I got to my truck I was burning up. I had to take my jacket off just to cool down. At the time, I thought I'd gotten hot from staying in the office too long. I never thought the conversation could cause so much internal heat. In any case, the seed was planted.

The years rolled by, and the deliveries piled up. Carmen got pregnant twice, and I couldn't help thinking devilishly why any man in his right mind would want to get that woman pregnant. At the time, I definitely felt she was a two-bagger.

Carmen and I got to know each other in five-minute increments, five days a week. Then, when Diane and Alana went through their problems, I found myself spending more and more time with Carmen. I never talked about my problems at home. We just joked around and had fun and talked about softball, or anything on our minds. Some days, I'd find myself spending up to a half-hour with Carmen. I didn't realize it at the time, but since my home life was in such a mess, it felt good to go in Carmen's office and escape from the reality of my troubles. She helped me get through those bad times. Carmen and the other friendly faces on my route gave me a ray of hope. I was at a point in my life where I wanted to run away, have an affair, or just kill myself and end it all. At the time, I can honestly say, I never once thought of having an affair with Carmen. I also didn't want to run away or kill myself and miss out on our daily chats. Renee was my reason for staying at home and battling to the end. Carmen was my reason for going to work.

"I've got a delivery for you today," I'd sing, as I walked in the door of Carmen's office.

"Ahhhh! I can't wait," she said, in her sexiest voice.

"Where would you like it, baby?" I propositioned.

"How about in the back door," Carmen said seductively.

"Sounds good to me," I agreed, handing her my clipboard.

"How long will this delivery take?" she questioned.

"Don't you mean, how long will this delivery be?" I joked.

"Well, that too, I guess," Carmen laughed.

"This delivery will be just long enough to satisfy the inner reaches of your soul, and it will take at least two hours of heavy breathing," I fantasized.

"You are a true delivery man, aren't you?" Carmen complimented.

"That's what they tell me all over town," I bragged. "Of course, that's just from the guys."

Carmen laughed and messed up her signature. "Now, I'm worried about you," she added. "And, all this time I thought you were after me."

"Actually, it's your husband I crave," I continued. "I like the way he fits into those jeans."

"You are sick!" Carmen exclaimed, as she handed me my board.

"Do you have anything for me downstairs?" I asked, setting her up.

"Wouldn't you like to know?" she teased.

"That's why I asked the question," I said more seriously. "I would really like to know."

"Not only do I have something for you downstairs, but there's something for you upstairs, too."

"You naughty girl," I scolded her. "You may have to be spanked for that one."

"Promise?" Carmen said, bating her eyelashes.

"You better be careful," I warned her, "someday I might take you literally."

"Promise?" she repeated.

Usually, by that time, I'd be getting pretty hot, so I'd have to change gears and get out of there. "I better go see what you've got downstairs," I said, clearing my throat.

"If it's too dark for you, just holler and I'll help you feel your way around," she teased.

Of course, when I got downstairs, I couldn't resist. "AHHHHHHHHHH!"

It was so much fun flirting with Carmen, and the funny thing about it was when I would leave her office, I'd never have a second thought about it. Sometimes, I'd wonder if she subconsciously might be serious, but I never dwelled on it, because I really wasn't interested in her. Carmen had a way of getting me going, though. Many times, I left her place with an erection from the things we'd talk about. It was not only sexual teasing, but we'd actually discuss our sex lives and other private matters that most people wouldn't even tell their best friends.

I always enjoyed talking to women more than men. Maybe it was because I was a Momma's boy. Women are just a lot more interesting than men, and they're a hell of a lot more fun to flirt with. Women are more sensitive. They care about people and their feelings. And, more importantly, women listen. I guess, my mother instilled a sensitivity and honesty in me that women can relate to. Not to mention my voracious sexual appetite.

As my relationship with Carmen advanced, so did our sexual play. We got to the stage where we'd playfully tickle, punch, pinch, or slap one another. It was all in fun, but when an errant touch would inadvertently hit a vital part of the anatomy, it made it even more exciting. In reality, it seemed like I was setting myself up for a horrendous sexual harassment lawsuit, but I didn't care. It was all in fun, and I had no ulterior motive for participating. I had no interest in her.

Then it happened. One spring she asked me to play on her coed softball team. I only played in a couple of tourneys a year because I was coaching my daughters, so I decided to take her up on her offer. Besides, Carmen was always telling me how great she was at softball. She said she batted a thousand one year when she was pregnant, but I didn't believe her. I missed playing and wanted to get back into it, but I also wanted to see Carmen Dellinger, All-Star third baseman.

I'll never forget the first game we played together. Carmen took ground balls off the arms, chest, stomach, or any other part of the anatomy in an attempt to stop it and throw someone out. When she batted, she hit line drives. Not little pop-ups or squibbly ground balls. She played softball like a lesbian, but I knew damn well she was heterosexual. I was impressed.

One night, after a softball game, Carmen and I decided to play some tennis. It was more of a challenge match, since she threatened to beat me. I had to uphold my masculinity. Actually, we mostly hit the ball back and forth and goofed around. I just tried to keep the ball in play, and she tried to blow some shots by me.

What seemed so unusual about us just hitting the ball was the fact I always had to play games and keep score. Never had I wanted to play a sport just for the heck of it, or for the shear entertainment value. With Carmen, I was perfectly happy to "goof around". When she blew some backhand shots past me, I was impressed again.

Suddenly, I was looking at Carmen in a different light. No longer was she this homely secretary I knew in an office. She was this tart and sassy jockstress, who turned sporting maneuvers into sexual overtures. Needless to say, I was infatuated with her at this point. The score was love-love, and I was beginning to fall.

We continued to play softball once a week, and we tried to play tennis twice as much. We had more fun playing tennis. After each encounter, I found myself wanting more. At the softball games, I had to stand next to her in the dugout. Slap her hand first when she did something good, or exchange fake punches when we got bored. On the tennis court, I had to impress her with how I got to every ball, or make her laugh with my jokes and antics. It was Sister Bernadette all over again. If anyone made Carmen so much as chuckle, I had to outdo him.

One game, Diane came to watch. That was a mistake. She saw Carmen and I flirt around the diamond, slapping each other with our gloves as we walked to our positions. Diane took notes, and she didn't like the way they read.

"So, who's that Carmen girl who plays third base?" she asked on the ride home.

"What do you mean, who is she?" I evaded. "You just said her name."

"How do you know her?" Diane corrected.

"She's the one who asked me to play," I responded. "She works in Hagerstown."

"So, you deliver to her everyday," Diane pried.

"Well, what do you mean by deliver," I kidded.

"You know what I mean," she said annoyed. "Do you see her everyday?"

"Yeah, they have a pick-up account at the office where she works," I answered.

"That explains why she was flirting with you," Diane said calmly.

"She wasn't flirting with me," I protested. "We were just goofing around."

"From where I stood it looked like flirting," she responded. "I think she has the hots for you."

"Get outta here!" I laughed. "I was goofing around as much as she was."

"You have the hots for her then?" Diane asked point blank.

"No!" I lied. "She's twelve years younger than me, and besides, she's not that good looking."

"Oh, you know how old she is?" Diane trapped me.

"Yeah, I think she told me somewhere along the line," I stumbled.

"Well, age doesn't matter you know," she reasoned. "I still think she has the hots for you."

In one short seven-inning softball game, Diane had felt the same thing that took me two months to realize. I was falling in love with Carmen.

TENNIS, ANYONE?

I couldn't be falling in love. I was a married man of over twenty years. Diane and I were actually communicating, and we survived her depression and the "Dickbert" debacle.

There's no way I could be falling in love. Why did I need to look elsewhere? In over twenty years of marriage, I'd never ever seriously considered adultery. Sure, I'd seen or met women I thought would be great to get in bed, but I never had a second thought about them. Now, I was dwelling on the thought.

How could I be falling in love? She was twelve years younger than me. When I was graduating from high school, she was in first grade. Sure, she flirted with me, but she flirted with a lot of other guys, too. Did she think I was too old? Did she really have the hots for me? God, I wish I knew.

It had to be a mid-life crisis. Male menopause. That was it! I was just trying to reclaim my youth by being interested in a younger woman. So, what'd I do? I bought a bright-red Miata convertible to help me forget about my lust. It didn't work.

It was the empty-nest syndrome. Both of my daughters were in college away from home, and I was feeling useless as a parent. Carmen had two young sons and I loved playing with them when she brought them to the games. That's why I was drawn to her. Skyler was still in the baby stage and not too mobile. I was using Carmen's kids to keep me young. I'd just have to wait it out.

By the next softball season, Skyler was walking around just like Carmen's kids. I loved playing with him just as much as my own, but it didn't lessen my feelings for Carmen. I was running out of excuses for my behavior. Could I really love her? Could I love two women at the same time? Could I possibly ruin my marital track record by having an affair? The more I thought of the questions, the more the answer seemed to be edging toward "yes".

Diane could see the threat that Carmen posed to her. She found out that I'd been playing tennis with Carmen frequently and she didn't like it. I'd conveniently forgotten to tell Diane whom I'd been playing with, so it wasn't like I was lying to her. I just wasn't revealing the truth. Finally, after one of our softball games, the two women in my life got a chance to meet.

"C'mere, Diane," I coaxed her. "This is Carmen, the woman you've heard so much about, and Carmen, this is my wife, Diane."

"I hear you two have been playing some tennis together," Diane attacked.

"Oh, just a little bit," Carmen smiled and giggled.

"From what I hear, it's more than a little bit," Diane challenged.

"Oh, it's not that bad, Diane," I tried smoothing over. "We only play about once a week."

"Well, that's one time too many," Diane stated.

"We're just having fun," Carmen intervened. "We're not doing anything wrong."

"Well, in my book, when a married man and a married woman are 'just having fun' together, it can lead to something wrong," Diane lectured.

"You won't play tennis with him," Carmen said, defending her actions.

"That has nothing to do with it," Diane shot back. "There are plenty of men around for him to play tennis with. He doesn't need to be playing with a woman."

"Yeah, but she's so much better looking than the other guys," I kidded.

"Real funny," Diane said impatiently.

"Well, we don't have to argue about tennis right now," I said, trying to change the subject.

"That's right, because you don't need to be playing tennis with her anymore," Diane came to her ultimatum.

"Why not?" I laughed.

"You know why," Diane threatened.

"I better be going," Carmen said sarcastically.

"Wait a minute," I said to keep Carmen there. "We're still going to play tennis."

"I don't know about that, Philzy," Carmen teased.

"We'll see," Diane added.

"That's right," I said half-mad. "We'll see."

"Nice meeting you, Diane," Carmen kidded.

"Wish I could say the same," Diane struck back.

"Hey! Be nice!" I tried to tame.

I couldn't believe it. Because of me, two women who'd never met were now complete enemies. In another situation, they could've been best friends. It was flattering to see Diane fight for me so vigorously. I'd never seen her jealous before. But, to keep the peace, my tennis dates with Carmen would have to be fewer and more secret. Things were getting difficult.

WHEN THE CATS AWAY...

Just as Diane had feared, the verbal foreplay of Carmen and I escalated into physical contact. At first, it was an innocent tap on the shoulders or pulling hair. We'd hand wrestle or try to gently slap or flip each other in the face. We were like two junior high school kids trying to find a release for our sexual frustrations. We were both married and knew we shouldn't indulge in sex games with other partners, but there was this mutual attraction we couldn't deny. We were alike in so many ways, yet there were so many circumstances that separated us. Not only were we married; we lived in different towns, went to different churches, and were involved in different schools. It was like we were the last two people on earth, standing on opposite sides of the globe. How far would we have to go before finding each other?

Sometimes, to keep from touching each other somewhere else, we'd just hold each other's hands. It was a rush. I'd held Diane's hand many times, and still did, because that's what I was supposed to do. Holding hands with Carmen was illicit, and it excited me. I just had to tell her how I felt.

"You're something special, you know that?" I told Carmen uncomfortably.

"What do you mean?" she asked.

"I mean...I've never met a girl like you before," I stumbled. "You've got a great sense of humor and a great personality. I can talk to you about anything, even some things I wouldn't talk to guys about. And, you're a good athlete without being a lesbian."

"Wow, what a great compliment," Carmen said sarcastically.

"No, that is a compliment," I corrected. "Not many women have that combination. That's why I think you're really special."

"What's with all the compliments all of a sudden?" Carmen questioned.

"I don't know," I copped out momentarily. "Well,.. the truth is . . ."

"What?" she said impatiently.

"I think... well... I think I've fallen in love with you," I finally spit out feeling terribly vulnerable.

"Yeah, right," Carmen said, trying not to be surprised.

"I'm serious, Carmen," I assured her. "This isn't something that just hit me last night. I've been battling this for the last year and a half, trying to tell myself it wasn't true, and even if it were true, there's nothing I could do about it."

"You're crazy," she said trying, to avoid reciprocation.

"I know I am," I agreed. "This whole deal's been driving me crazy. I just felt I had to tell you, no matter how you felt about me. I mean, it'd be a shame if I went on feeling this way and never ever told you about it."

"That would be a shame," Carmen almost mocked.

"I don't know about you, but this whole relationship has occurred backwards for me," I philosophized. "Most guys see a girl and they say, 'Hey, I wanna have sex with her,' so they ask her out and they date until they finally have sex. Then if they're lucky they become friends over the course of a long time, and finally get married. Then after several years of marriage, they become indifferent to one another, or actually, get to the point where they don't like each other."

"You've got it all down to a science don't you?" Carmen kidded.

"Just listen," I insisted. "With you, the first time we met I didn't even like you."

"Thanks a lot!" Carmen pouted.

"It's not that I didn't like you, it's just I was indifferent about you," I tried to explain. "I had no opinion about you. I had no reason to impress you, because I thought you were . . ."

"Were what?" she pried.

"Were, . . well, I just wasn't attracted to you," I tried getting out of it without saying "homely".

"Thanks a lot," Carmen pouted again.

"But, eventually we became friends, and I wanted to spend more and more time with you, and after I saw you play softball and tennis I knew I was, well . . I fell for you. The whole process was backwards."

"You're wasted," Carmen said, to avoid telling me her feelings.

She never did tell me how she felt about me. She was either being nice, or was afraid to admit to loving me. In either case, our junior high relationship continued. It even progressed. Carmen would stick her hand up my pants leg or seductively unbutton my shirt. I'd rub the ass of her pants or skirt and get the occasional quick feel of her breast. We'd even bite each other in various places and leave hickeys that we'd have to explain by some other means.

One time, things got steamy. We were wrestling around as usual, when I got her on the floor and found myself on top of her. I had her hands pinned on each side of her head, and I started pulling up her shirt with my teeth. She told me to stop and to get off, but I knew she didn't mean it. Carmen was strong enough that I knew she could get away if she really wanted to. She put up a good fight, but she wasn't getting away.

When I got her shirt up around her neck, I started on her bra. All the while we laughed inadvertently, as we struggled. Carmen always wore a sports bra, so it was softer and lighter than a normal bra, and it pulled up a bit easier. I'd just uncovered the nipple of one of her breasts and was ready to put my mouth on it when it hit me. I couldn't do it. It felt wrong and indecent. It was that damn Catholic upbringing. Sister Paula was looking over my shoulders. I was inches away from bliss and who knows what else, and my conscience got the best of me. Maybe if Carmen hadn't still been struggling I would've kept going, but I could tell it wasn't right for her. I rolled off of her laughing, and she reorganized her clothes.

We continued our foreplay for another year or more. Sometimes, I'd get in a self-pity mode and wouldn't talk to her for a few days, but then I'd jump right back in. I kept trying to get back to the lifted bra stage, but we never let it get that far again. Things were frustrating. I wanted her, and I was almost sure she wanted me, but we couldn't cross the line. I began to fantasize about Carmen's husband and Diane being out of the picture. Then Carmen and I could make love without any regrets or guilty conscience. Wishing two people dead would make me happy? I felt like such a cad for even harboring the thought. I still loved Diane, even though she was mostly grumpy. I'd be lost without her. In fact, my innocent flirting with Carmen made me realize I needed Diane to keep me honest. I prayed to God if anyone should die; let it be me, so I could be freed from this frustrating love triangle.

I endured months and months of Carmen teasing me and never committing to anything. I had to confront her.

"Why haven't you ever told me how you feel about me?" I demanded.

"Why should I?" Carmen asked to avoid the answer.

"Because I've told you so many times how I feel about you, and I've given you things and written notes to you, and I never get anything out of you."

"I gave you that lucky penny, didn't I?" she laughed, to change the subject.

"Big deal!" I shouted. "If you don't love me, just tell me. I'll leave you alone and won't bother you again. At least it'll be better than being kept in the dark."

"I can't go there," she said, looking away. "Because I know if I do, I won't want to stop."

"I know what you mean," I said with joy, at finally getting a decent response out of her. "I feel the same way. I want you so bad, but I know we shouldn't be doing anything like that."

"My parents would kill me if I wanted to marry someone else," Carmen lamented. "Besides, I'd be afraid of losing my kids."

"I don't think that would ever happen," I assured her. "I just want to make love to you so bad I can't stand it. And, the only way I'd do it is, if I knew positively that you loved me. I couldn't do it without knowing that."

"I just keep thinking of the mess we could be causing," she added.

"I know what you mean," I agreed. "We're like the star-crossed lovers in a novel who never get the chance to express their love to each other. We're so much alike, and we became friends over such a long period of time that it just seems unfair we can't take it to the next level. I just feel we were meant to be together."

"It's all so frustrating," Carmen added.

The phone rang in the office, which usually meant our visit was over. I realized, for the first time I was holding both of Carmen's hands. They were warm and sweaty, and as I looked into Carmen's eyes, I leaned forward to kiss her. She turned her head, allowing me to kiss her cheek. Once again my expectations had been cut short.

"I guess you better answer the phone," I said after the fourth ring.

She left to go to work, and I went to finish my route.

Just because we happened to be married before we ever met shouldn't be enough to keep us apart for the rest of our lives. Or, should it? So many people today have affairs at the drop of a hat, and we couldn't even think of having one after five years of falling in love.

It wasn't fair. I wanted to give Carmen my life, but I couldn't live with myself if I abandoned Diane. Why couldn't I be a prick like most men and just have the goddam affair and not worry who I hurt? God, I hated being Catholic. Why couldn't I be a Mormon?

Things cooled off after that. It wasn't that our feelings dwindled, but we knew if we got started with foreplay again, we might not be able to stop. We were in love, but too afraid to do anything about it. Too afraid to take a chance

Three years later, I retired from SOL. I still didn't get a kiss from Carmen, but she did cry a lot on my last day. Eventually, we didn't play softball or tennis together anymore. She had her two boys to raise, and I had Skyler to think about.

Still, I dream of seeing her again one day, when both of our situations change and we can be a little freer with our time and attentions. I envision seeing her across the room at a gathering where a lot of people are present. I can feel my heart pound now, just like it would at that moment. I'll walk towards her, ignoring all the people who talk to me or try to keep me from her. I'll grab her warm hands and look into her eyes like I did so many times at that Hagerstown office. Without saying a word, I'll steal that kiss I wanted so many years ago. I'll hold her tightly, and as I run my hands through her hair, I'll whisper in her ear. "I never meant to fall in love."

SKY, STARS, AND A LOT OF SON

I was fortunate to have Skyler. He could always take my mind off my troubles. Work, love, marriage, hobbies, whatever went wrong in my life, I knew that Skyler was depending on me to be there, and I was depending on him to make me forget.

Before I had children I wanted a boy. I wanted to raise him in a sporting environment so he could make the teams I was always cut from. I wanted him to live the life I was denied. It was probably a blessing I had two daughters. If my son were interested in ballet and basket weaving, I would've killed him! Having daughters was a happy medium for me. If they were interested in ballet, I'd have to accept it. Fortunately, they chose softball, track, swimming, and a couple years of grade school basketball. I never regretted having daughters.

I trained Skyler from the beginning. As a baby we'd roll balls back and forth on the floor. When he learned to walk, we'd toss balls in the air and catch. When he could run without falling down, I taught him to dribble a mini-basketball and shoot at an eight-foot goal. Skyler picked it up naturally, and just like Renee, he taught me a lesson.

I was getting frustrated trying to teach him to shoot right-handed. The shots would veer-off to the right or left, not even getting close to the basket. Suddenly, he yelled, "I want to do it this way!" And poured in five straight shots with his left hand. Needless to say, I was amazed. He'd always eaten with his right hand, and colored with his right hand, so I assumed . . . In any case, I cultivated the use of both hands. I wanted Skyler to be as much ambidextrous as possible.

It was an adjustment having a kid in the house again. I relished the idea, while Diane tolerated it. She still had depression problems and I'm sure any situation would've upset her. Alana finished college and got a teaching job at Centerville. She and Skyler continued to live with us to save money, but I did make her pay $100 a month rent. The money went straight in an account for their future.

By the time Skyler hit pre-school, I retired from SOL and got a job writing for the local paper. I could spend a lot more time at home, so Diane went back to work to keep herself occupied. Either that or she was trying to stay away from me. But once again, I could be there to help raise one of my kids.

"Gramps," Skyler said seriously one day during lunch.

"Yeah, Sky," I answered.

"So, where'd you say my dad is?" he asked.

"Well, we don't know exactly where he is, we just know he left," I said, half-afraid Skyler wanted to see him.

"So, is he ever coming back?" Skyler continued.

"We haven't seen or heard from him in five years, Skyler," I said objectively. "I can't say he'll never come back, but I don't think he will."

"Is that so," he said straight-faced.

"Yeah, I'm afraid that's the way it is."

"If he won't ever be coming back," Skyler reasoned, "then would it be ok if I called you dad?"

"What?" I exclaimed, spilling soup on my shirt.

"Can I call you, dad?" he repeated. "Everybody at school has one."

"Well, I'm actually your grandfather," I reasoned.

"I know, but when everybody else talks about their dad, I wanna tell them about you," Skyler complimented. "I don't think they'll understand if I call you Gramps."

I was so choked up I couldn't speak for a moment.

"Tell you what," I finally said, "if your mom doesn't mind, you can call me anything you want. Except late for dinner."

"Great!" Skyler exclaimed. "I already asked her."

"What'd she say?" I wondered.

"She cried," he answered. "I guess that meant yes."

I had to leave the room to get a tissue. From then on I was Dad.

"SKY" KING

By kindergarten, Skyler had advanced to a regular size basketball and a 10-foot goal. I could tell by his hands and feet he was going to be taller than me someday. It was the only good attribute his father would ever give him. We practiced on basketball constantly. Not because I wanted to, but because he enjoyed the sport and the time we spent together. I never forced him to go out and shoot. I was so afraid of turning him against the sport, I'd let him go a week before I'd suggest we go play ball.

Skyler Velcroed to basketball. He struck out at wiffle ball, and never got used to an odd-shaped football, but put a round ball in his hands and he controlled it like an extension of his own body. I had Skyler do ball-handling and shooting drills whenever we went out to play. It was astonishing watching a pre-schooler maneuver a basketball better than some adults I played against.

I had Skyler doing the Mikan drill, where you repeatedly shot bunny shots, as fast as you could. He'd shoot with his right hand on the right side, and his left hand on the left side, and he'd rarely miss. He wasn't the quickest at it, and since he was so small it took him longer to get the shots off, but he used the backboard every time and made that net sing.

As we moved farther away from the basket, Skyler developed a bad-shooting habit. He shot the basketball in a line drive fashion trying to get it to the goal. I explained to him in order for the ball to go through the hoop, he needed to arch it in the air, so it would fall straight down into the basket. He'd do it right for a couple times, then he'd go back to flinging line drives. Finally, after a week of unsuccessful teaching, I became frustrated.

"You have to push the ball up in the air," I scolded him. "You're pushing it straight out, and it's barely getting ten feet high."

Skyler did a couple shots right, but soon flattened them out again.

"Let me show you something," I said in disgust. I had him support a hoola hoop on the ground. "If I stand in front of the hoop and try to throw this basketball through it, it's pretty easy, isn't it?"

"Yeah," he answered confused.

"Now, if I stand over here," I said, moving over to the side of the hoola hoop, "it's not so easy to throw it through the hoop, is it?"

"Not unless I turn it around," Skyler speculated.

"That's right," I agreed, "and there's no way to turn a basketball goal around, so you have to shoot it so it falls straight down in the basket."

He tried it again, and again. He did it right three times and then reverted back to the line drives.

"Dammit, Skyler!" I finally blew. "Shots are precious! If you're going to shoot then you've got to give it a chance to live. You're killing these shots before they're ever born! Now, do it right! Every time!"

As soon as I said the words, I regretted it. Fortunately, Skyler didn't cry. He just got mad. He took the basketball and launched an arching shot that must've peaked about thirty feet in the air, brushed against a tree limb, and rocketed down toward the goal and straight into the hoop.

"That's it!" I shouted for joy. "I don't care how high you shoot the ball, just give it a chance to fall in."

I passed him the ball and he launched another 20-foot shot that clipped the same branch in the same spot, and fell through the same hoop. I couldn't believe he did it twice. I kept passing him the ball and he kept arching it skyward to the tip of the limb and down to the hoop. I made him move around the perimeter. He didn't always hit the limb, and the shot didn't always go in, but each time it was pretty damn close.

"I don't ever want to see a line-drive shot again. Do you understand me?" I emphasized.

He shook his head yes, as he launched another 3-pointer. That night, I got my saw and cut down every limb within forty feet of the basket. There weren't any limbs in the high school gyms around the State, and I didn't want him to become dependent on the target. It didn't faze him a bit. As long as he arched the ball high in the air, he was sure to at least hit some iron. I felt Skyler had found his basketball niche.

For the next couple of years, I became a professor of basketball. Now, don't get me wrong, I'm no James Naismith, but I knew how to play the game, and I knew what it took to be successful at it. I didn't always work on offense either. I knew the importance of defense, and I taught it religiously: The concepts of zone and man defense, the defensive slide, the trap, when to stop the ball and when to go for the steal, and most important the defensive block-out. Skyler didn't always like working on defense. No basketball player ever does. It's the difficult part of the game many coaches and players slough over or forget completely. College and pro teams use the shot clock as a defensive replacement. As a result, it's a dying art.

While schooling Skyler, I also looked for signs of one of the most important aspects of the game. Basketball sense. Like common sense, basketball sense is the innate ability to know what to do and where to be every second on the basketball court. If you're smart enough to get out of the rain, you have common sense. If you know to move to the opposite side of the goal from where a shot is taken to block out and rebound, then that's basketball sense. Unfortunately, unlike common sense, most players don't have basketball sense.

I watched Skyler play basketball with his friends. In fact, I'd stage basketball parties for his classmates just to see them play and to get them some experience. Skyler would anticipate a pass. He'd move without the ball. And he could calculate the destination of a rebound faster than a Geometry professor. Skyler had basketball sense. And, amazingly enough, so did a few of his friends. In fact, there were four in particular who had a lot of potential. Whenever the five of them would get on one team, it would be a massacre. So, usually I'd split them up just to make it competitive.

The next year, the Indiana High School Athletic Association, decided to initiate a four-class system into it's basketball tourney. Previously, every high school in the State played to the death until one champion was crowned. Now, there would be four champions, and they'd be separated by school attendance. The new system was good for small schools. No longer would they compete with the giants. The new system was bad for tradition. Now, the state title would only be a watered-down version of the original. For better or worse, the new four-class system was initiated for a five-year trial.

MAKE YOUR MOVE

In the summer before Skyler entered third grade. The summer before he played in youth league basketball for the first time. The summer Skyler and I were having so much fun. Alana hit me with a bolt of lightning.

"I've been offered a job in Anderson," Alana announced.
"What?" I asked in disbelief.
"In Anderson!" Diane added in shock.
"Yeah, I sent out a few resumes a few months ago, and it looks like Anderson needs a History teacher," Alana said calmly.
"Are you going to take it?" I hesitantly asked.
"Yeah, I think so," Alana said cheerfully. "It's more money."
"Money isn't everything, Alana," I reasoned.
"Anderson's a big school, too," Diane added. "It's bigger than Richmond, and there could be a lot of problems with delinquent students."
"That's a long drive, too," I chimed in.
"Well, I'd probably move there," Alana hit us again.
"Move! You can't move!" I demanded. "What about Skyler?"
"You're not going to take him out of Centerville, are you?" asked Diane.
"Well, . I guess, . that's what I'd planned on," Alana said overwhelmed. "He is my son you know."
"You can't do that, Alana!" I exclaimed. "It'll kill him! It'll kill me!"
"Well, what do you want me to do?" Alana said close to tears. "You want me to live here the rest of my life? You want me to be a single mom the rest of my life? I do have a sex-drive you know. It would be nice to bring a man home and not have to worry about waking up your parents!"
"We just hate to see you go clear to Anderson and find out you don't like it," Diane reasoned.
"It's less than an hour away!" Alana shouted. "You act like I'm moving half-way around the globe! Oh, never mind! You guys don't understand."
Alana left the room in tears. After giving her a few minutes alone, I went in to join her.
"Are you alright?" I quietly asked.

"Oh, for a future old maid, I guess I'm doing fine," Alana responded between sobs.

"Maybe we overreacted," I tried to apologize. "We should be proud you were selected for a higher paying job somewhere else."

"That's what I thought you would be," Alana said, looking up from her bed.

"We are! Don't misunderstand us," I explained. "We've gotten so used to you and Skyler being around, we can't even fathom the thought of you guys leaving."

"We've got to leave sometime, Dad," Alana said. "We can't live here forever."

"I wouldn't mind it," I smiled.

"It's just that sometimes I feel like such a failure because I'm not married and I don't have a home of my own, and my parents are helping me raise my son," Alana rambled in one breath.

"You are not a failure!" I scolded her. "If anything, you're one of the better success stories to come out of Centerville. You've graduated from college, you've got a damn good job, and you're raising a son as a single parent."

"But, I wouldn't be anywhere without you guys," Alana lamented.

"That's what parents are for," I explained. "If we sat by and didn't help you get established, then we wouldn't be doing our job."

"I just feel I have nothing of my own," she said.

"I was over forty years old before I owned my first house," I told her. "My parents helped us for a long time. Not because we necessarily needed or demanded it, but because they wanted to. It was their way of saying I love you."

"I know," Alana agreed. "I should be thankful for you guys."

"I understand what you mean by having a place of your own," I explained. "Everyone feels like that. Is this new job in Anderson about money?"

"That's a start," she responded.

"Well, I guess I should let you in on a little secret," I confessed. "That one hundred dollars you've been giving me a month for rent has been going into an account for you and Skyler to use later on. You can use it for a down payment on a house, or for college tuition, or for whatever. So, there's your extra money. If you're moving to Anderson just for that, then you may as well stay right here."

"Yeah, but you and Mom have got to be sick of sharing your home with a single mother and her son," Alana assumed.

"Not a bit," I quickly answered. "If you're happy with your job at Centerville, then I suggest you think twice about pulling up roots and leaving. And, think about the affect on Skyler. He's got it tough enough without having to make new friends."

"Well . . . I don't know," Alana stumbled.

"Don't decide anything now," I reasoned. "Just think about it, and make a decision in a couple days. Clear your head, and let the idea sink in."

Alana looked at me and smiled. "Ok," she whispered, "I'll think about it."

LEARNING THE GAME

When it was time for youth league basketball that winter, Alana and Skyler were still at Centerville. Alana met a handsome new teacher, and along with his efforts, we convinced her to stay.

For some silly reason, I decided I wouldn't coach Skyler in the third and fourth grade level. I'd been coaching him on basketball ever since he was old enough to stand, so I thought it was time he got a different viewpoint.

Skyler's first basketball coach was Todd Farmer. After his first practice, he came up to me and said, "With Skyler on this team, we've got the season in the bag." And, after seeing the first game, Todd was right. Skyler's team won 28-5, in a rout. Skyler scored 24 points, and it was obvious to see why. He was the only one handling the ball. Todd set up an offense where every player on the team would set picks to get Skyler free. All Skyler had to do was drive and shoot, drive and shoot, drive and shoot.

They won their second game 33-8. Same offense. Same ball hog that scored 28 points. Third game, 31-2. Skyler made a basket at the wrong goal in the first quarter, or else it would've been a shutout. Skyler was high point man for both teams. I felt a lot of unrest among the parents. It was supposed to be a team sport, and Skyler was making it a one-man show. After his third game, Skyler had a talk with me.

"Dad?" Skyler questioned, while he was doing his dribbling drills in the driveway.

"Yeah, Sky," I answered.

"Some of the guys on the team are calling me a ball hog," he said matter-of-factly.

"Well, it does seem like you're the only one handling the ball," I said, taking the other players side.

"I know," Skyler shot back, "but Coach tells me to. He doesn't want me to pass."

"Is that the way the game's supposed to be played?" I questioned.

"No," Skyler answered. "If there's five people on a team, you should use them."

158

"And if you want to play a sport by yourself . . .?" I asked.

"Take up tennis," Skyler finished. "But, what should I do?"

"Well, right now, Coach Farmer's got the whole offense keyed on you," I explained. "Tell your teammates to start picking for each other, and see if you can get them the ball."

"Yeah!" Skyler's eyes lit up, as he quit dribbling. "Maybe I can get some assists."

"And, every assist is worth two points for two different players," I added.

"What if Coach Farmer tells me not to pass?" Skyler wondered.

"Just take it yourself a few times, then start passing again," I suggested. "If you guys score big, the Coach won't care. He's just worried about winning."

"Gotcha!"

The next game, Sky put our plan into action. The third time down the court, the forwards set back picks for the guards, and Skyler sent a bounce pass through the lane.

"What are you doing?" yelled Coach Farmer.

One of Skyler's teammates grabbed the pass on his way to the basket and laid it in for a 4-0 lead.

"Oh," Farmer nearly whispered. "Nice pass, Sky."

The two teammates slapped hands on their way to play defense, smiling all the way. Parents in the stands were applauding the play and amazed how the pass ever made it through the lane. Every third time down the court, Skyler would find a player streaking through the lane. They didn't always score, but everyone on the team got to touch the ball for a change. After a 38-20 win, all the kids gave each other high fives for the first time. All the parents milled around in the stands talking about the game, and how all but two kids had scored. Skyler was high-point man again, but he only had 14 points. He was happier about the outcome than the boys who'd scored points for the first time.

"Coach Farmer must've changed offenses," one of the parents said to me.

"Yeah, it looks like it," I smiled.

"It's nice to see the other kids touch the ball," the parents added.

"That's why they call it a team," I said.

As Skyler and I were leaving, Coach Farmer stopped us.

"Hey, Sky," he said. "Nice game today. Really liked the way you were passing. But, if we ever have a close game like this again, I want you to handle the ball all the time."

"Todd," I said in disgust, "you won by 18 points. In this league that's like a 40-point win. Let Skyler get a few assists. You saw how happy the other kids were, didn't you?"

"Yeah, I guess so," Farmer sighed. "That's probably the best team we'll play, anyway. We can afford a few passes. See you at practice, Sky."

After Coach Farmer walked away, Skyler looked at me seriously. "Will you coach me next year, dad?"

"I guess I'll have to, Sky," I answered putting my arm around his head. "We're the only ones who know the game."

The next year I did coach Skyler. It wasn't easy, since I was coaching junior-high girls too, but I felt I had to do it. Once again, Skyler's team went undefeated, and although I worked hard with all the kids teaching them the basics, I didn't feel like my being coach was a deciding factor. Heck, the year before they won all their games with a bad coach. Which just goes to prove my theory. Good athletes can overcome bad coaching, but mediocre athletes need the best coach possible.

During that fourth-grade year, I found Skyler's backcourt mate. It was Shane Best, and next to Skyler, he was the best ball handler in elementary. This was the best thing that could've happened to Skyler, because he no longer had to be the only dribbler. Shane became the point guard and inherited ball handling duties, and Sky became the shooting guard. Sky worked on setting picks as well as receiving them. It helped his game immensely.

Once we realized what we had, a couple of us fathers (and grandfathers) got together and put the kids in an AAU basketball program. Along with Shane and Skyler, we had Emile George who was a tall kid and a good rebounder. Once he learned the geometry of basketball rebounding, he became a basketball magnet. Not only would he get in the right position, but his height and long arms gave him a tremendous advantage.

Then there was Vance Worth. He was not exceptional in any aspect of the game, but to his credit, he did them all well. He was almost as tall as Emile, so he could rebound. Vance could score if he wanted to, he could handle the ball, or he could set a mean pick.

And, to round out the team, there was Buzzy Gray. At best, he was an average player, but when you put him with all the others, he became the missing link. He was a smart ball player who could see the whole court. He could play guard or forward and still be effective. Since he could see the court so well, he was a natural for taking the ball out-of-bounds. He had an instinct for finding the open man, and chalked up quite a few assists.

GETTING IN THE GAME

The other fathers and I were convinced that these five kids would one day constitute the starting line-up at Centerville High School. We played them together in AAU as much as possible. They won over 85% of their games, but each time, a loss was hard to take. We made sure they didn't pout about losses either. We insisted they accept them and vow to do better next time.

Occasionally, at halftime or at the end of a loss, I'd let the boys coach themselves.

"My bad, guys," Skyler apologized after a close defeat.

"Pipe down, King!" Shane retorted. "You act like you're the only one who can win these games or somethin'."

"Yeah, give it a rest, Sky," Emile added. "We were out there too, ya know."

"None of us set the court on fire," Vance chimed in.

"I took some shots when I shoulda passed," Skyler lamented.

"You take a LOT of shots when you oughta pass!" Shane kidded. "I forget what a leather ball feels like."

"No, sh . . . sugar!" Buzzy stumbled. "I'm blocking out and setting picks. And it feels like a freakin' wrestling match out there. I didn't even know we had a ball!"

"Hey, we'll be better for this next time," Vance encouraged. "This team will never beat us again."

"Unless we got Mr. Cape Canaveral over here launching shots every twelve seconds," Shane smirked.

"Houston, we have a problem," Buzzy mimicked.

"At least I don't dribble with my head down," Skyler shot back, fighting off his rejection. "Are you lookin' for the pennies the fans are throwing at you?"

"At least I'm not a black hole," Shane kept poking.

"I didn't know Shane had fans," Vance rambled.

"If we keep this up, none of us will have fans," Emile reasoned.

"Yeah, we gotta play more as a team," Vance added.

"Team, team, team God — bless it! Team, team, team!" Buzzy chanted.

"Don't get him started," Skyler shook his head. "He'll be doing 'two bits' before long."

"Two bits, four bits, six bits…!"

"Can it!" the other four yelled simultaneously.

Sometimes, a little mindless chatter, and an attitude of not being afraid to lose was the best coaching an ailing team could get.

Ironically, Skyler had several chances to win games on a last second shot, but he could never get one to fall. One game, he scored 33 points, shot 60 percent from the field, but missed a 12-footer to win it. In three years, I bet Skyler missed six chances to tie or win games at the end of regulation and couldn't do it. He always took these games hard, but I made him realize that without him, they wouldn't have been close in the first place.

Finally, as seventh graders, the boys won a state title in AAU. The game came down to a last second shot. I heeded the warnings of the "Skyler Jinks" and set up a play for Emile. Skyler was to drive toward the right baseline and presumably get double-teamed. Emile would get a double pick from the left side of the lane, and Sky would loft a pass in the middle for a tying basket. The play worked perfectly. Not only did Emile score, he was fouled in the process and sank a free throw with two seconds left to win the game. The kids loved it. And, the best part was Skyler didn't care he was overlooked for the last shot. He was just glad to have a state title, and he now knew, he didn't have to take the last shot every time in a close game. (Knowledge that would benefit him later.)

That same year, we got some good coaching news for the high school. Jim Reiser was hired as the varsity assistant.

"Welcome to Centerville," I said, shaking his hand.

"You're the first, and probably the last," Jim replied.

"Hey, with what we've had, all you have to do is win a couple games a year and you'll be a hero," I kidded. "After Dick Stern, any direction will be up."

Dick Stern was the Varsity Coach at Centerville, and the ridicule of the community. He'd been the Coach since Skyler was in the first grade, and the program had gone steadily downhill ever since. Oh, one year, he had a team finish 15-6, win the TEC title and actually beat Richmond in the regular season. Everyone had high hopes for the Sectional against Richmond. They even made t-shirts that read, "I love you, man" on the front, and "But, you're not winning this Sectional" on the back. Needless to say, Stern and his team weren't ready for a rematch and got their asses kicked. Royally.

"Just between you and me, I've seen Stern coach," Jim said softly. "It's not a thing of beauty."

"That's an understatement," I added. It's like he's a disciple of the cult '101 ways to lose a ballgame'."

"And, he's followed it well," Jim chimed in. "He only plays his favorites in the game, and then subs for non-favorites when they start to do well."

"Amen, brother."

"We played Man the entire game against Stern last time, and I only saw two picks set by his players," Jim lamented. "His teams are lazy and selfish, and it's evident none of the players respect him."

"You must be psychic if you know all that," I said. "Your analysis is right on."

"Doesn't take much to figure him out," Jim said. "He's pretty one-dimensional."

"So, what does an old basketball coach from Union County do about Dick Stern?" I rhetorically questioned.

"Cry a lot," Jim kidded. "Send your resume to other schools. Beat your head…"

"Seriously," I interrupted. "He's a 'dick' in the literal sense. How do you change anything?"

"Very slowly," Jim whispered. "I know Dick well enough that if he thinks he's being undermined, he'll run you into a brick wall; even if it means making an ass of himself. I've got to make him feel he's coming up with ideas to make his team better. I've got to plant a helluva lot of seeds."

"You came here to become 'Jimmy Basketball Seed'?" I joked.

"Don't laugh," Jim said. "I've got a couple reasons for being here."

"And, they are . . .?"

"First of all, the administration at Liberty was getting too involved in the coaching," Jim stated. "Too many administrative kids getting cut from the team or not getting enough playing time, etcetera. I had to get out of that hassle. And, the most attractive part of coming here was . . ."

"ME!" I anticipated.

"No, you're not attractive, Phil," Jim said, without breaking stride. "What is, is the prospect of getting to coach that group of boys you have."

"No way," I doubted. "You came here for that?"

"There's not a coach in Indiana who hasn't heard about that seventh grade group," Jim said. "Skyler alone is getting rave reviews. They say he passes like Larry Bird, dribbles like Steve Alford, shoots like Rick Mount, and scores like Damon Bailey. And, everyone salivates at the thought of coaching him. There's even rumblings of a few college coaches around the state wanting to see Skyler."

"You've got to be kidding me!" I exclaimed.

"I'm surprised you haven't been offered an SUV or a million-dollar contract yet," Jim kidded.

I felt my hair follicles tingling. My grandson was in high demand. I felt so proud, yet I envied him terribly. In school, I could never make the team, and Skyler was on the verge of stardom.

"So, all the coaches are salivating over Skyler?" I repeated.

"Unfortunately, their taste-buds have to stomach Dick Stern in the process. No easy task, mind you. He's got tenure in a small school system."

"And," I added, "he plays all the school board kids."

"Exactly," Jim emphasized. "Why would the board even consider getting rid of him? He may never win another game, but he's got a lock on the system."

"Thanks," I grumbled. "Now you're making me nauseous."

"It's not a pretty outlook," Jim said. "But, that's why I'm here. I thought I could make a difference."

"You came here to get frustrated!" I exclaimed.

"Partially."

"Did I ever tell you, you're my hero?" I sang.

"Please, spare me," Jim laughed. "I can still resign, you know."

"Don't do that!" I shouted. "We need you bad. Thanks for coming."

"Don't thank me yet," Jim added. "Wait till I get something done about Stern."

Stern hadn't won a sectional game even with the four-class system. As a result, attendance at the games slowly dwindled. It got to the point where the only spectators were band kids and the parents of the players. And, the band would leave after the half-time show. I went to a few games and felt like I was at a wake. Empty seats everywhere, and very little to cheer about. Most of the time, the opposing teams brought in more fans than the hometown Bulldogs. Our cheerleaders spent more time flirting with the studs in the stands than they did trying to conjure up spirit. Hell, there was no spirit to conjure up.

I did see three old guys at every game, three of the faithful, who weren't related to a player. Following them out after one game though, I felt their loyalty waning.

"Why the hell do you keep bringing me to these games?" Milo asked his two friends.

"You know you love it, Milo," Kenneth kidded.

"Love it!" Milo recanted. "This is downright painful!"

"I hate to admit this, but I tend to agree with him," George added. "If this team was a horse, we'd have to shoot it."

"That's right," Milo perked. "A mercy killing is well overdue."

"Give 'em a break, guys," Kenneth consoled. "Every team has a few down years before they can regroup."

"Yeah, but we're having a down decade," Milo said seriously.

"We need a fresh coaching approach," George theorized. "We're not getting anything out of this guy."

"Well, don't call Dr. Kevorkian yet," Kenneth kidded. "We've got some good athletes coming up, who will resuscitate this program."

Coach Stern appeared to be the type of guy who was true to his name, but it was only on the surface. His discipline was lax at best. Players smoked, drank, stayed up past curfew, and skipped practices. There was always the threat of suspensions, but if you were a star player, there wasn't a worry. Needless to say, none of the players respected him. And, to top it off, Stern never taught basketball. The team never ran an offense. They never set picks against a man to man, and they didn't move the ball against the zone. No one liked Stern, but unless he did something stupid, Centerville was stuck with him. That is, until Jim Reiser came to town.

"Too bad, you didn't come here about 35 years ago," I told Jim. "Maybe I could've made the team."

"I've seen you play, Phil," Jim responded. "It would've taken a pretty good bribe to get you on the team."

"Hey! I used to play some pretty good basketball in my day!" I defended.

"Yeah, but you were thirty years old, too," Jim added. "That's a bit elderly for high school ball."

I hadn't seen Jim in over two years, and with comments like that, I wasn't sure I was glad to see him now. Actually, Jim was only ten years older than me, so it seemed like we were more friends than teacher-student. There was one thing about Jim I never understood. He never married. He'd always been a handsome guy, but I'd never even seen him date. I felt pretty confident he wasn't gay, but I guess you never know anyone completely.

Jim was older, grayer, and a little paunchier now, but he had a good personality and mature good looks and still wasn't married. I never asked him why, because I thought it was none of my business. If he wanted to tell me, I guess he would have. In any case, it was good to have Jim at Centerville. I knew it could only benefit Skyler.

Another bit of news we received during the summer before Skyler went into eighth grade, was the IHSAA decided to return to the one-class system in basketball. Attendance was way down for the Tournament and everyone was losing money.

For its first few years of existence, the four-class system was a boom. The small schools could fight among themselves for a State Championship. And since there were four champions, attendance and interest was up.

Unfortunately, to make everyone happy, the IHSAA instituted a "Tournament of Champions" to be played the week after all four classes crowned a state winner. Class "A" champ played class "4A". Class "2A" played class "3A". In other words, there was still only one team in the State who would win their last game of the season. It should've been called the "Tournament of Losers", since 75% of the participants went home in defeat. By trying to please everybody, the IHSAA just pissed everyone off.

With dwindling interest, the big shots at Indy had to swallow their pride and admit they were wrong. As much as it favored the big schools, the one-class system was unique in its simplicity. Fans lived for the day when their "Davids" would knock off the "Goliaths", even if it took a half-century. Once again, the IHSAA heard the cries, "If it wasn't broke, then why'd you try to fix it?"

It was a bittersweet announcement. With four classes, Skyler and company could've easily won a 3A state title. Now, they'd have to fight for their lives just to win a Sectional.

IF THERE'S SOMETHING WORTH DOING...

As Skyler started his eighth-grade basketball season, something disheartening was happening. Skyler was getting lazy. His passes weren't as sharp. He launched off-balance shots. He wasn't moving without the ball to get open, and his defense was lackluster at best. Not only was Sky lazy, his attitude trickled down to the other members of the team. Sure, the team was winning all their games, but not by the margins they should've been. Twice they had to go into overtime and actually play hard to get a win. They expected to win by walking on the court. They were just going through the motions.

When I talked to their coach about it, he said, "Don't worry, they're saving the best for last." When I talked to Diane and Alana about it, they said, "Oh, you just expect too much." Finally, when I talked to Jim Reiser, he agreed.

"I saw their game last night," Jim said. "It looked like a case of how poorly can I play and still win."

"I'm glad somebody else can see it," I said relieved. "It's driving me crazy. What can we do about it?"

"They won't be playing that way next year, I can assure you of that," Jim stated.

"Yeah, but what do we do now?" I wondered. "I'm afraid if we let it go on all year, they'll assume they can lay down all the time."

"I'm going to a practice tomorrow night," Jim assured me. "I'll see what happens, talk to the coach, talk to the boys, and see if I can get some motivation out of them."

"Great!" I exclaimed. "I'll talk with him, too. I can't stand to watch those games, even if they are winning."

It wasn't as easy to talk to Skyler as it used to be. He was a teenager now, and Alana and I had to ward off the Joshua syndrome in him. If he challenged authority too much or just wanted to be lazy about everything, we blamed it on his dad.

I'd always been glad I had daughters because, for the most part, they were easier to handle. If I got angry with them, I could scare them into doing what I wanted. With boys, it was a little more difficult trying to intimidate them. I felt I'd end up killing a son in anger when he refused to do what he was told.

"So, what's up with you guys this year?" I asked Skyler, as we shot around in the driveway.

"What d'ya mean?" Sky snapped, as he popped in a long three.

"You guys just haven't been playing that well this year," I accused. "You've barely been beating teams."

"We've been winning, haven't we?" Sky sarcastically asked.

"Yeah, but you're playing like crap," I shot back in anger.

"Well, don't worry about it, dude," he said disrespectfully. "Doesn't seem to bother coach."

"It bothers me!" I answered. "And, it should bother you. I'd think you guys would want to play the best you can, not just well enough to survive."

"Surviving's all that matters," Sky reasoned. "As long as we win, who cares?"

"I've always said if you're going to do something, than . . ."

"Yeah, I know. Do it to the best of your ability," Skyler mocked. "Well, I say if you can slide by at half speed, than go for it, old man."

I grabbed a rebound, slammed the basketball against the garage, and sent it past the driveway into the barn lot.

"Listen here, *young* man!" I shouted, trying to control myself. "Until you can beat me at one-on-one, I don't think you need to be calling me *old* man! And, if you want to play basketball at half speed, then I suggest you do the sport a favor and remove your sorry ass from the court!"

Skyler looked at me, teetering on the verge of defiance and compliance.

"Maybe I'll quit," he finally whispered sheepishly.

"You should!" I yelled, not meaning it. "You're taking advantage of the game. You don't appreciate it anymore. You need to step back and take a look at what you're doing with what you have. I never got a chance to get in the game. Hell, I never made the Team! But, I got more respect for basketball than you ever will. With the talent you have, there's no excuse for slacking off. And, if you think you've reached the pinnacle of your ability, then you're sadly mistaken, young man!"

We looked at each other intently without saying a word. I was trying to read his eyes, hoping he couldn't see the fear in mine. If Skyler gave up basketball I might as well end my life.

"Go get the ball," I said softly, after the long pause.

Skyler stood there for five more seconds. Then he turned and walked away to retrieve the basketball. We shot around for a while longer and played some one-on-one. Skyler stood just a couple inches under six feet and had thick brown hair. I towered a meager five feet eight inches and sported a gray cap. I still beat him 20-17. Maturity can outlast talent. For the time being, I'd won the battle of wills, but I didn't know how long it would last.

A couple nights later, Jim Reiser got his turn at Skyler. The eighth grade team had just finished another lackluster win and their coach was giving them the post-game pep talk.

"It wasn't pretty boys, but it's a win and I guess, that's what matters. Get a 'W' and go home. I've got a commitment tomorrow night, so we won't have practice. Let me see. What else was there?"

"Excuse me coach," Jim Reiser shouted, as he entered the locker room. "Mind if I talk to the boys for a second?"

"...No," he said hesitantly. "Go for it."

"Thanks coach," Jim said seriously. "Boys, you may have gotten a win tonight, but you guys stunk up the gym! No organization, no teamwork, no hustle, no enthusiasm, and most importantly, *no heart*! Does everyone here enjoy playing basketball?" Jim resounded, as the boys shook their heads. "Then why don't I see it on the court? Shane you dribble like a dyslexic! And, the way you telegraph your passes, Helen Keller could pick one off."

"Who's Helen Keller?" whispered Shane.

"Emile! Has the thought of jumping for a rebound ever entered your mind? You better hope for a job in television, because that's the only airtime you're ever gonna get. You might be tall now, but in two years you won't see a rebound, unless you get those sneakers off the turf. And, speaking of sneakers, are you wearing any Vance? I've seen paraplegics get up and down the court faster."

"They got wheelchairs, man," Vance responded, making the players laugh.

"And you'll need one too if you play for me, cause with that attitude, you won't get out on the court! You understand me?"

"Yes, sir," Vance whimpered.

"Skyler! You shoot the ball like you're on Valium. Get the ball off. Get it to the basket. You're getting shots blocked and out hustled to every spot on the court. Take some pride in what you're doing, and it wouldn't hurt to pass the damn ball, every once in a while."

"The black hole of space," Shane whispered.

"Buzzy's the only one putting out a decent effort," Jim continued.

"Yeah, baby!" Buzzy jumped up and raised his hands in the air.

"Don't celebrate yet," Jim scolded. "Not until you learn what a block-out is."

"Sorry," Buzzy squeaked, as he sat down.

"Instead of playing freshmen ball next year, I was looking forward to moving you five up to JV," Jim stated. "Not now! Not now. You five better show me something these last three games. You better show me something over the summer. You better show something next year in tryouts or else you five will be on the wrestling team."

"As long as we wrestle girls," Shane whispered.

"Do you boys understand this?" Jim screamed into Shane's face.

"Yes, sir," they said in unison.

"Good," Jim sighed. "I want to see something special tomorrow night at practice."

All the boys looked at each other and at their coach.

"Uh, Jim," The eighth-grade coach stuttered, "I have a prior commitment tomorrow night, so I told the boys we wouldn't practice."

"You have a commitment to this basketball team," Jim shot back.

"Well… I can't get out of it… you know, wifely things," the coach muttered.

"Maybe you can get out of this coaching job next year," Jim said irritably.

"Reiser doesn't know what a wife is," Shane snuck in.

"I don't know what you said, Shane, but you've just set the tone for tomorrow night's practice!" Jim boiled. "There will be practice right after school, right before the JV. If you don't show, you won't play in the next game. If nobody shows, then the reserves will play the entire game. It's going to be run and fun, so I wouldn't dare miss it. Thanks for the time, coach."

Jim stormed out of the locker room.

"I don't think I like him very much," Skyler said calmly. "But I like you even less Shane you loud mouth idiot."

"Don't you know when to shut up, you freak!" Emile added.

"Yeah!" Vance yelled. "We're dead tomorrow night!"

"Don't worry guys," their coach said shyly, "I'm your coach; he can't make you do anything."

"What an idiot," Shane whispered. "How'd he ever get a coaching job?"

"Hey guys," Buzzy said, "he almost liked me. I play better than the rest of you."

Jim Reiser lived up to his coaching threat. The next night at practice, the eighth grade team ran for ninety straight minutes. No breaks, no drinks. They ran drills, they ran sprints, they ran circles, they ran diagonals. And, not once did any of them lay hands on a basketball.

JUST PASSING BY

One day, I was doing a story in Hagerstown. On my way home, I passed by Carmen Dellinger's office. Her car was the only one in the parking lot and I knew she was alone. I hadn't seen Carmen in over three years, and I debated on whether I should stop and see her. I debated to the point that I passed her office at least seven times before I decided to pull in.

I shook like a groom at the altar. I doubted if she even wanted to see me now. As I got to the door, I chickened out and turned back toward the car, but I was afraid she might've seen me walk up, so I knew I had to go in. As I walked in the door, I could feel my knees wobbling. I took a deep breath and shyly said, "delivery" as I walked around the corner to her desk.

Carmen stared at me, as her mouth opened in disbelief. "Oh, my God!" she finally exclaimed.

"No, I'm not God," I kidded. "It's Philzy."

"Oh, my God!" she repeated, as she pushed her chair away from the desk.

"If you're praying I can come back later," I joked again.

"What are you doing here?" Carmen asked, as she stood up.

To see her stand up was an unusual sight. Carmen had always stayed in her chair most of the time, when we flirted way back, when she evidently felt it was a safeguard against going too far with me. Now that I looked at her, I saw a woman who was not quite as skinny as the one I knew. She was fuller in the right places. Her hair was thicker, longer and darker than I remembered, and she had the slightest hint of makeup, which highlighted her freckles. She was beautiful.

"I came to see you," I complimented. "Why else do you think I'm here?"

"I can't believe you're here," Carmen said, as she walked over and put her arms around my waist. "God, it's been so long."

I felt I was dreaming. I'd only hugged Carmen twice before. Once was at the funeral home, when her grandmother died, and the other was when I retired.

"It's been about three years," I exhaled, as Carmen squeezed the breath out of me. I put my arms over her shoulders and rubbed her back with my palms. Please God! Don't let me wake up.

"I didn't think I'd ever see you again," Carmen seemed to sigh.

"I didn't think you'd ever want to see me again," I said, hoping for a rebuttal.

"I've missed you so much," she whispered. "It hasn't been the same since you left."

"Is that really you, Carmen?" I joked, not believing the woman I knew, who possessed so much self-control, could be saying those things.

"It's really me," she sighed, looking up and kissing me on the cheek. "And, it's really you."

"Damn!" I exclaimed. "I should've come back a long time ago!"

Carmen laughed slightly and kissed me on the lips. My face and torso immediately hit inferno temperatures. I didn't know if it was shock or sexual excitement, but I really didn't care. All those years I'd wanted to kiss Carmen and never had any success. Now, I just walked in the door and she was sticking her tongue in my mouth. Needless to say, I didn't interrupt her to find out what had changed.

"What the heckle and jeckle you trying to do to me?" I asked Carmen when she finally quit.

"I'm just so glad to see you," she replied. "Can't I be happy?"

"Knock yourself out," I encouraged.

Carmen kissed me one more time, then let go to grab a tissue.

"Are you crying?" I asked.

"No," she lied, as she wiped her eyes.

"So, how you been?"

We talked for half an hour about what we'd been doing the last three years, and what we'd done together before that. Carmen answered the phone a couple times, but the calls didn't take long.

"Will you lock the front door for me, Philzy?" Carmen said, in her patented sexy voice.

"Sure thing," I answered like a whipped puppy. I noticed it was only 4 PM and Carmen had never closed before five. When I got back to her desk, she turned on the answering machine to the telephone. "Are you closing early?"

"I am now," she answered.

"You want me to leave?"

"No," Carmen almost shouted. "I still want to talk to you. I have to make some copies downstairs. Come with me to the dungeon to keep me company."

I went with her downstairs and watched from behind, as she made her copies. She had a short sundress on that showed off her strong thighs. I could see her strap from her sports bra sticking out from both of her shoulders. Her left leg swung back and forth, as she made her copies, and I couldn't stand it anymore. I walked up behind her and grabbed her shoulders.

"You still drive me crazy, you know that?" I whispered, as I kissed her on the right side of her neck.

"I was hoping I would," Carmen replied slyly.

"Why's that?" I asked, as I rubbed my hands up and down her arms.

"Well, I was hoping I wouldn't repulse you," she giggled.

"You are so beautiful, I can't stand it," I said automatically, as I nibbled on her ear.

Carmen just let out a soft moan, as I put my hand under her dress and rubbed both sides of her hips. The friction against her pantyhose made a rubbing noise.

Suddenly, I realized Carmen wasn't resisting. Usually, at this point she'd be playfully pushing me away or biting me or slapping me, but here she stood with her back to me, enjoying every caress I advanced towards her body. I'd always counted on Carmen to let me know when to stop. Now, she wasn't stopping me, and I was scared. What would I regret more now? Stopping myself, or going for all I could get?

Slowly, I began to unbutton her dress. After each button, I'd kiss and lick and suck on the newly exposed skin. I was spending two or three minutes a button, and there were seven of them. I kept waiting for Carmen to spin wildly around and run upstairs, but all she did was turn her head occasionally and kiss me.

As I got to the fourth button, Carmen reached behind her and began rubbing my leg. By the sixth button, she was rubbing my crotch. By the time I freed the last button, Carmen had unbuttoned and unzipped my pants. I didn't foresee her stopping me in the near future.

Using my teeth, I pulled Carmen's dress slowly off her shoulders. Finally, it fell down her arms, over her breasts, and onto the floor. She stepped out of her shoes and kicked the dress away.

"I've waited for this all my life," I exaggerated, as I turned Carmen around and kissed her.

"I've been waiting even longer," she whispered, as she pulled my pants down over my waist and onto the floor.

I stuck my fingers in between her pantyhose and underwear, and slowly began to work the pantyhose over her hips. As I got lower, I knelt down and kissed her inner thighs, as I progressed. Then I kissed them on the way back up.

"It's my turn now," Carmen said, as she started unbuttoning my shirt. She alternated kissing my chest and my lips as she went. Somehow, I kicked off my shoes in the process and got my feet out of my jeans. Soon, we were both standing together in our underwear. I turned Carmen back around and pressed my hips against her ass. I grabbed both of her hands in mine and began rubbing her midriff, as I chewed on her neck and ear. Slowly, I moved our hands around, up and down, as they caressed the cups of her bra and the midsection of her underpants.

"What are you doing?" Carmen seemed to purr.

"Just giving both of us a chance to feel ecstasy," I whispered.

Carmen just gave out a long, giggly moan, as I continued. Soon, it appeared as though her nipples would rip out from under her bra. Her panties were soaking wet, and I felt it was time to progress. At the same time, I put our right hands down her underpants, and slid our left hands inside her bra. Carmen turned her head and gave me a passionate French kiss, as she slightly spread her legs apart. Our left fingertips rubbed over her nipples while our right ones delved inside of her. She methodically thrust her hips back and forth, as we banged against the copy machine. I felt the wetness in my own underwear, as Carmen came to a climax. I turned her around and kissed her, and I could tell she still wanted more.

"Are you sure you want to do this?" I said like an idiot, as I rubbed both my hands over her ears and through her hair.

"Just shut up," she said, as she lowered my boxer shorts.

With the same methodic motions, I gradually pulled her bra straps down and eventually revealed her breasts. Once again, I began kissing uncharted skin, making sure to avoid her nipples, which were already erect and ready. Finally, I slowly pulled down her panties. And, after what seemed like an eternity, we were both naked in each other's arms.

I felt like I could explode at any moment, so I knew I better take it slow. Carmen was ready to jump on me, but I had to hold her off. I kissed all over her face and went down to her breasts. As I stuck one hand between her legs, I began sucking her breasts and softly biting her nipples. After about five minutes of straining on her toes, she gave out several long moans ending her second orgasm. We were both soaked in sweat.

Carmen made me lie on the floor, and she began to explore my body with her mouth. Soon, she was sucking on the main course, and it was a struggle not to cut loose. I briefly thought that if I did have a climax like that, then Carmen and I wouldn't have actually had sex. (The Bill Clinton Theory). But, I figured I'd gone so far, I wasn't about to stop now.

I pulled Carmen up to me and made her sit on my waist. Both of us said "Oh, my God" when it went in. Carmen couldn't control herself any longer, as she bounced up and down on my frame. I took turns squeezing her breasts and sucking on them, as she worked her way into a flourishing third orgasm.

Finally, I got on top of her and did my best exercise routine. We went quite a while before climaxing together for the grand finale. In sheer exhaustion we laid there.

"You were supposed to stop me," I said caressing her.

"I did once, and look where it got me," Carmen softly replied. "I lost you for three years."

"Isn't that what you wanted?" I asked.

"This is what I've wanted," she sighed. "I was just too hung up to let it happen."

"I've missed you so much, Carmen," I pledged, as I stroked her hair. "I never stopped loving you."

"I love you, too," Carmen said kissing me. I couldn't believe it. After all this time, she'd finally said the words I wanted to hear most.

As we both dressed, there was a hint of embarrassment in the air.

"Carmen, I don't know how you feel," I said, taking her hand, "but whether this happens again or not, I swear to you I'll have no regrets. I've wanted this for so long that there's no way I could ever think evil about this moment."

"I know," she said with a strained smile.

"We were meant to be together," I assured. "This was destined to happen."

"It always seemed to be going in that direction," Carmen added.

"I never in my wildest imagination expected anything like this today," I said, pulling up my pants.

"You're not the only one," Carmen said with a deep breath.

"I hope your husband doesn't ask you what went on at work today," I laughed.

"Well, I don't think he will," Carmen said seriously. "We've been separated for about six months now."

"You're kidding!" I exclaimed.

"No, I assumed you already knew that," she said.

"No, I had no idea," I said, still surprised.

"I thought for sure someone would've told you," Carmen added.

"I swear, no one told me," I said again. "I hope you don't think I came here to take advantage of that."

"If you did, then you succeeded," she laughed.

"I swear to God I didn't know," I said seriously, as I grabbed her by the shoulders. "I would never take advantage of you in a weak moment. You know that don't you?"

"Yes," Carmen smiled. "I know that."

I kissed her one last time and finished getting dressed. It was 5:45 PM, and we both had some explaining to do.

I don't remember driving home. There was a kaleidoscope of emotions running through my brain. I was happy, but I was ashamed. I'd just destroyed the sanctity of a 32-year marriage, but I got the opportunity to make love to the woman I wanted for so long. Man, was I messed up. And, if Diane found out about this, I was a dead man.

I couldn't face Diane when I got home. I gave her an excuse about having to wait to interview a guy, and then I left to go play basketball. I didn't even talk to Sky. I felt like a heel. I even stunk at basketball. There was no turning back now. I'd finally become an adult. I was an asshole.

KISSIN' COUSINS?

I saw Carmen once the next week. Then twice the following week. We were on our third week of our torrid affair and I had seen her three times in five days. I couldn't believe what Carmen was doing to me. I was giving up my nights of playing basketball just to be with her. I may as well have given up food. I was so in love I even wrote her a song.

I used to be lost in a relationship frost
That froze me to the bone.
With no one to laugh or be a better- half
I dwelled in the Twilight Zone

My existence was void, all the others annoyed
And never turned on any lights.
Alone in a maze, all my feelings just haze
My love never reached the heights.

Then we met, you said hi, what's your name sexy guy?
Sending my heart rate on the rise.

Now, when I'm with you I don't have to fantasize.

Don't have to dream about or scheme about
A love without the lies,
Don't have to wish for a touch that means so much
I've got it right before my eyes.
You came in my life, can I make you my wife, cause much to my surprise
When I'm with you I don't have to fantasize.

To me a true love was someone above
Who never existed in this life.
A friend to the end whose devotion won't bend

Or give you any strife.

A dreamer at best, I gave up on the rest
Creating a goddess of my own.
She'd walk by my side as a spiritual guide
And our friendship we would hone.

Then we met, you said hi, what's your name sexy guy?
Sending my heart rate on the rise.
Now when I'm with you I don't have to fantasize.

Don't have to dream about or scheme about
A love without the lies,
Don't have to wish for a touch that means so much
I've got it right before my eyes.
You came in my life, can I make you my wife, cause much to my surprise
When I'm with you I don't have to fantasize.

You brightened my tomorrows by loving me today.
You vanquish all my sorrows with everything you say.

And I don't have to dream about or scheme about
A love without the lies,
Don't have to wish for a touch that means so much
I've got it right before my eyes.

You came in my life, can I make you my wife, cause much to my surprise
When I'm with you I don't have to fantasize.

When I'm with you...I don't have to fantasize.

 When I sang it to her in my best Garth Brooks voice, she cried. A much better reaction than I got from a poem several years before. Each visit with Carmen was like a breath of fresh air. And, every time I left, I choked in the smog of reality.
 "I love you, Carmen," I whispered to the naked woman in my arms. "You're so cuddable."
 "I love you too, Philzy," she sung back at me. "In all your luscious nutridity!"

"I wish we could stay like this forever," I fantasized.

"We could, you know," Carmen whispered back.

"I know," I answered in depression. "I just don't know what to do. I mean... I know WHAT to do, it's just I don't know how to go about it, or how to handle it, or..."

"I understand," Carmen interrupted. "It's not easy. You've been married so long you don't know anything different. I knew what I was inviting in three weeks ago. I knew I might never call you my own."

"At least we can have a piece of each other," I rationalized.

"I hope so!" Carmen squealed with joy.

"No. Not that kind of piece!" I corrected. "I want you to be a part of my life."

"I hope so," Carmen repeated.

"So, how's your divorce going?" I directed the conversation.

"Really well," Carmen sighed. "It seems my husband has had more affairs than I."

"And, just how many is that?" I wondered.

"Does the term 'Casanova' ring a bell?" she joked.

"Vaguely," I answered.

"Let's just say my soon-to-be-ex makes Wilt Chamberlain look like a hermit," Carmen added.

"A hermit who has to duck when entering his cave, I take it," I said, trying to be funny.

"I love you," Carmen glowed, as she squeezed tighter. "You make me so happy."

"I'm trying, baby," I kidded.

"Just keep on trying," she sighed.

"So, just how many affairs HAVE YOU had?" I pried.

"Oh, at least one," Carmen teased.

"Anyone I know?" I asked.

"May...be," She droned in a baby voice.

"Man, I want to be with you," I wished, as I squeezed her tighter.

"You want to be with a man?" Carmen misquoted.

"Yeah, I do," I teased. "I'm coming out of the closet."

"Wake up and smell the mothballs," said Carmen. "I'm outta here."

"Oh, no you don't," I squeezed. "You're stuck with me."

"I'm stuck on band aids," Carmen joked.

"I want to be with you forever, but I don't know what's going to happen,"

I lamented without getting Carmen's joke. "What if my daughters disown me? I talked Alana into staying at our house and now I'm thinking about moving out myself. I may never see Skyler again. He'll hate me for that. Can I throw away all…"

"Just shut-up Philzy," Carmen purred, as she cuddled closer. "Let's just enjoy the time we have left, today. You'll figure something out, someday."

I closed my eyes and ran my hands up and down Carmen's naked back. "I love you."

Three hours later, when I came home, Diane had a surprise for me.

"Guess what I found out today?" Diane said with a straight face.

I swear to God, my heart stopped. She knew. Someone told her about Carmen. Maybe even Carmen told her. She's getting a divorce. She could be trying to break Diane and I up. No, Carmen wouldn't do that. She's not that kind of person. In either case, I was had. What was I going to do? What was I going to say?

"I have no idea," I answered her sheepishly, as I looked away.

"Well, you won't believe it," Diane built it up.

"Tell me already," I said, annoyed with the delay.

"I was doing some genealogy today and found out something interesting."

I gave out a sigh of relief. She was talking about genealogy, not adultery.

"What on earth could be interesting about genealogy?" I happily asked.

"Five generations back, I found we have a common grandparent," Diane announced proudly. "You and I are cousins."

"What?" I said, laughing.

"We're cousins," Diane repeated proudly. "It may be several times removed, but we're really cousins."

"We're committing incest!" I joked. "No wonder our kids are retarded."

"I knew when I found out your dad was from Kentucky, I should've avoided you."

"That means our marriage is null and void, doesn't it?" I tried to ask seriously.

"I don't think so," Diane disagreed. "You're stuck with me."

"Yeah, but we broke the law," I continued. "One of us should go to jail."

"I'll call the sheriff and have him pick you up," Diane answered, as she leaned over to kiss me. I tried to back away, but I knew I must accept my doom.

Nothing was there. I felt no passion; I felt no love. I want to run away.

MY FRIEND DAD

Just like everyone does, my parents got older. Most of the time, you don't notice it because you're growing old yourself. When I was forty, my parents seemed the same to me as when I was four. Now, they were in their eighties, and the cloak of time had finally started to appear.

My dad had long since retired from farming. He came to a virtual standstill in his life and he didn't go crazy. My parents traveled a bit, but always returned home within two weeks because Dad would get homesick. They played golf together, went to card parties, and basically enjoyed the senior life. It was everything I never thought my dad would do. He never had time for simple pleasures when he was young, but now, he had all the time in the world for his wife and his three children.

"What're you doing here, Phil?" Aaron said, surprised to see his son.

"Just came to shovel off your sidewalk," I responded. "Don't want you to get snowed in."

"Don't worry about that," Aaron waved off. "It'll melt by spring. C'mon in and get some breakfast."

"Well, hi honey," Betty said to her youngest child. "Are you hungry?"

"Sure, I could use some breakfast," I conceded.

"You want biscuits and gravy? Bacon and eggs? Waffles?" Mom wandered through the menu.

"No, no," I interrupted. "A piece of toast and coffee will do."

"Are you sure?" Mom asked.

"I'm positive."

My mom was as spry and healthy as ever. She was a bit slower and forgetful, but she always tried. Even with the wrinkles and thinning hair, my mom was still as beautiful as she seemed to me as a youth. It wasn't the physical beauty that showed, but the inner glow she possessed that made her so appealing to me. Even before Sister Bernadette, I fell in love with Mom.

"So you keeping busy Dad?" I began our conversation.

"Are you kidding?" Dad said in his loud voice. "Just sittin' in the rockin' chair wastin' away."

"It'll be golf weather soon," I encouraged. "You'll be losin' your balls before ya know it."

"Betty said I already have," joked Dad.

"Aaron!" Mom scolded. "Watch your language!"

"That's the way she is, Phil," Dad responded. "Won't ever let me have any fun."

"That's what wives are for," I threw in.

"I was gonna run in that Boston marathon last time, but Betty tied me up so I couldn't leave the house," Dad prodded.

"You can barely make it to the mailbox Aaron, and you're talking about a marathon," reasoned Mom.

"I can still catch you."

I always knew my dad had a great sense of humor. I just never got the chance to enjoy it as a youth.

It was good to see my parents so happy. They had survived life, they weathered all their storms, and they were finally able to sit back and bask in the glory of it all. I envied them so much. Would I ever be able to have what they did?

I guess I could've held a grudge against my dad for not playing with me when I was young. I could've hated him for the rest of my life for not being there. But, I stuck with him and he finally came through. It was actually my dad, who got me writing again in my middle thirties. One day he surprised me with a word processor for no particular reason. If I ever get published, it's all thanks to Dad.

I found my dad late in life, but we still enjoyed so many years together. It saddened me to think his time might be running short.

SING ALONG

"I can't believe I'm just now leaving Hagerstown when Skyler has a game. I only have 15 minutes to get there before it starts. Carmen's killing me. It's a good thing I gave Carmen the disc of my book. If Diane ever found out what's in it, she'd kill me. I need to put in a tape. Where the hell's Hootie? . . .SHIT!"

>I won't dance, you won't sing.
>I just wanna love you
>but you wanna wear my ring.
>But, there's nothin' I can do,
>I only wanna be with you.
>You can call me a fool,
>I only wanna be with you.
>Hootie & The Blowfish

HEAVEN CAN WAIT

According to the Catholic religion, there are four places you can go when you die. Heaven, Hell, Purgatory, and Limbo. These four potential destinations are easy to understand, when you put them in everyday context.

Limbo is where you go, when you haven't been baptized. It's like the waiting room at a doctor's office. Clean, sterile, and very indifferent. It's not a bad place to be, but it's not much fun either. Since you have no place to go, you might as well waste your time there. Every once in a while, a nurse will stick her head out the door and say, "Just checking to make sure you're still here." Unfortunately, in Limbo, you never get to see the doctor.

Purgatory is that same waiting room at the doctor's office. Only this time, the room is overcrowded with sneezing, coughing and vomiting patients, with their kids who run all over the place and bump into everything. You've read all the magazines, and your chair smells like a disposable diaper. The nurse sticks her head out every once in a while and says, "We'll be with you in an hour." Finally, at the end of the day, you get to see the doctor.

Hell is the exact same waiting room as the one in Purgatory. Only this time, each patient takes a turn sneezing, coughing, and vomiting on you, and each of their kids take a turn kicking you. All the magazines are from the '80's, and they're in a foreign language. You're sitting on a disposable diaper. At the end of each day, a nurse sticks her head out the door and says, "I'm sorry, we can't get you in today. Can you come back tomorrow?" You end up spending the night.

So, what is Heaven? Heaven is when YOU snap on the rubber glove and say, "Ok, Doc, bend over and spread your cheeks!"

END OF AN UNDEFEATED SEASON

The eighth-grade game was nearing the end of the first quarter. Centerville was leading Union County by fifteen points. Skyler already had hit three 3-pointers, but scoring wasn't the top priority on his mind. His dad hadn't made it to the game yet, and he was never late. Phil always worked his schedule around Skyler's games.

In the huddle after the first quarter, Skyler scanned the bleachers with his eyes as the coach gave his instructions. Phil always sat on the top row center with a bag of popcorn in his hand to munch on as the game progressed. He was nowhere in sight.

"Where's your dad?" Buzzy whispered to Skyler.

"Don't know," Skyler whispered back.

"You guys care to listen to what I have to say?" the Coach shouted at the interruptions.

As the second quarter started, it was evident that Skyler's mind was somewhere else. He began missing easy shots, even shooting an air ball. And, his passes were being intercepted. He'd make a play and look in the stands. Let his man cut open, and look in the stands. Union County was catching up and the Coach was furious.

As the coach chewed out King during a time-out, Skyler noticed the junior-high principal talking to Alana and Diane. A minute later, as he tried to play on the court, Skyler noticed they were gone. Now, he was really worried. He felt his family had abandoned him.

As he took off down the court on a fast break, Skyler saw Alana and Diane out in the concession area talking to a police officer. He stopped dead in his tracks. A long pass flew by Skyler's head and sailed out of bounds.

"What the heck are you doing, King!" the Coach yelled. "Thompson! Go in for King!"

As Skyler's heart pounded in his stomach, he walked toward his mom and grandmother.

"King! Get over here!" the Coach yelled.

Skyler didn't hear. As he neared the exit, everyone in the gym began to quiet down. They couldn't believe they were watching a star player walk off the court in the middle of a game. Everyone had to watch and hear what would happen next.

As Skyler reached the double-doors leading out of the gym, he grabbed the middle section for support.

"Where's my dad?" he asked everyone standing there. All of them turned and looked in surprise at finding him there. Alana and Diane were crying.

"Where's my dad!" Skyler demanded, as he ran his right hand through his hair.

"Oh, Skyler!" Alana and Diane nearly said in unison, as they approached him with open arms.

"Where's Dad?" Skyler said pathetically, as he fell into their arms. "Tell me he's all right."

Some of Skyler's teammates began making their way to the exit. Vance, Emile, Buzzy, Shane.

"What the hell's going on?" the Coach wondered out loud.

"Skyler, there's been an accident," Diane finally said.

Skyler broke away from their arms. "Where's Dad, dammit! Where's he at!"

Alana and Diane couldn't answer. There were only more tears.

"Tell me where he is!" Sklyer yelled at the police. "Tell me!"

"Son. There's nothing . . ." the policeman tried to answer.

"I've got to find him!" Skyler shouted, as he ran to the outside exit.

"Skyler!" Alana yelled to stop him.

"We'll get him, Mrs. King," Buzzy said, as the four teammates began their pursuit.

Alana and Diane continued to cry on each other's shoulder.

"I assure you Mrs. Belcher, your husband didn't suffer," the state trooper tried to console. "We'll help get your son, and then we can take all of you to . . . to the . . ."

"He's not my son," Diane sobbed through her hand.

"Pardon me."

"He's not my son," Diane repeated and pointed at Alana. "He's her son."

"I see," the trooper said, totally confused.

"He called his grandfather "dad" because he's the only father he's ever known, Diane said through the tears. "And . . .now . . .he's gone."

"We'll go get him," the trooper assured, while tapping his partner on the shoulder. "C'mon, let's go."

Parents from the gym were coming out and surrounding Alana and Diane. With a strange combination of curiosity and sympathy, they wanted to help.

The game with Union County was never finished. Never rescheduled. Centerville forfeited.

PIPE DREAMS

The state troopers caught up with Skyler on Centerville Road. He had outrun all his teammates. They couldn't get him calmed down until they agreed to take him to the hospital.

"I wanna see my dad! I wanna see my dad!" was all he would say.

The troopers used the lights and sirens to get Skyler to the hospital as fast as possible. When they arrived, the troopers convinced Skyler to see an emergency-room doctor. The doctor gave him a muscle relaxer to calm him down, and eventually, the troopers were able to take Skyler to Aaron and Betty Belcher's house.

Alana and Diane were at the funeral home. The undertaker was keeping them busy with questions and forms to fill out. The two women held each other's hand, as they alternated staring off into space and crying.

"When do I get to see him?" Diane asked out of nowhere.

The undertaker was taken back by her request. He looked at her speechless momentarily, then, finally replied, "There won't be any need to identify him, Diane."

"How do you know it's him?" Alana asked.

Once again the undertaker paused before answering, "Well, it was his car, and his wallet and personal affects were found on him."

"That's still not positive proof," Diane argued. "It could've been someone else."

"Well, we've also sent some of his dental work to be identified," the undertaker hated to say.

"Oh, God!" Diane sighed at the thought. "I can still see him, can't I?"

Feeling very uncomfortable, the undertaker once again paused before answering. "It was a very nasty accident, Diane. Didn't the state troopers tell you any of the details?"

"They just said he was hit head-on by a semi," Alana answered for her mother.

"That's part of what happened," the undertaker said uncomfortably. "A metal rod came loose from the front of a semi, and it rolled off on a curve, just as Phil was coming by. The rod went through the windshield and out the back of the trunk. And, with the car's momentum, and the fact the rod was still attached in the rear of the semi, well, it acted like a lever and whipped Phil's Miata around the back of the semi, and, it was struck by another tractor trailer that was behind the first one."

"The trooper said he was killed instantly," Diane nearly pleaded.

"Yes, that's right," the undertaker said quickly. "There was absolutely no suffering at all."

"How could he be killed instantly, if his car was whipped around like a carnival ride?" Diane wondered.

"It all happened so quickly," the undertaker assured. "There was no time . . ."

"What was the cause of death?" Diane asked.

"There's no need to go into details, Diane," the undertaker pleaded, trying to spare her.

"What was the cause of death?" Diane demanded.

"I assure you he didn't . . ."

"I have a right to know, goddamit!" Diane cried. "How did he die?"

The undertaker took a deep breath. "The metal rod was ten inches in diameter. When it went through the windshield, it . . .hit him in the face. There was nothing, . . .we were lucky to find any teeth for the dental records."

"Oh, my God!" Diane sighed, as she covered her face. "Oh, dear God!"

"I . . .I didn't want to have to tell you," the undertaker stumbled.

Alana and Diane held each other again. No one in the room said a word until the undertaker stood up and looked at the hallway door.

"Please, come on in."

Alana and Diane looked up to see Renee walk in the door. Her face was red and her eyes were nearly swollen shut. In her quiet voice, she could barely be heard.

"Where's daddy?"

REISING TO THE OCCASION

Jim Reiser ascended the stairs to the porch like a man on his way to the guillotine. He knew what his mission was, but he had no idea how to carry it out. He raised his hand reluctantly and tapped gently on the screen door. Jim took a deep breath and attempted to squelch the cowardice that lurked within him. He raised his hand again and pounded harder.

"Can I help you, sir?" Betty Belcher said, as she opened the door.

"Yes, Mrs. Belcher," Jim stumbled. "Sorry to bother you, but I'm Jim Reiser. We met several years ago at Liberty when Phil was in school, and…"

"Oh, Jim," Betty said, wiping her eyes. "Yes, I remember you. Come in, please."

"I heard what happened, and I'm sorry to bother you, but I heard Skyler was just…"

"Stop apologizing Jim," Betty nearly scolded, "I'm so glad you're here. We don't know what to do with poor Skyler. They gave him a sedative, but I still think he's going to have a seizure or something."

"This is just awful," Jim nearly cried. "I just saw him yesterday."

"We can't, believe, …" Betty broke down. "He's my baby!"

Jim put his arms on Betty's shoulders, as she laid her head on his chest. As the sobs echoed out of her body, tears were silently rolling down Jim's cheeks. Jim closed his eyes and tried to disappear into another place, another time. He opened them to find a man standing in the doorway.

"Mr. Belcher?" Jim wondered, as Betty raised her head.

"Yeah, I'm Aaron," he replied.

"I'm Jim Reiser, sir," he said, holding out his hand.

"He's come to see Skyler," Betty sobbed, as she mopped her cheeks.

"He's a mess," Aaron responded, extending his arm for a weak and reluctant handshake. "I hope you can help."

"Follow me, Jim," Betty said, as she began to walk in the other room.

Jim followed through two rooms full of antiques until they finally came to the family area. The television was playing a Purdue basketball game with the volume all the way down. Beside the TV was Skyler. He sat on a stool with a basketball in his hands. He faced the wall and rocked incessantly back and forth while asking.

"Where's my dad? Where's my dad?"

"Skyler?" Jim whispered, as he leaned over toward the boy. "Skyler. It's Coach Reiser. I've come to see how you're doing."

"Where's my dad, Coach? Where's my dad?" Skyler repeated, as his red eyes rose to glare at Jim's.

"Now, Skyler. The police told you. Didn't they?" Jim prodded.

"Yeah, yeah, yeah!" Skyler sobbed, as he rocked faster. "Is he…is he…is he…dead?"

"Yes, buddy. He was killed in the car crash," Jim strained through his teeth as he grabbed Skyler around the shoulders.

"I want my dad! I want my dad!" Skyler shouted, as his entire body began to shiver within the grasp. "I need my dad, Coach! I need my dad!"

"All of us will miss him, Skyler," Jim lamented. "I've lost one of my best friends."

"I can't take it! I gotta get outta here!" yelled Skyler, as he fought to break free from Jim.

"Settle down. Listen to me! Settle down!" Jim fought. "Settle down and I'll tell you why I never got married."

The strange words seemed to quiet Skyler's plight. "What?" He asked in confusion.

"I'll tell you why I never got married," Jim repeated. "I know you guys make fun of me because I'm not married."

"We…don't…make...fun," Skyler stuttered, as he calmed down.

"I know, but you do wonder, don't you?" Jim said, as Skyler shook his head yes. "That's what I thought."

Jim cocked his head backwards and let out a deep breath, as if he were preparing to go into battle. Three times in one day seemed a bit much.

"I was married at one time. A long time ago. I know it's hard to believe, but it's been close to forty years now. Her name was Marilyn. She was my high school sweetheart. We went to prom together, we went to each other's sporting events; we did pretty much everything together. All the guys said I was whipped, cause I always wanted to be around her. I didn't care. It felt great to be whipped.

So, we went off to college together. Took a lot of the same courses. Both majored in education. It was great. After our first year of college we couldn't stand it. We got an apartment so we could always be together. The next three years were the best. I only worked part-time, went to school, and spent all my free time with Marilyn. It was the three quickest years I've ever spent. As soon as I graduated, I asked Marilyn to marry me. I guess, we both knew we eventually would, but I'd never really asked her. She still cried. I'd never seen anyone in my life be so happy, yet still cry. We were married in June. Marilyn still had a semester to go, so she wanted me to wait before applying for jobs, since it might separate us for a while. But, being the stubborn man, I sent out my resumes all over the state so we could get a jump on finding our new home. In late July, I got a nibble. We were supposed to drive to Evansville for an interview, so we thought we'd just make it our honeymoon and drive on down to Kentucky and Tennessee. Marilyn was happy for me, but she worried about my getting the job. If I did, I'd be stuck in Evansville, while she was in West Lafayette finishing up school. She briefly tried to talk me out of going, but we always supported what the other did, so she didn't harp on it or anything. She tried to talk me out of going… We never made it to Evansville… We started driving late at night so we could get there early in the morning for my interview… We were tired… And, somewhere on the way… I fell asleep. When I woke up, the car was underneath a semi. I was trapped between the console and the roof of the car. I could just barely feel Marilyn with my right hand. She wouldn't answer me. We were stuck under that semi for ninety minutes. How could ninety minutes seem longer than the three years we lived in the apartment together? I prayed for three years…. When they finally pried me out, the police tried to pull me away from the car. I had to help get Marilyn out. I had blood all over me, but I just wanted to help. The weird thing was, I didn't have a scratch on me. It was all Marilyn's blood… When we hit the semi, I was apparently slumped over on the console… Marilyn was sitting straight up… She didn't have a chance, Skyler."

"Goddam, Coach!" Skyler empathized. "That's awful!"

"It happened again today, Skyler," Jim lamented. "We lost part of our souls today…. But, I can help you, if you help me. I can't take reliving this all over again."

"I'll help, Coach." Skyler whimpered. "We need each other."

Jim and Skyler held each other with their heads buried in each other's shoulders. Jim had come to Centerville to get a chance to help Skyler. He never anticipated being the recipient.

"Will you lay down for me now, Skyler?" Jim coaxed.

"Sure Coach," Skyler answered. "I'm beat."

Jim walked Skyler upstairs to the bedroom.

"How about you Coach?" Skyler asked, when his head hit the pillow. "Who'll take care of you?"

"You already have," Jim responded.

As Jim turned to leave, he met Aaron and Betty at the bedroom door.

"Jim, I overheard your story to Skyler," Betty consoled. "I'm so sorry for what happened."

"It was a long time ago," Jim sighed. "I don't know if I have any tears left."

"I was supposed to take him to the River Boat next week," Aaron added. "We went there occasionally to lose money."

Jim put one arm around Betty and one arm around Aaron. Together they cried.

LOVE THY ENEMY

Fifteen years ago, Phil Belcher wrote his own obituary for a journalism class. He had himself dying at the age of 69, of cardiac arrest, after a night of sexual escapades with three prostitutes. His career highlights included corroborating with Mel Brooks on the movie script "Delivery". (Due out in the Fall.) Unfortunately, none of Phil's predictions came true. Our real lives never really stack up to our fantasies.

The Belcher wake was quite a large one. In just over a half-century, he had touched a lot of lives. Twenty-five years of coaching can bring you in contact with a lot of people. Many of them came to say goodbye.

Carmen Dellinger came to say goodbye. Diane Belcher saw Carmen enter the funeral parlor, and it turned her tears to anger. Even though Diane knew nothing about their affair, it was disturbing to have Carmen crash this sad occasion.

"Why is SHE here?" Diane whispered to Jim Reiser who was standing beside her.

"Let it go," Jim answered, as he put his arm around her. "There's nothing to fight about, anymore."

As Carmen's place in line slowly advanced toward the closed casket, Diane could see she was crying. Carmen was also alone. There was no one in line with her to help ease the pressure of attending a wake. In her loneliness, Carmen would occasionally dab her eyes or nose, then tearfully look in her purse for another tissue.

By the time Carmen made it to the front of the line, Diane actually felt sorry for her. With blood-shot eyes, red nose, and swollen lips, Carmen looked so pathetic.

"I knew your dad from Hagerstown," Carmen barely whispered to Renee and Alana, as she hugged them. "He talked so much about you two, I feel like I already know you."

"I'm Alana and this is my sister Renee," Alana said to the stranger.

"I know," Carmen sighed, as she moved down the line. Renee and Alana could only look at each other and shrug their shoulders.

"Mr. And Mrs. Belcher. . ." Carmen choked. She couldn't think. She only bowed her head and cried, as the Belchers patted her on the back. "Where's Skyler?"

"He's . . .asleep," Aaron answered.

"I'm Jim Reiser," Jim intervened, as he grasped Carmen's limp hand. "I used to coach Phil at Union County."

"Phil always talks so highly of you," Carmen muttered.

"I've done the same for him many times," Jim returned.

Diane extended her right hand toward Carmen.

"I'm so sorry, Diane," Carmen sobbed, as she grabbed Diane's hand with both of hers. "I just don't know what to say."

"There's nothing to say," Diane replied, somewhat surprised at Carmen's sorrow. "I guess we've both lost someone special."

"You were so lucky to have him," Carmen whispered through her tears. "He really cared about you."

"He cared for you, too," Diane reluctantly admitted. "I could see it in his eyes."

"I'm sorry I made you angry by playing tennis with him," Carmen apologized. "That got us off on the wrong foot."

"I shouldn't have been angry," Diane let go. "I should've just appreciated what I had. Maybe he wouldn't have needed you?"

"But, I'm so glad I got the chance to know him," Carmen sobbed.

"Thanks for coming, Carmen," said Diane, as she gently pulled her closer. "I know it wasn't easy."

Carmen vaguely smiled, then trudged toward the casket. She dropped on the kneeler and sobbed. Carmen's tears caught the attention of many people in the parlor. Diane's eyes strayed from the reception line to watch. Carmen's grief made Diane feel inadequate. Had Carmen lost more?

BROKEN DREAMS

Skyler continued to suffer. In one swift blow, he'd lost his dad and grandfather. Skyler was sedated throughout the wake and funeral service. When Phil's ashes were cast to the winds at a local softball diamond, Alana and Diane literally held Skyler back to keep him from running after them.

Skyler spent the rest of his time in bed. If only he could sleep, maybe he'd eventually wake up from the nightmare he'd been living. Between the drugs and depression, Skyler couldn't tell what was real and what was fantasy. For a full week, Skyler faded in and out of consciousness as Alana and Diane took turns tending to him and forcing him to eat.

One day, Skyler became particularly restless. He called out for his dad several times without getting an answer. Finally, as he slipped off into a fantasy, he made up his mind. He would never play basketball again.

Skyler jumped from his bed and went outside to the garage. He grabbed a ten-foot ladder and one of Phil's old softball bats and took them to the basketball goal. He set up the ladder, and with the bat in his hand he climbed until his waist was above the rim.

"If I can't have my dad," Skyler screamed to the sky, "then I don't need this goddam game!"

Skyler swung the bat like a madman. Again, and again, and again. The rim was bending slightly with each blow.

"Damn you!" Skyler yelled to the heavens. "Why did you take him from me?"

The backboard cracked and splintered. Alana and Diane rushed out of the house hearing the racket.

"Stop it Skyler! Stop it!" they both yelled. "Get down from there!"

With a last Herculean blow, the rim and backboard popped off its bracket and jumped toward Skyler. The ladder tilted, and all three objects gave way to gravity. Skyler's leg slid through a step, as they turned upside-down. The goal fell last, and through the middle of the ladder acting as a vise. With a snap, Skyler's leg was broken. It snapped just like the limb Phil cut down, so Skyler could arch the ball higher.

The pain! The confusion! The panic! The ambulance! The hospital! It was all happening so fast, yet, it seemed to be taking so long. The worry! The anesthetic! The operation! "Don't worry about him playing basketball, just be glad if he can walk!"

It all exploded away. Skyler was back in his bed. His leg ached. He couldn't move it. It was a lead weight. Skyler couldn't even raise his head. The painkillers had him so doped up that nothing seemed like reality. He kept reliving his nightmares, and denying they were the truth. He dozed off.

Something, . . . or someone . . . was tickling Skyler's good foot.

"Stop it," he mumbled incoherently. The tickling continued, but he didn't dare move suddenly, for fear of hurting his leg. "Quit it."

"Get up Sky."

"No, . . I can't . . I don't feel good," Skyler whined.

"Get up, or the pterodactyl will get you."

Skyler looked up as quickly as his dizzy head would allow. "Is . .is that you . . Dad?"

"Who else would it be?" Phil answered. "So, what the heckle and jeckle have you done now?"

"Uhhh, it's my leg," Skyler said, rubbing his eyes. "I broke my leg."

"Looks like you did a bang up job on it, too," Phil kidded. "You pretty much wiped out our basketball goal."

"I'm sorry," Skyler whimpered. "I was mad. I didn't want to play basketball ever again."

"After all the time and effort we put into basketball, and you want to give it up!" Phil scolded.

"Dad. Are .. are you alive?" Skyler wished.

"I was alive until you tore my basketball dream out of your heart," Phil said. "How can I stay with you if you give up the one thing we spent so much time on?"

"You were dead!" Skyler cried. "I don't care about basketball! I just want to be with you!"

"You can be with me if you want," Phil explained. "But we have to do it through basketball now. Are you interested?"

"Yes," Skyler sobbed.

"Then don't give up on our dream," Phil said. "You've got a chance to do great things in this sport. Greater things than just getting in the game. If you put your mind to it, you could be one of the best Hoosier basketball players ever."

"But, my leg," Skyler moaned. "It'll take forever to heal. I don't know if I'll even be able to walk."

"If you promise me you'll dedicate yourself to basketball, I'll see what I can do about your leg," Phil propositioned. "Is it a deal?"

"Yeah, sure, but what about you?" Skyler asked.

"You'll have to do this on your own now, Sky," Phil said. "That's the hard part."

"But, I don't want to do it myself!" Skyler whined. "I want you, too!"

"Dammit, Sky!" Phil yelled. "You're old enough to do this yourself! Just like I knew you could arch the ball higher. If you don't try, you'll never succeed. So, promise me you'll never give up."

"I won't give up, dad," Skyler cried. "I won't give up because I love you."

Skyler felt his dad tickle his foot one last time. Then, he fell asleep.

It was a short nap. Skyler woke with the pain in his leg. It tingled and felt extremely heavy. He tried to move it, but he couldn't.

For some reason, Skyler seemed more alert than he'd been in days. Maybe the painkillers were wearing off. Skyler raised his head slowly to look at his leg. He saw the two family cats, Fishy and Swoozy, lying on top of his leg. No wonder he couldn't move.

"Get off!" Skyler yelled, as he tried moving his leg.

The cats lay there staring at him.

"Get off!" he said louder, to no avail. Skyler grabbed a pillow and tossed it in their direction, scattering the cats. He slowly slid his leg to the edge of the bed. For the first time in five days, Skyler wanted to get up. His leg still tingled and felt like a useless appendage, but there wasn't any pain.

Skyler sat up and looked down his torso. There was no cast or brace! There were no scars or stitches! His leg was clean. Skyler slowly bent his knee and rotated his ankle. He set both feet on the floor and carefully stood up. Just tingling. No pain.

"It's not broke," Skyler whispered to himself. He limped away from the bed. "It's only asleep!" he yelled, as he bounced up and down on his toes. "IT'S NOT BROKE! Mom! Mom!"

"What's wrong Sky?" Alana said with fear, as she ran into the room.

"It's not broke!" Skyler yelled, jumping up and down.

"What's not broke?" Alana asked.

"My leg! My leg's not broke!" he said, sticking it up in the air.

"I know," Alana said, laughing.

"Dad said he' take care of it, and he did!" Skyler explained, as he grabbed his sneakers and a t-shirt. Alana couldn't answer. She didn't understand. All she knew was that Skyler had said more words in the past minute than he'd said in a week.

"I've gotta go play ball!" Skyler screamed, as he streaked out of the room.

Diane was nearly knocked down by her reenergized grandson.

"Gotta go play ball, Grandma!"

"What the hell happened to him?" Diane asked Alana, when she got over the shock of seeing Skyler off his feet.

"I have no idea," Alana confessed. "He just said Dad took care of it."

"Hey guys!" Skyler yelled through the outside door. "My goal's still up, too! I don't believe it!"

"Whatever happened, don't second guess it," Diane told Alana. "To see him out of bed like that, . . it's a miracle."

THE SECOND COMING

As the Freshman Basketball Season approached, Skyler and his 6' 2" frame were ready to take on the world. But, Skyler and his four friends would never see a Freshman game. Vance Worth, Buzzy Gray, Emile George, Shane Best, and Skyler King were all moved up to junior varsity. JV Coach, Jim Reiser couldn't have been happier. Unfortunately, his dynasty lasted only two games before Head Coach, Dick Stern, moved Emile George and Skyler up to varsity. The fact they didn't play much their first two games on varsity didn't sit well with Reiser.

"Coach, if you're not going to play George and King, then let them play JV ball," Reiser reasoned.

"I'm trying to give them varsity experience, Jim," Coach Stern answered.

"But, if they only play four minutes a game they're not getting that much quality time," Reiser lamented. "At least let them play half-and-half, so they can get more playing time."

"Look. I'm calling the shots here, and I say they stay on varsity," Stern threatened. "If they want more playing time, they'll have to earn it."

The varsity team was having its troubles. Most fans attended the JV game, but once everyone saw Skyler wasn't playing, they lost interest. The gym resembled an abandoned fortress.

Before the fifth game of the year, the varsity lost four of its starters to alcohol consumption. Coach Stern tried to keep the raided party quiet, but too many teachers and administrators had heard the news. The four players were suspended for five games for their violation, so Buzzy Gray, Vance Worth, and Shane Best were promoted to varsity.

The anticipation for the next generation of Bulldogs was great. This time, as the JV struggled in their first loss, the fans slowly began to fill the stands. The gym was far from full, but it was a welcome relief from the scattered support they were used to. The first-half was a disappointment for everyone. None of the freshman stars saw the court, and the varsity reserves ineptly cruised to a 19-point deficit.

Some of the fans left at intermission, not even bothering to finish their popcorn. Others waited to see if Coach Stern was a complete idiot.

"So, what do I do now, Coach?" Stern asked Coach Reiser, after chewing out his players at halftime.

"You really want to know?" Reiser asked him.

"I know what you're going to say," Stern answered. "I just don't believe in playing freshman."

"Then why the hell you got them up here?" Reiser went off. "Send them back to the freshman team and let them get some playing time."

"Look! I'm not the one that got caught drinking!" Stern tried defending himself. "This shit has ruined my team!"

"And, you did the right thing by suspending them," Reiser tried buttering him up. "At least use what you got on this team. If you're not going to play five people, then we might as well go home right now."

Stern rubbed his chin with his left hand. "Ok. I'll give your goddam freshman a chance. But, they've only got four minutes to show me something. I'm not about to get embarrassed on my home court." Stern stormed out of the locker room.

"Thank you, God!" Reiser shouted with both arms raised to the heavens.

When the second half started, the gym was nearly empty. Fans were still in line at the concession stand, and the student band was taking their break. Luckily, for the freshman, most people missed their first minute of varsity action. Two turnovers and a missed three-pointer by Skyler were the highlights.

"Well, what do you think about your freshman, now?" Stern ridiculed.

"Give 'em a chance Coach."

When word got out who was playing, some of the fans began to file back in. Skyler hit Emile for a backdoor lay in. Buzzy stole the inbounds pass and hit Skyler on the right wing for a three. Cowan missed their next shot and Vance led a 3-on-1 fast break which ended with an Emile dunk.

The few Bulldog fans in the gym were going crazy. Everyone else heard the noise, and vacated the concession stand in a mass migration. Even most of the band members returned to find their seats.

The Bulldogs were pressing and stole the ball again.

"Who told them to press?" Stern grumbled.

"You did, Coach. In the locker room," Reiser lied.

"I didn't tell them to press," Stern retorted. "Did I tell them to press?"

Skyler came off a pick and hit another three. Centerville was down by ten. Fans were running to get back inside.

"Oh, holy night. The stars were brightly shining."

(The fabulous Freshmen were on a roll.)
"It is the night of our dear Savior's birth."
(Skyler hit a three.)
"Long lay the world, in sin and error pining"
(Shane stole the ball and threw a behind-the-back pass)
"Till he appeared and the soul felt it's worth"
(Skyler comes off a pick to hit a three)
"A thrill of hope, the weary world rejoices"
(Fans applaud wildly)
"For yonder breaks, a new and glorious morn"
(Vance sets a mean pick)
"Fall on your knees"
(The Cowan Coach dropped, begging someone to play defense)
"Oh hear the angels voices"
(The Bulldog cheerleaders yelled with a new enthusiasm,)
"Oh, night, divine, oh night, when Christ was born"
(The fans cheered their new King)
"Oh night, Divine Oh night, Oh night divine."
(Centerville beat Cowan by 15 points.)

PEP TALK

In the locker room, after the game, the "fab five" was enjoying their feat.

"How'd ya like that shit, boys?" Buzzy strutted. "Did we put on a show, or did we put on a show?"

"We SHOWED UP big time, dude!" Shane boasted, as he slapped Buzzy's hand. "Those Cowan kids looked like they were in a coma!"

"After my first dunk, that short kid was saying the 'F' word," Emile laughed. "I don't think he's ever seen a dunk."

"Hell, there ain't been a dunk in this gym since before we was born!" exclaimed Vance, as he stuffed his shirt in the laundry tub.

"Did you guys see that piece-a-shit Stern on the sidelines?" Buzzy broke in. "He looked like he'd just swallowed a big fat terd!"

"I don't think he likes us," Emile smirked.

"Doesn't make sense," Skyler added. "We play our hearts out, turn around a ballgame and win, and the Coach looks pissed."

"He's a total dick," Shane said bluntly.

"Maybe, but wouldn't you think a Coach would be glad to get a win any way he could?" Skyler worried. "He didn't enjoy it at all."

"Well, I goddam enjoyed it enough for both of us!" Buzzy shouted.

"Ten-four good buddy on that!" Vance added, as he grabbed Buzzy's hand and shook them defiantly in the air.

"It just worries me," Skyler wondered. "He's the Coach, and he can really screw things up."

"Quit worrying," Emile assured, "I'll step on his ass."

"Everybody gather up!" Coach Stern screamed, as he entered the locker room. "C'mon, get together, now!"

All the players rushed to the center of the locker room, where they gathered for pre and post game talks. Coach Stern glared over his team as if he were a judge about to sentence a hardened criminal to life in prison. His forehead was furrowed and his eyes squinted beneath his brow. In the background stood Coach Reiser with a silly grin on his face.

"Sit down, Shane," Stern grumbled.

"I'm pumped, Coach!" Shane answered.

"I'll pump you if you don't sit down!" Stern threatened with his fist, as Shane lowered himself into a seat. "So, you guys won."

"Ten-four good buddy!" Vance celebrated by high-fiving Buzzy.

"Shut-up you redneck!" Stern ordered.

"Quick. Someone pull the cob outa his ass," Shane whispered.

"You freshmen might think your hot stuff now, but you've only got four more games before the real starters come back," admonished Stern. "Have your fun while you can, cause it won't be long before you're back on the JV. There's no place on a varsity team for one freshman, let alone FIVE!"

"Depends on the freshman, Coach." Reiser objected from behind, as Stern turned to glare at him.

"What's up, Coach?" Buzzy questioned. "We won the game."

"Won the game!" Stern echoed. "Is that all you care about?"

"Aren't you here to win games?" Buzzy asked.

"Don't get smart with me!" Stern yelled, as Jim tapped him on the shoulder to calm him down.

"How can we get smart with HIM?" whispered Shane.

"You won the game alright, but it takes more to become a good team," Stern fumbled. "You need teamwork. You need unselfishness. You need . . ."

"A Coach," Shane added quietly.

"What game was he watching?" Skyler wondered out loud.

"What did we do wrong, Coach?" Buzzy shot in. "Was winning wrong? How about next time we lose?"

"That does it!" yelled Stern. "You're out of the next game! You're suspended"

"Fine!" Buzzy yelled back.

"Settle down Coach," Jim said, as he grabbed Stern's arm. "They're confused on why you're yelling at them."

"You want to handle this?" Stern returned in anger.

"I could do better," Jim shot back.

"Fine! You take it!" Stern said in disgust. "I'll be in my office."

Stern walked away and slammed the door behind him.

"And, don't come back," Buzzy jumped up and said.

"Thank God!" Shane exclaimed.

"Coach. We won," Skyler broke in. "What did we do wrong?"

"Let it go," said Jim. "There's a lot of pressure being a Head Coach."

"He needs more head," Shane whispered.

"I didn't hear that, Shane," Jim scolded. "You guys played a great first game. Slow start, but you got into it and did the job. I, for one, am proud of you. Now, get dressed and get out of here."

"Am I suspended, Coach?" Buzzy asked.

Jim thought for a second and smiled, "I doubt it."

Even though Coach Stern begged them, the four seniors who were suspended for drinking never came back to the team. After losing its first four games of the year, the Centerville team finished the season with a 12-9 record. It was the first time in five years a Bulldog team had finished above .500. In the first year of Indiana's return to the one-class tournament, Centerville drew the unenviable task of facing Richmond in the first game of the Sectional. Centerville stayed even with Richmond in the first quarter by a score of 12 to 12. But, in the second quarter, Coach Stern began subbing for the freshmen. By halftime, Centerville was in a 34 to 24 hole.

During intermission, Reiser coaxed Stern to go back to his starters. With four minutes left in the third quarter it was 45-41. Stern again began subbing, as if he planned to throw the game. With eight minutes left, the Bulldogs were down 62 to 49.

The fourth quarter was a roller coaster. Subs every thirty seconds. Stern messed the line up so bad that with four minutes to go all the freshmen were back in. Two minutes later, they trimmed a fifteen point Richmond lead to eight, by sheer determination and pressing on their own. Then, the unthinkable. Stern pulled Buzzy, Emile and Skyler out of the game. Reiser jumped up fuming, had a few words with Stern, and stormed off the court. As Centerville bled to death, the fans booed Stern every time he stood to shout instructions. Final Score, Richmond-88, Centerville-73.

The next morning, Coach Stern was in the office of the Centerville Athletic Director, Bean Kreg. By the time Stern emerged from the heated office two hours later, it was decided that he would no longer coach boys' basketball. The stage was set for the future.

DON'T BE BOARD

On the night the School Board was to vote on the new varsity coach, the five Freshmen attended the meeting. Sky King was allowed to make a comment.

"My teammates and I know you have three finalists for the new head coaching job, and since we are to become the beneficiaries of how you vote, we would like for you to hear our recommendation. We, in no way intend any disrespect toward the school board, or pretend to bully our opinions on anyone present. But, if Jim Reiser is not voted in as the next Centerville Boys Varsity Coach, then my four teammates and I will not be playing basketball in our sophomore year, or any year to follow. Thank you."

"Right on, brother!" Buzzy added.

"Ten-four from all of us, yeah!" Vance included.

"Shut up guys, their heads will explode," Shane hissed.

For a few moments, the entire School Board was speechless. Stew Siler, an avid basketball fan, knew the severity of the statement he had heard. He also saw looks of resentment beginning to form on the faces of the other board members, at being told what to do by high school boys.

"In that case," Stew said, breaking the silence, "I make a motion, we select Jim Reiser as our new Boys Varsity Basketball Coach." Still no one else spoke. Stew nudged the lady next to him. "There's a motion on the table, Sarah. You're supposed to follow suit."

"Oh! . . .I. . .I second the motion," Sarah reluctantly said. "I guess."

"All in favor?" the Superintendent asked.

"Aye, aye, aye,"

"All opposed,"

"Nay, nay,"

"By a vote of three to two, Jim Reiser is the new Varsity Coach."

The soon-to-be sophomores celebrated with high fives, and pats on the back for Coach Reiser. The two losing candidates left disgruntled.

"Congratulations boys," Stew said relieved. "Now, bring us home a Sectional Title!"

The sophomore season was one of promise. The Bulldogs finished the season with a 17-6 record. Skyler averaged 29 points per game, and the fans began to come back in droves. Even though they ended up second in the TEC, and even though they lost the Wayne County Tourney Title to Hagerstown, and even though Richmond beat them by nine points in the Sectional Championship game, basketball was fun again at Centerville.

RELATIVELY SPEAKING

One summer day, Diane Belcher got a call from her mother-in-law. It was urgent. Get there as quickly as possible. When she arrived at the Belcher House, it looked like a family reunion.

"What's going on?" Diane asked, completely lost.

"It's taken a long time, but June's finally found her daughter," Betty Belcher said proudly.

Diane looked around more intently at the gathering of people. There was only one person who didn't belong. "Oh, my God!" Diane said, covering her mouth. She was looking at Carmen Dellinger.

"You two know each other?" Betty asked.

"I told you that, Mom," June scolded, "Phil used to deliver to Carmen's office in Hagerstown."

"Who would've known?" Carmen shrugged, looking directly at Diane.

"I wish Skyler wasn't at basketball camp this week," Betty said regretfully, "he'd really get a kick out of this."

Diane watched, as Carmen connected with the entire Belcher family. It was as if Carmen wasn't a stranger at all. She laughed and reminisced with June and Betty, she coaxed Aaron to crack a smile, and Carmen seemed to find a special bond with April. Diane felt like an outsider.

"Betty, you don't need to do that," Aaron complained, when Betty brought out family photos of Randy and Phil.

"Calm down Aaron," Carmen soothed, "I need to see these."

The Belchers had a large meal and a grand celebration. As it finally wound down, Diane was able to talk to Carmen alone.

"This just boggles my mind," Diane reiterated the shock.

"Tell me about it," Carmen reassured.

"I don't know if I'm happy to know you two were related, or if I'm sad, because Phil isn't here to find out," Diane tried to explain.

"You don't know how hard I cried when I found this out," Carmen said, "I still haven't gotten over it."

"Maybe that's why you two were attracted to each other," Diane reasoned,

"You know; blood is thicker than water."

"It could be," Carmen said uneasy. "We had a lot in common."

"How did you take all this?" Diane wondered. "I mean, when June found you."

"I don't think it's really sunk in," Carmen replied, "I always knew I was adopted, but I never had that urge to find my real mother. June and I had a nice meeting, but she's a stranger right now."

"This must be quite a shock to you?" Diane questioned.

"You have no idea how shocked I was," Carmen understated, "now if I could just find out June's a millionaire, I'd be all set."

"Wouldn't that be lovely!" dreamed Diane.

"It's just nice to finally know why things happened."

"So, you're divorced now?" Diane reiterated.

"Yes, I'm divorced," sighed Carmen, "and, no potential suitors just yet."

"How about children?" Diane pried.

"I've got three boys," Carmen smiled, "they wear me out."

"What ages?" persisted Diane.

"Sixteen, fifteen, and ... half past the terrible twos," Carmen hesitated, "I left them at my mom's today, well, my adoptive mom, that is. Didn't want to overwhelm everyone at the first big reunion."

"That's a big age difference," Diane noticed. "What's up with that?"

"It's called one last fling before getting divorced," Carmen eluded, "I finally mustered the strength to get away from a dickbert of a husband."

"Dickbert?" repeated Diane. "Phil used that term, too."

"That's where I got it," Carmen admitted.

"What are your boy's names?" confronted Diane.

"David, Michael, and... I hope you don't mind, but I named the youngest one after Phil," Carmen apologized.

"You two must've been very good friends," Diane insinuated.

"He was one of my best friends," Carmen said, almost choking up. "When my husband and I started having trouble, he was the only one who made me feel I deserved better."

"You're little son, Phil, is he..." Diane stopped herself to keep from appearing ridiculous. She knew her husband had a vasectomy. There was no need dredging up impossible scenarios, now that Phil was dead. "Is he a cute little boy?"

"He's a darling," Carmen glowed. "When he smiles at me, it's like everything is great."

"Babies have a way of doing that," added Diane.

"Little Phil actually saved my life," remembered Carmen. "Just after ... your Phil died, I found out I was pregnant. It was the only thing that got me through."

Once again, Diane found herself wanting to ask the impossible. To think of the disgusting. She couldn't bear to make herself look stupid.

"On the night Phil was killed, he was coming home from Hagerstown," Diane redirected her thoughts. "Had he been to see you?"

"Yes, I saw him that night," said Carmen, refusing to lie. "I guess I was the last one to see him alive."

"Why was he there to see you?" Diane nearly grumbled.

"I told you. We were friends," Carmen tried to smooth out. "I was in the process of getting a divorce, and I needed someone."

"Were you in love with my husband?" Diane demanded.

"Yes, I loved him," Carmen surprised herself. "Whenever you can talk to someone with such honesty and caring as we did, then you really have something special. It's as if we felt our biological bond."

Diane hadn't expected Carmen's honesty. She had prepared to argue over possible lies, but she was getting hit in the face with the truth.

"Was Phil in love with you?" Diane whispered.

"I hope he was," Carmen reminisced.

"Did you have an affair with Phil?" Diane said matter-of-factly.

"He's my Uncle," Carmen joked. "How could I?"

"You didn't know that, then," Diane grumbled.

"Phil was a good friend," Carmen repeated. "We didn't do anything wrong."

"I'm sorry about all these questions," Diane lamented, as she put her hand on her forehead. "I'm just jealous Phil needed another woman to confide in. We had a long marriage, and we had our problems like most couples, but..."

"He told me several times, if it weren't for you and Skyler, he'd be lost," Carmen reassured.

"Maybe Skyler," Diane added. "He had basketball with him."

"You said yourself you had a long marriage," Carmen rationalized. "Not too many people get that."

"That's all I have left," thought Diane out loud, "memories of what we did have."

Diane allowed a brief smile to break her mood.

"Well, interrogation over," Diane sighed.

"Did I pass?" asked Carmen.

"I guess so…welcome to the family," Diane said, as she hugged Carmen. As the two embraced, Carmen laughed, as tears rolled down her cheeks. "I'm sure Phil would've loved this."

BULLDOG MANIA! CATCH IT!

The junior year for Skyler and his gang was one of great anticipation. The maturing of the 'fab five' was something everyone wanted to see. Emile was a gangly six foot seven inches tall. Vance sprang up to a stout six foot five. Buzzy put on enough beef to set a pick on a bulldozer, and Shane and Skyler were as sharp and quick as ever.

All-sport ticket sales were at an all time high. By the third game, Centerville ticket takers were turning away fans. Opposing teams did their best to avoid Lee Outland Gymnasium, short of forfeiting. Not only was it a sure loss, but whenever a certain Bulldog hit a three, the PA announcer would scream, SKYYYYYYYYYYYYYY King!

"We need a motto," Skyler suggested, after one practice.
"How about 'kiss my ass'?" Buzzy volunteered, as he slapped his butt.
"Take this ball and shove it!" Vance misquoted his favorite oldie.
"Something a little less volatile," Skyler reprimanded.
"Volatile!" Shane repeated. "Boy, we're using such big words now."
"How about, 'this dunks for you'?" Emile threw in.
"Here's a good one," Coach Reiser interrupted, while passing by his smelly players. "Hit the showers!"
"Booooo!" the Team hissed in unison.
"Too clean, Coach," Shane kidded.
"We need a congratulatory slap, too," Skyler directed the conversation.
"A what?" Vance asked.
"You know, like a high five, only something special we do," Skyler explained.
"We could rub our asses together," Buzzy ridiculed.
"Get off the butts!" Skyler said annoyed. "Too gay."
"Chest butts," Vance thought out loud.
"Head butts," Shane brainstormed.
"We could slap each other on the forehead," Emile added.
"Been done, too dangerous, too three Stooges," Skyler rationalized. "Let's grab each others index finger and shake."
"If we start getting a rash of jammed fingers, you guys are dead," Reiser

yelled from the background.

The five players looked at each other for a second, "Hit the showers!"

Reiser was in coach's heaven. To have five top-notch ballplayers in the same class was a dream come true. Most coaches didn't have five true ballplayers in all of the four high school grades. With the talent came a price. Worry. Worry about injury, worry about apathy, worry about the stall. Reiser spent entire practices working against the stall. His philosophy -- be patient and wait for the gradual kill. If a team came out in a stall, his boys were to stick to the basic hard-nosed defense and wait for the turnover. On offense, he instructed them to work the ball around the perimeter until a lay-up or dunk materialized. Once the Bulldogs worked their way to a ten-point lead, the stall was worthless. Three times, teams came out in a stall. In each case, by the end of the first quarter, the game was over.

Reiser still worried. At mid-season, the Bulldogs weathered another crisis. They were 10-0 at the time, when Skyler developed a girlfriend and an attitude. According to rumors, the girl was just interested in adding another conquest to her resume, and the fact she pulled it off on the most popular kid at school made it even sweeter.

One day, Skyler showed up twenty minutes late for practice with his girl in his arm. Coach Reiser wasn't happy.

"What are you doing here?" Reiser asked, as all the players stopped running.

"I came for practice," Skyler answered.

"You're a little late, aren't you?" Reiser alluded to the obvious.

"So," Skyler shot back, as he threw his arms in the air.

"So, if you can't show up on time, then we don't need you here," Reiser said in anger.

"What?" Skyler said in disbelief.

"Get out of here!" Reiser shouted. "We're trying to practice."

Skyler was shocked and hurt by the words. He looked at his coach fuming, and saw the look of disappointment in his teammates eyes. Skyler grabbed his girl and stormed out of the gym.

Skyler wasn't at practice the next day either. By the time the players made it home for dinner that night, everyone in Centerville knew. No one in the King house got any sleep. First, the whole basketball team came visiting.

"What's all this?" Skyler asked, as the players filed in.

"We came here to kick your ass, you dip shit!" Buzzy responded.

"What'd I do?" Skyler played innocent.

"What'd I do? What'd I do?" mocked Shane. "You're ruining our team you selfish little bastard."

"We're damn-near undefeated Sky," added Vance

"Are you coming back?" pleaded Emile.

"Yeah, I'm coming," injected Skyler.

"When?" Buzzy demanded. "We play Friday night."

"Notice the 'WE', Sky," Shane mocked. "We play Friday night."

"Soon," Skyler stumbled. "Soon as Reiser apologizes."

"What?" Buzzy exploded. "You outta your mind?"

"Sky, I may be stupid, but you're a moron!" Vance threw in.

"We got something good, Sky," Emile added, "you leave and you screw it up for all of us."

"Let's just kick his ass right here, guys," Shane suggested, "end of problem. We kick ass and make him eat crow."

"What's it gonna be, ass munch?" Buzzy threatened.

Diane Belcher made a strong appearance. Phone calls from all over the county burned up the lines. And, eventually, Coach Reiser showed up.

That night, Skyler dreamt about a red Miata crashing over and over again. The next day at school, Skyler had to make a decision.

"You don't need that stupid basketball team, anyway," Skyler's girl said. "We can spend more time together."

"We've probably been spending too much time together," Skyler reasoned.

"What does that mean?" she demanded.

"Just what it sounds like," Skyler said.

"Well, you better meet me right here at the locker after school so you can take me home," she insisted.

"Yes, dear," Skyler mocked, as she stormed off to class.

That afternoon at basketball practice, a girl burst into the gym interrupting the drills.

"Skyler King! You're a son-of-a-bitch! You hear me, you son-of-a-bitch!"

As the players laughed, the girl stormed out.

"Well, I guess she didn't tell us anything we didn't already know," quipped Reiser.

Skyler sat out the two games scheduled for that weekend. It was a costly weekend, as the Bulldogs finished the season at 18-2. Fortunately, neither game Skyler missed was a conference game, so Centerville finished undefeated in the TEC. Most people felt Reiser planned it that way.

In the Sectional, Centerville waltzed through the first two games and now faced Richmond in the finals. It was a classic battle of Richmond's size and power against Centerville's finesse and teamwork.

The first three quarters were textbook basketball on both sides. Few turnovers, good execution, fair shooting. Richmond led 20-15 after one quarter, and 45-42 at halftime. By the time the third-quarter horn sounded, the score was tied 68-68.

Then, something happened in the fourth quarter that no one would've ever expected. Coach Reiser decided to try something he'd done little of all year. Press.

Richmond had pressed on and off all game, but with Shane Best and Skyler to handle the ball, it was a fruitless effort. Richmond didn't expect to taste its own medicine. The Red Devils were shaken and tired. Within three minutes, they were down by ten points. The Richmond Coach called his second timeout. One minute later, the Bulldogs were up fifteen.

The Centerville fans, and all the fans from all the other small schools, were rocking the gym. They had the Tiernan Center bleachers swaying so swiftly that the PA Announcer had to warn the crowd to sit down. Richmond had to foul and throw up desperation shots to get back in the game. Centerville kept inching away. Richmond called its last time-out.

For four solid minutes, the Centerville fans were able to celebrate a sure victory. High fives, hugs, kisses. And, most with complete strangers. Milo, Kenneth, and George were leading the cheers in their section, and tried miserably to organize a wave.

98-77 is the damage Richmond suffered. The Centerville students rushed the court, hoisted their heroes on their shoulders, and toured the entire gym. It had been seventy years since Centerville had won a one-class Sectional at Richmond. At the moment, it seemed worth the wait.

In the Centerville locker room it was a massive celebration. Hugging, screaming, flying jerseys, and towel flips on bare asses. Everyone joined in except Skyler. He stood at his locker trying to grin.

"Ain't it great!" Vance screamed in Skyler's face.

"Super-duper," Skyler said matter-of-factly.

"Sky! Get excited!" Buzzy demanded. "We just won the goddam Richmond Sectional!"

"Buzz, for crying out loud," Shane kidded. "Don't use the Lord's name in vain. You want lightning to strike the locker room? Mess up our celebration?"

"What's up, Sky?" Emile asked seriously. "Aren't you happy?"

"Of course, I'm happy," Skyler admitted. "It just worries me."

"He's worried about making the all-tourney team," Shane joked.

"Why, you selfish bastard!" Buzzy overacted.

"No, it's not that," Skyler said. "We're only juniors and we won the Sectional. How we gonna top this next year?"

"Win the damn thing again!" Vance suggested.

"What if we don't?" Skyler thought. "We'll be failures."

The team stopped for a second and thought about the worst.

"Shut the hell up, Sky!" Buzzy finally interjected. "That's a year off! If you can't celebrate now, then I'm stuffing you in this locker."

"Yeah, wake up and smell the jock strap, Sky!" Shane shouted, as he shoved a supporter in Skyler's face.

"BULLDOGS RULE!" Came the roar from the back, as Coach Reiser entered the locker room. Everyone screamed like girls, formed a circle around Reiser and raised their fists to the sky.

Centerville went to the Regional and won their first game. In the nightcap, they lost by two points when Sklyer missed a long three on the top of the key to potentially win the game. It was disappointing, but the Bulldogs had broken through a barrier that seemed insurmountable. They were proud, the School was proud, and the Town looked forward to one more year.

SUMMER SCHOOL

Skyler stood at the plate with the bases loaded. Centerville was down by one run with two outs in the bottom of the last inning. On the mound stood the mighty Hagerstown relief pitcher. It was the same athlete who guarded Skyler in the Finals of the Wayne County Basketball Tourney. Skyler scored 38 points on him.

The first pitch was launched. Skyler swung and missed the arching curve. The next two pitches were also curves, but down and away for balls. After each pitch, the batter and pitcher glared each other down. The 2-1 delivery streaked toward the plate. Skyler swung and drove the ball down the left field line. It landed three feet foul and bounced off the fence. Skyler came that close to winning the game.

With the count— two balls and two strikes— the Hagerstown pitcher wound up for the next pitch. The ball started for Skyler's head, but then took a sharp left turn and headed for the catcher's mitt. Skyler swung with a mighty heave. He missed the ball. Strike three! Ballgame.

As the pitcher came off the mound, he made a detour to purposely walk past Skyler.

"So, the mighty Sky King can't hit a curveball," the pitcher ridiculed.

"Since we live in Indiana, I only got one thing to say," Skyler rebutted.

"What's that, loser?" the pitcher asked.

"Let's play basketball."

A CHANCE MEETING

It was Thanksgiving at the Belcher home. A bittersweet time of celebrating family. How often we overlook the good times, when everyone can be together. Randy and Phil were missing. Diane was at her own parents to celebrate. But, Carmen came. She felt it was the best way for her to get back a little of what she once had.

"Skyler, it's so nice to see you again," Carmen said. "Remember me? I'm your long lost aunt."

"Yes, M'am," Skyler replied. "We met briefly last Christmas."

"Please don't call me M'am. It makes me feel too old," Carmen teased. "My name's Carmen."

"Ok, Carmen," Skyler replied. "Who's that you have with you?"

"This is my little Phil," Carmen said proudly. "I named him after your father."

"Everyone said you knew my father pretty well," said Skyler.

"Yes, I used to see him five days a week at my office when he delivered," Carmen smiled. "Can you say 'hi' to Skyler, Philzy?"

"Hi, Skywer," Phil answered.

"Hi buddy," Skyler said, rubbing Phil's hair. "Were you good friends with my dad?"

"Me?" said Phil.

"I think he means me, honey," laughed Carmen. "We were real good friends, Skyler. I've never known another man who I could talk to so freely."

"I guess, us men are hard to communicate with sometimes," Skyler joked. "Either that, or I just haven't found the right woman yet."

"It takes time," Carmen warned. "It was a long time before I met your dad."

"He talked to me about you before," Skyler remembered. "You're the third baseman that plays ball like a man."

"That's me," Carmen admitted.

"He said if I had half the heart for athletics as that third baseman did, I could excel at anything."

"He actually said that about me?" Carmen choked.

"Yeah, he was really impressed with your enthusiasm," added Skyler. "He said there are so few people who put out an effort that's worth bragging about. He said if you find them, you should never let them out of your sight cause you can learn so much."

"Stop it. You're making me cry," Carmen kidded, as she sobbed.

"You really loved him, didn't you?" Skyler asked, causing Carmen to shake her head yes. "It's too bad for all of us."

"Both of us could sure use him here today," Carmen said, as she wiped her eyes.

"So, you're the one who takes care of Mom now," Skyler bent down and stroked Phil's arm.

"Uh, huh," Phil replied.

"He's my whole life," Carmen added.

"You're so lucky, Carmen," thought Skyler. "You've still got a piece of Phil to enjoy."

Carmen smiled and nodded her head.

"C'mon, Philzy," Skyler encouraged. "Let's go see if there's any pumpkin pie with our names on it."

THE TYLERS-TWO

It was senior night. The last game of the year for Centerville. The last game Skyler, Vance, Emile, Buzzy and Shane would play in Lee Outland Gymnasium.

The town fire marshal prepared for the large turnout by inspecting the bleachers and fire exits the week before. He also showed up early to count the number of tickets sold. Even though the east wall of the gym had been knocked down and temporary bleachers installed, there were never enough tickets all season long.

But, the Bulldog fans were not to be denied. A group of industrious Freshmen had wedged a rarely used back door open, and were escorting anyone turned away from the game to their secret entrance for half the price. The Freshmen cleared over $200.

Tim and Jim Tyler, the twin terrors of the junior high, had a more exciting finale planned for the undefeated Bulldogs. Their mission was simple: sneak past security, scale a restraining gate, make their way to the maintenance room, and plunge the entire gym into total darkness. Why? Just because they were the twin terrors.

Getting past the guard was simple. The Tylers bought a Coke, and paid a friend fifty cents to give it to the guard, while they slipped past. It was getting over the accordion-style gate, which only had a six-inch gap at the top, which was going to be difficult.

"Now what," Tim whispered loudly to his brother, as they stared down the gate.

"No problem," Jim replied. "I'll give you a boost, so you can climb over the top."

"Are you kidding!" Tim said disbelieving. "There's not enough room to get through!"

"Don't be a pussy," Jim goaded. "You can make it. No problem."

Not wanting to be a pussy, Tim decided to give it a try. Jim held onto the flimsy gate and let Tim climb up his back. Tim got his leg through easily, but as he tried to squeeze in his torso, his chest became pinned between the ceiling and the top prongs of the gate.

"I'm stuck! Tim cried, as the gate pressed against his breastbone. "I can't get out!"

"Just squeeze through!" Jim demanded.

"I can't!" Tim said desperately. "It's gonna break my ribs! Get me outta here!"

"Shut-up!" Jim yelled. "Somebody's gonna hear you!"

"I can't breathe, Jim!" Tim panicked. "I can't breathe!"

In a fit of anger, Jim jumped on the gate and climbed to the top. He grabbed the top prong, which had Tim stuck to the ceiling, and gave it a mighty tug, as he pushed on Tim's body with his other hand. Tim sprung from his trap and fell sprawling to the floor on the opposite side.

"There, you big pussy," Jim said disgusted.

"Oh, shit!" Tim moaned, holding his chest. "You broke my ribs, you bastard!"

Jim stuck his leg through the gate, and then with one swift motion, he pulled the top prong across his chest. Jim jumped off the gate, landing next to his brother. Without hesitation, he kicked Tim in the butt with the side of his foot.

"That's how it's done, you weenie!" Jim said proudly. "C'mon, get up and let's get going before the game's over."

Tim got up slowly, rubbing his chest. Fueled by adrenalin, the boys rushed down the darkened hallways, stopping only to carefully look around the corners.

"If we turn right at this next corner, the control panel should be halfway up the hall," Jim said panting for air. "Let me check around this one."

Jim pressed his body to the wall and slid his head around the corner, to check out the last stretch of hallway.

"Let's go," Tim whispered impatiently.

Suddenly, Jim jerked his head back as quickly as if he'd been kicked in the face. With his arms wide, his fingers dug into the wall, in an attempt to blend with the plaster and wood. The more he moved his fingers, the wider his eyes opened.

"What's wrong, Jim?" Tim whispered to his brother.

Jim put an index finger up to his puckered lips, and motioned to the corner of the hallway with his thumb. Tim pulled himself over his brother's stiffened frame, and stuck his head around the corner. By the light of an "exit" sign, Tim could see the outline of a man standing next to the breaker box.

"There's a man down there," Tim exclaimed, after jerking his head back.

"Be quiet," Jim reprimanded, as he put his hand over Tim's mouth. "If we get caught, we're dead."

Jim looked around the corner again to convince himself what he'd seen. The man stood motionless in front of the breaker box, as if he were reading the cover.

"He didn't see us," Jim said with relief.

"Who is it?" asked Tim.

"I don't know," Jim answered. "Could be Marvin, the janitor."

Tim stuck his head around the corner to get another look. "That's not Marv. Marv's a lot bigger."

"What's he doing here?" Jim asked, with a quiver in his voice.

"Maybe they suspected us," Tim speculated. "It could be a trap."

"Let's get out of here," Jim said in fear, as he grabbed Tim's arm.

"After coming all this way!" Tim said in defiance. "No, way. You're the one who's a pussy."

"So, what now, smart ass?" Jim asked, trying to save face.

Tim lay down on the floor and slid out toward the edge of the corner. "I'll watch from down here until they decide to leave."

"What if he comes this way?" Jim wondered.

Tim shrugged his shoulders. "I guess we'll run like hell."

Tim pulled his way along the floor until he was in position to see. Jim sat nervously beside him, trying to think of an excuse to leave. As they waited, a slow methodical noise began emanating from the location of the unknown intruder. Jim listened intently, as each noise matched the pounding of his heart. Finally, Jim slapped his brother on the leg to get his attention.

"What's wrong?" Tim said, as he slid back.

"I don't know," Tim answered. "Sounds like he's eating something."

"Let's go!" Jim pleaded.

"Just a couple more minutes," Tim stalled. "Besides, this was your idea."

Tim slid his head back around the corner to watch his apparition. Jim curled beside his brother and wiped some sweat off his forehead. The two boys were in for a long wait.

SAYING GOODBYE

As each senior was introduced, they walked to center court with their parents. Typically, they saved the best for last.

"Our next senior this evening is, Skyler King!"

The crowd, already on its feet, broke into a thunderous applause, drowning out the PA Announcer, as he read through Skyler's achievements. Skyler walked out with his mother in one hand and his grandmother in the other. As they took their spot on top of the Bulldog at center court, Skyler's grandmother let go of his hand and took a step away. There was just enough space between them for one person to stand.

After what seemed an eternity, the applause died down.

"Ladies and gentlemen, I present to you the senior basketball players and cheerleaders for 2015." The crowd, still on its feet, began to applaud again.

Earlier, the seniors were told to leave the floor after the acknowledgments, but for some reason they stayed. The five basketball players knelt on the center circle and simultaneously kissed the Bulldog. They stood up, shook each other's index fingers, and raised their fists in the air. Cheers and whistles greeted them. Skyler walked toward the scorer's bench, asked the PA Announcer for the microphone, and waited for the applause to die down.

"As representative for the seniors being honored here tonight, I would like to express our love and admiration for the parents, relatives, friends and coaches, who are responsible for everything we've achieved."

A heart-stopping roar reverberated through the gym, as Skyler nodded to his mother, grandmother and Coach Reiser. As he prepared to speak again, the crowd became silent.

"And, . . . personally, I'd like to thank my father, Phil Belcher. I wouldn't be here tonight if it wasn't for him."

Once again, the basketball-hungry fans obliged the pre-game ceremony by setting a new decibel level for applause. As Skyler set the microphone back on the scorer's table, the lights in the gym went out. Total darkness slapped the crowd in the retinas. A few screams and intermittent murmurings could be heard. Most fans sat back down quickly to regain their equilibrium, while others clung to those nearby for security.

"What the hell's gong on?" Principal Bates asked his athletic director.

"Why are you asking me?" responded Kreg. "Do I look like an electrician?"

"Where's Marvin?" Bates demanded.

"Out in the hall," Kreg shot back.

"Go get him, and I'll make an announcement over the PA," Bates demanded.

"If the power's off, the PA won't work either," Kreg rationalized.

"Just get Marvin!" Bates said in anger.

Kreg felt his way out to the hall to find the custodian. Bates scratched his head for a few seconds, then decided he better calm the noisy crowd before someone got hurt.

"May I have your attention please!" Bates screamed at the top of his lungs. "May I have your attention? Please, everyone stay in your seats! We've had a power failure, and we'll get things fixed as soon as possible, so we can start the game."

The few cheers Bates received for his speech did little to relax him.

"I found Marvin!" said a voice out of a flashlight.

"What's going on, Marvin?" Bates demanded.

"I'd say the main breaker's kicked out," Marvin said matter-of-factly. "The whole school's dead, but I can see lights all over town."

"Well, let's find that main breaker. Now!" shouted an irritated Bates.

Bates followed Marvin and his flashlight down the hall toward the iron gate, which separated the school from the gym. When they arrived, Bates tried to move things along.

"Hurry and open this thing up, Marvin," Bates said impatiently.

"Well, you'll have to hold my flashlight for me," Marvin answered.

"Yeah, sure," Bates said, as he grabbed the light.

"Well, let's see. Which one of these devils is the right one?" Marvin wondered, as he pulled out a key chain containing over fifty keys.

"Dammit, Marvin! I've got over 3,000 people sitting in the dark, and it's hard telling how long it'll be before some old lady in a walker decides to take a piss and ends up rolling down the bleachers and killing herself!"

"Think I got it right here, Mr. Bates," Marvin said with a proud smile.

"Oh. Great," Bates said embarrassed.

Marvin stepped toward the lock and slowly inserted the key. But, before he could unlock the gate, Jim and Tim Tyler came flying out of the darkness and crashed into the gate.

"Let us out! Let us out!" both boys screamed in unison.

The shock of the Tylers, coming out of nowhere, sent Bates sprawling backwards, causing him to throw the flashlight down the hall.

"Jesus Christ!" Marvin prayed, as he closed his eyes and bent the key.

"Let us out!" the boys screamed. "There's someone chasing us!"

"What the hell's going on?" Bates barked with a crack in his voice, as he crawled for the light.

"There's a man after us!" Jim yelled. "You've got to let us out before he gets here!"

"Who's after you?" Bates asked, as he shined the light in their faces.

"Just some man!" Tim whined on the verge of tears. "Let us out!"

"What man?" I don't see anybody down there." Bates contradicted, as he shined the light down the hall. "What are you boys doing over there in the first place?"

The boys just stood on their side of the gate, shivering, keeping a white-knuckled grip on the bars. Without warning, a swift gust of air, accompanied by a fine white mist passed by all four of them.

"What was that?" Bates asked, as he shined the light on the two boys. "Did you two set off a smoke bomb or something?"

Neither one answered. When Bates heard a dripping sound, he lowered his light to discover Jim had urinated down his blue jeans.

"Jesus Christ, boy!" yelled a disbelieving Bates. "Dammit, Marvin, open this gate!"

Marvin's face was ashen and his handful of keys jiggled wildly, as he kept trying to unlock the gate.

"Now, what's wrong with you?" Bates said in disgust.

"Did you see it?" Marvin asked in a somber tone.

"See what?" questioned Bates.

"Did you see his face?" Marvin asked again.

"What face?"

"I've seen it before, but I can't place it," Marvin said in shock.

"Get out of my way!" Bates said in anger, as he took over jiggling the keys.

Bates unlocked the gate and slid it across the hallway. As soon as the exit was presented to them, Tim and Jim Tyler took the opportunity to set a record in the mile run.

"You boys come back here!" yelled an angry Bates. "You're in a lot of trouble, and I know who you are!" When the boys wouldn't stop, Bates turned to Marvin. "Who were those boys?"

"Never seen them before," Marvin responded.

"Come on. We've got to get those lights on. Now!"

The two nearly ran down the hall until they reached their destination.

"This is the main breaker box right here," Marvin said.

"I'll hang those brats by the flag pole for shutting those lights off," Bates fantasized.

Marvin tried pulling on the door to the breakers, "This is the box that needs a key. See. I can't open it. There's no way those boys could've shut the power off."

Marvin unlocked the box and flipped the main breaker. When a security light popped on right above them, the two men nearly jumped in each other's arms.

"Well, at least we have some light," Bates said sheepishly.

Marvin locked the box and backed up to leave. A crunching sound could be heard on the floor.

"Look!" exclaimed Bates. "Popcorn! That proves those boys were down here."

"Yeah, but there's no way they shut off the lights," Marvin said again. "And, if they did, why would they run back this way where we were standing?"

"Well, if they didn't do it, then who did?" Bates sarcastically asked.

Marvin stared at Bates' face, but he was looking right through him. After what seemed like an eternity, he answered, "If I could remember that face, I'd tell you."

MOOD LIGHTING

During the blackout, there was very little activity in the gym. Some of the parking attendants had come inside with their flashlights to help those who lost their bearings, but for the most part their meager beams only made the darkness seem more ominous.

The High School Band played through most of the delay to help soothe the nerves of those uneasy about their blackened environment. Skyler sat in front of the scorer's bench and talked to the officials between songs. Some say during the National Anthem, which everyone was asked to remain seated for, they could hear Skyler fighting back tears.

When the lights finally came back on, the crowd let out a cheer, which drowned out the band. Since the lighting was mercury vapor lamps, they came on dim at first and then slowly built up to full power. Skyler got off the floor and started walking toward the locker room with the rest of his team. Before he made it very far, he heard a loud distinct voice call out his name. Skyler stopped and looked into the stands. The lights were still dim and fuzzy, but he could make out a lone figure standing on the last row of bleachers. He couldn't tell who the man was, but he was eating a bag of popcorn. One kernel at a time.

"What?" Skyler yelled back to the crowd.

The figure made one sweeping wave with his right hand, then put his thumb and forefinger together to signal his approval. Staring at the figure, Skyler made his way to the steps and started climbing to the top.

"Dad," Skyler said softly, for fear of embarrassing himself. He began jogging up the steps, as his chest pounded with excitement. "Dad," he said louder, as he reached the halfway point. "Is that you?"

As Skyler got closer to the top, people began standing up to shake his hand or cheer him on. In the confusion, he lost sight of the figure. When he reached the spot, there was no one he recognized.

"Did anyone see my . . . ?" Skyler stopped before he said something totally absurd. He looked over the fans one last time and smiled. "I thought I saw somebody I knew."

Just before turning to leave, Skyler noticed half a bag of popcorn sitting on the footrest of the top row of bleachers.

"Whose popcorn is that?" he asked, as if he'd punish the culprit. Everyone looked at Skyler with a pathetic stare. "Whose popcorn is that?" he shouted.

Finally, one fan picked up the bag and held it out to Skyler. "It's nobody's. But, you can have it if you want."

"Nobody up here's even had any popcorn," another fan answered. "I sure didn't notice it when I sat down."

Skyler took the popcorn and felt the kernels in the bag. They were still warm.

"He was here," Skyler said quietly. "I know he was here."

Skyler rolled up the bag and ran down the steps. When he reached the basketball court, he turned to the fans he'd just left, raised his fist containing the popcorn into the air, and disappeared through the locker room door.

SOMETHING FAMILIAR

Marvin had locked the security gate and was walking back toward the gym. He hoped the excitement for the evening was over, so he could relax and enjoy the game like everyone else. As Marvin walked past the trophy case on his way to the concession stand, something made him stop in his tracks. It was a picture of Phil Belcher.

After the Sectional Trophy from last season had been placed in the case, Skyler sneaked in a picture of his father. It was his small tribute to the man who had given him the inspiration.

Marvin stared at the picture for several minutes, reading Skyler's inscription over and over. Marvin's breathing suddenly became shorter and more pronounced. The keys dangling from his waist started to jingle, even though his feet were stationary. Finally, the blood rushed from his head and began pounding against the walls of his heart. It looked as though he'd seen a ghost.

PRE-GAME RITUAL

As Skyler ran into the dressing room, he was jumped by a playful band of teammates and wrestled to the floor. First, they pulled his basketball trunks to his knees and started working on his jersey. Buzzy pried the sack of popcorn away from Skyler and began celebrating.

"I got his popcorn! I got his popcorn!" shouted Buzzy. "Now, I won't have to go to the concession stand!"

"Give me that back!" Skyler shouted, as his jersey covered his face.

"Sorry, buddy," Buzzy replied, "no snacking before a game."

"Give it to me!" Skyler blurted, as he struggled. "Give it here!"

Skyler jumped up wearing nothing but his jock and basketball shoes, and dove toward Buzzy. With his shorts still around his ankle, Skyler tripped and landed head first into the side of the lockers. He hit the floor with a thud and lay motionless, as his teammates prayed for a sign of life.

"Sky! You all right?" Buzzy ventured. "Skyler! It's time to play ball!"

Skyler didn't move. "Oh my God!" Vance panicked. "He's dead!"

"There goes our undefeated season," Emile joked, hoping it wasn't true.

"Go get Coach!" Shane said nervously. "Or, a doctor, or something."

Buzzy knelt down beside Skyler, putting his hand on Skyler's shoulder to roll him over. "Skyler? You all right?"

Skyler whirled around and grabbed the crumpled bag of popcorn away from Buzzy.

"You son-of-a-bitch!" Buzzy yelled. "I knew you weren't hurt!"

"What the hell's going on in here?" Coach Reiser's voice echoed, as he opened the locker room door.

Everyone froze and looked at the Coach, but no one answered. Reiser saw Buzzy and Skyler arm in arm, with Skyler wearing only his jock.

"What is this? Gay night at the Centerville Gym?" Reiser sarcastically asked. "Since the lights are on now, I suggest you guys get your asses on the court and warm up."

Without hesitation, the ballplayers bolted for the door. "You may want to check your wardrobe, Skyler?" Reiser suggested.

Emile tossed Skyler his shirt and shorts, so he hurriedly put them on.

"Should I ask what this was all about?" Reiser ventured. "Oh, never mind. Just get the hell out of here."

Skyler tossed the popcorn in his locker and headed for the court. During warm-ups, Skyler seemed to be disinterested. After missing several shots, even the fans could tell it wasn't going to be a good night for Centerville.

"Did you see that?" shouted Milo, as he pointed his bony finger toward the court. "That's the fifth shot in a row he's missed!"

"Who did?" George calmly asked, as he eyed his program.

"Sky King! That's who!" Milo shot back. "He's missed five shots in a row, and he's moving like he's wearing a yoke."

"Don't worry, Milo," George said, without looking up. "It's not game time, yet."

"Don't you ever watch warm-ups?" Milo screamed, as he stood up and slapped the program out of George's hand, causing it to fall under the bleachers. "He's not the same out there, I tell ya. Something's wrong."

George looked longingly at his program that lay a mere five feet from his grasp. "Dammit, Milo," he said in a monotone. "I wasn't finished with that, yet."

"It doesn't matter, George," rebutted Milo. "If Sky plays like this, then you're not gonna want a souvenir."

"Three popcorns to go," said a cheerful Kenneth, as he approached his two companions.

"Take it back," Milo demanded. "Get your money if you can. This game's gonna ruin your appetite."

"What's wrong with him, George?" asked a perplexed Kenneth.

"You see that program?" George pointed. "I can't read a word of it from here."

"The game's over," Milo told Kenneth. "Sky's in slow-mo instant replay tonight."

"Maybe he's just a little senile," Kenneth joked. "I hear that's been going around lately."

"It doesn't matter what he's got," Milo lamented. "We may as well forfeit this one."

"Now, now, Milo," Kenneth calmed. "We've won nineteen in a row. I'm sure we can scrounge up one more win."

"Not tonight," Milo rejected. "Hagerstown's got our number."

"I can't read anybody's number without my program," George whined, still staring under the bleachers.

"Forget about it!" Milo shouted, as he grabbed a program from the man behind him. "Here! Here's a stupid program! Now, watch the warm-ups."

"Why, thank you," George said to the man behind him. "I've saved one of these from every game this year."

"What'll you wager this game, Milo?" Kenneth asked.

"Well, if King gets more than thirty points," Milo stated, "I'll, . . .I'll tell you what I'll do . . ."

When the buzzer sounded, sending the players to their benches, you could almost hear the entire gymnasium take a deep breath. In less than two hours, Wayne County could have its first undefeated team in regular season, or Hagerstown could have an upset.

The Bulldog huddle was tense. Reiser's hand shook, as he diagramed on the grease board. Most of the players were bouncing up and down on the balls of their feet or chewing gum, as if they were trying to extract some teeth. On the other hand, Skyler seemed aloof. He sat on the bench with both hands on his knees, staring straight down. It looked as if he were meditating. Reiser noticed Skyler wasn't himself, but he didn't dare ask what was wrong. He was afraid of what the answer might be.

As Reiser babbled on about the game plan, Marvin Statler, the School Custodian, came up to the huddle and tried to get Skyler's attention by waving his hands. Skyler didn't notice him, but all the other players and Reiser did.

"Dammit, Marv! What do you want?" Reiser shouted with a nervous anger. "We're trying to play a ballgame here!"

"Uh, . . nothin'," Marvin stuttered. "Never mind."

Marvin started to walk away, but he decided to stay with the huddle. As the PA Announcer began giving the starting line-ups, Marvin pulled Skyler from the huddle and put his hand up to his ear.

"This may sound crazy," Marvin hesitated, "but I think I saw your dad."

"You what!" Skyler lit up.

"Out in the hallway during the blackout," Marvin explained. "I'm sure it was him."

"I saw him, too," Skyler smiled, realizing he wasn't going crazy. "In the stands."

"That's great," Marvin smiled back. "He's come to see your last game here."

"And, at the other guard, Skyyyyyyyyy King!"

"Give 'em hell, Sky!" Marvin said slapping him on the back.

Skyler ran out on the court and nearly knocked down each of his teammates with high fives. Then he tried to dislocate their fingers. Reiser sighed with relief. He knew Skyler was ready to play. As the teams walked to center court, the two Hagerstown players assigned to guard Skyler, surrounded him.

"You guys ready to go?" Skyler smiled, as he put his arms around both of them. "We're not playing baseball, now!"

The two Tigers gave each other a puzzled look. It wouldn't be the last time Skyler would make them look stupid.

END OF AN ERA

The gym was empty. It took two hours after the game for everyone to filter out. Everyone, except one lone figure who sat top row, center court.

Coach Rieser sat in his small office next to the locker room. His feet rested on an open drawer, as he slumped lazily against the chair. After the game, while talking to the media, fans, and players, Reiser had chosen his words carefully. He let on, as if nothing significant had occurred. Inside, he knew better. Still, the emotional high was beginning to wear off, and reality began to settle in.

(What does a Coach do after leading his team to a perfect 20-0 record? Isn't an undefeated season the pinnacle? You've won a Richmond Sectional. Where do you go from here? Is it possible to win a Regional, a Semi-State, or, God forbid, A STATE? Could a small county school repeat Milan's 1954 win?)

As Reiser's brain began to scramble, he pulled his aching body out of the chair. He felt like he'd played four quarters against Hagerstown. Reiser didn't have time for pain, though. He had a celebration to attend, and he was an hour late. After securing the locker room, he strolled through the gym to get to his car. Reiser thought he heard a voice whispering from the top of the bleachers, but since all the other lights were out he couldn't see that high.

"Who's there?" Reiser shouted, trying not to sound scared.

The whispering stopped, and a long silence followed. "Just me, Coach." A familiar voice echoed.

Reiser rushed to the switch and turned on one of the upper lights. On the top row he saw a young man squinting at the bright intrusion. It was Sky King.

"What're you doing here?" Reiser said relieved.

"Oh, I live here Coach," Skyler answered. "Didn't you know that?"

"Were you talking to someone?" Reiser asked, not expecting the long pause.

"Do you see anyone else up here?" Skyler finally asked in his defense.

"Just a minute," Reiser said, as he began to ascend the bleachers. He took the steps two at a time until he was next to his player. "Don't you have a celebration to go to?"

"Yeah, everybody's meeting upstairs at Jody's, but it'll wait," Sky said.

"I guess, you caused quite a stir in the parking lot after the game," Reiser smiled.

"What do you mean?" questioned Skyler. "I wasn't even out there."

"Oh, Milo Wilkes lost another bet on us, so he was out there directing traffic in his boxer shorts," Reiser laughed.

"That guy will never learn," Skyler added.

"I'm glad you're still here," Reiser said. "I've been in the office thinking, and I'd like to thank you for making the last three years a piece of cake."

"You added a little icing yourself," Skyler complimented.

"No, not me," laughed Reiser. "All I've done is direct traffic. A player like you comes along about as often as Haley's Comet, and I'm just the lucky stiff who got to coach you. Actually, the last half-hour, I've been seriously considering retirement. We won the Richmond Sectional; we're undefeated this year, what's left to prove? Centerville will never see a team like this, or another player like you. I don't know. This may be my last hurrah."

"It's not over yet," Skyler said with confidence.

"It may not be for you, but I'm on the verge of stepping on the down elevator," Reiser joked.

"When you got this job three years ago, didn't you say it was a dream come true?" Skyler lectured.

"Absolutely," answered Reiser.

"Well, if these three years have been as easy as you say, then you haven't had to do much coaching," Skyler reasoned. "So, you need to take a team with no talent and turn them into a TEC contender. Earn some of that money they been paying you."

Reiser's face gradually turned to a smile, "Have you ever considered a career in Psychology?"

"I sure as heckle don't want to be a basketball coach," Skyler laughed.

"We better go on that note," Reiser laughed, as he slapped Skyler on the shoulder. "Jody's rarely stays open past eight, so we better take advantage of it."

As the two of them walked out the door, it marked the end of an era. The Lee Outland Gymnasium would never witness the likes of it again.

SKY REIGNS OVER HAGERSTOWN

The Saturday morning paper was later than usual, but there wasn't a sole in Centerville, who didn't already know the news.

"The entire population of Centerville came out to see a basketball game last night. What they witnessed was a piece of Hoosier Hysteria History.

In a flawless 24 minutes of action, Sky King, the high arching, southpaw guard for the Bulldogs, single handedly outscored both teams on the court. It was King 78, Hagerstown 71. It was King 78, the rest of the Bulldogs 59. It was a performance fit for, well, a King.

The Tigers received a momentary reprieve, when a blackout delayed the start of the game by 15 minutes, but when power was restored, King proceeded to turn the lights out on Hagerstown. From the opening tip, when King took a pass off a double-pick to sink the first of his 15 three-pointers, it was basketball at its best.

The Hagerstown Tigers (15-5) were playing for a tie in the TEC, and the best record in over 20 years. What they settled for was second place.

With his 78 points, King demolished his own school record by 16, and still had enough teamwork to dish out eight assists.

"I was inspired tonight," King understated after the game. "I can't explain it without sounding stupid."

That's exactly how the Tigers must have felt.

Mercifully, Centerville Coach Jim Reiser pulled King after three complete quarters, much to the displeasure of the hometown fans. Reiser was booed and verbally abused for not letting King conquer the century mark.

"I should've sat him down sooner," said a calm Reiser. "But, with the Sectional coming up, I wanted to give the starters as much playing time as possible. It was, without a doubt, the best performance ever by a high school athlete."

On the other hand, King had no objection to his bench time.

"I'm surprised he let us play that long," said King. "Coach always emphasizes team, not individual goals. Having an undefeated season is much more important than being high point man."

Centerville becomes the first Wayne County Team to register a perfect season, and considering how long it took, they may be the last.

"This team is not just me," King emphasized. "Everybody plays a big part. We've been playing together since fourth grade, so we know each other well."

The supporting cast included ten points and 21 assists by point-guard, Shane Best, who solidified his position as the all-time Bulldog assist leader by dishing out 14 of those to King. Emile George pulled down 17 rebounds in route to a 19-point performance. Buzzy Gray took time to drop in 11 markers somewhere between his eight steals, and Vance Worth was consistent in all departments while notching 19 points.

For the tigers, Larry Song scored a career-high 33 points, but it wasn't nearly enough to restrain the Bulldogs who were on a mission.

Centerville's next challenge will come in the Richmond Sectional, where they reign as champs. The Bulldogs will play Union City in the 8 PM Game, Tuesday night.

"Even though we knew we were capable of it, our goal was never to have an undefeated season," Reiser explained. "We just wanted to be in a position at the end of the season, where we were playing our best ball. After tonight, I guess you could say we're there," and How!"

BE TRUE TO YOUR SCHOOL

For the first time in decades, Richmond was excited about a Sectional. The Bulldog Championship last year had revitalized Centerville, but it also brought a new awareness to the city of Richmond. Now that the one-class system was reinstated, they wanted their Sectional back!

Since Richmond had lost only two seniors to graduation, their record improved to 17-3, including an NCC (North Central Conference) Championship. There was a drive on the team, which fans hadn't seen before. As a result, the support for the Devils reflected its inner strength.

There wasn't a store window in Richmond that didn't have a Devil logo or cheer. And, each cheer targeted a particular breed of canines. Bulldogs.

When Richmond let school out early the day before the Sectional for a pep rally, most students attended. What they witnessed included the chain sawing of a mock-Bulldog mascot to mix with all the other team mascots to concoct a tasty Red Devil goulash.

Richmond basketball was alive and well.

If the fan support in Richmond was a hit, then the support in Centerville was a grand slam. It wasn't every year Centerville had the opportunity to root on a Sectional champ. Especially, one with all five starters back.

Not only were businesses decorated, but houses, trees, lampposts, and anything that remained stationary for five minutes along Main Street, was painted royal blue and white. Businesses set up Sectional pools on the average winning margin of the Bulldogs, naming the winners of each game, or coming closest to Sky King's point total for the Tourney.

The School Board approved a motion, to let out one day of school for each tourney-victory. Naturally, the days would be added to the end of the school year, but no one cared. The town board passed a resolution to erect a new basketball goal and backboard in Maplewood Park for each victory in March Madness. They also declared March, "Bulldog Month" and promised to contract a Bulldog Memorial if they won the Sectional again.

The high school was an exploding crepe paper factory. Blue and white spider webbed its way across every hall, and remaining spaces were covered with posters. Even teachers got in the party mood by declaring Sectional time, "No homework week".

Every air of enthusiasm is not without its realm pessimist. Some fans had a hard time agreeing on the Bulldog fortunes.

"There's no way they'll repeat!" Milo shouted, as he lowered his hand on the restaurant table. "It can't be done."

"Oh, fiddle farts, Milo," George answered, as he waved his fingers in front of Milo's face. "All five starters are back from last years team. How could they lose?"

"That don't mean diddly!" Milo countered. "We're talking about Richmond here, and you don't beat Richmond two years in a row in the Sectional, AT Richmond."

"Fill us in on your theory, Milo," Kenneth said with a smile. "Have you calculated this on a slide rule."

"There ain't no calculatin' to it," Milo shot back. "It's the law of averages. You can't beat the law of averages. Either that, or they'll pay off the referees to screw us."

"And, if that fails, they'll have snipers strategically placed in the stands to pick off our players when they go in for lay-ups," Kenneth chuckled.

"They could put that glass lid on our basket, so every shot bounces back out," George added.

"Joke if you want, boys, but mark my words. Centerville's goin' down," Milo said grimly.

"Put your mouth on the line, Milo," Kenneth goaded. "You can't get off that easy."

"If Centerville wins, I'll . . . I'll push you down Main Street in a wheel barrow at noon, . . . while wearing a dress," Milo threatened.

Kenneth and George looked at each other and smiled.

"Deal," said Kenneth, stretching out his hand.

BE PREPARED

As Coach Reiser watched the last practice before the Sectional, he felt an insecure apprehension. One wrong turn, one hard elbow, or one errant pass could end the Bulldogs chances. Still, Reiser knew there was no letting up. It takes a lot of ingredients to make a winning team. The most important one is luck.

"That's enough!" Reiser yelled with a sigh of relief. "Everybody sit down!"

"It's a miracle," Buzzy said. "He's letting us off ten minutes early."

"Don't get your hopes up," Vance responded. "We could still run suicides."

The ballplayers sat on the bleachers, waiting for their traditional post-practice pep talk. Only, this time, there was no joking around. Reiser paced back and forth in front of his players.

"Is he expecting one of us to have a baby?" Shane whispered.

The Team Managers gathered up the sweaty towels and basketballs, trying to make a quick exit. One Manager dropped his load of basketballs, and the bounces rang out like gunshots in a tunnel. Reiser damned the Manager with his piercing stare.

"Sorry," the Manager squeaked as he retrieved the balls.

Reiser turned back to his team, but still couldn't find the words. He was a scared champion, and the thought of being dethroned nauseated him. Last year, his team was the underdog, and everyone was taken by surprise. This year, every team in the Sectional would be gunning for them.

"I don't want an answer to this question," Reiser yelled, causing his players to jump, "but what do you boys have left to accomplish? What's left to prove? You've won a Sectional Title. That hasn't been done in seventy years! Now, you've played a 20-game season without losing. Shouldn't you be content? Can't we all go home?"

"Let me tell you a story of three words. Satisfaction. Complacency. And, Pride. When you become satisfied with your position in life, then you're destined to stay there. If you're satisfied with an undefeated season, then that will be the highlight of your year. We're done!

"Complacency will get you killed. Go ahead. Be cocky. Be self-assured.

Don't worry about Union City until they hit a half-court shot that beats you. Every team in this Tourney wants to beat us, because we're Champs. You become complacent, and they'll do it.

"Pride will keep you achieving. If you have enough pride in yourself and your team to do your best every time, then you're destined to move one notch higher. Have the pride to not be satisfied with your last game, or complacent about your season, and go out and achieve greatness. You guys pick the word you like best."

Reiser walked away from his team, as he ran his fingers through his hair. He flung the locker room door open, causing it to smash into the concrete wall. None of the players moved. They didn't know if he was mad or nervous. After about a minute of silence, one player broke the silence with a loud fart.

"What the hell was that?" Vance yelled in disgust.

"It was a kiss for you," Buzzy replied.

"Yeah, and it tastes like your girlfriend, too," Vance added.

"Don't you wish you knew?" Buzzy defended.

"Hey, Emile," asked Skyler, "What word did you pick?"

"Meat-loaf!" Emile shouted. "I'm hungry as hell."

"You're meat ain't been loafin' all year," Vance added. "Just ask the cheerleaders."

"Hey guys, before we leave, maybe we should do a cheer or something, so Coach knows we're serious," Skyler suggested. "Let's get in a huddle and put our hands together."

"That's gay!" Shane kidded.

"Then you should feel right at home, Shane," Buzzy ridiculed.

"Shut-up, you homo!" Shane shot back.

"C'mon, guys," Skyler encouraged. "Let's get this over with. On three, we'll give a cheer."

"What're we gonna say?" asked Emile.

"Everybody just say what's on your mind," Skyler suggested. "Yell for the one thing you want most out of this Tourney. Ready. One, two, three . . ."

"SEX!"

THE SPIRIT WORM RULES

The sign on the gym door read, "Pep Rally 2:15", but no one needed a reminder. After the 2:10 bell, it was an instant migration to the gym.

The Pep Rally was an assortment of skits, unnecessary introductions, and acknowledgments. Emile played a priest, who exorcised the gym of the "Red Devil" virus. Shane hunted down a Union City Indian while blindfolded, and plucked his feathers. And, Skyler dressed as a well-endowed cheerleader, who had the hots for the Bulldog mascot.

Even Coach Reiser got into the act. He had to lie on the gym floor while the "Victory Worm" slowly and methodically made its way over the top of him. The worm consisted of ten kids under a string of bed sheets, wearing flippers on their feet. If one foot of the worm descended on top of the poor Coach, it meant certain doom in the Sectional. If all the feet cleared, it symbolized a tourney title. Just as the rear end of the worm was preparing to scale the prone Coach, one leg hoisted in the air and deluged him with a seltzer spray. To add insult to injury, the worm then squatted and dumped several mud logs on his face. But, the worm's feet never touched the Coach. Despite relieving himself, the worm had spoken.

GETTING DOWN TO BUSINESS

The bus-ride to Richmond was short, quiet, and uneventful. The Bulldogs were the Blues Brothers of Centerville, Indiana. They were on a mission from God.

There was little commotion in the locker room, except for a brief search involving Buzzy's jock strap.

"Just use a thimble instead," suggested Vance. "Why waste all that material on such a small pecker?"

Reiser was subdued, and his pre-game speech was brief and to the point.

"Union City doesn't belong on the same court with you guys, but if you get beat tonight, then all our names are gonna be shit," Reiser said bluntly. "Let's go warm up."

Apparently, the Bulldogs had a strong disliking for shit. By the end of the first quarter, the game was over. Centerville jammed in 34 points in the first eight minutes, while Union City barely mustered ten. Sky King only accounted for 19 of those points since he had a bad first quarter. He missed two out of ten shots.

Three nights later, Centerville had to face Hagerstown for the third time. No matter how bad you beat a team, Reiser knew it was difficult to beat them three times in one season. He was nervous. So nervous he had trouble urinating. Actually, stopping the urine was the problem. Reiser dribbled on the front of his pants, and in a feeble attempt to clean it up, he made the spot bigger. He spent warm ups and the entire first quarter with his suit jacket draped over his moist leg.

Aside from needing a diaper, the rest of the evening was drip free for Reiser. King canned 67, and Hagerstown was toasted by halftime. Alana even won the game ball in a raffle.

Once again, Skyler and his troupe sat out the fourth quarter. And once again, the Bulldog fans let their disapproval be known. After the game, a reporter asked Reiser how he handled the harsh treatment from his own fans.

"If I take in anymore "boos", they'll have to give me a Breathalyzer before

I leave here."

The stage was set for the Championship Game. For the second year in a row, Centerville squared off against Richmond. The Red Devils had disposed of their opponents, almost as easily as the Bulldogs. Beating Northeastern by 45, and Randolph Southern by 33.

Unlike last year, Richmond had established itself as a team in contention. They finished first in the NCC, the strongest conference in Indiana, just ahead of the Marion Giants. They were rated eighth in the State, and their 19-3 record indicated they were survivors.

Richmond was a hungry team. Last year in the Sectional they'd been embarrassed on their home court. Richmond was out for revenge.

Coach Reiser did something he'd never done before. After victories on Tuesday and Friday night, and with a championship game only hours away, he scheduled a practice on Saturday afternoon. Nothing serious. Just one last chance to prepare for history. None of his players complained about coming in early.

The practice session didn't last long. Once word got around, it became a community event. First, came the cheerleaders. Then, parents of the players filed in. Students came in a steady stream to get an early start on the celebration. But, when townspeople began showing up, Reiser knew practice was over. What started out as an instructional practice, turned into an impromptu pep rally.

Reiser was amazed to watch all the people in the Gym milling around and talking about the upcoming game. Never had there been an event in the Town that could bring so many people from so many age groups in one place at the same time. Reiser's Basketball Team had done something that no laws or ordinances could ever do. It had brought the town together.

Before ending the big party, Reiser turned on the PA system and gave his flock one last sermon. "I'm not one to make promises of victory. But, with support like this, there's no way in HELL we're going to lose tonight!"

SHORT TRIP. LONG NIGHT

Five miles separates Centerville High School from Richmond High School. In most Februarys, it was nothing more than a long walk to the guillotine. This five-mile jaunt had an alternate destination in mind. The Bulldogs were defending champs, and they carried a confidence no one thought imaginable.

Five miles is a short trip, but sometimes you want it to last forever. Everyone in Centerville wanted to savor it. There was a seventy-year gap between their first and second Sectional Championship. In the last one hundred years, Centerville had only notched four Sectional wins over Richmond. With those odds, very few people would ever see it happen again.

This five-mile trip was not a caravan. It was an event. The Wayne County sheriffs and the Centerville police closed down the eastbound lanes of National Road. It took seven officers to direct the traffic out of the crammed parking lot. Led by a John Deere tractor decorated to look like a Bulldog, it took a half-hour to make that five-mile run.

"If a thief ever blew a great opportunity, it was on that night," Kenneth Hatfield would later say. "Nobody was minding the store. They coulda walked off with the whole damn town and no one would've noticed."

It was suspected that anyone with dishonest intentions was outside Tiernan Center scalping tickets. Some were going for $75 a pop.

Once inside the gym, it was unimaginable how the scalpers even possessed any tickets. It was standing room only. The first sellout since Tiernan Center was built in 1985.

Even the fans of the teams who were eliminated came to the championship game. It wasn't often a county school had a better than average chance of winning the Sectional. They weren't about to miss it.

"This is Chet Brimly with the Y-95 pre-game show, and right now I have with me Jim Reiser, the Coach of the Centerville Bulldogs. Coach Reiser, your Team is the reigning Champion of this Tourney, you have all five starters back from last year, and you're coming off an undefeated season. How do you feel going into this game?"

"Well, Chet, after listening to you, overconfident!" Reiser joked. "But, you'll notice I haven't asked for the trophy yet. We have thirty-two minutes yet to play in this tourney, and unless Richmond forfeits, we're going to have a hard fought battle."

"Last year, you blew the Devils out in the fourth quarter, yet once again you're billed as the underdog. Does that bother you?" Chet questioned.

"Not in the least," Reiser responded. "The last twenty-two games we've played, we've been the favorite, and it's scared the heckle out of me. There's nothing worse than expecting to get something and having it taken away. I like the role of underdog. It takes the burden of winning off your shoulders and you can go out and make the other team sweat."

"What happens if the Red Devils shut down your Sky King scoring machine?"

"I guess I'll call the Maytag repairman," quipped Reiser. "You have to remember, Sky is second on the team in assists. If they put three men on him, there's two guys wide open. I love to see Sky in those situations."

"With the kind of season you've had, is it surprising you're not rated any higher than eighteenth in the State?"

"I've never put much faith into polls, sportswriters, or radio announcers. Sorry about that, Chet," Joked Rieser. "Our position makes no difference to me. In fact, I'm glad we're at the bottom. It's the kiss of death to hit number one."

"No team other than Richmond has won two of these Sectionals in a row. Would you like to go down in history as the only Coach to do it?"

"Yeah, you could put my name right next to Napoleon, and Alexander the Great."

"It would be a great feather in your cap, though."

"Don't start plucking any chickens yet," Reiser downplayed. "I was just in the right place at the right time, and if I don't cause any collisions while directing traffic, then there's no way we'll lose."

"What do you think of this crowd?"

"This is Indiana basketball," said a proud Reiser. "When we had the four class system, you couldn't even fill the lower level of bleachers for a Sectional Championship. Now, we have all six schools waiting to see what happens. Fortunately, most of them are on our side."

"And, if you don't win tonight . . .?"

"Every able bodied sole in Centerville will help me pack," Reiser responded.

FULL MONTY

As Charles Dickens might've put it, the locker rooms were a contrast of, "the best of times and the worst of times."

Richmond dressed methodically as a mist of tension lingered within every breath. Petty bickering over bench space and senior rights was occasionally preempted by an irate chant of "Kill King!"

On the other side of the gym, naked bodies hung from chin-up bars as they dodged the snaps of a wet towel.

"Don't aim for the philberts!" one nudist cried. "I've got a family life to look forward to."

"That's not what your girlfriend says!" hollered Vance.

Another Bulldog pulled his athletic supporter over his head.

"Hey, Emile, I always thought your nose was the same size as your penis," Buzzy commented.

"You oughta know, Buzz!" yelled Emile. "You've had your hands down my shorts enough."

"Hey, guys, no gay talk, please," Vance whined.

"Wait a minute, guys!" shouted Skyler, as an idea popped into his head. "Here's an exercise my dad and his cousins used to pull. Everybody line up." Skyler did his best to direct traffic. "Now, ready. Drop those jocks and jog in place!" Skyler did a high-knee jog as he stood stark naked in front of the team. "C'mon guys, make those dickies bounce."

All the players were laughing hysterically as they watched the usually subdued Skyler look foolish.

"C'mon guys!" Skyler encouraged. "You'd do it for the cheerleaders, wouldn't you?"

One by one, the team began dropping their jocks and joining their leader in a bare-butt run around the locker room.

"That's more like it!" yelled Skyler. "Now, sway from side to side. C'mon, side to side. That's right. Slap that baby against those legs. If you slap the leg of the guy next to you, then consider yourself a real man!"

As most of the team swayed in naked synchronization, Coach Reiser came in the locker room. A mad scramble ensued, as all the players tried to find their jocks in a hurry and put them on. Reiser stood in disbelief at the door. He rubbed his nose and eyes with his hand, trying to figure out what to say or do.

"I don't want to know," Reiser finally said. "It doesn't matter to me what kind of pre-game ritual this is. Just so it works. But, I would suggest putting on your shorts, because we're due on the court. NOW!"

As the team hurried to finish dressing, a few mistakes were made. Dusty Meyer, the tenth man on the squad, held up a jock strap that could've wrapped around his waist twice.

"I've either shrunk, or I've got Emile's jock," Dusty said with a smile.

SHOWDOWN

The eight thousand plus fans in the packed Tiernan Center cared little about what went on in the locker rooms. What they'd been waiting for was the tip-off.

Emile slapped the ball to the left of Skyler, who was back defending the Richmond goal. As Skyler hustled to run down the ball, an over-zealous Richmond player slammed into him in mid air. Skyler went sprawling backwards. He kept his balance momentarily with a few awkward steps, but gravity took over and hurled him blindly toward a collision.

It all seemed so humorous at the time. The clown-like steps, followed by a silly Pratt fall. But, no Centerville fan was laughing when Skyler landed headfirst onto the edge of a metal bleacher.

The clock stopped at 7:58. So had the heart of everyone clamoring for a second Sectional upset. In two seconds, Tiernan Center went from a New Year's Eve party to a wake. The silence was deafening.

The entire gym was on its feet, waiting for fate to run its course.

"Oh, my God!" shouted a lady amid a sea of royal blue.

On the other side of the gym, a high school student with a red and white face, raised his fist triumphantly in the air. "Yesss!"

"He's all right," Alana wished, as she folded her arms in denial.

"He's not moving," worried Diane, as she held her hands over her heart.

"He's a tough kid," added Renee. "He'll get up."

The Red Devil who sent Skyler toward the bleacher stood defiantly facing his prey with his fist clinched at his side. For a brief moment, he waited for a decision. A standing eight-count wouldn't do. It must be a TKO. As the trainer arrived at Skyler's side, the Red Devil turned and strutted away. He was greeted with high fives from two of his teammates.

Coach Reiser was in shock. He stood in front of the bench with his hands on his hips, but he knew he couldn't show fear. Reiser's face was hot. Beads of sweat were forming on his forehead to squelch the flames. His hair follicles were standing on end, and he felt certain he looked like a man who'd been electrocuted.

"We're dead!" lamented Dusty. "If he's out, we're dead!"

"Shut-up, you guys!" Reiser yelled. "Shut the hell up!"

Reiser finally decided to walk over to where Skyler was. The other four starters were huddled around their teammate waiting for a verdict. Reiser wanted to divert their attention. As he reached the halfway-point, he could see Skyler moving his arms and legs.

"Coach. You need to get a sub in the game, or else we'll have to charge you with a time-out," A referee coldly intercepted Reiser, before he could get to Skyler.

"What's the call?" Reiser asked, happy to have a diversion.

"What'd you say?" the referee responded.

"What's the call?" Reiser repeated.

"We've got red ball," said the referee. "White carried it out of bounds."

"Carried it out of bounds!" shouted Reiser. "He was bulldozed by that son-of-a-bitch to get him out of the game."

Vance and Emile heard their Coach's complaint and got up to lend him moral support. In fact, everyone in attendance heard the Coach and waited for the response.

"Coach. Either attend to your player or go sit on the bench," the referee said calmly.

"How about a foul! An intentional foul!" Reiser demanded. "You should throw him out of the game for a hit like that! He's not even a regular starter!"

Skyler was sitting up. He was holding the top of his head, but he was sitting up. Buzzy and Shane got up to join their Coach. Reiser's plan was working. With Skyler getting up, and his entire team raving mad over a flagrant foul, the Red Devils would see a Hell like they'd never seen before.

"Don't start like this, Coach," threatened the referee. "We've got a whole game to go, and it'd be a shame to start it with a "T".

Reiser felt a renewed confidence. He was gaining momentum with every word.

"A technical!" screamed Reiser. "Why don't you give them a goddam technical?"

The referee made a "T" with his two hands and signaled the official scorer. "We've got a technical foul on the Centerville bench!" he said, turning back to Reiser. "One more Coach and you can spend the game in the locker room."

"You dumb ass!" shouted Buzzy. "Your pea-brain is smaller than the one in that whistle."

Once again the referee made a "T". Reiser knew things were getting out of hand. He grabbed Buzzy by the back of the shirt and pulled him away.

"Sit down!" Reiser yelled. "All of you sit down!"

The crowd was getting into it. Richmond was yelling for Reiser to take a seat, and the rest of the gym was giving the referee hell. "Homer" was a popular term.

"Coach, I suggest you get your team under control so we can get started," said the referee.

"I'll take care of my team," Reiser pointed his finger angrily. "Just keep your eyes open out here."

With the trainer holding his left arm, Skyler shuffled up to the Coach. He still had his hand on his head, but Reiser seemed unconcerned.

"Let me see," Reiser said pulling Skyler's hand from his head.

Blood rolled down Skyler's face and into his eyes. He swooned forward, into the arms of his Coach. The blood covered Reiser's white shirt like an exploding tube of paint on a fresh canvass.

"Jesus Christ!" shouted the referee.

"Give me the towel!" Reiser screamed to the trainer.

It was too late. The trainer had already vomited in the towel. The Centerville bench cleared. A lady in the first row fainted. And, Sky King was unconscious.

IT HURTS ME MORE THAN YOU

{I remember one time when you were five years old, Skyler. We were outside on the gravel drive playing a game to ten baskets. You were upset because I was beating you. One time, I stole the ball from you and you stomped your feet and yelled, "dang it Daddy, quit it!" I laughed so hard I nearly wet my pants.

Anyway, the next time you had the ball, you tried driving around the right, but you slipped on the gravel and went down hard.

I always hated it when one of my kids got hurt. When your aunt and mom were little it used to drive me crazy whenever they'd cry. I never knew what to do. I'd always freeze and get mad at the fact it even happened. I didn't want to make wimps out of them, so I'd just make a joke out of it. Then they'd get mad at me, and we'd have to make up later.

One time, I was throwing softballs to your aunt Renee. She and your mom were two of the best softball players ever to hit Centerville. Renee threw a ball past me, so I pretended a player was trying to hit an inside-the-park home run.

"She's rounding third and heading for home!" I yelled in my best play-by-play voice. "And, here's the throw to the plate!"

My throw was hard and a little low, so Renee crouched down to dig it out. It took a bad hop and popped straight up into her nose. I swear my heart stopped.

As her nose bled like a fountain, I couldn't hold her close enough, or tell her how sorry I was. I felt like the lowest form of human.

Renee got a swollen nose and a black eye out of the deal, and I actually think she was proud of it. Like a battle wound that signified she'd been through the softball wars.

But, after you slipped on the gravel, I tried to play it down like nothing. I think I even picked up the loose basketball and drove in for the winning lay-up. Then, as I cheered, I called you a wimp for not getting up.

Well, I got that sick feeling again, when I rolled you over and there was that hunk of glass sticking in your calf. I couldn't love you enough or apologize enough for letting you get hurt. Even though both incidents weren't my fault, I felt guilty and helpless, as I watched both of you bleed.

This time, Skyler, I can do something about it. If you'll have the courage to help me, I can get you back in the game. I know you won't give up, because it's not in your nature. Just remember, things don't always go your way, and it's not a weakness to look for help. Just promise me you won't give up, Skyler. Promise me, Skyler. Skyler. Wake up!}

Skyler opened his eyes like an alarm had gone off in his head. The team trainer and manager were looking over him, as if he were a corpse. The bleeding had stopped, and the trainer held an ice bag on his head.

"I promise, Dad," Skyler whispered, as he slowly sat up. "I promise."

"Hold on there, Skyler," the trainer said, trying to hold onto the ice. "We just got the bleeding stopped. Don't do anything to get it flowing again."

Skyler looked slowly around the room. He eyed the manager, then the trainer, then the manager again. Finally, he looked down at his blood-soaked jersey.

"What happened?" he whined on the verge of tears.

"You're all right," the trainer assured him. "You cut your head open on the bleachers. Don't worry, we got an ambulance coming to take you to the hospital."

"It'll take too long at the hospital!" Skyler said instinctively. "I've got to get back on the driveway, now."

The trainer and manager gave each other a puzzled stare.

"Where's everybody at?" Skyler worried.

"They're still on the court," said the manager. "It's probably the second quarter by now."

"I've got to get out there!" Skyler jumped to his feet.

"Hold on!" the trainer yelled. "You've got a gash in your head that won't quit."

Skyler raced to the mirror and looked at his wound. "Oh, God!" he sighed. "You got any gauze?"

"Sure," responded the trainer.

"Any tape?" Skyler interrogated.

"Sure," echoed the trainer.

"Let's patch it up," Skyler recommended, as he sat down on the bench.

"I can't put tape over all that hair," lamented the trainer.

"Then get the scissors and cut out what you don't need," hurried Skyler.

"C'mon, we don't have much time."

The trainer got his equipment and began his repair job.

"Go see what the score is," Skyler said to the manager, as he pushed him toward the door. "And, see how much time's left!"

As the trainer put the finishing touches on Skyler's racing stripe, two ambulance attendants came in the locker room.

"Somebody call for an ambulance?" one of them asked.

The trainer looked at the two men, not knowing what to say.

"They need you in the other locker room," Skyler said calmly. "They'll be some Richmond bodies to take out as soon as this game's over."

"There's two minutes left in the second quarter!" shouted the manager, as he busted through the door. "The score's 46-32.

Skyler didn't have to ask who was ahead. "Shit!" He yelled, as he jumped off the bench and crashed through the door, hardly bothering to touch the floor. He had half a game to keep his dream alive.

As Skyler came out of the tunnel, the first thing he noticed was the scoreboard: 48 to 32, and Richmond had the ball. He wanted to run like a madman toward the scorer's bench and report in immediately, but he stayed calm and quickly walked to the bench.

As Skyler approached, a few scattered cheers began to emanate from the crowd. The farther he went, it followed him like a wave, getting louder with each step. Reiser noticed his stars return when the players on the bench stood up and went berserk. Reiser felt like doing a back handspring, but he kept his cool.

"How you doing?" Reiser shouted in Skyler's ear.

"Not bad," he replied. "I think I'm ready."

"Nice hairdo! There's just a minute left. No need putting you in now," Reiser reasoned. "Have a seat and wait for halftime."

Skyler sat down to his awkward situation. He'd never been on the bench with his team behind. Never, in his life. He was used to only seeing the bench in the fourth quarter with a thirty-point lead. Skyler sat uneasily on the bench, sweating from the anxiety.

On the other hand, Skyler's return began to affect the play on the court. One by one, his teammates caught a glimpse of his presence, and the relief of knowing he was back was enough to raise the level of their play another notch. To Richmond, it was an enormous letdown.

With 1:20 left in the half, a Red Devil who'd just seen Skyler, threw a lazy pass to a teammate. Vance Worth intercepted the sphere, took it the length of the court, and kissed it off the glass.

Richmond missed a 10-footer, and the Bulldogs started a fast break. When the defense cut off the lane, Emile fed the ball to Shane on the right of the key. He rattled in a three-pointer.

After a back-door lay-up for Richmond, Shane banked in a three from the top of the lane. Every Centerville fan smiled about that one.

With thirty seconds on the clock, Richmond decided to go for one shot. As they worked the ball around the perimeter, Reiser screamed "FISH". Shane yelled it out to his teammates, and Vance repeated.

When the clock hit :15 seconds, Richmond made their move. The Bulldogs denied the feed inside, so with :07 left, the Red Devil guard panicked and fired up an awkward 18-footer. As it spun in and out, Emile grabbed the ball at rim level. Before he hit the ground, Emile fired a backwards, two-handed pass over his head, towards the Centerville goal. Shane caught the ball at half court with three seconds left. With two Devils in hopeless pursuit, Shane laid the ball over the front of the rim.

After the buzzer, the Bulldogs were celebrating as if they'd won the game. It had been a good run, but they were still behind 50 to 42. Reiser scolded his team for their antics and reminded them they still had sixteen minutes to play.

There was no half-time talk. Reiser knew he couldn't say anything in the locker room that would match the adrenalin rush displayed on the court. He didn't want his team becoming complacent.

Reiser fought a half-time show of Devilettes for space on the court. He eventually won out amid a chorus of "boos" from the Richmond section. It didn't bother him, though. He'd been booed by his own fans earlier.

Reiser had some subs rebound for Skyler, as he shot around the perimeter. None of his shots were falling. In less than ten minutes, Reiser had to decide whether to go with Skyler, or stick with who was playing.

"Well, we got Sky back, but we're still going to lose," lamented Milo.

"We're on our way back, Milo," Kenneth challenged. "That boy you hired to take out Sky didn't get the job done."

"Did you do that just to win your bet?" questioned George.

"I did no such thing," Milo denied. "I just knew Centerville could never win two Sectionals in a row."

"Don't be gloating yet," warned Kenneth. "In fact, you may want to go out and buy a Regional ticket about now."

There were two minutes before the start of the third quarter. Skyler walked over to the bench and sat down by himself. He was a little dizzy still, and his shot was off. His team was in trouble.

"I've got to score if we're going to win," Skyler thought out loud. "I've got to score. I've got to score."

Skyler bent over, putting his forehead in the palms of his hands. He felt so light headed.

{What do you mean, YOUR team? This is the Centerville Bulldogs. Not the SKYLER Bulldogs. One man doesn't make a TEAM. You've got four other players on the court. Use them! You want personal glory; go play tennis! You want to win ballgames? You need to pass. You need to pass.}

"You gonna pass out?" asked Emile, as he grabbed Skyler on the shoulder.

Skyler looked up slowly and in a daze. "I'll pass more," he said. "Emile, have the guys come over here."

When the rest of the team got to the bench, Skyler filled them in.

"Shane, if you pass me the ball, I want you to cut to the basket. Your man's going to double-team me, so you'll be wide open." Skyler coached. "Buzzy, don't worry about setting any picks for me. See if you can get Emile open off the baseline. And, Vance, I'm going to set a few picks for you, so be ready. If I've got two men on me, there's no way your man's going to be able to follow you through the middle. Let's do this right guys."

Everyone finger wrestled and slapped hands, just as Reiser arrived at their meeting.

"That's great!" Reiser approved. "We need to get fired up here. Sky, I've got you in, but I need you to look for the open man. They'll be expecting you to shoot, but it looks like your shots off. You might even set a few picks out there, too."

Everyone on the team got a silly grin on their faces.

"What's wrong?" Reiser said perturbed.

They all burst out laughing. "Coach, we been around you too long," Emile chuckled.

Centerville was down by eight. Their star player was injured. And, they were playing Richmond. It seemed peculiar for the fans to see their Bulldogs laughing in the huddle. But, there were those who could interpret what it meant.

"Dammit!" muttered Milo at the sight. "There's another damn bet I'm going to lose."

Both Coach and player knew what they were talking about. With two minutes left in the third quarter, Sky King still had no points. He did have seven assists. His last one was a perfect feed to Shane streaking down the middle, which knotted the score at 67 all. The Richmond Coach had seen enough. Time out.

As the Devils plotted to play a straight up man-to-man, the Bulldogs were ready to gamble on their star.

On the next three Centerville possessions, Skyler swished three baskets. All from twenty-two feet. After an Emile miss, Richmond finally canned a 15-footer with thirty seconds on the clock.

Reiser knew better than to call for one shot. With Skyler's past history, it would be a waste. The Bulldogs worked the ball around for only ten seconds until they found Skyler open from downtown Richmond. His 27-footer exploded from his cannon-like arm as if it would ascend forever. It reentered the earth's atmosphere and found nothing, but net.

Richmond squeaked in a tip-in at the buzzer to save face, but they were now down 79-71 with one quarter to play.

"Don't lose your focus," Reiser warned in the huddle. "It's far from over. If we let up, they'll catch us. Take whatever you can get."

The Centerville fans were ready for a rout. It never materialized. As Reiser feared, their concentration abandoned them. Skyler missed his next four shots, and combined with a handful of turnovers, it added up to a Richmond rally.

After a long uphill battle, a Red Devil dunk at the three-minute mark tied the game. The Red Sea was on the rise.

There were three ties and three lead changes the rest of the way. It was a fan's delight and a Coach's nightmare. Centerville found themselves with the ball, and a one-point deficit. Forty seconds on the clock. Once again, it was not their intention to go for a last shot. Still, they worked twenty-five seconds off before Skyler found Emile wide open in the lane. Skyler was double-teamed, but he fired a perfect no-look pass. It sailed right through Emile's hands and out of bounds. It was Richmond's ball.

The Red Devil Coach called timeout to set his escape route. The Bulldogs were desperate.

"Oh, God, guys! I'm sorry! I'm sorry!" Emile apologized nearly in tears.

"You're not sorry for anything!" Reiser scolded. "We've got a game to win and you're the one who's going to do it! So, get your head out of your ass!"

"My fault, Emile," consoled Skyler. "The pass was too hard."

"That's great," ridiculed Reiser. "We can kiss and make up in the locker room. Now, listen! Stay man-to-man. We need to steal the inbounds, or foul immediately. Make sure you go for the ball so they don't call intentional foul. Believe it, guys. I'm not going home a loser!"

Richmond got the pass inbounds, and even ran off seven seconds before Buzzy could foul their center. As they lined up for a one-and-one, Centerville called time out.

If Richmond missed the first free throw, Centerville had eight seconds to get the ball down the court and score a bucket for the win. If Richmond made the first free throw and missed the second, Centerville could go for a tying "two". If Richmond made both free throws, Centerville had to shoot a three-pointer to tie. Everyone stared at Skyler when that situation was discussed.

The two teams lined up again for the free throw. Again, Reiser called time out.

The same plans were discussed for the second time.

A third time, the teams went to the free throw lane to decide the game. Time out, Centerville.

"Coach, that's your last timeout," the referee told Reiser.

"Real classy, Reiser," the Richmond Coach snarled.

"Class has nothing to do with it," Reiser shot back.

Reiser was so nervous in the huddle he could barely speak.

"Make . . .make damn sure we. . . get this rebound! We have to have the ball!" Reiser commanded. "Believe it. Believe it, and do it. Let's go!"

For the fourth time, Richmond and Centerville prepared to end the game. Richmond had two players at half-court to defend the Centerville goal, and two players on the foul lane. Centerville had all five players on the lane, praying for one last rebound.

After what seemed like an eternity, the free-throw attempt was in the air. Richmond hoped to build on their one-point lead. It bounced off the rim.

Emile pulled down the rebound and passed it out on the left side to Shane. Skyler broke down the right side, and Emile trailed up the middle.

Two defenders met Shane at half-court, but a behind-the-back dribble and a quick cut right left them jockless. As two other Red Devils came to cut off Shane, there were four ticks left. He fired a pass to a wide-open Skyler on the right side. One step in front of the three-point line.

Skyler went high in the air for the shot. A last second shot. Four red bodies streaked to block the attempt. None of them would make it. As Skyler hit the pinnacle of his jump, he saw Emile flashing through the lane. {Pass} For the second time, he fired a bullet. Emile caught this one, about rim high. Without wasting any motion, Emile rammed it through the hoop on his way up. As the buzzer sounded, Emile knew he was never coming down.

Emile did come down, and was tackled to the floor by the entire team. The student body joined the pileup and nearly crushed Emile beneath its weight. Red bodies lay strewn across the battlefield. Red fans slumped back in their seats. What had been the anticipation of an 18-foot shot with a 50-50 chance of going in, turned out to be a high percentage dunk.

While the Red was bleeding its way across Tiernan Center, the Royal Blue bounced off the rafters like so many overheated kernels of popcorn. Anyone who had a shred of blue on his or her body was out on the gym floor. All of them wanted to be a part of the history they'd just seen.

Even though this was Centerville's second Sectional Title, it didn't dampen the enthusiasm. A small school was never supposed to win a one-point game against Richmond. It had been a war, and "David" had slain "Goliath" again. Centerville waited seventy years for a second title, and now they had two in a row. Everyone celebrated as if it were his last day on Earth. They knew this would never happen again.

Reiser was last seen bouncing down the sidelines like a kangaroo on a pogo stick. He didn't care the Richmond Coach abandoned the post-game handshake and headed straight for the sanctity of the locker room.

After his rocket pass to Emile, Skyler had slid back on his rear end. He watched the shot, heard the buzzer, then flopped on the court in relief. It took the crowd a few moments to get to him, but as they hoisted him on their shoulders to honor their basketball god, they could see Skyler was bawling like a baby.

At first his teammates didn't know what to make of Skyler's reaction. Was he hurt? Was he happy? In twelve years of school, there was only one other time they'd seen him cry.

"Are you okay?" Shane questioned Skyler, as he gave him a hug.

"Oh, man! This is the greatest!" Skyler exclaimed between sobs.

"What's wrong, Skyler?" Emile jumped in to ask.

"You okay?" Vance added.

As Buzzy and the others joined in with their concern, Skyler gained his composure.

"Ever since we won last years Sectional, I've been scared," confessed Skyler. "I thought that might be our high point. I didn't want to graduate a loser. Everybody knew if we could do it once, we should be able to do it again. I've been scared to death of letting everyone down."

Once again, Skyler sobbed. And, like a chain reaction, the rest of the team followed suit. With their arms around each other, they huddled and cried.

Reiser finally broke away from the crowd with his life. He gave his team a few peaceful moments together, and then he interjected.

"All of you earned this," Reiser said, as he joined the huddle. "You'll be remembered as long as basketball is played in Indiana. This may be just a game, but it's a precedent that will follow all of you for the rest of your lives."

Reiser huddled with his team for another minute, while pandemonium reigned around them.

In the stands, a few small skirmishes erupted between opposing fans. One lucky punch knocked out the two front teeth of a Centerville boy. Maybe one day, he would have a son, who would have a grandson, who would lead his team to a Sectional Title.

"Coach Reiser! Coach Reiser!" Radioman, Chet Brimly persisted. "What's your feelings on your win tonight?"

"I'm pissed off!" Reiser kidded, causing the Radio Station to bleep him. "I had a Scrabble Tournament I wanted to go to next week."

"What?" Chet asked, perplexed.

"Just kidding, Chet," Reiser laughed. "You may as well shoot me, cause I'll never be any happier than right now."

"Is this win better than your 21-point victory last year?" Chet queried.

"Having two Sectional Titles is like having two children," Reiser philosophized. "I love them both the same. It's just that this one was born, so it's getting all my attention."

"Emile George!" Chet wondered. "You slammed those last two points home. Were you worried about missing that shot?"

"I didn't have time to think about it," Emile laughed. "I was just going in for a possible rebound, and all of a sudden, Sky fires this pass at me. The shot was easy. I was worried about catching it."

"Sky King. Why did you pass the ball instead of shooting it?"

"My shooting percentage for last-second shots is pretty poor," Skyler joked. "I'd much rather have Emile be the goat instead of me."

"Coach. Final thoughts on the game," Chet demanded.

"It was a helluva battle," Reiser stated. "To lose your top scorer for the first half and still stay in the game, it's a tribute to this Team. We not only have the top scorer in the State, we have the best team-effort in the State."

"Speaking of the top scorer, Coach," Chet continued, "can you stay in the Tournament long enough for Sky King to surpass Damon Bailey as the top all-time scorer in the State of Indiana?"

"Nothing against Skyler, but I could care less about that," Reiser said bluntly. "I've taught team basketball the last three years. Not Sky King basketball."

"Is a State championship within your reach?" Chet wondered.

"This is our State championship," Reiser declared. "Anything after this is gravy. There's a lot of nightmarish losses floating around in this gym. But, after this game, I think every small school in Indiana will sleep well tonight."

Centerville was primed for a major celebration. A town that usually folded up at 9 PM, was open for business.

Sky King missed the festivities. He was sent to the hospital for observation and stitches. Milo Wilkes joined Skyler in the emergency room. He lost his bet with Kenneth, but was a little too happy about it. After running up and down the bleachers, he was hit with chest pains. Milo made a miraculous recovery, though. The next day at high noon, traffic was stopped on Main Street in Centerville as a peculiar looking man in drag pushed Kenneth Hatfield in a wheelbarrow. They made the front page of the newspaper.

While most fans celebrated undaunted, there was one who tasted the bittersweet joy of the moment.

Joshua King had been in the crowd, and he watched his son win a Sectional Title. He felt proud at watching Skyler's accomplishments, but saddened he couldn't be a part of it.

As he left the gym, Joshua made a point to walk past the celebration.

"Skyler. Skyler!" Joshua shouted. "Nice game!"

"Thanks!" Skyler said, barely looking.

"I'm your dad, Skyler."

"My dad's dead, man," Skyler said disgusted and walked away.

He tried to pat Skyler on the back, but he never got close enough. On their way to congratulate the Bulldogs, Diane and Alana walked past Joshua. Alana stopped in her tracks at the sight of him. More out of shock.

"All of you deserve this," Joshua said weakly.

"Let's go," Diane said, as she pulled Alana toward her son. The two of them had pleasanter things to concern themselves with.

As they passed by Joshua, the pungent odor of stale whiskey and marijuana reeked from his body.

"What a worthless waste of humanity," Diane mumbled to herself.

NO STOPPING NOW

Surprisingly, Centerville won the Regional and Semi-State easily. They beat New Castle for the Regional Championship by fifteen points, and Anderson at the Semi-State by twelve. Centerville was going to the STATE. Needless to say, it was a March that a small town in east-central Indiana would never forget.

The Bulldogs won their first game at the State, and were to play Marion in the Championship game. Marion finished second in the North Central Conference to Richmond. But, Marion was the only team to beat Richmond on their home court. It wouldn't be easy.

With six seconds left in the game, Centerville was behind by two with a Marion player on the free throw line to shoot two. He made both. Emile threw the ball into Shane, who hurried it up the court. When he got to half-court he threw it to Sky on the right wing, and he immediately launched a three. For some unknown reason, a Marion player tried to be a hero and block the shot. He missed the block, but knocked Skyler down in the process. The referee's whistle blew. The ball arched high in the air as it sailed for its destination. If it landed on target, and Skyler hit his free throw, the game would be tied. It was a last-second shot. Skyler was way overdue…The ball hit the back of the rim and bounced away.

The Marion players and fans rushed the court. Their celebration had begun. The Centerville players slowly made their way back to the bench. Reiser rounded up his players and huddled with them one last time. It was reminiscent of the scene after their Sectional win. As a continuous roar of celebration went on around them, the Bulldogs conducted their private meeting.

"Coach," one referee interjected, "Coach, we have three free throws to shoot out here."

"The game's over, bud," Reiser said solemnly. "What's the use?"

"We have to shoot these free throws, Coach," the referee answered. "Tourney rules. I need number twelve out here."

Reiser looked at his star, "Go, Sky."

As Skyler went to the free throw line to shoot, the Marion fans started heckling him to make him miss. "Loser!" "Ball hog!" "Choker!"

Reiser was at the scorer's bench when he heard the news. His eyes lit up like hundred watt bulbs. He turned to his player standing alone on the court and prayed.

"Skyler!" Reiser yelled, getting his attention. "Skyler! Make these and shut these people up."

Skyler made the first three throw, and the Centerville crowd gave out a roar. Marion's heckling persisted. Skyler made the second free throw, and again, Centerville celebrated. Marion still had one last chance to annoy their opponent. They gave it their best. Skyler arched the third free throw and sent it to the bottom of the net. This time Centerville exploded in a roar that drowned out Marion completely.

"Ladies and gentlemen," the PA echoed, "let me introduce to you the new IHSAA basketball scoring champion. SKYYYYYY KING!"

The Centerville fans and players were ecstatic. Sky King had passed scoring champion Damon Bailey by one point. Marion stood and stared in quiet awe. The players mobbed Skyler on the free throw line. It was as if the Bulldogs had won after all.

EPILOGUE

"They're gonna lose," Milo predicted, as he sat in his recliner pouring a Coke.

"Oh, shut the hell up!" Kenneth said nervously, as he pointed to the TV. "This is for the National title."

"Who taught you how to pour a Coke?" George wondered. "Why you holding the glass at an angle?"

"Oh, it's an old trick someone taught me," Milo answered. "It saves the carbonation."

"Be quiet!" Kenneth shouted. "They're going back to the game."

"We're ready for play to resume," the TV Announcer declared, "North Carolina leads by two points with ten seconds on the clock. Purdue has the ball and needs to go the length of the court for a tying or winning shot. Wilson gets the ball inbounds to Simpson. North Carolina applies pressure in the backcourt. Simpson gets away from one, now two defenders. Here's a long pass to Lester. He puts up a three. It's blocked! The ball's loose! There's a scramble for the ball! George slaps the ball out of the pack! King picks it up for Purdue and fires a three! There's the buzzer! ITS GOOD! Purdue wins the National title at the buzzer on a shot by senior, Sky King! He sank it babyyyyyy!"

Skyler ran around the gym with his arms in the air. He ran around the gym three times before any of his teammates could catch him. After they mobbed him mercilessly, Skyler ran up in the stands. Diane, Alana, Renee and Jim Reiser met him halfway on the stairs.

"We did it!" Skyler yelled, as he hugged his mother.

"I'm so happy for you Sky!" Alana cried. "You deserve this!"

"I don't believe it!" exclaimed Diane, as she grabbed her grandson.

"Great shot, Sky!" beamed Renee. "I've seen you hit those a thousand times in the driveway!"

"That was a last second shot!" Jim said, as he hugged his former player. "You were due, man! You were due!"

"I wish Dad could see this," Skyler quietly told his gathering of fans.

"He would've been proud of you!" Diane added.

"I'm sure he didn't miss this one," Alana smiled.

"It's been a lot of hard work," Jim added. "He got you here."

"So did you Coach....so did you.... I gotta go! Gotta get back to the team! Be back in a bit." Skyler ran to rejoin his team. He didn't touch a step on the way down.

"I'm so proud of him, Jim," Diane said close to tears.

"We all are," Jim answered, as he gave Diane a kiss on the lips.

Billy Packer was interviewing the Purdue Team at courtside. It was one big party.

"Was that a planned play?" Packer joked. "The blocked shot and all."

"That's the way coach drew it up in the huddle," laughed Wilson.

"Emile George! You've played with Sky King longer than anyone here! Did you think he had that shot in him?" Packer asked.

"I knew it was in him somewhere!" Emile responded. "Trying to get it out was the hard part."

"Sky King," asked Packer, "Is that the most important last-second shot you've hit?"

"That's the ONLY last-second shot I've hit!" Skyler kidded.

"Four years ago you were Mr. Basketball, yet you missed the Indiana State Championship by one point," Packer continued, "what does hitting this shot today mean to you, Sky?"

"This celebration's for everyone who helped get me here," Skyler said, as he looked into the camera and took a deep breath. "It's for someone who never got in the game."

THE END!